Mackinac Island Beacon

Mackinac Island Beacon

Mackinac Island Romances Series

By CARRIE FANCETT PAGELS

Hearts Overcoming Press

Copyright Carrie Fancett Pagels 2024

Portions of this story were published originally as part of a novella, "Love's Beacon" (© 2018, Carrie Fancett Pagels) published in The Great Lakes Lighthouse Brides Collection from Barbour Publishing

ISBN: 978-1-7366875-9-8

Hearts Overcoming Press

United States of America

Praise for Carrie Fancett Pagels' Books

Mackinac Island Beacon
Once again author Carrie Fancett Pagels deposits us among friends as they negotiate the trials of orphaned women with strings of hope attached to lighthouse beacons and promises. A tale of home and heart as we gather for the revealing of secrets and dreams.

> ~**Marguerite Martin Gray**, award-winning author

In *Mackinac Island Beacon,* Carrie Fancett Pagels weaves tender love stories, desperate searches for lost loved ones, a struggle to recover repressed memories, and joyful reunions all in locations so descriptive that I want to see them for myself.

> ~**Susan F. Craft**, award-winning author, The Great Wagon Road series

Behind Love's Wall
Carrie Fancett Pagels creates a wonderful story of intrigue and romance in *Behind Love's Wall*. Set on the amazing historical Mackinac Island, the author makes a creative balancing act of time periods and characters, bringing it all together in one story that I found hard to put down. I believe readers will enjoy the twists and turns, and I highly recommend *Behind Love's Wall*.

> ~**Tracie Peterson**, bestselling, award-winning author of over 125 novels

My Heart Belongs on Mackinac Island
An enchanting love story, *My Heart Belongs on Mackinac Island* is sprinkled with warmth and humor, grace and faith. A highly enjoyable read!

> ~ **Tamera Alexander**, *USA Today* Bestselling Author

Dear Reader:

Portions of this story were published originally as part of a novella, "Love's Beacon" published in *The Great Lakes Lighthouse Brides Collection* from Barbour Publishing. About fifteen percent of this novel was culled from that novella. I hope that this new expanded, fully fleshed novel, with multiple story lines will bless the reader!

My favorite Bible verse is Romans 8:28 *And we know that in all things God works for the good of those who love him, who have been called according to His purpose.* This verse is the inspiration for weaving together all the backgrounds on my characters to show what God can do with their outcomes.

You can find Author's Notes and Acknowledgements in the back of the book.

Dedication

To Ruth Hill, who was a bright spot in my middle and high school years!

A wonderful baton twirling coach, chorus teacher, singer and pianist, and so much more!

A true inspiration to so many.

In Memory of

Joyce Ann (Carroll) Hart (1933-2023) my long-time literary agent, CEO of Hartline Literary, who was an incredible blessing to me. She loved my Mackinac stories and encouraged me in my writing ministry. Joyce is greatly missed not only by myself but by many in the Christian Fiction writing community. Joyce was like a second mother in so many ways. She stepped into the breach after my mother passed away in 2010. I'm sure they are getting along famously in heaven!

Characters List

Hero: **Paul Scholtus**
    Hetty – daughter
    Mary & Jack Scholtus – parents
        Ronald "Ron" – brother
Heroine: **Valerie "Val" Fillman**
    Dorcas and John Fillman – parents
        Timothy – Fillmans' son
        Mabel – Fillmans' daughter
Hero: **Lawrence Zumbrun**
    Christian Zumbrun – father
Heroine: **Susan Marie Johnson**
    Evelyn Marie (Singleterry) & Henry Clay Johnson – parents
Jack Welling – Lawrence's running protégé
    Peter Welling – father
    Ada/Adelaide Fox Welling – stepmother
        Satilde "Sally" Welling – Peter and Ada's daughter

Sugarplum Ladies' & Families:
Lady Eugenie Mott Gladstone Marchioness of Kent – Founder of the Sugarplum Ladies
    Lord Percival "Percy" Gladstone Marquess of Kent
        Georgina "Georgie" – daughter
        Nathan – son
Carrie Booth Moore – One of the original Sugarplum Ladies
Tara Mulcahey – One of the original Sugarplum Ladies
    Bertie Mulcahey – husband

Others:
Father Joseph – Head of Mackinac Island Orphanage
Sister Mary Lou Kwiatkowski – nun at orphanage
Mrs. Deanna (Tumbleston) Stevens & Colonel Benjamin Stevens – Veterans' Home Managers
Billy Lloyd – dockworker & boat handler
Robert Swaine – Ship's captain, owner of a fleet and of businesses
Sadie Duvall Swaine – wife and nurse
Madame Marguerite Mirandette – revered island matriarch and catechism teacher

Prologue

Mackinac Island Orphanage
September, 1897

*T*he scent of laundry soap shrouded the washroom where Susan Johnson had brought baskets of clothes from the line—taunting her that this was to be her life. She stood at the long white table where she folded clothes as Mrs. O'Brien worked nearby. Susan felt as wrung out as the nightdress the Irishwoman just finished.

"Did ye see tha' peculiar woman from the lighthouse as she ran from service last Sunday?" Mrs. O'Brien shook her head. "As if the devil himself were chasin' her off—her eyes all ablaze with an evil fury."

"I had just invited her daughter, Val, to our coffee fellowship, with the two younger ones."

"Poor souls. I wonder wha' caused tha' boy's limp."

And quiet Mabel had difficulty hearing. "Their father rushed them out of church after the mother left."

"That lighthouse keeper—he's a strange one, too, aye." Mrs. O'Brien tipped her jaw down. "But not so odd as his wife."

The door to the laundry building creaked open, and Sister Mary Lou peeked inside. "Father Joseph asked if you have sufficient disinfecting agents."

"Aye." Mrs. O'Brien wrung out a pair of dark trousers.

Susan couldn't resist asking, "Why does he wonder?

The nun entered the building, bringing an inflow of cool air with her. "Terrible illnesses going around, dearie."

"The flux? It's not even late autumn for such illness." Susan folded a tiny black dress.

"Best be ready for some new children, dearies." Sister Mary Lou's voice held sorrow.

"You mean people are already dying?"

Mrs. O'Brien straightened and wiped her wet hands on her apron. "Aye, that's the way of this dread disease, though some fare well."

The pretty nun nodded. "Most do, thank God."

Not Susan's parents, all those years ago—yet she hadn't gotten sick. Why had Susan been the only survivor in her family? And why hadn't more people in the downstate area around Shepherd been ill then?

Mrs. O'Brien sighed. "Many recently succumbed on the mainland afore I come over here."

Susan pressed her hand on the stack of clothes.

"Even before you joined us last month?" Sister Mary Lou pushed her new spectacles up her small nose.

"Aye." The red-faced woman rubbed the back of her hand across her brow. "In St. Ignace parish and Mackinaw City, too." She made the sign of the cross, as did Sister Mary Lou, who then pulled out her rosary and kissed the crucifix.

"May God rest their souls." Sister Mary Lou slipped her dark beaded rosary back in place. "This week we have some St. Anne's members who've gone from bad to worse overnight."

Mrs. O'Brien again pushed a wet piece of clothing through the wringer. "Aye, that illness surged quicker than Lucifer playing his fiddle on Halloween."

The nun closed her eyes. Sister Mary Lou had a strong aversion to Halloween. Instead of a Halloween Festival, which other children on the island had celebrated, the orphanage would celebrate Harvest Festival. An All Saints' Day celebration would be celebrated in the parish hall on the day after.

"I know you'll do a wonderful job helping any new children, dearie." Sister Mary Lou tucked her hands into her black habit's pockets, a sure sign she was done speaking with them. She headed out of the building.

"You're a blessin', that'd be for sure." Mrs. O'Brien finished the last of the wash and set the tiny trousers in a basket of wet things.

Susan ran her hand across her damp brow. "We could use a little break before we hang the last of the laundry outside." The September breeze would have them dry in no time.

"Aye."

The two of them sat on the wooden bench against the wall and stretched their legs.

The older woman pulled a wax-paper-wrapped object from her pocket and handed it to her. "That's one of me own creations—an American-style biscuit filled with pumpkin—so be careful afore ye bite into it."

Susan wasn't a girl, but a spinster approaching twenty-three. "Thank you. I'm sure it will be heavenly."

"Heavenly might be a wee stretch o' the truth. But my old man says it's the best he ever et."

She'd save her cat a tiny bit. Her calico, Lizzie, was excellent company in her attic room—and a good mouser. "Let's see. I bet he's right."

Susan bit into the middle. The sweet and spicy taste of pumpkin custard brought to mind Mrs. Scholtus, her childhood neighbor. That dear lady had fed Susan pumpkin custard pie after her parents had died. Moisture filled Susan's eyes. Her best friend, Paul, had sat across from her at his family's big oak table.

"Oh, my dear, it's not that terrible is it that my treat is makin' ye cry?"

Susan swiped at her eyes. "No, it's truly wonderful." So good that she was tempted to not save Lizzie that last bite. "Just brought back memories of the last time I tasted something so fine." *And had such a dear friend.*

A year older than her, Paul lived on the neighboring farm. They'd been inseparable.

Susie, you want a lift? Paulie held out his hands, fingers interlaced, as she eyed the tree they were about to climb.

"It's too high."

"You can do it. I'll help." He playfully stomped his heel in the dirt.

"All right." She arranged her skirt around her and lifted one foot as he bent.

"Up ya go!"

She reached as high as she could and grasped the limb. "What if it breaks."

"It won't. Ron was up there last night."

Paulie's older brother was almost twice their size. She pulled up, grabbing another branch to steady herself, as Paulie gave her an extra boost.

She scooted firmly onto the branch and looked down.

"Ya did it!"

With help from him, she had. She swung her legs, thrilled at her accomplishment.

Mrs. O'Brien massaged her red knuckles. "Come down to the kitchen tonight, after the children are in bed, and I'll show ye how it's done."

"What would Cook say?" Susan was already in trouble with the feisty head cook.

"Och, no one needs be the wiser."

"I'd love that." She rolled her lips together. If she ever got out on her own, she needed to cook.

"If'n yer interested," the laundress pulled a flyer from her oversized apron pocket. "This next summer, that new Social Affirmation Society is lookin' to start a cooking program here on the island."

"Social Affirmation Society? The ones who are doing all that construction?" The influx of workers and materials had begun almost as soon as the summer season had ended. And the clamor of saws and hammers had commenced down the road from the orphanage.

"Aye. That group of ladies wishes to better the world through helping unfortunates—like our orphans—to get some skills for life."

Sounded a bit like the group her mother had worked with before she'd married. Frankly, it sounded like they helped people like herself. "So it's worth all the commotion the workers are making."

"Ye might wish to register. People comin' from all parts."

"But I'll be watching the children or doing chores." *Unless Father Joseph has other plans for me—like kicking me out.*

"Leave that in the good Lord's hands."

The Lord's hands were neglecting Susan, though. Still. . . others had it even worse than she did. A roof over her head, three meals a day, the best calico cat in creation, a steady job and pay—some of which she could save. She took another bite of the pumpkin treat, savoring the sweetness—but truly Mrs. O'Brien's friendship was even sweeter.

"Och, if you could get yourself some more trainin', I'd bet my grandmother's lace shawl, God rest her soul, that ye could get out there and make a livin' for yourself. Meet some other young people your own age."

"Most people my age have families."

"Not all."

"True." But they were few. "And I've got Lizzie to keep me company."

"She's a beauty, that cat."

"Except that she thinks she's a dog—and always wants to run after the strays that come by in the yard."

"Ye better find ye a man who likes cats, young Susan," Mrs. O'Brien advised.

She laughed. "I've garnered no male interest whatsoever, so I think Lizzie is quite safe. But I do like the idea of expanding my skills."

Susan couldn't rely upon the goodwill of the priest forever.

She wasn't even Catholic. And one day the dire need for her services, which overrode her religious affiliations, could end. Then where would she be? She shivered.

She'd not end up out on the streets. She'd come close to being in that situation years earlier, until Sister Mary Lou had stepped into her life. She'd brought Susan with her from St. Ignace when Father Joseph had been sent to "clean out" the staff who'd been unkind to the Mackinac Island orphans.

No, she couldn't depend upon this position to continue.

4

Time to renew her search for another job.

Lansing Youth Health Program
Lansing, Michigan

Lawrence Zumbrun scanned the basketball hall floor, where over two dozen youngsters were engaged in calisthenics and other physical fitness activities. Pride infused him at their progress.

"Zumbrun, you've done a fine job with the young fellows here." Mr. Blodman, the superintendent for the youth recreation program had shown up unexpectedly this afternoon. The scent of stale cigar smoke still lingered on his wool suit.

"Thank you."

Blodman's nose crinkled as if he smelled something bad. Maybe he'd gotten a whiff of his own odor. "But I'm afraid the funding has disappeared with this recent downturn in the economy."

Lawrence jutted his chin back. "But we've built a wonderful program here in the capitol."

"A model program, we're told." Blodman shrugged. "But money speaks, doesn't it?"

He was tempted to challenge the man to a boxing match. How could they pull the plug on this program? On him? What about the work he'd done with Jack Welling, Michigan's premier runner, who'd be going to the Olympics? Should Lawrence mention that?

He couldn't argue with Blodman. None of the colleges in Michigan offered a health and fitness degree. *Not yet.* Lawrence had spent his career since he'd graduated with a biology degree from the University of Michigan working on the health and welfare of young people. Young men, that was. He'd even studied with John Kellogg on his notions of food as fuel for good health.

"Did you hear me, Zumbrun?"

"Sorry."

The older man pulled at his handlebar moustache. "I said it'd be best if you begin looking for a new situation."

Over five years of his life invested in these young people. Lawrence couldn't hold back. "What about Jack Welling and his training?" Surely, they'd not abandon the boy.

There was a rumor his parents were well off, but the boy lived on a rural farm north of Lansing. Lawrence didn't put much stock in that story.

Blodman tapped his walking stick on the wood floor. "That's their problem, I'm afraid. He'll have to find some new sponsors."

This gymnasium, filled with happy young men, would soon be empty. "Where will my fellows go for healthy recreation?

"Maybe they can help their families around their homes instead of flibbertigibbetying here."

The man's cold words struck Lawrence. So that's how Blodman felt about the program. Had he undermined their efforts here? Heat surged through Lawrence's chest, and he fisted his hands.

"I'd suggest you inform young Welling sooner rather than later, so you don't leave him dangling, Zumbrun."

Lawrence couldn't force any words past his clenched teeth. Instead, he hurried out to the middle of the floor before he did something he'd regret. He clapped his hands. "Come on, gentlemen, let's all run some laps around the gym."

Their groans were music to his ears, for they didn't really begrudge the task—otherwise, they wouldn't be here.

As they queued up and began to run, Lawrence closed his eyes. *Lord, help me and these young men, and give me the words to share with Jack and his family.*

Jack deserved better than this.

Lawrence would have to find a way to keep coaching the star athlete.

But first he'd need to find a new job.

Chapter One

Round Island Lighthouse
September, 1897

Sun glittered diamond reflections on the water as a light breeze carried Valerie Fillman, aboard Billy Lloyd's skiff, to Mackinac Island. Thank God for the fair weather, because on a wild stormy day they wouldn't have stood a chance against the Straits of Mackinac's temperamental nature. And she must get to the pharmacy as quickly as possible.

"You all right, Miss Fillman?" Billy, not quite fifteen, skillfully piloted his boat toward the channel.

"Fine." She clutched the edge of the seat. There was more space without her family on board.

"Look! The superintendent is coming across." Billy pointed to Dardanes' vessel, as it sailed toward them.

"No! They shouldn't go in there." She pushed down on her skirts and was about to stand to warn them when Billy's shocked expression made her stop.

"Stay seated!"

"They could get sick, too!"

"You could tip us over. You want that?"

"No." She just wanted to get the medicines that could help heal her family.

"Don't worry about Dardanes. He's smart. Knows what he's doing."

"I should have left a sign on the front door."

He shrugged. "He'll know better. Lots of folks are sick. Lots have d—"

His voice trailed off as he clamped his mouth shut.

As the boat skimmed over the water, she was struck by how easily she could have drowned. "Died?" She croaked out.

"A few."

"How many?" she called over the flapping sails and the water rushing beneath the boat.

"Maybe six or seven." He shook his curly mop of hair. Amazing how it always looked the same, no matter the weather.

"On such a small island?" Would the death toll be four on Round Island? Not if she could get their fevers down and their coughs under control.

"Did you do the light last night?" He didn't answer her question.

"Yes." Their assistant would manage now that he was over the dread illness.

Since he'd recovered, using medicine from the pharmacy, then her own family should, too.

But they all looked so very bad.

Billy gestured toward the fort, now decommissioned and a state park. "See how pretty the leaves are?"

Gold, red, and orange leaves mixed on the hardwood trees in the park below the fort. "They are beautiful. I always enjoyed it when the trees surrounding our lumber camps changed in the fall." There was something magical about the bright, hopeful color of the leaves and how they swirled to the ground. When they were younger, Tim and Mabel loved to jump in the leaf piles. *No, that memory is not of Tim and Mabel.* As they surged over the water, the recollection blew away—just like the leaves would.

Soon, they reached the wharf, and her wobbly legs struggled to disembark. A big man on the pier, with calloused hands, helped her up.

"Thank you."

"*Ole hyvä.*" He ambled away toward a fishing boat.

Billy Lloyd leaned in. "He said 'you're welcome.' He's Finnish."

"I thought I recognized that accent." From one of the lumber camps they'd once lived in. "Thanks for getting me here, Billy. I'll be back before long. But let me pay you the first part." Her hands shook badly as she struggled to pull the coins from her reticule.

"You can wait. And remember what I told you."

"Meet you back at the wharf in an hour."

"Yup. Got errands to run for my boss."

Something nudged her, maybe the way his bottle-green eyes fixed on the Doud's Grocery Store sign, so she handed him half the payment for the trip. "Here, take this." She knew he shouldn't be hungry, since Mrs. Lloyd was the head cook at Astor's Restaurant, but he was a growing youth, like her brother.

"Thanks." He grinned. "Gotta fortify myself with a cup of coffee and a roll before I do Captain Swaine's errands."

"Coffee?" At his age?

He thumped his chest. "I'm a working man."

Valerie blinked at him. Thank goodness Mum hadn't made Timmy go search out work. But then again, she'd always kept her children close. Kept an eye on all of them. "You know where the pharmacy is, Billy?"

He wiped his sleeve across his nose, which eliminated the notion of him as a working *man* and returned him to the boy he was. "Yup." He pointed west down the main street.

Val hurried toward her destination—her source of hope, Island Pharmacy. On this autumn day, not many islanders walked the wooden sidewalks that fronted the buildings on the main street. Pulled by a team of gray Percherons, a dray filled with cedar boards and shingles rolled past. Two brawny red-haired men sat at the back, scowling.

When she reached the pharmacy, she quickly stepped inside. Her breath caught in her chest. The scent of camphor mingled with beeswax and a hint of bay rum and brought to mind someplace, somewhere, long ago.

A tall man.

She stood on the thick entry mat, overwhelmed by the vague recollection and the prospect of being inside a store. It had been years since she'd been allowed to enter a mercantile with her parents—and then under the strictest of instructions to not dawdle but to get what her parents had come for and to leave promptly.

Valerie forced herself to move across the wide-planked oak floor and toward the counter. She took her place in line behind a petite woman attired in black, from her booted heels to the cap perched atop her coil of white hair. Was she in mourning?

Would Valerie, too, soon be attired in black?

Lord, help me.

She focused hopefully on the bottles of medicines, elixirs, and teas displayed in the case behind the counter that might send this scourge fleeing.

Is it too late?

Days earlier, Valerie had pleaded with her parents to allow her to come to Mackinac Island for medicine, fearing the worst for Mabel and Tim. They'd refused. Only after they'd become nonresponsive had she been able to leave Round Island when Billy had arrived. Tim and Mabel hadn't taken much more than hourly sips of water in the last day. She blinked back tears.

Dear God, my family is so sick. Please enable me to help them.

The illness had gone on so long and somewhere deep, so very deep, in her soul a recollection of a similar illness in a large household had emerged. An image of a huge room of children, feverish, some crying, some calling out for their mothers, had made her wonder if somehow she'd already experienced the dread sickness now ravaging her family at the lighthouse.

Sometimes, she wondered if she'd been in an orphanage and her mother had not wanted Valerie to remember.

The elderly woman received her package and left the counter, casting a quizzical look at Valerie as she passed by. Did the stranger know of her family? She'd once heard them described as "A queer lot" by someone who'd not realized she'd been listening.

Valerie's hands shook as she pulled the list from her reticule.

"May I help you, miss?" The young man behind the counter gazed at her, concern reflecting in his dark eyes.

Niggling anxiety nipped at her as she thrust out the sheet of paper.

"Do you have an account here?" He cocked his head to the side.

"No." She clutched her reticule hard. "I'll pay cash." Her parents never kept accounts at stores.

He dipped his chin. "I'll take this back to the pharmacist." He turned and went through a set of heavy golden-yellow, fringe-edged, curtains to the back.

The jingling of the doorbells startled her.

A pretty blond woman entered, holding tight to a toddler's hand. The child looked up, hazel eyes shining. Attired in a fashionable bonnet and matching rose-colored coat, the young mother smiled at Val. When the stranger greeted her, Valerie couldn't find her tongue. The only time she was out around people was at the occasional church services they'd attended and even then, her parents swept them all out and away immediately after service ended.

The stranger blinked at her. Val realized she'd been staring and averted her gaze as she whispered, "Hello."

The stranger didn't respond. Perhaps she'd not heard Valerie.

The clerk returned and looked past Valerie. "Mrs. Swaine, or should I call you Nurse Swaine?"

A nurse? Maybe she could help. And Swaine? That was Billy's boss's name.

"I'm just 'Mother' to a sick boy today, Henry."

"Well, I've got something for little Robbie's sniffle." He pushed his black sleeve garters higher then bent and retrieved a paper-wrapped parcel from behind the counter.

The young woman accepted the package and slid it into her bag. "Thank you."

"I'll put that on Captain Swaine's account."

Trained as a nurse, married to a captain, and has a young child. All those things the young woman enjoyed were out of Valerie's reach. Right now, though, instead of focusing on her selfish jealousy, Valerie should be praying for her family. And asking this nurse a few questions.

"Have a blessed day, Sadie—I mean Mrs. Swaine." Henry's cheeks reddened.

"Every day I sure am blessed—thank you." She smiled at the clerk. "And tell your mother I'll come check on her next week, once Robbie has recovered."

"I shall, thank you."

Someone called from the back, and Henry swiveled away from them.

"Excuse me, may I ask you something? As a nurse?" Valerie chewed her lower lip.

The young mother turned and faced Val, her blue eyes darkening. "Have we met?"

"My father is the lighthouse keeper, ma'am. And he's very sick as is my entire family." Even though this young woman likely wasn't much older than her, Val cast her eyes downward, as her mother had drilled into her.

"What would you like to ask?"

"Have you seen many people with this terrible flux?"

Twin blond eyebrows drew together. "Many."

"And is there anything I can do? Anything besides the medicine that might help?"

Valerie studied Sadie's face, which seemed to twitch ever so slightly. "You've made them comfortable and given them plenty of fluids? They're resting in bed?

"Yes. All of that."

"And you opened the windows?"

"My mum wouldn't allow it, but I did for my brother and sister."

The nurse's mouth dropped open, then she closed it. "At least they are getting fresh air. So many older folks refuse to listen to reason."

Mum had never listened to reason. Maybe on a rare occasion.

"Give them their medicine. Make sure they take it. Get some strong black tea into them, too." She exhaled a sharp breath. "And pray."

"Yes."

The Swaine's toddler extended his tiny mittened hands to Val, and something inside her soul quickened. She longed to have someone reach for her like this. Her mother had instilled into Mabel and Tim that she'd not lift them up—they must get around on their own once they could toddle about. Her father wasn't much better.

Just as Val bent and was about to pick the boy up, his mother lifted him onto her hip.

The toddler sneezed.

"Oh my!" His mother leaned away.

"Bless you."

"Thank you. Well, I best get this boy home." Arms full, the young mother headed out as a man entered.

With strikingly handsome features, the man stood over a head taller than the nurse.

"Sadie Swaine, *guten tag*." He bent and patted the boy's head.

Mrs. Swaine arched an eyebrow. "Good day, Friedrich. How's Maude?"

"She's started closing out the books and readying the hotel for the off-season. Our last guests depart today."

"It will be quiet at the inn after that."

The man chuckled. "Not once the new baby arrives."

"No. And I can't wait to help with the delivery."

Robbie arched his body toward the door and whined.

"Here, I will get the door." Friedrich held the door ajar for Sadie. "Your driver, Cousin Stan, looks like he's ready to take you back to the Canary cottage."

"Yes. I'm grateful to have him there to help me. Thank you and good day, Friedrich."

Was this what normal social exchanges were like? Friendships? Helping one another? Val felt like shrinking inside of her old coat. Every time she'd had the opportunity to be around other people, inside the lighthouses they'd lived in, she'd tried to pay good attention. Tried to soak in what she'd been deprived of in their isolated life. Now, though, if her father succumbed—what would become of them?

The clerk returned with several brown bottles. He quickly wrapped them in paper and then placed them gently in a bag before tying the parcel with twine.

Did those bottles contain her family's only hope?

Shepherd, Michigan

If that wasn't a sight to behold on a brisk September morn, Paul Scholtus didn't know what was. Young Jack Welling, the nation's best candidate for a medal at the Olympics, ran up their long drive at top speed, clutching something. If the runner had been anyone else but the fifteen-year-old, who preferred to run rather than walk anywhere, Paul would have been concerned.

He shielded his eyes from the sun. The youth slowed as he approached the porch. If Paul wasn't mistaken, that was a newspaper the boy held. Maybe there was some important news.

Jack waved. When he reached Paul, he bent over, hands on legs, his breath puffing out mist in the chill air. Still, the kid hadn't broken a sweat. "Hiya, Mr. Scholtus."

"Mr. Scholtus is my dad. Call me Paul." As a widower with a small child, even though only twenty-four years old, he must seem ancient to the younger fellow.

"Yeah, Paul, well I need to see your pa." He grinned. The kid had a cocky but endearing smile—the kind that a lot of young women might eventually fall for as he matured.

"Sure thing, but what's going on?"

Jack waved the newspaper. "Aw, something about that lighthouse up at the Mackinac Straits. My dad said Mr. Scholtus would want to read about the light since he's afishinado of such things."

"Aficionado?"

"That's what I said, ain't it?"

Paul pulled the paper from Jack's hands.

"Hey!" the boy protested. "That's for your dad."

"No, this is for me." Paul scanned the newspaper. Was there an opening at one of the lighthouses up north? He'd been waiting so long.

Nothing on the first page.

The door behind Paul opened and then closed. "Hello, Jack. Did you run all the way out here?" Ma's gentle voice made Paul feel embarrassed at his rudeness.

"Sure thing, Mrs. Scholtus. Dad told me to share the latest issue of the Mackinac Island newspaper with your husband."

Paul glanced up to encounter the boy's glare. "I believe he meant me."

Jack's eyes narrowed. "You said your dad is Mr. Scholtus—not you."

"But I'm. . ." Paul was the resident lighthouse enthusiast. His parents knew of his interest but weren't happy about his desire to secure a lighthouse keeper's post and leave the farm. "I'm the one who enjoys reading about lighthouses."

Ma descended the steps and came alongside him. "Oh my. Look at that article about Sister Mary Lou."

"Isn't she a nun at the island orphanage?" Jack rubbed his nose.

Ma took the paper from him. "She's overseeing the children at the orphanage and has a harvest festival planned. She grew up here and was a wonderful young lady."

"She's kinda old now." Jack's lips twitched.

Paul shot him a warning glance. The kid was basically implying that Ma was old, too, which she wasn't.

"Look!" Ma raised the paper. "There's a picture of her and it says the person beside her is Susan Johnson. That's got to be our Susie. Your old friend, Paul." Ma's mouth dropped open.

It couldn't be. Paul leaned in. Alongside the nun stood a dark-haired willowy young woman, her hands clasped at her waist. Beneath the photo, the caption read *Sister Mary Lou and her assistant Miss Susan Marie Johnson chair the Harvest Festival committee.* "I'll be darned."

"Watch your language." Ma cautioned.

Jack waved a hand. "I've heard a lot worse, especially down at the Mackinac docks when I run between the drays. Never got hit by one, though."

Paul couldn't help chuckling at the boy's comment.

Or had his spirits lifted because he finally knew where his old friend had gone? His dear childhood friend was safe on Mackinac Island. A long-held burden lifted.

In the barn, the horses whinnied, as if they, too, were happy. More likely, they wanted out again.

"Guess what, Mrs. Scholtus?" Jack flexed his shoulders.

"What?"

"We'll be going up to Mackinac for the summer this year, too."

Paul frowned. "I thought your sister and her husband were operating the family's inn." Mr. Welling had devoted his livelihood to running Winds of Mackinac Inn with his former wife, who'd died. Then his daughter had inherited the property and others, which she and her husband now ran. Jack would inherit his share when he was older.

"They are." Jack rubbed his neck. "But my stepmother is helping some social crusaders to get a summer cooking program going on the island."

Ma cocked her head. "Do you cook, Jack?"

"Nah. I'll get me a wife one day to do that."

Paul snorted. *Maybe not with that attitude.* "Do you think you just pick them like you do your races you run?"

"Maybe." The cheeky kid grinned, and Ma mussed his hair.

"Maybe I'll pick me out one early up there and keep her on hold like they let you do at the mercantile."

Paul shot him a look of disgust.

"I mean, after all, we'll live in our house near the property where the program will be. I'll see all those girls who wanta be cooks. One day that house will be mine. It's called Butterfly Cottage." Pride mixed with something else, tugged at his fine features.

Ma patted Jack's back. "What a pretty name."

He shrugged. "It's not all that big, but it's got a real nice view. It's up on the East Bluff."

"Can you see the new Round Island Lighthouse from there?" Paul couldn't help asking, even though Ma scowled. She wasn't happy about him renewing his notion of taking up lighthouse keeping.

"Sure ya can. That lighthouse is like a beacon to all the people comin' up there to the island! Ya ought to come up and see me. I'll show ya around Mackinac—when I'm not running."

"What about your training, though, if you go to the island? I thought your coach was here." The coach, Zumbrun, was just a little too good-looking for his own good and his subtle air of aloofness suggested he thought himself above the countryfolk who lived in the area.

The boy shrugged. "My folks are hopin' Lawrence will come help with the program up there, too. And then he can coach me."

14   *Mackinac Island Beacon*

Paul had met Zumbrun before he'd become Jack's coach, at the sanitarium in Battle Creek. Paul never divulged to anyone any of the people he'd seen while employed there. "So he may follow you north?"

Jack held up his hands, both having fingers crossed. "Here's hoping."

Paul prayed that Zumbrun and his friend, Georgina, had sorted out their troubles. Lawrence Zumbrun had been a regular visitor. Surnames weren't used on the patients' charts and Georgina's family didn't visit. Staff members circulated rumors that they were aristocrats who resided in England. But she had a Midwestern accent. Still, some would mockingly refer to the disturbed young woman as "Lady Georgina" behind her back.

"Lawrence likes helping young athletes, like me. He's like a big brother."

What had happened to Zumbrun's friend in the sanitarium? Had Georgina ever recovered from losing her younger sister?

Lord, wherever Georgina is, bring peace and healing to her and her family. Paul had prayed that prayer many times.

"If Mr. Zumbrun comes to the island, those kids will get an awesome summer athletics program." Jack punched the air in emphasis, as if he were a boxing champion. "It's the place to be."

Susan was there on the island. Jack and his family would be heading there. Paul's dream of tending a lighthouse could possibly be met there.

Time to re-submit his application to the Lighthouse Commission. This time, he'd emphasize that he'd be willing to accept a position even as a second assistant.

Not much money. But it was time to move on. And closer to something else.

And maybe to *someone* else.

Chapter Two

Mackinac Island Orphanage

Susan wrestled her shoulders into the blue-and-white, sailor style, jacket that had come in the last donation barrel. If she didn't flex her arms, then maybe she could keep from popping off any more of the buttons. The garment had lost one before she'd found a spare sewn into the seam and replaced it. Couldn't lose any more, though. A size too small, the coat was still far superior to her previous fall jacket, which was terminally past the patch-and-darn stage. She carefully pinned her hat in place, cringing as she heard some stitches pop on her jacket.

Today, on her free day, she'd ride the staff bicycle around the island. Time to enjoy the changing leaves and have a little picnic by Lake Huron. She'd return and grab her books to return to the library, and then would pick up cookies from the Christys' tea shop for the youngest group. The classes all took turns for their cookie week because Susan didn't want to trespass on the baker's generosity. Although the proprietors, her friends, always insisted on donating the baked goods, Susan kept money to cover the goodies—just in case.

She headed down to the first floor to depart.

Sister Mary Lou emerged from her office, her face aglow. She waved a missive. "I've received a special letter."

The nun loved receiving correspondence but seemed especially excited about this one.

"From your cousin in Ohio?" Sister Mary Lou often traveled there to visit.

"No, it's from someone with whom we're both acquainted, dearie." She beamed.

"Oh?" Susan raised her eyebrows. "One of our orphans?"

The sweet nun clutched the envelope to her chest. "From a hometown friend, a bit older than me, who'd encouraged me to become a nun. Mary Pelletier was her name, but she then married John Scholtus—"

"Mrs. Scholtus?" Susan blurted.

"Yes."

Bittersweet memories resurfaced.

Her best friend, Paulie Scholtus, found Mother's book on the floor under the table where they were playing hide and seek.

"That's not good for reading—it's an autograph book," Susie told him.

The two of them popped up from beneath the tablecloth.

"What's an ottergraph book, Mrs. Johnson?" Paul held the book up.

Momma laughed. "No, not like those adorable otter pups in the river. This is an autograph book. When someone signs their name, it's called their autograph."

Momma opened the book and smiled. "It was fashionable, when I was young, for people to write a little sentiment to you in these books. A darling young girl who helped me when I was working with the Sugarplum Ladies, gifted me with this book."

If only her mother could have lived long enough to be reunited with all those Sugarplum Lady friends.

"I remember Shepherd being a beautiful place to live." Until her parents had passed away so suddenly.

"It was." Sister Mary Lou sighed. "But back to this letter. Mary saw our pictures in the paper."

"The Mackinac Island paper?"

"Yes. That running boy from the island, Jack Welling, lives on a nearby farm to hers now. He brought it over. Goodness, I haven't heard from dear Mary in many years."

"I'll never forget her kindness." Nor Paul's friendship.

Mary says you and her son, Paul, were friends."

"Yes, we were great friends." Until. . .

"He sends his regards."

That was all? A pang of disappointment pierced her.

"I believe so."

"Oh." Was she so forgettable? She must be.

"He married another of your friends. Annabelle." Sister Mary Lou's face grew solemn. "And they had a little girl."

"Had? Did something happen to their daughter?" How terrible that would be to have a child succumb.

"Not to the child." The nun took her hand. "But, dearie, your friend has passed away."

Susan tried to make sense of what she said. Since Paul had sent his regards, he couldn't have died. "Annabelle?"

"Yes. She's been gone for almost three years."

"Poor Paul."

"Yes, but he has his family gathered around him."

"What a blessing to have their comfort."

"Mary says he's growing restless and may move on and away from where his memories haunt him." She shook her head slowly.

Susan nodded. "Thank you for telling me. I'll pray for him."

"Prayer availeth much."

"Would it be proper for me to send Paul a condolence note?" How silly of her. She'd not kept up with him all these years. "But this may be late for that kind of card." She'd known where he was. She could have sent a letter to keep in touch. But she'd harbored some resentment toward him and his family for not taking her in when her parents died.

Sister Mary Lou smiled. "That would be thoughtful to send some kind of note—I don't think it's too late—to him and his mother. I could include that with my correspondence."

"I'll do that as soon as I return from my activities, later this afternoon."

"I'm sure he'd be glad to hear from you." Was that a smug look that flitted over the nun's face? Surely, she wasn't playing matchmaker for a mail-order bride scheme.

No. She wouldn't do that.

"Well, I'm off. Is there anything I could pick up for you when I stop at the Christys' shop later?"

"Yes, thank you. I'm almost out of black English breakfast tea."

"I'll purchase some. And don't offer to pay—you're always sharing with me. It's my turn to buy more for our tea times."

"If you insist."

"I do." It was Susan's turn to allow her own smug smile to tug at her lips. Sister Mary Lou was forever doing for others—good to bless her in return.

Soon, Susan situated herself on the bike. She glanced to the left, where a racket commenced from the construction down the street. The new buildings were going up quickly. She drew in a deep breath as she rode past the work area to Arch Rock. She stopped, compelled to pray for her old friend and his little girl.

May God direct their paths to where they need to be to heal.

Val headed outside the pharmacy to the crisp scent of autumn leaves that carried on the light wind. The street was quiet, save for a handful of people shopping. Billy wouldn't be back for a while yet.

Right now, there was nothing she could do for any of her family members. But with this freedom of movement, she'd not waste her brief opportunity to explore possible work options. She crossed the street and headed toward the mercantile.

A lacy blouse with mother-of-pearl buttons was displayed prominently in the center of the window. A fringed purple and red paisley shawl, fine brown leather gloves, and a jaunty purple hat with a plume on the side surrounded the fancy shirtwaist. No point in imagining herself owning any of those fine things. She ran her hand over her ill-fitting garments. She couldn't go in there and ask about a job looking like this.

From somewhere nearby, apples must be roasting or cider brewing. She looked to the left, where a tobacconist shop crouched between the two pharmacies. When she looked to the right, her heart leapt—there was a sign for the Christy Tea Shoppe. She would buy her brother and sister those cookies she'd promised. Valerie marched down the walkway and entered the shop, enveloped by the apple scents.

A dark-haired young woman, near Valerie's age, stood at the counter as the lady behind it filled a wax-paper-lined box with cookies. "Thank you, Mrs. Christy, for providing these. The children at the orphanage just love your cookies, and so do I."

It was her new friend from church who had welcomed them— before they'd been rushed out the door by their father.

"Susan? Miss Johnson?" Valerie eked out the words.

Susan turned and a smile blazed across her pretty face. "Valerie! I'm so glad to see you. What brings you to the island mid-week?"

Her temporary joy vanished. Valerie patted her bag of medicines. "My family is very sick, and I came to get medication."

Was the Fillman family ill with that terrible flux? Susan stepped closer and patted Valerie's shoulder. "I'm sorry to hear that. Is there anything I can do?" This illness was deadly serious.

"Pray."

"I will." She closed her eyes. *Lord, help this family—Thy will be done.* Hadn't she just prayed a similar prayer for Paul and his daughter? Valerie's prayer was more urgent, but did God look at things that way? Thank goodness He was capable of anything and didn't have any trouble answering all kinds of prayers—as He willed, of course.

Mrs. Christy placed the cover on the cookie box. "I hate to eavesdrop, but I'll pray, too."

"Thank you." Valerie's smile trembled.

What her new church acquaintance needed right now was to be distracted from her worries. At least Susan could do that and give her a brief respite. "Let's send some cookies to your family." She rotated back toward the counter. "Rebecca, I'd recommended your excellent sugar cookies to my new friend."

"New friend?" Valerie's tone sounded startled, but her eyes were wide with pleasure.

"Anyone who meets our dear Susan becomes her friend." Rebecca Christy beamed at her.

What a kind thing to say. Susan had many acquaintances on the island, but she'd not had a bosom friend, for which she'd longed.

The baker retrieved a half dozen cookies and set them inside a small box. "There's one extra in there for your assistant, Miss Fillman. I heard he's finally recovered."

Susan accepted her own box for the orphans and stepped aside as Valerie went to the counter.

When Valerie reached for her reticule, the proprietress raised her hand. "This is a gift from us. Any friend of Susan's is a friend of ours, too."

"Thank you so much."

"You're welcome."

"I need some English black tea for Sister Mary Lou, too, and I absolutely will pay for that, Rebecca. No arguments." Susan pulled the money from her jacket pocket and placed it on the counter.

The shopkeeper raised her hands in surrender. "Yes, ma'am."

Susan grinned as Rebecca turned to the counter behind her and located the nun's favorite tea.

"And I'm going to have you girls sit down and try my newest apple cider recipe," Rebecca called over her shoulder. "You will be the first ones to try it. Garrett is up at the Grand working on an armoire."

Garrett Christy was a gifted craftsman and in charge of creating unique pieces for the hotel. "Seems like last year he ended up making massive hutches for the dining room during the off-season."

"Right. And, like now, he couldn't be my taste-tester during the day, when I tried out new items. And of course, the children are at school."

"Well, we're here, and that cider smells heavenly." Susan pulled a watch from a chain on her blouse. "I have time. The younger children are in religious instruction right now. I can still get these cookies to them before the class is over."

"I have to get back to the wharf within a half hour." Valerie shrugged.

Rebecca had already poured cider into two mugs and set them on a tray. "Go sit by the window and watch the leaves drifting. They're pretty right now."

"The maple by the orphanage is scarlet red. I love its vibrancy."

Susan led Valerie to a round table by a large window and they both sat down, setting their parcels aside. Rebecca's skirts swished as she bustled a tray to them. Not only the two steaming mugs of wonderful-smelling cider but additional cookies.

"And those are my apple gingersnaps." The baker grinned like a young girl. She loved her work. "Let me know what you think."

"Thank you. You're a blessing to me and the orphans."

"You're very kind." Rebecca adjusted her apron and then returned to the counter.

"What's it like living at the orphanage?" Valerie asked.

Susan exhaled a slow breath, surprised that Valerie hadn't yet focused conversation on her family's illness. But how Susan longed to ask for details. She didn't want to upset Valerie, though. "I relish working with the children, and I enjoy helping Father Joseph and Sister Mary Lou." Susan gazed at the patterned tin ceiling. "I wish I could learn some more skills though—like cooking and baking."

"Perhaps Mrs. Christy could help you."

Susan inwardly cringed, recalling their failed attempts. "She keeps busy with her family. But Mrs. O'Brien, our washerwoman, enjoys baking and she's offered to teach me when our kitchen isn't in use." *Although we'll have to sneak to do so.*

Valerie tilted her head. "Don't give up."

Susan flexed her shoulders and heard more stitches pop on her jacket, so she relaxed them immediately. "I won't. I am determined to learn more skills."

"Well, I cook most of our meals, but I can't say I'm a good cook." Valerie shrugged. "I do the best with what we have."

"There's a program coming next summer that will offer different classes, including cooking and baking. In fact, they're constructing the buildings for it now." *And we hear them banging all day long.*

"I will be out at the lighthouse then with my family."

Would Valerie still be there? Many had succumbed to the dreaded illness. Susan sipped her cider. "Now this cider is something I'd like to learn how to make."

Valerie drank, too. Her violet eyes widened. "It's like happiness in a mug."

A laugh escaped Susan. "We need to be sure to tell Rebecca that, and I agree."

"Let's try the cookies at the same time." Valerie's enthusiastic smile transformed her face from pretty to beautiful. "On the count of three."

This was fun. "One, two, three."

They both raised their cookies to their lips and took a bite.

Their sighs of enjoyment were accompanied by a gust of wind that swirled autumn leaves against the windowpanes.

"You're going to have a rough trip back, I'm afraid."

"I fear you're right."

"Let me walk you back to the wharf after we finish. It's on my way to the orphanage."

Mrs. Christy patted Valerie's shoulder, her hand warm and firm. "Praying the waves calm and your family's health improves." She cleared their table, and they said their goodbyes.

Susan accompanied Valerie to the docks. A sudden stiff chill breeze pushed Valerie's skirt even higher than its already short length. *Oh no.* The Straits were back to their temperamental nature. She swiped at her skirt's coarse fabric, pushing it down toward her ankles. *How embarrassing.*

At the wharf, Susan gave her a quick hug goodbye. "I'm glad to see you and enjoyed our little visit. If you need anything, please send word to the orphanage."

Other than Tim and Mabel's hugs, when was the last one she'd received? "Thank you. I will. I hope to see you again, too."

They parted ways, and the loss felt like a warm cloak had blown off. As Valerie reached the boat's mooring spot, she spied the lighthouse inspector, Mr. Dardanes, arguing with Billy, whose face was red.

As she neared, she caught Dardanes's words. "Miss Fillman can't return and that's settled."

She stepped closer, clutching the medications to her chest. "What's going on?"

The lighthouse inspector grabbed Valerie's arm firmly and turned her away from the young boatman. "You'll need to stay ashore."

"I need to get these medications back to my family. They're relying on me." Although her parents hadn't exactly said so. They'd not been able to speak.

The superintendent shook his head, his hat remaining firmly in place. "I've just returned and spoke with the assistant while I was there. . ." His dark eyes softened but he still steered her away from the dock.

"What is it, sir?" She hugged her thin coat closer as the wind increased.

Perspiration dotted the man's brow but he didn't stop walking toward the boardwalk. "It would be best if you stayed in town tonight."

"Until they're better? But I have medicine for them." They must be highly contagious, which was as she'd suspected. Only Val had withstood the onslaught of the vicious illness. The brief recollection of a smooth pale hand, so unlike Mum's, stroking her brow, flitted across her memory and she almost tripped on her skirt hem. She righted herself with assistance from the dark-haired man.

"I'm afraid no one can go in there."

"But where will I stay? The lightkeeper's house here in town?" She'd never seen it.

Dardanes's gaze flitted nervously around the wharf. "I'm afraid it's not been readied yet."

"Then where?"

"Ask Father Joseph to put you up."

A tiny jolt of happiness swept past her strong apprehension. She'd be with Susan. "But I've. . . I've never been away from my family."

"Not even for a night?" His dark brows drew together.

Valerie wasn't normally allowed any separation from her family. Today was the first time she could remember. As a young child, she'd had ongoing nightmares of being taken away from them. Perhaps those memories, though, were of being taken from an orphanage with many other children there.

Her head began to ache.

"I have a daughter about your age, and she's been away from us many a night." The superintendent frowned. "You must be about twenty or so?"

"I, uh, yes." Val blinked rapidly. "We've never celebrated my birthday."

"You can't be serious." His dark eyebrows raised high.

"I am." She moistened her lips.

"My nineteen-year-old daughter gives me a list well in advance of her happy day."

She bit her lip as she considered when last she'd had a truly happy day. The time spent with Susan today had been so. And her time with her brother and sister, when not interrupted by Mum, could be happy.

For a moment, she allowed herself the old fantasy—that somewhere out there were parents who truly loved her. A family where she was allowed to be a child instead of treated like a servant. Valerie closed her eyes and pushed aside the uncharitable thought. Of course her parents cared for her. They needed her. Hadn't they told her so many times?

"Who will help my parents if I don't get this to them?" Valerie held up the package.

"All I know is that you shall not return." His lips compressed into a line. "If you pray, now's the time to do so."

Chapter Three

Mackinac Island Orphanage

Susan startled as Valerie, a dazed look on her face, stepped out of Father Joseph's office. *What's she doing here? Something must be wrong.*

Sister Mary Lou stepped out of the office. Her body was bent in the manner that meant she heavily felt sorrow in her spirit. She touched Valerie's back and pointed toward Susan, prompting Susan to join them.

"Miss Johnson, I understand that you are acquainted with Miss Fillman?"

"Yes."

"We'd like you to share your quarters with her, dearie, while we learn of her family's. . . circumstances."

Susan's breath caught in her throat. "I. . . yes, if you'll follow me, I'll show you to my room." Not quite how Susan hoped to meet with Valerie again.

The lighthouse keeper's daughter followed Susan and Sister Mary Lou up to the attic. Embarrassment warred with anticipation of companionship.

Susan had occupied the garret room since she'd arrived on the island. Then it had been dismal. But it had been her own, unlike her previous placements. At the top of the stairs, she opened the paneled door that led to her room. Susan stepped aside so the other two could enter.

"Could you make up your extra bed for our newcomer?" Sister Mary Lou inclined her head toward Susan as she stepped into the center of the garret.

Valerie Fillman's doe eyes scanned the attic room. Was she comparing it to her room at the lighthouse? No doubt that was full of comfortable new furniture and bedding instead of shabby cast-offs. Still, Susan had done her best to make her little space cozy. There were framed pictures, an afghan a parishioner had made for her, quilts from two adoptive families of the children she'd cared for at the orphanage, and a small vase of season's end hydrangeas.

"Welcome, Valerie. I'll make up your bed and fluff the pillow." Susan clasped her hands at her waist. "I'm really sorry about your family being so ill that you clearly can't return today."

"Thank you." Valerie still clutched the package from the pharmacy, the small box of cookies, and her reticule.

"I can loan you a fresh nightgown and things," Susan's cheeks heated, despite the many times she'd offered undergarments to girls who'd come to the orphanage. But never to someone who was becoming her friend and near her age.

Valerie blinked several times. "I'd not thought of that."

"Of course not." Susan went to the closet and pulled out a shawl and offered it to the other woman. "It gets chilly in here, so you'll need this."

"Isn't that yours, though?" Valerie accepted the shawl.

"It was a donation. And I have another I can get down." Susan treasured that shawl and the hat she kept stored high in the closet.

One year at the Michigan State Fair, many years earlier, Susan's foster family had taken her and had 'allowed her to roam' while they rode some of the rides and ate the fair food with their own children. When dark clouds had clustered later that day, Susan shivered near a hot apple stand. How she'd yearned for coins to purchase some food. Then she'd recognized a voice nearby.

"I tell you, that is Susan Johnson," a familiar boy's voice insisted.

"It is not."

She turned to see Paul Scholtus and Annabelle, both older now but recognizable. They walked arm-in-arm. Annabelle was wrapped in a pretty pink, hunter green, and peach shawl.

"Paul? Annabelle?" She could scarcely believe it. Even though her heart hurt at having lost her dear friend, joy skittered through her at seeing Paul again.

Maybe it was her imagination, but Annabelle's nose seemed to wrinkle as Susan moved forward to take Paul's hands in hers and shake them.

"It is you, Susie."

"Yes."

"What are you doing here?" The way Annabelle posed her question sounded as if Susan had no right to be at the fair.

"My foster family is here."

Both Paul and Annabelle looked around.

"Where are they?" Concern etched Paul's maturing, now deeper, voice.

Susan shrugged. Then she shivered.

"You're cold." That same strange glint shone in Annabelle's pretty eyes like they had when Susan had first met her. Annabelle

removed her beautiful wrap and handed it to Susan. "Here, put this around your shoulders."

"Oh, I couldn't."

But Annabelle draped the soft woolen fabric around her, and it felt so good. Perhaps Susan had misjudged the girl.

Paul cast Annabelle a strange look, then removed his hat, a knit blue Frenchman's cap, and passed it to Susan. "You should put this on, too, Susie, so you don't catch your death of cold."

"Susan?" Valerie Fillman touched her shoulder. "Miss Johnson?"

"Oh, sorry, I was just recalling a memory from long ago." She went to the closet and pulled out the cedar box that held her special treasures, then removed the scarf. "I received this beautiful shawl from a. . ." Annabelle wasn't exactly a friend. "From someone I used to know." Susan draped the soft cloth around her shoulders.

Valerie moved closer. "May I touch it?"

"Certainly."

The newcomer ran her hand over the fabric and then rubbed it between her fingers. "It's very fine wool, isn't it?"

She heard the unspoken word, *expensive.* "It is."

Sister Mary Lou moved forward. "That's merino wool—a generous gift."

"That person must have cared for you." Valerie gave Susan a gentle smile. "Maybe like Mrs. Christy does."

"I'd like to think so."

"It's a blessing to have friends to help you."

"Yes," Susan agreed. Yet there'd been something in Annabelle's eyes and the way Paul had acted toward her that had always made Susan feel there was something she'd not known about the gift.

"I think Mrs. Christy is right, that you make friends easily."

"I'm glad you two young ladies got to chat at Mrs. Christy's shop earlier." Sister Mary Lou dipped her chin. "And I agree, our lovely caring Susan attracts friends."

Instead of bemoaning that I have few chums my age, I should appreciate those I have. "That's kind of you, Sister Mary Lou." Susan wiped a smidge of dust from a nearby picture frame.

"Only speaking God's truth, my dear."

Susan's cheeks heated from the praise. "Have you ever received a special gift, Valerie?" She knew Sister Mary Lou regularly received gifts mailed to her from family on the mainland.

"Yes, I, uh, maybe. . ." The young woman's voice dropped to a whisper. "Sometimes I remember, or maybe it's a dream, about someone giving me something very special. And I remember a boy, he was older than me who'd drawn a picture for me. It was for a card that I still have."

"Oh?"

Valerie fished around in her reticule and pulled out a small folded card. "I can't remember his name, but he was kind to me."

Lansing, Michigan

Lawrence Zumbrun paced the floor of his apartment, located conveniently near the capitol building. He'd miss this place. But his prospects, both career and otherwise, had come to a close, along with his job. Things would change now that he'd accepted a position managing the newly formed Social Affirmation Society. What a wonder that a position had so quickly become available for him.

God's grace, pure and simple.

He paused in front of his hearth. Image upon image of his brothers' families full of tiny Zumbrun children looked back at him solemnly—an unusual look for his nieces and nephews, to be sure. Two of his brothers had followed in Father's footsteps and become lawyers. The others, like Lawrence, were accountants or bookkeepers. *Will I one day have a photographic image placed upon my siblings' hearths?*

Perhaps he should have a new photograph taken since he'd not be there for the annual Zumbrun family celebrations. How cold would it be on Mackinac Island this autumn? Once he made this transition to his new job, within the month, he'd be stuck on the island for the winter. Once the ice came in, he'd not be able to travel to see his family. It should be interesting, though, to see how young Jack Welling performed with his runs back in his old stomping grounds. Thank God, Lawrence could continue coaching him and that the Wellings had offered him a room at their new quarters until the lodgings were ready for the summer program.

Lawrence was beginning a new life.

A life that, hopefully, could make room for a spouse.

That would require you to stop searching out the Gladstone's lost child.

A muscle in his chest tightened. The family had finally ceased their quest. How many young ladies had been put off by Lawrence's fascination, which they called obsession, with finding the girl? He ran his hand along his jawline.

This was it. This last lead. This would be the end. No more.

And he had peace about it.

Finally.

Peace.

He'd never forgotten the Gladstone's youngest daughter, who was three years old when the family had departed for England, where her father had inherited a title and a vast estate. They'd said their goodbyes at the Zumbrun's home in Detroit, with his four brothers and sister there, too.

Lawrence reveled in drawing. His friend Nathan's little sister, the youngest Gladstone child, enjoyed watching him, with her wide pretty eyes. They were like purplish-blue wildflowers. He'd drawn violets and a bluebird with his colored pencils on a simple white card for her. Then he'd written, 'Goodbye,' on it.

He wished he'd never written that word. Why hadn't he put, 'Best Wishes,' or something like that?

Because he'd never thought it would be a final goodbye. Although he'd seen Nathan again when the Gladstones returned, Verity Gladstone had either gotten lost or had been stolen—although no ransom demand had ever been received. Once Nathan's father unexpectedly became the Marquess, and the family moved to England, Lawrence had lost touch with his friend. When Georgina, Nathan's older sister, returned to the States, and later entered a sanitarium, Lawrence regularly visited her and developed a bond.

And now that Georgie was doing better, he'd introduced her to the man who'd soon become her husband.

Time for all of them to let Verity Gladstone free from their minds. She'd likely flown on to heaven all those years ago. Better to accept it. Wasn't it?

Shepherd, Michigan

"What a bountiful harvest this year." Paul's father stood in the middle of the now-bare corn field and gestured far and wide across the expansive Scholtus farm acreage.

Paul's brother, Ron, tucked his thumbs under his suspenders and snapped them. "And we got top dollar, too."

"Time to celebrate." Dad clapped his large work-roughened hands.

The only celebration Paul wanted was one where he'd received a letter offering him an interview for a lighthouse keeper position. Weeks had passed by. Would he never hear from the commission? He'd worked one summer as an assistant lighthouse keeper. But his brother had been injured that following planting season and Paul had to come home. Then later he'd gone to the sanitarium to work and afterward, returned home and got married. Then the baby, and the loss of Annabelle.

"Why the long face?" His brother elbowed him.

Maybe because I'm raising my daughter without my beloved wife beside me. Or because I need to get away from all the memories of her. Or because this is not the life I've wished to live. "Nothing. Just tired."

"Grampa will help tonight if Little Miss gets up again with an earache." Dad patted Paul's shoulder. "Right now, though, I'm going to figure out what your mother wants to do with all this." He raised a handful of money.

Ron shook his head. "Tell you to put it in the bank."

Dad had switched banks after Annabelle died. Her parents were cruel to Paul and wanted nothing to do with Hetty. Paul had taken away the bank owner and his wife's only child. It still hurt. Yes, they'd loved Annabelle, but so had he.

"Come on, boys, let's head back to the house."

Paul and Ron moved alongside their dad.

"Your mom has fed us aplenty all through the season. Maybe we men can roast a pig like our neighbor, Lee, from the Carolinas does."

The Southerner wasn't very popular with his farming neighbors, because of his tinkering with his loud engines. But Dad sometimes invited him over for a night of euchre. "He's not here right now."

"I heard he has a lady friend and may be getting married." Ron winked. "Maybe he'll move away with her."

"Or go stay back near his factory in Detroit with his buddy, Grant." It might be unkind to wish, but the neighbor's experiments were not good for the animals.

"All right, boys." Dad patted his belly. "Hey, I haven't made my famous barbecued beans for ages."

"Don't!" both Ron and Paul called out as they followed Dad toward the house.

"I'll do a big pan of roasted potatoes," Paul rushed to offer. His belly hadn't forgotten the last time he'd eaten his father's beans.

"I'll make a huge pan of cooked apples with cinnamon and sugar." Ron's overly large smile was a dead giveaway that he was holding back his real thoughts.

Dad rubbed his chin. "You boys do the sides then."

If Annabelle were still alive, she'd have sulked over the upcoming gathering. She'd likely have taken their daughter and retreated to their bedroom for the party.

An ache formed at Paul's temple. They'd had plans. Plans to get away from here. Bigger plans for their future.

And now that was all gone.

A wisp of smoke curled from the house's chimney.

Somehow, that trailing smoke taunted that Paul had never fulfilled his wife's expectations. Would he ever have done so?

If not. What would it have been like to have lived out a life with someone whom he never could please?

"Son?" Dad, now a good fifteen feet ahead of him, turned. "You all right?"

"Just thinking about Annabelle."

And not in a good way.

God forgive me, I know it's not right to speak ill of the dead. Was it wrong to even think bad thoughts of them?

Until recently, he'd never allowed any such ideas to slip into his mind. Why now?

Because of the newspaper picture of Susan. And the reminder of how Annabelle had really thought of his old friend. And the mean things she had said about her.

As much as he'd loved his wife, he'd also been blind to her defects in character. Not that Paul was perfect, but he tried to treat all people as he'd wish to be treated. "Love thy neighbor as thyself," as the Bible said.

How right it felt to be rekindling a friendship with his old neighbor. If he obtained a lighthouse assignment in Northern Michigan, perhaps he'd even be able to see her in person regularly again.

And he needed to put his memories of Annabelle to rest. But could he? Would the distance and the isolation bring healing?

He couldn't help sensing there was something more he'd need.

Chapter Four

Mackinac Island Orphanage

"Wake up, Valerie! Wake up!" Susan called, from where she stood getting dressed.

"No! Too many people! So many!" Valerie tossed and turned.

Fearful of approaching and touching Valerie in case she became combative like some of the orphans with nightmares, Susan tried calling out again. "Valerie! Can you hear me?"

"Don't want the train. Too long!" She flailed her head from side-to-side. "That horse cart is too small."

"Valerie, please stop!"

She sat straight up in the bed, perspiration dampening her forehead. "Oh, my, where am I?"

"It's me, Susan, your new friend. You're at the orphanage."

"Yes, Susan." She puffed out a breath. "I'm sorry." She pressed a hand to her chest.

"What were you dreaming about?"

"I have this nightmare a lot." Valerie pressed a hand to her head. "I'm traveling and traveling but it feels like I'm going nowhere. Then finally I'm back to a place that's somewhat familiar."

"I'm so sorry."

"I wake up and wonder what the dreams mean—they seem so real."

"Nightmares can be like that."

Valerie nodded.

"Do you feel up to joining me for breakfast? Might perk you up."

"Yes. Thank you."

Soon they both were dressed and headed downstairs.

The buzz of youthful voices surrounded Susan as she and Valerie weaved through the cafeteria. Although tempted to sit at "her" table, where most of the younger orphans sat, Susan carried her breakfast tray to a nook in the corner. Valerie sat across from her. Two of the older children, seated nearby, cast quizzical glances in their direction. Susan said grace and the two tucked into their hot oatmeal with raisins.

Valerie set her spoon down and sipped her coffee. "Such a cheerful room."

"Usually." Susan inclined her head toward the older children. "Several older orphans have realized they'll likely remain there until maturity. Adoption is unlikely, unless a farmer has need of a strong boy for work."

Valerie's eyebrows lifted. "I can guess how they'll be treated if they're only considered laborers."

That had been Susan's case, but she didn't want to say so. *Not here.* And from Valerie's comments, her parents treated her like a servant. "A few have returned here to work at the docks or as street cleaners. They've said that at least they learned how *not* to treat others."

"We have to ask God to help them—help us." Valerie yawned, then set her coffee cup down. "To overcome life's difficulties."

"Yes." Susan took another spoonful of her oatmeal. "The cooks need someone to help overcome the bland taste of this porridge. One would think they wouldn't recognize a sweet spice if it jumped up into their hands."

The corners of Valerie's lips tugged. "I was thinking something similar but wasn't about to say it. I'm just grateful to be here."

Susan reached across the table and squeezed her new friend's hand. "We're glad to be here for you. And I'll let you in on a secret."

She released Valerie's hand and felt in her pocket for the two tiny vials she brought with her on the oatmeal breakfast days. She showed them to Valerie. "Cinnamon and ginger from my friend Mrs. O'Brien. Want some?"

Valerie laughed. "Definitely."

She passed the tiny glass bottles to her. "Don't let the children catch you, though."

As she looked around, Valerie's mouth twitched. "All's clear." She tapped some of the spices into her bowl. "Thank you."

Susan accepted the vials back. "We're trying to figure out a kind way to ask the cooks to add some to the oatmeal. Until then, we're also working on the exact amounts we think are needed."

"Probably a budget issue." Valerie stirred the cinnamon and ginger as Susan poured some into her own bowl.

"I imagine so. But still. . ." If they'd let Susan review the budget, she'd probably find a way to save money from wasteful things that the children wouldn't eat—like sardines.

"We have supplies brought to the lighthouse and anything extra like that I have only so much I can budget for to cover extra spices and more sugar for Tim and Mabel's cookies. So it's probably like that here at the orphanage." Valerie took a spoonful and grinned. "So much better. Thank you."

"So you ordered the food?"

Valerie blinked rapidly. She had dark rings beneath her eyes today. "Only at the lighthouse. My mother has been getting. . . worse with some confusion recently."

The way the lighthouse keeper's daughter spoke, with a serious low tone, convicted Susan that her suspicions about Dorcas Fillman might be correct.

They ate their oatmeal and had just finished their coffee when Valerie's eyes widened as she looked over Susan's shoulder. Sister Mary Lou entered the room with little Francesca by her side. The child waved at Susan and then ran straight toward her and Valerie.

When she reached Susan's side, Francesca pointed to Valerie. "Is Miss Fillman, yes?"

"Yes." Susan squeezed the child's slim hand. She was doing a good job with her English.

Her dark, almost black eyes, wide, Francesca stepped around to Valerie. "*Scusate, ma padre Giuseppe desidera vedere la signorina Fillman venire nel suo ufficio.*"

Susan tried to keep from frowning at the girl, who'd lapsed into her native tongue. They'd have to step up their efforts to encourage her English mastery.

Valerie pushed back from the table, trembling. "Susan, would you please come, too?"

"Where?"

Valerie gestured toward Francesca. "This little girl asked me to go to Father Joseph's office."

Francesca beamed, but when she caught Susan's eye, she stared down at her tiny boots.

"You understood her?"

Valerie shrugged. "Italian people in the lumber camps taught me a little."

"I sorry I no say in English like Sister ask me."

Susan stood and patted the girl's shoulder. "It's all right."

Francesca pointed an index finger upward, her way of requesting to say something.

"Yes?"

"I think Padre Giuseppe, Father Joseph, he has something," she closed her dark eyes, "*molto brotto*, ah, how you say?"

Even Susan, with her limited understanding of Italian, knew molto meant much and brotto sure sounded like something bad.

The color left Valerie's face.

Much badness?

Oh no, this was not going to be good. Father God, prepare us, make a way before us.

"I'll come with you, Valerie."

Valerie bit back a sob. The worst kind of news? Had her entire family succumbed? But the Italian orphan had not said, "*peggio*." Peggio in a sentence always sent Italian lumberjacks scrambling.

"I go eat." The adorable little Italian girl ran off.

The two women joined Sister Mary Lou, who'd lingered near the dining hall entryway. "Good morning, ladies."

"Good morning, Sister Mary Lou. I asked Susan to join me if that's all right."

"We'll ask Father Joseph when we get up there, dearie."

They departed the dining hall and entered the corridor. Valerie followed Sister Mary Lou and Susan down the hallway. Exhaustion pulled at her, slowing her steps somewhat. Or maybe it was dread exerting its emotional control.

Forcing herself to breathe, Valerie walked determinedly toward the priest's office, which she'd visited the previous day upon her arrival at the orphanage. Sister Mary Lou knocked on the door then peeked inside. She motioned the other two forward. When they entered, Father Joseph had his back to them as he faced out the mullioned window. Gray skies loomed dark in the Mackinac skies.

Sister Mary Lou held her hands clasped at her waist. "Miss Fillman wishes for Susan to be here with her."

He turned, nodded, and pointed to the nearby settee. His facial expression reminded Valerie of an expression she'd read about—the proverbial blank canvas. She couldn't get a read on what he'd say.

Valerie sat and arranged her skirts around her, and Susan sat beside her. Sister Mary Lou stood behind them.

Father Joseph sank onto a nearby chair, positioning himself on the seat's edge. So precarious was his perch that she couldn't help wondering if he'd fall off onto the carpeted floor.

"Miss Fillman, I'm afraid I have bad news."

She closed her eyes. What would she do if her family was gone? All gone?

A thin memory, a ghost of an image clouded her mind. Mum, very young then, crouched in front of her.

"They've gone. They've all left you. And all you've got is me!" She shook Val's shoulders hard. "Do you understand? I'm your mum, and we've just got each other for now until I find your da'."

But Father and Mother were getting on a big boat. Why hadn't she gotten on it, too?

The memory didn't make sense then to her young mind, nor did it now.

"Your parents succumbed to the illness."

Valerie pulled in a shuddering breath and pressed her hand to her mouth. She opened her eyes. "My brother and sister?" Sometimes she'd prayed that she could find a way to take care of Tim and Mabel by herself, but she'd never found a way to break free on her own.

Father Joseph stared hard at Sister Mary Lou, who placed a hand on Valerie's shoulder.

"Only time will tell." He cleared his throat. "They're in the hospital in Saint Ignace, receiving the best care that can be given."

She exhaled a long breath. There was still hope.

Sister Mary Lou leaned in. "We'd like to have you remain here with us and if—"

"*When* the children recover, then we'll have them join you here." Father Joseph's even features were fixed in an almost stern expression.

"Yes." Sister Mary Lou removed her hand from Valerie's shoulder. "When they're recovered."

"Until then, they will remain on the prayer list for healing."

"And Susan can share her room with you."

"Yes," Susan agreed.

"Miss Fillman, we know this is a shock." Father Joseph rose. "We'll wait until later to discuss funeral arrangements and plans for the mass."

"Of course." Valerie stood, sensing that she was being dismissed. "But is there a way for me to see my brother and sister?"

His dark eyebrows rose high. "Oh no. They are too contagious for anyone other than special nursing care to tend to. No visitors until—"

"Until they are feeling better?" She chewed her lower lip. Would they beat this dread illness?

"Until then, we'll let them get the medical care they need."

How would she pay those medical bills?

Valerie needed to find a job so that she could support her brother and sister. She'd need to be able to support them when they came home.

But they had nowhere to come home to. Their parents were dead.

Valerie would find a way. She'd find a place.

She'd failed to get the medicine to her parents. It had been too late. Too late.

She fought back the black blanket of grief.

She had to be strong for Tim and Mabel. But all she wanted right now was to sink into a soft bed, cover herself with quilts, and sleep.

Sister Mary Lou patted Valerie's shoulder. "Come down to my office and let's take tea. I've found a good cup of chamomile can settle one's nerves. That and some time spent in prayer."

Susan examined her timepiece, which hung from a gold chain. "I'll need to go and teach my ten o'clock class, Sister Mary Lou."

"You do that, dearie, and I'll fetch Valerie some tea from the kitchen."

"And I'll see you later." Susan gave Valerie a quick hug, which surprised her.

"Yes. Thank you."

The nun led Valerie to a small office further down the hall. Inside, a narrow rounded-edge desk appeared to hunch beneath an open window. Children's playful voices carried from below.

"Have a seat, dearie, while I fetch us some tea."

"Thank you." Valerie sank onto the divan, which had an embroidered pillow at each end.

When the door closed behind the nun, Valerie closed her eyes. She was so very tired. Cotton candy swirls clogged her mind, pulling her down and away.

Sleep shrouded Val in misty visions.

Her mother, father, sister, and brother reached out to her from the lighthouse, but she couldn't clasp their hands. They were slipping away from her. She had to reach them. But she had to get on the boat to see Grandfather. But she had no grandfather, did she? Her family members' faces were changing, shifting so that she couldn't recognize them. She should go. No! They should stay.

Then another family strained in to touch her, to take her hand. The tall man who smelled so good and the beautiful lady beside him, whose smile made Val want to run to her. But she couldn't. Nearby, her older sister talked with another boy. Her older brother. They laughed. The servants carried luggage toward the ship. Two of the maids chatted nearby.

Someone grabbed her hand tightly. She looked up to see Dorcas, who pressed her fingers to her lips. "Don't!" she called out as the young woman pulled her down the street.

"Miss Fillman! Valerie!"

Val struggled awake to that scent of faint incense and lemon that filled the nun's office. Sister Mary Lou stood before her—her expression full of concern. Behind the sweet nun, an oil lamp illuminated the walls, which were painted a soft green. A crucifix and a painting of Jesus framed either side of the nearby doorway.

Sister Mary Lou fished a handkerchief from her black habit's pocket and passed it to Valerie.

Val accepted it and wiped her face, wet from tears.

"Thank you, Sister Mary Lou."

"You're welcome." The nun settled on the chair beside the settee. "You received quite a shock today."

"Yes." Valerie tried to shake off the strange dream. Her head ached.

"The superintendent left it to Father Joseph to break the news to you."

Tears welled up again. Her parents had perished within one day after she'd desperately left Round Island to obtain medication.

"Who is managing the light?" Strange that she should think of this, but it was important for the safety of the ships passing through the Straits.

"The lighthouse assistant stepped in to manage the light and Superintendent Dardanes is seeking temporary help until he can find a new keeper."

To replace Pa. A cold numbness trickled through her soul. How had God allowed this? Why had Mum and Pa refused to let her go when Valerie had first offered, five days earlier?

"This vicious flux has taken many lives in our parish." The nun patted her hand. "We're going to have to trust God."

Trust? Had Valerie ever trusted someone? *No. Perhaps long ago.* Maybe that was God she'd called upon as a young child.

But He'd never answered her prayers.

Could he answer prayers for her brother and sister? She'd add more—God was a big God. Was He big enough to help solve Tim and Mabel's other problems, too?

Surely, He could.

But why hadn't He before?

Marquessate of Kent, England
Gladstone Estate

"A Sugarplum Ladies reunion on Mackinac Island? A cooking school at a Christian retreat center?" Lady Eugenie Gladstone held the embossed invitation aloft near the windows as soft light flickered through the open velvet drapes. "And no signature?"

Her husband, Lord Percival, Marquess of Kent, set his newspaper aside on his mahogany desktop. "Tara Mulcahey has to be behind this, of course. She's been after you for years to come visit back in America. And she's never given up hopes of resurrecting your early years as a social reformer with your Sugarplum Ladies."

"They weren't *my* Sugarplum Ladies." She cast him a warning glance. "But the grandchildren will be here for most of the summer." All five of them.

"We can work things out. You, Carrie, and Tara haven't gathered together in ages. Years. Good heavens, can it be decades?" Percy's eyebrows drew together as he sipped his coffee and then set his cup back on the ivory china saucer.

"Not quite." *Over a decade.* Sixteen years or so? Was that even possible? Carrie Booth-Moore's successful husband had relocated the family from Detroit to New York shortly before she and Percy were to depart for England. Before that, the three lady friends had been happy as clams helping young widows learn skills after the war had ended. And they'd been joined by Evelyn Singleterry, who'd managed the Sugarplum Ladies' efforts with unbelievable skills. But she'd died too young—her husband, too. Where was her daughter now? Susan would be a grown woman.

Percy tapped his fingers on the table. "Wouldn't mind going to the States."

"Truly?" Eugenie's spine stiffened all the way up to her coiffed hair. Percy, too, had been devastated by the loss in their family all those years ago. Since they'd finally given up their search for their daughter, several years earlier, he'd become increasingly more distant.

She brushed at her skirt. "This could be a good trip for us both—especially since you're also on the invitation, darling."

"What?" He frowned. "Let me see."

He extended his hand, but Eugenie simply held the envelope aloft, faced toward him.

Percy scanned it. "That settles it. I'll get messages to my old friends to let them know."

"Christian would likely come up to Mackinac with us." The attorney and Percy had maintained their relationship for decades. Christian Zumbrun had been truly crushed that he'd not been able to help them find their missing daughter. But it wasn't Christian's fault. His youngest son, Lawrence, had stepped in, too, to help.

"Or we could stop in Detroit."

"Yes." Eugenie chewed her lower lip. "Sometimes I wish we'd never left."

Her husband came to her. He wrapped his arms around her from behind her chair and nuzzled her hair. "I wish that, too, my love."

Mackinac Island

Giddiness thrummed through her as Susan pressed her hand against the letter in her pocket. Mrs. Scholtus had written back to Sister Mary Lou, and Paul had included a brief note to Susan as well. The nun had passed both letters along to her that morning. She'd savored every word over her breakfast of eggs and sausage. Paul wished her well. He was glad to discover where she'd ended up.

It was kind of him not to ask why she'd never bothered to write him a note. After all, she knew where he and his family lived. Until recently, she'd lived in several situations that were less than desirable. She'd never have dared to share with him the difficult times she'd gone through before she'd connected with Sister Mary Lou and moved to the orphanage to help with the children here. Now, though, she could honestly tell her old friend that she was healthy, happy, and doing the Lord's work with these orphans. Still, she was lonely for that feeling of being with family. Paul certainly had had that in abundance—until his wife had died.

Father Joseph joined Susan and the children on the playground. "How's our new guest doing this week?"

She clasped her hands at her waist. "Miss Fillman cried last night a bit. She's asleep yet. I feared to wake her."

He shook his head. "She's been through a lot and has a hard road ahead of her."

"She's like a lost lamb."

"Like these young ones were."

Five-year-old Amanda broke from the group playing ring-around-the-rosy and ran toward them. Susan instinctively bent to be at eye level with the child. When she reached her, she pulled the pixie into a quick hug.

"How are you doing, Mandy?"

The precious child pointed to the gap in her lower teeth. "I lost a toof."

"Oh, my, you *have* lost a tooth." She tipped her head back to look up at the priest. "Can you believe that, Father Joseph?"

He extended his hand and opened his palm. "You'd best hand that tooth over to me. I'm sure the Walsh family might reconsider their adoption if you're missing some of your parts. We'll have to put this back in."

Mandy's lips quivered as tears pooled in her eyes.

"Father Joseph! I can't believe you'd tease her like that." Susan pulled the little girl close. "That fine family is so excited to get you, and they know baby teeth fall out and new big teeth come in. Apparently, Father Joseph doesn't. Maybe you should explain to him, Amanda?"

She released the girl and Mandy stuck her finger in her mouth, but said nothing.

Father Joseph shrugged and made a funny face. "I'm sorry, Amanda. My humor isn't always appreciated."

Mandy motioned for Susan to bend closer. The child cupped her hands around her mouth. "That wasn't funny, and I don't 'ppreciate it. That was mean."

Susan leaned back. "Hmm, I know, but can you forgive Father Joseph?"

The girl crinkled her nose. "Yes. I forgives him."

Before Susan or Father Joseph could respond the child raced back to her group who were now forming a human chain to wind around the yard.

"I'm going to miss little Mandy." Susan's heart ached for her own loss. "But I'm so grateful she'll be in her new home this coming Christmas." Only three months away but Susan had no plans for herself—only to make the orphans' celebrations happy.

"I best get back inside. Have to complete the limited memorial service plans." He raised his eyebrows. "With these contagious illnesses continuing, it seems odd to not have the normal mass services."

Fear of contagion, coupled with medical advice, had such gatherings reduced with the epidemic.

He rubbed his neck. "But we will still have a gathering in the hall, after the memorial."

"May Mrs. O'Brien and I help with the reception? By cooking, I mean." Her kitchen privileges were limited by the orphanage's cooks.

Father Joseph arched a bushy eyebrow. "I didn't realize you had an interest."

Mother, whom she'd lost at almost the same age as Mandy was right now, had been an amazing cook. She'd been trained at the Sugarplum Ladies Society in Detroit, despite becoming their manager. That had been before she'd met Father. "One of the few things I have from my birth mother is a receipt box full of recipes that I'd love to try out." That and Mother's autograph book—something her mother had occasionally brought out and had guests write sentiments inside accompanied by their signatures.

The first inscription, so sweet, always made her smile:

> To Miss Evelyn Marie Singleterry,
> A New Year's Wish -1868
> *May this book*
> *To thee bring*
> *Sentiments to*
> *Make your heart Sing*
> *Adelaide Fox – Your Sugarplum "Numbers Girl"*

"Did you cook or bake in any of your foster homes, Miss Johnson?"

"Not much," she admitted. "But I want to try. And Mrs. O'Brien is an excellent baker."

"Oh?"

"Yes."

He rocked on his heels, a sign he was cogitating. "I give you permission to check with the cooks and inquire as to when the kitchen is free. Then you may use it as long as your assigned work duties are completed."

"Thank you." Rebecca Christy must have kept Susan's catastrophes to herself, thank goodness.

"You're welcome."

The first thing she'd make would be the Eugenie Mott cardinal cake. "Is there a, um, budget for the funeral reception?" And would it be in poor taste to prepare a cake full of chopped red cherries? Expensive, and probably not the right choice due to its vibrant color.

Maybe the Tara Mulcahey brown sugar apple muffins would do. Her mother's dear friend, part of the Sugarplum Ladies catering group, had visited them at the farm not long before Susan's parents had passed away.

Why had Mrs. Mulcahey not tried to help Susan when her parents had passed away?

"Has everyone been notified about the deaths, Father Joseph?"

"We asked the Lighthouse Service to do that, but it wouldn't be a bad idea to send that out to the parishes. We've been told the family lived a very isolated life and had no relations here in the States."

"Yes. Valerie told me that, too. Her parents were immigrants from England." *East London.*

"And she's an adult. She can contact others. We'll help her once she's gotten over the shock."

Who had notified others for Susan's sake when Mother and Father had succumbed? She'd wondered, over the years, why none of her parents' friends had taken her in. But she'd been moved to a foster home very quickly. Mrs. Scholtus may have wanted to take her in, but with her large family, perhaps her husband didn't know how they could manage. And times were tough—her parents had said that not long before they'd fallen ill.

"I'll speak with the cooks and Mrs. O'Brien about working on reception foods."

The priest dipped his chin. "The Lighthouse Society Superintendent gave us a very charitable donation for everything but cautioned me not to expect many folks."

"Oh." So that might mean she could try Mrs. Carrie Booth-Moore's simple, but expensive seafood mousse, which was made in small batches. And it wasn't something prone to burning easily—at least not by Susan.

Susan was about to participate in her mother's legacy and it brought tears to her eyes.

If you're looking down from heaven, Mother, I hope to do you proud.

Chapter Five

Shepherd, Michigan

*W*as one of the letters in Ma's hands marked with the Lighthouse Administration's insignia? Paul, seated on the couch, set his daughter with her doll onto the carpet and accepted the mail.

"Dinner is in a half hour." Annoyance, mixed with sadness, tinged Ma's words.

"Thanks, Ma."

Once she'd left the parlor, he opened the first letter—from the Lighthouse Administration—which he quickly scanned.

His heartbeat ticked upwards. There was an immediate opening at Round Island Lighthouse, which was currently being manned by substitutes and an assistant. *Family quarters on one level.*

Paul pulled in a quick breath. This was what he'd been waiting for all these months. A chance to start over. A chance to live out his dream of being a lighthouse keeper on the Great Lakes. A chance to put Annabelle's memory to rest.

He read the rest of the letter. No mention of why the previous lighthouse keeper had left. But he'd need help to care for his daughter—which he'd need to mention in his application. Paul's heartbeat ratcheted up further. How quickly could he find someone if they offered him the position?

He drew in a steadying breath and opened the next envelope.

Susan had written, too. She talked about the children she worked with and inquired about what was happening with him. Sounded content. What a relief. All those years ago, he'd felt so bad that his family couldn't take her in to live with them. Those were hard times on the farm, but of course, no one talked about it back then.

He could ask Susan to help him find a worker. She may know someone. Maybe an older widow could help. The position also supplied a small home on Mackinac Island for the winter season, when the lighthouse wasn't operating.

Might be best to contact the orphanage directly and not bother his childhood friend. He needed to act quickly. He'd send a telegram to the Mackinac Island Orphanage and explain his needs. Otherwise, how could he take this job?

And he'd need someone kind who could cook and bake for them. Round Island Lighthouse, while technically not far from Mackinac Island and also the mainland, was still isolated enough that he couldn't simply head into town and purchase meals for himself and Hetty. In the winter, when the ice froze over, then yes. But until then, he'd need someone who possessed passable cooking skills.

Would there be anyone, cook or not, who'd be willing to come out to the lighthouse to help with Hetty?

This was already getting harder.

But God was bigger than all his problems.

Mackinac Island

Mrs. O'Brien took a dainty bite of the muffins Susan had prepared. Her eyes widened. "What on God's green earth did ye put in these?"

Susan pointed to the cooking preparation table.

"Did you put salt in the recipe 'stead of sugar?"

"It had both."

"A little salt and more sugar?"

"Yes."

Susan lifted a muffin to her lips and sniffed. *Salty.* She took a bite. "Oh no."

"Och *yes*, dear girl. Ye switched 'em around."

"I've ruined these."

"Och, ye'll not call me an Irishwoman if'n I cannot save these for use in something else. Won't take a *mealy praty*, a lump on me old noggin," she thumped on her head, "to come up with a use."

The door swung open and Valerie stepped inside. "Am I interrupting?" She cocked her head to one side, "You look upset."

Susan hung her head.

Mrs. O'Brien patted her shoulder. "Never ye mind, pet. This all takes a bit of learnin'."

"May I help?" Valerie moved toward them. "Did something go wrong?"

"Salt for sugar."

The young woman's lips compressed. "Common mistake for beginners."

Valerie had offered to help bake for the reception but both Susan and Mrs. O'Brien had refused her.

"Aye, and I'd gotten distracted working on these cakes, or I'd have helped poor Susan out more."

"Let's try those instead." Susan pointed to the long counter where five different cakes cooled.

Those violet eyes widened. "Oh my. Who will eat all of this?"

Mrs. O'Brien shrugged.

"The children will have it with their meal if it doesn't all go at the reception," Susan hurried to explain.

"They seem sweet." Valerie shoved her hands in the pockets of her dark gray work dress. They'd been unable to find her any black items, for mourning, in the donation barrel.

"They are very good children for the most part." Susan sighed as she grabbed her mitts and ran to pull her biscuits from the oven.

"Oh, those smell heavenly."

She pulled the large tray out and set it on a nearby rack.

"Perfectly golden brown."

"And no sugar in those." Mrs. O'Brien winked.

"Unless I put in sugar by accident instead of salt."

"Then we may have shortcakes."

Susan angled her head sideways. "Oh, yes?"

"Aye, most shortcakes have sugar in them."

Valerie leaned against the counter. "My mother rarely let me add sugar to my recipe because she believed the plain biscuits could do as well."

"Och. How much baking and cooking did ye do?"

"Almost all of it."

"Truly?" Susan couldn't imagine doing so.

"When I was younger, she did." Valerie chewed her lower lip. "But as soon as I was old enough, she taught me how to cook. She occasionally made stew or porridge for us."

The kitchen door creaked as a curly-haired child peeked in.

Mrs. O'Brien scowled. "By those red curls I'm guessin' it's one of the Clancy clan."

The eldest child, Sean, who was almost as tall as Susan even though he was only twelve, strode in, his thumbs hooked through his belt loops. "I smelled me some good cookin' in here and came to 'vestergate."

Valerie arched an eyebrow. "Investigate?"

"That's wha' I said, ain't it?"

Susan marched over to the lad, tempted to yank his ear. Of course she wouldn't. "Now don't be rude, Sean."

He shrugged, but his cheeks reddened. When his stomach growled loudly, sympathy surged through her.

A growing boy—but they were under strict mandates to ration servings to the children by age.

She touched his shoulder. "Come try a biscuit."

"Yeah?" He cocked his head.

She smiled at him. "I'm not so good at baking, though." She made a disappointed face before she swiveled around and walked back to the table.

"That's all right Miss Susan. You're the best at givin' hugs."

When was the last time she'd hugged Sean? She'd thought he'd grown too big for her hugs after story times. She'd have to rethink that notion. She turned to look at him, expecting him to be stifling a laugh. But he wasn't. Instead, his eyebrows drew together as though he was deep in thought. If she had a husband and a home, she'd take in an entire family, like Sean's. People didn't want to adopt entire families of children. But she would—in an instant if she had the means.

Valerie pointed toward a tall stool by the table. "Sit down. Would you like to try some fig preserves?"

He waved her suggestion away. "Just plain is fine by me, thank you." He looked pointedly at Sister Mary Lou.

She nodded approval, no doubt happy that he'd remembered his manners.

"Voila!" Valerie passed the boy a small plate with one biscuit.

His lips tugged. "I thought it was a biscuit. What's a vwellah?"

Susan chuckled. "Miss Fillman is using a French expression meaning, basically, here it is."

"I ain't never heard no Frenchies use that expression." He looked very serious. "Miss Fillman, you sure that's what it means? I don't want you getting tricked into saying something real bad."

The three women burst into laughter. He looked so very grown up when he was giving her new friend advice.

Eyes wide, he glanced at each woman, his cheeks even redder than before. "What? I'm just tryin' to be helpful." He rolled his eyes and then bit into a full third of the biscuit.

The ladies quieted. Susan awaited his reaction.

He swallowed and then shoved the rest of the biscuit into his mouth.

Valerie chuckled. "I guess you like it then, Sean?"

His small features tugged together, making him look, like his siblings did, almost elfin. "I dunno. I may need to try a few more."

Sister Mary Lou rolled her eyes upward. Was she praying for heavenly guidance? She placed another biscuit onto his plate.

When the second one disappeared as quickly as the first, Susan added a third.

"I don't think he likes them." Valerie's voice was deadpan, but her eyes twinkled.

Sean scowled as he finished off the third. "I'm not sure. I'm thinkin' we should have my brothers try them, too."

From the look on Sister Mary Lou's face, that was unlikely to happen.

Susan needed to soften the blow. "We only have this one small batch, Sean, plus some muffins that I ruined."

His young face seemed to instantly age. "I shouldn't have eaten those all. I shoulda split 'em in two and we all coulda had some."

The poor boy. Now he had a full belly but a topping of guilt to go with it.

Susan leaned in. "Say, Sean, would you be willing to help us again, and next time we'll let them try what we bake?"

"But you first have to tell us what you think of Susan's biscuits." Val crossed her arms over her chest.

Sister Mary Lou quickly dipped her chin. "Exactly. A deal is a deal. So what's the verdict?"

He crinkled his nose as he pointed at Susan "Guilty."

Susan pointed to herself. "Me?"

"Guilty of making the best biscuits I've ever had. And don't tell Cook, or I'll be in trouble."

Sister Mary Lou placed her index finger over her mouth.

"We won't say a word," Susan promised.

"Back to bed, young man." Sister Mary Lou inclined her head toward the door.

"You might not have finessed the art of baking muffins yet, but you have a wonderful way with the children." Valerie beamed at her.

"God has gifted us all with something to bring glory to the kingdom. And I think Miss Fillman has hit on yours, dearie."

Maybe Susan was right where she belonged. Maybe she was meant to be, for the rest of her life, at the orphanage. She could help with the children.

Why then had the Lord left this desire in her heart for more?

For her own family?

When she'd written that letter to Paul, she couldn't help but wonder what it was like to be surrounded by family, like he was.

"You look deep in thought." Valerie moved closer. "I would still be very honored to have you help with the memorial reception."

"Oh. You're kind. I guess I could serve. I just wish I could have helped more."

Mrs. O'Brien joined them. "Och, don't ye give up your efforts, Susan. I'll help with the food."

"Thank you, Mrs. O'Brien."

"Och, glad to help ye, Valerie." The older woman pointed at Susan. "And ye mark my words well, once that summer program up and starts, ye'll be cookin' like a professional chef. Otherwise, yer future family is gonna go hungry or have some broken teeth—or both."

Valerie and Susan gaped at the Irishwoman.

Then they all burst out laughing.

"I could at least make those fancy sandwiches—the Carrie Booth-Moore cucumber ones—if you bake the bread."

"Och, and you could manage the salmon spread, too, that goes on little rye bread squares. Perhaps those two recipes from Mrs. Booth-Moore could keep yer future family fed."

Her future family? She didn't even have a beau. But if they wanted to be hopeful, why shouldn't she? Wasn't that part of why she was so desperate to improve her skills? Yet she wasn't becoming more proficient. "If I pick up bread from Rebecca Christy to go with my salmon spread, then maybe they won't starve."

Wasn't love more important than her baking ability? Sean and his brothers were starving for love, affection, and attention. She had that in abundance.

Chapter Six

Chicago

*C*arrie Booth-Moore gritted her teeth as her two eldest daughters launched into singing *Sweet Rosie O'Grady*—their newest favorite popular and simply the most annoying song. "She's the sweetest little rose the garden ever grew," they chorused with gusto. Their enthusiasm overrode their lack of singing ability, so Carrie rose and closed the doors to her ladies' parlor room. *No wonder their husbands suggested they come over here to practice.* They sounded nothing like dear Evelyn Singleterry had. That young woman had the singing voice of an angel. *Gone too soon.*

Carrie settled at her Louis XIV desk, but the doors swung open, accompanied by more of Maude Nugent's song lyrics. "Close the door," she hissed to her youngest daughter, who held a cream-colored envelope aloft.

"Look, Mother! We have an invitation for the Sugarplum Ladies to meet up on Mackinac Island this summer."

Carrie arched her brow. "First of all, there is no *we*, as you were not a Sugarplum Lady. And secondly, how would you know what was in the note?" She extended her arm, dripping with gold bracelets, and accepted the missive.

Her daughter shrugged. "Cook taught me how to open a sealed envelope using steam."

Scowling, Carrie opened the note and read, then gaped. Could it be? Had Eugenie finally relented and was coming to visit?

"There's no signature, Mother."

"Pish posh—this is Eugenie Mott Gladstone, now Marchioness of Kent, pure and simple." Carrie fanned herself. "I'll need an updated work wardrobe." Work—her husband considered that a dirty word as far as his wife and daughters were concerned. He'd barely tolerated her time with the wonderful program which had helped numerous women get back on their feet after the war. Her daughters loved hearing about all the things she'd done then, but her husband opined that she should not encourage them in such interests and should help them find wealthy mates, not learn work skills. But times were changing—so should he.

"And what about me, Mother?" Her daughter wheedled. "Will I be allowed to help?"

She cast her a shocked glance. "I thought you enjoyed swanning around the West Bluff, having your maid change you five or more times a day."

"I could learn some new things." Her lips pulled to the side. "Especially if Father stayed home."

She ignored the later comment. "If you're certain."

"I am." She offered a smile that was half-smirk. "I've decided to become a modern young woman."

Was that what Carrie had been all those years ago? Eugenie had certainly been ahead of her time. A social crusader who'd swept Carrie into her scheme to help the widows of Civil War veterans and others affected by the schism in their country—Eugenie Mott, her bosom friend.

Eugenie back in the States. Would her children be with her? If only little Valentine, too, were there. Where had that girl gone to? Poor broken-hearted Eugenie.

Had some evil person snatched the little girl simply for the diamond bracelet Carrie had gifted the child with on her last birthday at home? Guilt had dogged her for years.

But she'd gifted that exact bracelet to her daughters and to Eugenie's girls, too—seven tiny diamond bracelets in all. *I never should have tempted the devil who took her.*

Too late for that now. But it wasn't too late to try to encourage her dear friend again.

This could be exciting. This could be a change. But her erratic heart beat out a different story.

As her youngest left the room, another verse made Carrie cringe. "I shall never forget the day she promised to be mine. As we sat telling love tales in the golden summertime."

A reunion with Eugenie and Tara. It was a shame dear Evelyn wouldn't be there.

But who was organizing this event? There were so many uncertainties. A woman in her position needed to be cautious. She'd dictate a response when her personal secretary arrived. *How did one respond to an anonymous writer who used a post office box?*

Carrie surveyed the room, where photographs of her days in Detroit with the Sugarplum Ladies dotted the walls. *The best days of my life.*

Evelyn had come on later with them and had proven to possess extraordinary management skills. Whoever ran this summer program couldn't compare.

Now come on, Carrie girl, Mother would have told you that such comparisons are unfair. She dipped her head.

Daughter of an Irish immigrant mother—like Rosie in the song—Carrie could help others directly instead of simply writing out checks.

But what will my heart doctor say?

Detroit

Tara Mulcahey smoothed out the wrinkled letters that she'd received from Evelyn Singleterry Johnson over the years. As the Sugarplum Ladies' business manager, Evelyn had kept their accounts in tip-top shape. The quiet dark-haired beauty, who'd lost her fiancé in the war, had married a little later in life. She'd met Henry Clay Johnson at one of the agricultural events the Sugarplum Ladies had catered. Before long, the married couple welcomed their daughter, Susan Marie.

Tara had visited the family annually and they'd been close. But then, one fateful year, Evelyn had ceased sending letters. And when Tara had traveled to the Johnson's farm, it had been sold—and their daughter Susan gone.

Hands trembling, Tara swiped moisture from her eyes. She had spent years trying to locate her friend's daughter—much like her dear friend, Eugenie Gladstone, had looked for Valentine. But unlike Eugenie's child, Susan had been taken away by a care society and then placed with a family. When the social agency refused to share information, she'd hired a private investigator through Christopher Zumbrun's legal firm. Her cousin was married to the prominent attorney, and Christian had been very helpful.

Tara had learned that Susan's first two placements—a foster family and then a Poor House—hadn't been far from the farm in Shepherd. When trouble came, the first family returned the child as if she were no more than an unwanted puppy. Tara had been so angry. All the investigators could find after that was that an itinerant farmer and his wife had taken Susan to the Upper Peninsula. Given that the peninsula stretched over five hundred miles across, and he had no other leads, he'd finally stopped taking her money.

But then a letter had come from her cousin's youngest son, Lawrence, the previous day.

> Dear Cousin Tara,
>
> I have good news! A young woman, listed as Susan Marie Johnson, was photographed for the Mackinac Island newspaper. I've enclosed the picture, and it appears as though she works at the island's orphanage.
>
> I have begun correspondence with the priest for the diocese to determine if this may be your friend's daughter. I am hopeful that we may yet reunite you with your goddaughter. I expect to arrive

on the island myself within a few weeks to begin work there.

I will update you as soon as I hear.

Sincerely,

Lawrence

Tara had been thrilled with the newspaper clipping. That young woman looked very much like Evelyn had. This Susan Marie had to be her friend Evelyn's daughter—she just had to be.

"Post is here, my love." Bertie, Tara's husband, clutched several envelopes in his beefy hands.

"Any for me?"

"All of 'em are, my sweet." He winked at her, handed her the letters, and then thunked down into his chair at the table.

"This is unusual."

"I'll say. Ya got one in there from them posh folks in England. Marchioness of Kent, what?" His Cockney accent thickened as he spoke.

"From Eugenie?"

"Tha's the one, lovie."

Tara quickly searched for, and found, Eugenie's letter. One post had Carrie's distinctive writing and the other held no address.

She tore into Eugenie's letter and scanned the missive. All was well with her friend and her husband. But after reading the next bit, she clutched the letter to her bosom. "I wonder what Eugenie means in her letter when she says she and Percy intend to go up to the Straits once they can arrange things."

He shrugged. "Maybe they're plannin' a trip."

"But then she said she'd see me—or us—there. Why would she write that?"

"Dunno, love, but would you like a cuppa? I'm gonna make myself one." He rose from the table.

"Some oolong with a teaspoon of that honey our neighbor gave us."

He saluted her. "Comin' right up, missus."

Tara re-read the letter but could still make no sense of it. She raised her hands. "I give up."

Bertie put the kettle on the stove. "Look through them other letters—maybe that'll help."

She didn't see how, but she didn't say so. Since the Gladstones lost their child, almost seventeen years ago, Eugenie's letters could be somewhat cryptic—but this one beat all.

Tara opened the next letter from Carrie Booth-Moore. "Carrie wrote me, too, and she says the same thing—that she hopes to possibly see me at the Straits of Mackinac. She asks if I've gotten the invite, too, and was I the one who sent it or Eugenie."

"Do ya think the two of 'em are puttin' ya on?" Her husband rocked back and forth on his heels as the tea kettle began to simmer and sputter.

"Why would they do that?"

"Dunno, love."

Tara blew an exasperated breath and reached for the ivory engraved envelope. Definitely no return address. She unsealed it, then gasped. A Sugarplum Ladies reunion! Carrie and Eugenie must have known how very much she needed to see them.

"Oh, my heavens, they've set up a Sugarplum Ladies reunion and a summer camp on Mackinac Island!"

She fanned herself with the heavy notecard. What fun they would have. What recipes they would make.

"Tha's all lovely, sweetie, but where'll we stay? We don't have a big castle-like cottage up on the cliffs like yer pals do."

"True. But it says that there will be accommodations."

"Lovely, pet." Her husband removed the kettle from the stove and poured the tea. "I think Uncle Horace has somethin' here with this whistle—that sounds in case ye let the water boil out."

"Too bad there's not a kettle that whistles when water starts to boil." She shrugged. "Then we wouldn't have to stand watch over it."

"I'll mention that to him in my letter."

"You do that, Bertie."

Lansing, Michigan

Lawrence packed his papers related to the two missing Sugarplum Ladies' children in his briefcase. At least he'd likely found Evelyn Singleterry Johnson's child for Cousin Tara. The letter from the priest would likely confirm her identity, and then he'd notify his cousin again.

The sharp rap on his apartment door had to belong to Mr. Peter Welling. When the door swung in, and Jack barged past his father, stepmother, and little half-sister, Lawrence's conjecture was proven correct.

"The train got here early, Larry!"

Lawrence cringed—he hated Jack's nickname for him. At least Jack's sister's nickname, Sally, made sense, since Satilde was an unusual name.

Jack tossed his cap toward the coat rack. When it hit its target, he threw his hands in the air. "Ringer!"

Ada Welling rolled her eyes, like a much-younger woman would have at Jack's antics, as she shifted her daughter on her hip. "Sorry we're early, but we caught a taxi almost immediately and thought we'd best come."

Jack jerked his thumb toward his sister. "Yeah, she's gonna need a nap soon." He made a snoring sound.

Peter Welling drew in a slow deep breath. "We're delighted to meet with you."

"Or they would be—if I'd stayed back on the farm." Jack winked. But then he went to Ada, took the one-year-old in his arms and inclined his head toward Lawrence's bed chamber.

Lawrence nodded his assent. "Make sure you put extra pillows around Sally. That's what I have to do when my nieces or nephews nap here."

Ada followed them, pulling off her gloves.

Mr. Welling hung his coat, and then sank onto the divan. "This your furniture or the landlady's?"

"I've only got a trunk, with my weights," he pointed to the corner, "some luggage. Pillow and clothing and all that, of course."

"Good, good." He ran a hand through his graying hair. "The Penwells, the railroad man and his wife, offered free transportation for all of us. Later they'll bring any children who come up for the program. But we don't want to impose on their goodwill with a request to transport a lot of furniture."

"I understand." Good thing he'd not accepted his parents' offer to furnish the apartment.

Mrs. Welling returned to the living area. "I'm delighted you're coming on with the program, as are the board members."

"They're nowhere near as demanding as that bunch of curs in Lansing." Mr. Welling's nose crinkled. Lawrence could see where his son got that habit.

"They think they're doing what is right, sir."

"Ha! They're doing what they think will get them votes. And save money they can spend on their schemes."

"Now, Peter, don't get excited over something you can't control." She sat beside her husband and patted his hand.

"Yes, dear."

Would Lawrence one day have a wife to utter those words to? "Have you got the building plans, sir?"

"Oh yes." Mr. Welling reached into his jacket and pulled out a pad of grid paper. "These aren't the blueprints. They're drawings to show you what's being set up on the island." He set drawings on the coffee table.

"Oh, I'm sorry—I should have mentioned that this coffee table belongs to me. A gift sent from England, from my father's closest friends."

"Tell Louis to make room for whatever Lawrence needs." Ada Welling's clipped tones made it sound like she was the railway tycoon and not Mr. Penwell.

Peter Welling faced his wife and mock saluted, then settled back against the divan. "Given what you're planning on bringing up for Satilde, I doubt it'd make much difference.

Adelaide shrugged. "A one-year-old requires a great deal of accoutrements that won't be easily available on the island."

"Never found it an issue for Maude and Jack," Peter grumbled.

She cast him a stern glance. Did she resent that his first wife had been well off and could afford to have extra goods shipped to Mackinac? Jack said a codicil in his maternal grandmother's will had prevented his father from owning properties that he and Jack's mother had operated for years. That was why when Peter remarried, he and Ada returned to his father's farm in Shepherd. Peter was definitely not a farmer, according to his son. Still, the couple had continued to pay Lawrence to coach Jack, and they'd hired other coaches prior to him. Mrs. Welling, who was in her forties, had worked long and hard and must have savings of her own.

"Enough complaining." Mrs. Welling pointed to the first diagram. "For Jack's runs this winter, the new gymnasium will have lots of room for those truly frigid days."

Peter feigned shivering, "When the Straits of Mackinac winds threaten to blow you away."

A grid drawing of a large rectangular room showed it surrounded by smaller rooms. "The gymnasium is where many of *our* summer activities will be held."

The way she said *our* made it sound as if she had ownership of the program. He was supposed to manage the physical activities for the children and would have his own staff. And there would be other managers for different aspects. He'd test a theory. "Will you and Mr. Welling have offices?" He pointed toward the smaller rooms that surrounded the gym.

She laughed. "Heavens, no. I have Satilde to chase after."

Peter glanced at his wife. "There's a young woman on the island that we, uh, that the foundation is hoping to hire."

Jack rejoined them. "She's asleep. I only had to sing *Bye, Baby, Bye*, twice." The boy lowered himself into the chair beside Lawrence.

"Thank you, Jack. You're a wonderful big brother." Mrs. Welling beamed at the youth, who blushed.

Peter cleared his throat. "Yes, he is, but let's do what we came for. In answer to your question about offices, you'll have your own right here." He tapped a larger office in a corner. "Your assistants will have offices beside you."

Ada tapped her fingers together. "There's room for equipment, storage for other miscellaneous things, and all the spaces that you suggested might be useful for physical activities and classrooms."

"This is an even bigger design than our building in Lansing. Will it be ready in time for next summer?" Lawrence tried not to frown.

The couple exchanged a meaningful look.

Jack flexed his long legs out. "Already underway. They started constructin' all the buildings."

Mrs. Welling raised her palms and flexed her fingers. "Not all."

"The gym, kitchen, and housing buildings." Mr. Welling turned the pages of the notebook. He stopped at a drawing of another rectangular space. "Later will come the music building."

"The arts and crafts building with larger classrooms will also be built later." The matron brushed at the mother-of-pearl buttons on her cuffs.

"But the housing and cafeteria are gonna be done, right?" Jack's nose crinkled, just like his father's had earlier.

Like father like son. In Lawrence's case, not so much. By following a path of working with youth and accepting low-paying positions after college, he'd distanced himself from his attorney father, who had hoped he'd pursue a more lucrative career.

"The cafeteria is in the kitchen building, son." Mr. Welling pointed to the kitchen area, whose circumference was ringed with linear notations of stoves and long worktables. "They'll cook there but over here is an area to eat." He tapped at the rectangular space in which long tables and benches were lightly sketched.

"Are they gonna try out their stuff on us, then?" Jack cringed. "When they're just learnin'? They might kill us with their lousy cooking."

A slow chuckle began in Mrs. Welling's throat and then built until she covered her mouth as she burst out laughing.

"A cook accustomed to serving large groups will provide planned meals for participants." Mr. Welling raised his eyebrows. "Of which you are *not* one, as you are not a participant in the actual program, and will have no say in the matter."

Jack's face turned crimson. Lawrence compressed his lips, lest he say something untoward such as defending the boy's normally good manners. But Jack had a habit of intruding himself into situations where he didn't belong, so Lawrence restrained himself.

Young Welling rose. "I'm gonna check on Sally." He headed toward the bedroom.

"Don't wake her!" cautioned Ada.

Lawrence shook his head. "This is astonishing how fast it's coming together."

Again, the two exchanged a long glance.

"This has been in the works for a while. The fact that you're ignorant—"

Mrs. Welling touched her husband's arm. "The fact that your position has ended is serendipitous for us, because we'd love to have you for the program. And the board wondered if it was unethical to lure you away from the Lansing health initiative."

"Now we don't have to." Mr. Welling dipped his chin.

If he'd been forced to choose, it would have been difficult. "I'm grateful for the opportunity."

"We're hoping Miss Susan Johnson feels the same way." Mrs. Welling beamed. "She helped manage the orphanage's programs for several years now and—"

"We think she'd be perfect." Peter Welling coughed into his hand.

"Susan Marie Johnson? From the Mackinac Island Orphanage?" Lawrence sounded like a parrot.

Adelaide touched the cameo at her collar. "You know her?"

He couldn't reveal that they'd been looking for Susan for years. "Not personally. But I did see a photograph of her in the Mackinac Island paper."

"She's not hard on the eyes, is she?" Peter laughed.

"Peter! She's going to be working with Lawrence." Ada playfully slapped at her husband's leg. "Don't be encouraging that kind of behavior."

The older man tried to look innocent. "What kind of behavior is that?"

"What Lawrence needs to know is she's extremely competent."

"What an attractive quality." Peter winked.

Attractive was precisely the word for the woman in the image. His face warmed. "Pretty is as pretty does, but a woman with intelligence and good character can outshine them all—as my mother says."

Jack crossed his arms, making a face of disgust. "If she ain't got any brains, she ain't worth the time."

"And you would know this how?" Peter focused his attention on his son.

Lawrence was suddenly grateful to have the spotlight off himself. The Wellings had become like a second family to him. They'd sponsored him as Jack's trainer. Taken him on travels with Jack to the Olympics and the marathon in Boston—thrilling events. And now they were bringing him on as a manager in this new venture.

He didn't deserve this unmerited favor. He could almost hear his pastor's voice—*That's why they call it grace.*

Chapter Seven

*T*his was truly Susan's favorite time of day—when all the orphanage chores were done and she and her new friend spent time together. Tonight, they were dressing each other's hair. Lizzie lay on the bed, licking her paws as if she, too, were participating in grooming.

"You have the prettiest dark hair." Valerie brushed Susan's long thick tresses. "It's so shiny and thick."

"Thank you. But you'll learn what Father Joseph thinks about that—vanity and sin and all the problems associated with pride."

"True," Val murmured, "but it's still so beautiful."

"Thank you. And of course, you know how much I admire your golden locks."

Valerie laughed. "I think you've said so a few times."

Susan adjusted the shawl around her shoulders. "I'm very sorry for your loss, but I am grateful for your friendship. I've not had that many close friends over the years." Not the bosom buddies that she'd so longed for in her life.

"Would you mind telling me about your friend, Annabelle? The one who gave you the pretty shawl?"

Susan exhaled sharply. "My closest friend, when I lived on my family's farm, was Paul Scholtus."

"A boy then, for your dear friend?"

"Yes. He was so much fun."

"And Annabelle later then?"

"Yes. Sort of." Annabelle felt more like an enemy at times.

"Tell me about your friends."

What could it hurt? "We loved to run all over the farms—his and mine—and climb trees. We'd take to the woods and make little shelters and eat sandwiches and oranges that our mothers sent with us." Those precious oranges had been quite a treat.

"You were adventurous, then."

"Yes, but I think we put our mothers in distress quite a bit. Like when we grabbed our own snacks and ran off to the woods to look for the very best place to build a winter shelter—which of course our parents would never have let us go stay in."

Valerie laughed. "No doubt your parents tracked you two down."

"Indeed, they did." Memories of those golden days flooded back to Susan. "I think it was the tree climbing that almost did them in, though."

"Susan Marie Johnson come down out of that tree at once before you break your pretty neck!" Mother called out in a most unladylike manner.

Susan clung to the branch in front of her.

Paul leaned down from above, his eyes glinting. "You can do it, Susie. Don't be afraid."

Climbing up had seemed easy, with Paulie pushing her when she struggled. But lowering herself back down? Not so easy.

"Push your leg all the way down straight until it touches that big bough, grab the sturdy branch in front of it, then step down."

"Then what?" Her voice hissed like Mama's when she was fed up with all the farm chores that had to be finished.

"Then lower your other leg, and you'll need to sit your bottom down on that bough."

"How?"

"Bend your knees and then fling your legs out while you hold the branch."

She wasn't much on flinging anything. And how did you fling your legs? But she trusted her friend.

Valerie gently touched Susan's shoulder. "Are you alright?"

"I was just recollecting. You asked about my friends. Paul had been my pal since we were babies."

"Really?"

"Yes, our mothers had regular tea together at each other's farms."

"That's lovely." Valerie pulled the brush carefully through Susan's long tresses, then stopped when she hit a tangle.

"Once Paul and I got older, we would meet at the fence and climb over to play."

"So he came from a good family? One your parents trusted?"

"They were good people. They'd farmed their land for generations. Mr. Scholtus was well respected in the community as was Mrs. Scholtus."

"You felt safe?"

"Always. My early childhood was wonderful, and they were part of making me feel secure."

Valerie's brow puckered as she began brushing again. "How old were you when you met Annabelle? And how did that happen?"

"Goodness, I think we were six, almost seven."

"You said you had no brothers or sisters, is that right?"

"I was an only child. That made Paul all the more special to me."

"I'd imagine so. And what about Annabelle."

Lizzie jumped down from the bed.

"I was playing with Paul the day Annabelle and her mother came to our farm for the first time. And my mother wasn't too happy to have to chase me down at Paul's farm."

"Oh?"

"I was supposed to have changed into a dress for afternoon tea when Annabelle came over. Her father was a banker and her mother was quite. . ."

"Proper?"

Susan raised her eyebrows. "That's one way to put it." *Proud, arrogant, and a snob.*

"I'd been up in a tree with Paul when my very irritated mother brought Annabelle over to the Scholtus's farm."

"I wonder what Annabelle's mother thought if she was so prim?"

In Susan's mind, she was six years old again.

"Jump, Susie!" Paul whispered to her.

Susan popped down from the lowest branch, landing in a crouch on the grass below.

A beautiful little girl, dressed in a frilly pink dress clutched a doll to her chest. A matching doll—with golden hair and glassy blue eyes and a similar dress as Annabelle wore.

"Hello!" Susan brushed off her pants.

Annabelle's mother fixed her with a disapproving glare.

A rustling and the thwack of a branch moving, sounded as Paul dropped down.

Annabelle's eyes widened.

Mama's cheeks reddened as she pointed to Susan and Paul. "This is my daughter, Susan, and her friend, Paul."

"It looks like they have free rein." The woman arched her brow. With coffee-colored upswept hair and a dainty velvet camp fixed on top of it, she looked like the pictures in Mother's magazines. But her mouth and eyes looked mean.

Susan placed her hands behind her back.

Annabelle stepped forward. "So, are you two best friends?"

A smile began to tug at Susan's lips as she waited for Paul to declare that they were—as he'd done to his many brothers when they teased them on the Scholtus's farm.

But there was only silence.

Susan turned to catch her dear friend staring at the new girl.

Mama laughed. "They've been friends since Susan was a baby."

"I've always wanted a best friend." Annabelle, a strange glint in her eyes, looked straight at Susan, then walked right past her, to Paul and extended her hands.

"Very nice to meet you, Paul."

Suddenly, everything changed.

Lizzie rubbed against Susan's ankles.

Valerie set the brush down. "If you don't want to tell me, that's all right. Annabelle must have been a special friend."

Susan shook her head. "I met her very close to the time my parents died."

"I'm sorry. I wish I hadn't pried."

"No. It's all right."

"Still, the way you described your friend, Paul, is it any wonder that Annabelle wished to befriend him?" Valerie's wistful voice pierced Susan's heart.

Lizzie purred loudly and Valerie petted her. She'd never been allowed a pet. Somewhere, though, there had been a dog, who'd always made her feel comforted. What would it have been like for Valerie to have felt safe and secure as a child, instead of in constant fear of her mother's bizarre outbursts? She shivered.

"You're right. Why wouldn't Annabelle have wanted to befriend him? Even as a child, Paul was trustworthy and so much fun." Susan sighed. "Annabelle became good friends with Paul, and I'm glad he had her companionship when I had to leave."

Susan's strained voice prompted Valerie to change the topic. "Didn't you say your mother was part of a large catering group?" She set the hairbrush down and sat beside her friend.

"Yes. My mother was one of the esteemed Sugarplum Ladies Society—a group of women in the Detroit area who learned catering skills after the Civil War ended."

The Sugarplum Ladies. The name triggered a sensation of knowing within Valerie. "I think I've heard of them." Val struggled to recall when or why.

"Mother became one of their administrators, setting up events and whatnot."

"Do you ever hear from any of her old friends?" Why hadn't one of them stepped in to help the orphaned girl? Not that anyone had ever helped Valerie with Mum—but oh, had she wished people had.

"My mother received letters. And one Sugarplum Lady came to visit several times." Susan lifted the top from a jar of pomade and dabbed some on her fingers. The rose scent wafted through the air as she rubbed her hands together and then smoothed the ointment through her hair. "Tara was her name. My mother said she was the closest thing to an aunt that I'd ever have, so she had me call her Auntie Tara."

"I wish I'd had an aunt or that my mother even had any friends. I could have used an Auntie Tara." Maybe she'd have rescued Val from Mum. Removed her from a place where screaming rants were a frequent occurrence. They only stopped when Pa threatened to leave if Mum didn't behave.

Susan pressed her hands to her mouth, then dropped them. "I believe I remember her last name. Mulcahey! I've tried for years to remember. When I tried reaching the Sugarplum Ladies Foundation, I learned that they'd closed their doors years ago."

"That's too bad."

"Yes. My letter was returned."

"Now that you remember, you can see if you can find her."

"What if she doesn't want to be found?"

"You're an adult. What harm could come of that?" Valerie gasped as she had her own recollection. She pressed her hand to her throat.

"What is it?"

"My mother did have a friend." She recollected a young woman and her family. "When I was very young, we went to live on a farm here in Michigan with some English immigrants. They spoke with the same accent as my parents did."

"Yet you have only the tiniest hint of an accent."

"Yes, and Mum's friends thought that was very odd." Valerie concentrated hard, sure that the name of the farmer was right on the tip of her tongue. *Winds. Wends. Winnah.*

"Honestly, I would think so, too."

"Maybe that's why we didn't stay there long. We left suddenly." There'd been a lot of shouting that day. "We never saw them again."

"Why do you think that was?"

"Maybe they asked too many questions." Valerie shrugged. But there was something darker than that which had triggered the move. Someone or something had died. At the time, she'd thought it had been the family's beloved horses, but when they'd left, they were out in the orchards.

"I do have a happy memory of that place, though." Valerie had been so excited to go visit a neighboring farm with her mother. "We brought some of our hosts' apples to the farm on the other side of the fields. And they had a daughter. She was older, but she was nice to me."

But while Valerie had waited in the kitchen, Mum and the farmer's wife talked about Mum signing something. Mum didn't want to, but the lady insisted. She seemed downright cheerful about it, but she'd been very persistent. Valerie had sat on a cushion on the floor, making a house out of blocks. The lady showed her book to Mum, who then started sounding interested. She asked a few excited questions. Then Mum's tone changed, like it did when she was about to get one of her moods. Her terrible moods. But she didn't yell, or throw anything, or hit the stranger. She did write something in and sign the book, though.

"It's good to have friendly neighbors—especially ones who share in the harvest. Our neighbors used to keep us supplied with apples, and we'd send over black walnuts from our trees. Those things were terrible to try to crack open." Susan sighed. "The Wenhams were so good to us."

"Wenham?" Was that the name? Or had it been something that sounded like that?

"Yes. Did you know someone by that name?"

"I think so. It may have been the name of those farmers who'd been my mother's friends but who turned us out. I'm not sure."

"I have only fond memories of our Wenhams." Susan sighed. "Sometimes friends can let you down, though. I know I was sad that none of our neighbors took me in after my parents passed away. I do know, from working at the orphanage, that there's a long process in taking care of the placement of orphans."

Fear clutched at Valerie's heart. "I need to find a way to make sure I can care for my brother and sister. I don't think they could manage being in an orphanage—especially if it was run by people who weren't kind like Father Joseph and Sister Mary Lou."

"They are exceptional, and I'm grateful the children here have them." Susan stopped brushing Valerie's hair. "You know something strange?"

"What's that?"

"Our Wenham neighbors had an accent. An English accent but not like in some of the books with the way aristocrats speak. More that Cockney way, like your parents had."

"Do you think our paths may have crossed before, Susan?"

"I don't know, but you have me wondering."

"Could you write to Mrs. Wenham and ask if she remembers my parents? If she's the same friend?"

"Yes. She still may want to know about what happened to your mother and father, even though they parted on difficult terms."

"Thank you. I have some things I'd like to ask her about."

"I'll send a note tomorrow."

Tomorrow. It felt like her life kept being put off until tomorrow.

Shepherd, Michigan

Still no word from the Lighthouse Administration about his application. No mail again today. He was stuck here.

Amazing how Paul's thoughts could make a perfectly beautiful place feel like a silken prison. As he rocked his three-year-old daughter in the parlor, he was surrounded by reminders of his late wife. From the afghan covering his daughter's legs to the cross-stitched pictures that hung on the walls, his home was occupied by a woman no longer with them.

Funny how it had only been in this very house that Annabelle had honed her domestic skills. His mother and sister-in-law had taken her under their wings. When Hetty arrived, the last remnants of the spoiled Annabelle were disappearing.

Soon, another woman far away could be taking care of Hetty. The priest from the orphanage had two possible candidates in mind for him, but he'd noted that one might not be available the following summer and the other possibility might not be interested. Paul exhaled a sharp breath. He'd have to trust in the Lord.

"Where's Momma?" Hetty, nestled in Paul's arms, patted his cheeks. Longing constricted the muscles in his chest. His daughter asked this question every time she was around other children, like her cousins, whose mothers were present. She'd spent the morning with Ronald's children.

"Your mother's in heaven."

"Where's that?"

Paul pressed his spine into the rocking chair cushion, knowing that any explanation was beyond his daughter's understanding.

Heavy footfalls on the porch were followed by the creaking of the front door hinges.

"Looks like you got your wish, Paul." His older brother's brows knit together as he waved an envelope embossed with a lighthouse insignia.

"What?" Paul swallowed hard. The mail was delivered to the main house on the family farm, a home his brother also occupied. But that didn't give Ronald the right to open Paul's mail. "Let me see it."

Instead of handing it over, Ronald held the letter out of reach, like he used to do when they were both much younger. "When were you going to tell us?"

"I applied. And it's none of your business." Paul leaned over and picked up Hetty's doll from where it had slipped to the floor and handed it to his daughter. "Run upstairs and put dolly to bed."

With eyes as wide as saucers, Hetty glanced between her Uncle Ronald and her daddy, but then hopped from Paul's lap and did as she was bid.

"It's all of our concern if you run off and leave your child with us."

"What?" Paul scowled. "I would never do that."

"And who would perform your farm work if you leave?" Ronald finally handed him the letter.

"Harvest is over." Paul made a shooing motion. "Go bother someone else." But his brother crossed his arms, the fabric of his canvas jacket straining across his shoulders.

Paul had dreamed of becoming a lighthouse keeper as a young man. He'd even served as an assistant keeper at a central Michigan lighthouse when Annabelle had gone off to a "Finishing School" back East after high school. He wanted anything but farm life and had tried his hand at other things, too—like his stint as an orderly at the sanitarium in Battle Creek.

"Well, open it and read what I saw."

Paul scowled at his brother, then opened the letter and quickly read the offer of employment. The compensation was good—more than good. He drew in a steadying breath. "This is far more generous than I expected."

"Much better than they gave you as an assistant, that's for sure."

Paul shook his head in wonder. "They'd pay for the childcare worker, too. I let them know I had to have help."

Gone was the accusation in Ronald's eyes, replaced by concern. "If you could have Annabelle back, you would trade that coveted lighthouse position in a heartbeat for her, wouldn't you, brother?"

Unable to manage a response, Paul blinked back the moisture in his eyes. Of course he'd want his wife back. *My first and only sweetheart.* Something in his spirit disagreed with that thought, but he quashed it.

From upstairs, the tinkle of Annabelle's music box played a sweet tune. Hetty must have gone into his room and gotten into her mother's things again.

Ronald sighed. "You know Grace and I would keep Hetty if you must go. If you need to get this out of your system once and for all."

Out of his system? He'd responded to the advertisement because he needed to get away from everything that reminded him of Annabelle. That he'd always wished to man a lighthouse was simply a bonus. But what about Hetty? How would this affect her? Still, he'd never planned to leave her behind. "I can't leave my daughter."

"Why don't you go up there and see if you can get a woman to help you with her?"

"So you're encouraging me to go, then?"

"Maybe. I'm probably being selfish wanting to keep you here. Could do you some good to get out of here for a while. But my kids are gonna miss their cousin. And what if you can't find good care up north?"

"As it so happens, there are two possible choices to help watch Hetty when I'm working." He'd not disclose to his brother that he'd been cautioned that neither might work out.

64

"Do what you need to do, little brother." Ronald tapped his booted toe. "But we'll be praying you tire of the lighthouse quickly and come back home."

With his mother, father, brothers, and sister all on the family farm, a lighthouse might be a lonely place. But as his eyes lighted upon his wedding picture in its ornate silver frame, he knew what his answer would be. "If I can't find help for Hetty, I won't accept the position. It's that simple."

"That's sensible."

He had to leave here, though. "I've accepted Louis Penwell's offer of a train ride up to Mackinaw City on the new railroad line. I'll need someone to watch Hetty while I'm gone." But instead of traveling for an excursion to get away, as his railroad friend had offered, Paul would use his time to interview the two women on Mackinac Island. While he was there, he'd speak with Susan and ask her opinion.

Susan no doubt knew the two candidates.

Or could it be that she was one of them? When they'd been children, they'd planned that one day they'd marry and have children and live in a lighthouse. None of that had happened for them together. What a bittersweet memory.

Affection for his childhood friend warmed him. *Lord, I don't know what you have planned for me, or for Susan, I do know that we can trust You. Please make a way for both of us. In Jesus's precious name, Amen.*

Chapter Eight

England

*E*ugenie Gladstone pulled a sheet of paper from her desk drawer and set it atop the blotter. Where should she begin? She'd accepted the invitation to reunite with her fellow Sugarplum Ladies on Mackinac Island for the benefit of the Social Affirmation group, but she'd not considered that their cottage was already occupied.

Percy, seated by the window, cleared his throat. "You know you've got to tell Colonel and Mrs. Stevens that you're coming. It is our place, after all—your father left it to you."

"I know. But they've occupied it for several years now."

"This is exactly why I told you we should have left it closed up."

"Wasted. Unused."

"Yes, but now you wish to return, and you'll have to—"

"Kick them out?"

"Exactly."

She crinkled her nose. "Did you get Christian Zumbrun to send a copy of the agreement with the Stevens?"

"I sent for it, and the terms were simple. Two months' notice. That's more than reasonable."

"But there are all those men to be moved elsewhere, simply for me to come—"

"For us to come. I'm not sending you by yourself."

"Yes, for us to go to the island for only one month. It seems selfish."

"My darling, it's *our* cottage!" Percy's raised voice put her on edge.

"It was my family's cottage, and you were never keen on going there. It was the children who loved it."

He raised his hands. "True enough."

He rose a moment later. "It belonged to the Mott family, and I leave it to you to determine how you wish to manage its usage."

"You're sounding peevish."

"I'm not. I am trying to be logical. I'm a Canadian barrister at heart still, my love, and I'm all logic except for when it comes to you and the children." He came to the desk, bent, and kissed her.

"You're not a Canadian barrister anymore. And I hate for you to abandon your duties on the estate for so long."

"We have a manager for that."

Too bad the man didn't seem to understand how to grow crops on the land. But she'd not mention that sore topic.

Percy jutted out his chin. "And I just might rent us a place in Windsor and set out my shingle once again, I'm so bored over here."

"You jest."

He turned and began to pace. "Yes, but I'm sorely tempted."

"Percy?"

"Yes, Eugenie?"

"Would you actually give them notice of intent to occupy or in our case, re-occupy for the summer?"

He turned, a sheepish expression on his handsome face. "I'd try to find them another place first, then I'd give them notice."

"Another place? Where?" She tapped her palm on her desktop.

"Ask Robert Swaine—he always knows what is going on around the island and especially up on West Bluff. If there are any homes vacant, he'll know."

"That's how Deanna ended up contacting me." She cast him a look of annoyance.

"Indeed. Trust it to Captain Swaine to set you on course."

"I'll send a letter to him right away."

"Do you think he's still angry about the advice I gave his mother all those years ago?"

"You can't seriously think that I pointed out it was you who advised her about her will and that horrible addendum she attached to it, do you?"

He laughed. "Be a good wife and never tell him, please."

"Yes, Lord Gladstone." She lowered her head in faux deference. "Your wish is my command."

"It's like you're back." He shook his head but was smiling. "Like I have my wife back again. With your joking."

"I. . . I've always been here."

But part of me has not.

How strange that it took letting go of darling Valentine's search to finally find peace again.

Could this trip to Mackinac undermine everything that had finally been overcome?

Sunlight warmed the late September morning, illuminating the vibrant reds, oranges, and yellows of the island's leaves as Susan stepped outside the orphanage doors with her friend.

She linked arms with Valerie. "I'm so glad we've got our free day off together."

Valerie beamed at her. "Me, too."

"And away from the sound of all that construction." Susan rolled her eyes.

"At least they waited today until after the sun rose."

Susan pointed down the street. "Mr. Danner kept his promise to send a carriage for us."

Valerie's cheeks glowed coral-pink. "This is exciting."

What Susan took for granted, a trip around the island on her free day—albeit normally on foot, Valerie embraced like a freed prisoner might.

"Tell me again about the West Bluff and some of the houses that we'll see. I'm sure they'll be beautiful up close—they were so lovely from Round Island."

"We'll get to go inside Canary Cottage." Susan leaned in. "Mr. and Mrs. Swaine have some donations to pick up at their home."

Valerie's eyes shone even brighter. "She's the nurse, right?"

"Yes. Sadie's a good one. Thank God the island has her services."

"I met her when I'd stopped at the pharmacy that day. . ." Valerie lapsed into silence.

My poor friend.

They walked on.

"I'm glad you heard your brother and sister are in good spirits and improving."

"Yes." Valerie drew a shuddering breath. "I'm grateful prayers are being answered."

"We'll keep sending them heavenward." Susan waved to Mr. Danner. "We have another stop today."

"Where?"

"We'll stop by Apple Blossom Cottage to see if the injured veterans anticipate any upcoming needs."

"But the fort closed some years ago, didn't it?"

"Yes. But Mrs. Deanna Stevens, wife of retired Colonel Benjamin Stevens, opened the home to some of the injured officers who needed care. Those who had no place else to go." Susan shivered as the wind blasted from the lake. "Sadie helps with some of their health concerns, too."

Valerie frowned. "The colonel must have come from a wealthy family."

"They don't own the place. The Stevens call it Tumbleston Refuge, after her family name, for the veterans. The cottage is named Apple Blossom Cottage. I think the Mott family owns it, but no longer uses the place."

"Mott?"

"They were a prominent Detroit family, but I don't know much about them." Susan shrugged. "I do have a signature in Mother's autograph book from a Miss Eugenie Mott. It was very nice."

> *To Evelyn Singleterry—our Sugarplum Lady*
> *Manager Extraordinaire!*
> *May the silken strands of godly friendship*
> *Bind us all firmly together*
> *Now and in the many precious*
> *Years to come and beyond*

"I'm not sure if she's from that same family, though. I'm not much on keeping up with that kind of thing."

Valerie shrugged. "Me either. Mum had the habit of burning any newspapers almost immediately after Pa had read them."

Mott. Valerie knew that name. But she'd not utterly humiliate herself like she had recently, by almost fainting in Father Joseph's office. She'd compose herself by taking slow deep breaths. It was as if her parents' deaths had opened a Pandora's box of crazy associations she could not pin down. Yesterday, that young man's name, Lawrence Zumbrun, had triggered a lightning-like reaction that was crazy. Now the cottage owners' name, Mott, started a throbbing in her head. Valerie rubbed her temple as Susan stepped into the carriage ahead of her. The names seemed so familiar, but she couldn't put faces with them no matter how hard she tried. They were like disembodied images of people floating around in her mind.

"Coming, miss?" Mr. Danner smiled down at her.

She got into the carriage and sat beside Susan.

"Stan, can you take us to Tumbleston Refuge first, please?"

"It'd be my pleasure." He flicked the reins, and the Percherons pulled the carriage out into the street.

They rolled past a forlorn-looking fine home.

Susan pointed. "That was once owned by Madame. Her place looks so romantic.'"

Valerie leaned forward. The two-story home with tall columns in front was very pretty, even closed for the season. "I was thinking it looked sad." It reminded her of some of the boarded-up homes near various lakes where her family had stayed.

"She did lose her husband early. But I've heard they had a good marriage."

Val squeezed her friend's hand. "Are you hoping to find true love one day?" This was the first time she'd heard Susan mention anything about romance.

As another gust of wind hit the carriage Susan pulled her shawl closer over her coat. "I don't have the luxury of contemplating such things."

"Why not?"

Her friend shrugged. "I'm pragmatic. But Madame LaFramboise is someone who has inspired me. She had amazing business acumen and ran a successful fur trading business long after her husband died."

"She did?"

"Truly."

Valerie hunched down in her seat to avoid the wind. "I'm unlike you. Not a pragmatist and I don't have your businesslike mind when you consider things." Valerie was more of a dreamer. "I mean, I certainly have no interest in getting married." *Ever.* Not after what she'd observed in her parents' marriage.

"No?"

She shook her head. "But that young man was handsome, don't you think?" She'd seen how Susan's soft brown eyes had followed him.

"Mr. Zumbrun? I thought you didn't want to talk about him."

"I don't. I just wondered if he had you contemplating romance."

When her friend's cheeks turned pink, Valerie averted her gaze, not wanting to further embarrass her.

The carriage rolled on past the park, with the fort on the hillside looming in the distance. She'd change the topic. "Did all of the infirm soldiers come from this fort?"

"As I understand it, yes. Many were brought here to the fort many years ago from out West. They served their enlistments out on Mackinac Island—doing light duty."

"But then the fort closed."

"Yes. Then the Stevens stepped in to help."

Mr. Danner directed the horses on. Valerie took in the shops, the stables, the milliner's place, Astor's Restaurant, a photographer's studio, the tobacconist, and finally the Grand Hotel. Although she'd viewed it from the lighthouse, she'd never seen it up close. "Look at that porch. It's so long."

"Longest in the world, I'm told." Susan held onto her hat as that stiff breeze swept through the bluff. "I imagine that helps promote business."

They rolled on past the massive hotel, also closed for the season. What must it be like in summer, to be there with hundreds and hundreds of guests all attired in their finest clothes and playing sports on the grounds below the hotel? Strolling through the rose gardens would be heavenly. Valerie could almost smell them.

Stan directed the horses past those beautiful cottages, mansions actually, that sat well back from the road. This close, they seemed familiar. But then again, she'd looked at them from across the water, so perhaps that was the reason.

Soon the horses pulled to a stop and the two women stepped out onto the curb. Catching a gust, Valerie's cape rippled around her, and she clutched it closer. She gazed at the walkway that led to a large Queen Anne-style home. Recognition stirred.

A hand holding mine. "Say goodbye for the season, darling."

A silver-haired man trimming the roses.

She broke free and ran back to the cottage. She touched the lion's head atop the heavy black iron pole and made her wish. She wished to come back that next summer and every summer after. Georgie chasing after her.

Her older brother yelled for them to help find the dog, who was hiding.

A hound dog.

A gift from their friends.

"Valerie?"

She pressed her hand to her chest where her heart beat rapidly.

"Are you alright? You've gone pale."

"This place reminds me of. . . something."

"Do you know it?"

Valerie shook her head, embarrassed. "I believe I do, but I don't know how. Sometimes I wonder if I'm losing my mind."

Susan's pretty face reflected concern as she linked her arm through Val's. "Come on. Maybe once we're inside, it will come to you."

Did she want the memories to come? What if the people she really belonged with were all dead? Wouldn't that be worse than not knowing? What if all these remembrances were simply fantasies of things Valerie had dreamed?

Susan stepped forward and Val did, too.

The evergreen bushes alongside the house were overgrown. They could use a good clipping.

A pretty woman with salt-and-pepper upswept hair came through the front door to the porch. "Good day, Susan." She waved at them. "Have you brought a friend? She doesn't look like a veteran to me— but you never know. I've heard of women disguising themselves during the war."

"Not this one." Susan grinned at Val. "But we have a few questions about the cottage, if you don't mind."

Her dark eyebrows shot upward. "Oh, well, I'll tell you what I can. Come in."

They followed her inside.

Val closed her eyes for a moment. There should be checkered black-and-white marble tiles with a wide staircase as soon as they came inside. And she'd run up after her older brother and sisters.

As soon as they entered, her knees went weak. The checkered marble tiles, dotted with a liberal coating of dust, appeared gray and off-white but were as she'd imagined. The chandelier overhead needed polishing. Threadbare carpet runners on the wide stairs needed to be replaced. But her older brother and sisters weren't there.

She sank onto a nearby wooden bench and tried to breathe. *I have an older brother. Older sisters. I. . . What is happening to me?*

Susan sank down beside her. "Valerie, what is it?"

She pressed a hand to her throat. "I. . . know this place. I think I may have lived here."

A crease formed between the matron's brows. "This was the home of the Motts. Mr. Mott died about thirty years ago and his daughter inherited it. Did you and your family ever come here for some reason?"

"I. . ." If she said she thought she'd lived here, would she sound crazy? Mrs. Stevens may have heard of the lighthouse keeper's wife being insane. Maybe she'd believe the same of her daughter. It was best that Val kept this to herself, at least for now.

Colonel Stevens ambled into the foyer, nodded at Susan, and then stiffened when he spied Valerie. "Everything all right?"

Deanna turned toward her husband. "This young lady says she remembers being here and obviously it has upset her."

"Oh?" He frowned.

Susan rushed to explain, "Valerie recently lost her parents—they were the lighthouse keepers on Round Island."

"I've heard about that. Such a pity." Colonel Stevens' lips pulled in.

"Should we send for Nurse Sadie to come over?" Mrs. Stevens brushed at her skirt.

"I don't think so. Valerie has had a few episodes like this, and she recovers quickly." Hopefully, she would now, too.

The scent of roses wafted as a paunchy man, wearing slippers, shuffled past with a vase in his arms. "Mornin' everyone."

"Good morning, lieutenant."

"Glad I don't have to salute, Colonel. My arms are full." The man laughed at his own joke as he continued past.

Valerie shook her head as if shaking off cobwebs. "I wish I didn't have these spells. Right now, I feel certain that to the right, I'd enter an elaborate dining room, the table set with china, silverware, and crystal."

The colonel and his wife exchanged a quick glance. "We don't set the table with the family's china and so on, but yes—"

Deanna shot her husband a warning look. "We do have a dining room there, as do many homes."

"Why don't I give Valerie a tour of our yard while Miss Johnson catches you up on the orphanage?" Colonel Stevens offered. "That way Valerie can get some fresh air and clear her mind a bit."

Deanna nodded curtly. "Do you feel up to that, Valerie?"

Valerie rose, her cheeks flushed pink. "I'm so embarrassed. Please forgive me."

"There's nothing to forgive, my dear. We'll go see the last of the autumn roses before they're gone."

Once the front door closed behind the two, Deanna took Susan's hand and squeezed it. "What do you know about this girl?" She released her hand.

"I know she has nightmares." *That slipped out too quickly.*

"Our men here do. From battle experiences." Deanna pointed toward the left. "Let's go sit in the parlor."

Soon, they were seated in front of the fire, on two velvet settees, facing one another over a low carved cherrywood table.

"Now tell me why you stopped here today."

"I brought Valerie to see the view from here on the West Bluff."

"This is one of the best views on the island and we're grateful to be here."

"I always loved walking up to West Bluff and today Mr. Danner offered us a ride, which we accepted."

Deanna leaned in. "You say she thought she'd been here before—in this very cottage?" A muscle jumped in the woman's cheek.

"She seemed very distraught, like she is after she wakes from her nightmares."

"Susan, do you know the history of this house?"

"I know you and the colonel have been running the veterans support society since I've come to the island."

"What do you know of the current owners?"

"Nothing, other than they must be generous, kind people to offer the use of this home."

"Do you know about their missing child?"

"Missing child?" Shivers coursed down her arms. "No, I don't. From here?"

Deanna shook her head. "Not from the island. But the cottage owners stopped coming here around fifteen years ago—after their child went missing."

"Oh, my." *Could Valerie be that child?*

"Susan, I hate to tell you this, but early on, once we'd moved in, several people came by here and claimed the child with them was the missing child." Deanna rolled her eyes, making her look much younger. "Of course the children were not."

"Why would people do that?"

"Because she's the daughter of Lord Gladstone. He married Mr. Mott's daughter."

"Gladstone? Like Gladstone, Michigan?"

Deanna blinked, then laughed. "Well, yes like that name, but this aristocrat lives on his estate in England with his family. And he'd offered a huge reward if his daughter was found."

"You wonder if Valerie might be a fortune seeker?"

"Well, it sounds crass with you putting it that way, but is it possible?"

"I don't think so."

"You're an excellent judge of character."

"Thank you." One advantage to being a practical person.

"We'd better check on things, and verify facts, before making any assertions that your new friend might be that missing daughter."

A man wearing pajamas with a long robe tightly tied at the waist limped into the room. "Coffee or tea?"

Deanna turned to him. "Are you offering or asking, Wiggins?"

"Offering, milady," he rolled his hand forward and bent at the waist, chuckling.

"Roll in that cart with sugar and cream, too, please."

"At your bidding, your highness."

The older woman swiveled back around, a smile stealing over her pretty features. "What I have to put up with around here. I remember being a youngster and peeling potatoes in the kitchen at our inn in Kansas and hauling slop pots out." She shook her head. "Sorry—didn't mean to offend you with those images."

"No offense taken. I still do that type of work if needed."

"Now I'm even sorrier." She gave a curt laugh. "But back to Valerie. What can you tell me about your impressions of her?"

"She's struggling. It's as though she'd been released from prison."

A wrinkle creased Deanna's forehead. "How so?"

"Her parents kept tight control over her, and they always lived in remote locations. So she's learning how to be around people. But she also suffers from nightmares as though she's once had another life— possibly with a different family. She's wondered if she was adopted."

"Or abducted?" Deanna angled her head downward.

"Several of her nightmares are of being in a huge crowd and of traveling by train and by horse cart. Of traveling and traveling but going back to a place that was somewhat familiar by the terrain and the water features."

Her hostess raised her hand to her mouth.

"What is it?"

She dropped her hand. "You don't think she's fabricating these dreams?"

"No. She calls out, and I hear her. She's still asleep while she's talking about them."

"Lord and Lady Gladstone's child went missing in a crowd at New York harbor."

From outside, a gull squawked as if agreeing.

"New York?"

"They were en route to England, to his ancestral home to visit his parents."

"How horrible to lose their child. But how did that happen?"

"They don't know. Their older children were keeping watch over Valentine and there were nursemaids and other staff at the dock who were traveling with them who should have kept watch."

"Valerie said she was in the crowd, and then someone took hold of her hand. It was someone she knew. Sometimes she's said it was her mother other times with that nightmare she calls her by her given name."

Deanna shrugged. "Sometimes children call a parent by their name, but that's unusual."

"I agree."

Wiggins rolled the cart into the room and set out tea before them. He poured for each of the ladies. The ivory china teacups were embossed with a large "M" presumably for the Mott family. Had this once-grand mansion been Valerie's family's? Still was?

"Tell me more about what you know about Miss Fillman. I'll send a letter to the solicitor from Detroit who'd asked us to keep an eye out should the Gladstone's daughter ever show up here. Honestly, I never thought I'd see the day." She raised a cautious hand. "And I may not have, yet."

But what if they now had?

Chapter Nine

Straits of Mackinac, Michigan

*L*awrence pressed his hat on his head as a gust of wind threatened to blow it overboard. With his other hand, he held onto the rail.

He leaned toward Jack. "I can't believe we're heading to Mackinac."

"Yup. Best time of year." A wistful look flicked across the boy's face. "Autumn through winter. Best of all, you're here with us." He thumped his chest.

Mr. Welling jostled his tiny daughter on his shoulder. "We're on one of the last ships of the season."

His wife arched a brow. "The last planned ship to port, I believe."

"I wouldn't be too sure of that, Mom." Jack winked at his stepmother then leaned over Lawrence and pointed. "That's the Grand Hotel. My sis worked up there one summer."

"For a very brief part of the summer." Ada Welling sniffed.

Jack laughed. "Before you canned her."

She raised her eyebrows.

Lawrence wouldn't poke that hornet's nest. The Round Island lighthouse came into view. He was tempted to whistle but didn't. "She's a beauty, isn't she?" He'd always found lighthouses fascinating. Their lights were the beacons that brought sailors safely through difficult waters.

Jack flexed his shoulders. "That new lighthouse is not only a beaut, but she's useful. I've always vowed that despite my good looks, I want to be a useful man, too."

Both Mr. and Mrs. Welling stared wide-eyed at Jack. Suddenly they all burst into laughter.

Mrs. Welling dabbed at her eyes. "Oh my."

Jack's sister pulled free from Peter's shoulder and cast her brother a strange look—almost like Sally was incredulous. The boy extended his arms and the child leaned toward him. He took her. "See? Like I'm being useful right now."

"And, Son, surely you've wanted to work on being humble, too, eh?"

"Humility is overrated, Dad." He elbowed Lawrence. "Ain't that right, Larry?"

"Huh?"

"Well, you're always saying I need to have the mindset of a winner. That I have to see myself as the best on the track field."

Lawrence shifted his weight, finding himself at a loss for words. He certainly didn't want to get himself in trouble with Jack's parents.

Mr. Welling cleared his throat. "I imagine that Lawrence intends for you to apply that way of thinking specifically to your running."

"And not to the entirety of your life." But Adelaide Welling's lips still twitched with mirth.

Jack gently rocked his sister back and forth. "I'm pretty good at this, too, ya gotta admit."

Suddenly, his sister let forth a squall. Jack held her at arm's length. "What?"

The girl reached for her mother, who took her into her arms and settled her on her lap. Immediately, the child ceased crying.

Jack jerked a thumb toward his sister. "Yeah, well, I'm not her mother. Moms pretty much have a leg up in this game, right coach?"

Both Lawrence and Peter shook their heads.

Before long, the boat docked and then they disembarked the ship.

Peter touched Lawrence's elbow. "Don't forget that you're tasked with delivering donations for the orphanage."

"Of course. Happy to do so." This was one way to return the Wellings' kindness in hosting him over the winter.

The family headed to their cottage in a taxi while he approached two stocky porters, both of whom could have used a good shave. "I need you to bring all those marked goods to the church orphanage."

They nodded, and soon the three of them headed away from the wharf and toward the orphanage, to the right.

A sense of peace and quietude had settled over the island, despite the business at the docks. The place seemed very unlike when he had traveled there in the summer with his family. As they walked, the brilliant autumn leaves threatened to drop the last of their fiery artistry soon. A hint of snowfall rested on the crisp air.

The white, wood-sided, rectangular orphanage loomed ahead. The three-story structure was capped by a steeply pitched roof to help shed winter snow. A large yard, strewn with leaves, paralleled the length of the building to the left and was currently filled with the building's young occupants. Happy children's voices carried over that of the horses' hooves from a nearby dray conveying hay down the main street. The clanging noises of metal and pounding on wood carried from the construction occurring farther down the street. The children playing in the yard seemed unperturbed, though.

"You're to bring those trunks to Father Joseph," Lawrence reminded the porters.

They cast him a look that suggested he was insulting, stupid, or both. His cheeks heated. They'd already been told. Of course they remembered.

Beyond the waist-high fence that surrounded a large yard, a group of children played kickball. Others jumped rope while the rest tossed a ball into an apple crate from a distance of about eight feet. The wind lifted the cap covering a young lady's sable brown hair. She reached for the hat, but the wind scurried the head covering away.

When the beautiful brunette turned and looked at him, Lawrence's breath caught in his throat. Attired in well-made clothing that was some years out of fashion, she carried herself in dignity and grace even when chasing down her felted hat. She bent, grasped the hat which sported a jaunty yellow feather, and then brushed it off.

"You comin', governor?" The dock porter was clearly mocking Lawrence, so he ignored him.

The two porters then took the trunks into the building.

To Lawrence's surprise, the lovely woman stepped toward him at the fence. "May I help you?" Her voice was soft yet firm.

"I'm. . . I'm just. . ." His face heated. "I work with children, and I was admiring how you—"

"Mr. Zumbrun?" The priest emerging from the building cut into Lawrence's inept explanation.

"Yes. I'm Lawrence Zumbrun." He turned to the young woman. "And you are?"

"I'm Susan Marie Johnson," the young woman whispered, before she turned away.

Susan Johnson. Cousin Tara's goddaughter? She had to be.

The priest waved him over. "Come in, young man. We're hoping to hear your plans for the summer program."

As tired as he was from the journey, he longed to speak further with Miss Johnson, but he followed the priest into the building. "Did you receive my letter, Father Joseph?

The priest cast a guilty look over his shoulder. "I'm afraid I'm well behind in my correspondence. But I had heard from the Wellings via telegram, so I knew you'd be coming today."

Lawrence followed the man down the hall. What was it like to dress in clerical clothes every day? What did Catholic priests call those things? Cossacks? No, that was Russians or Slavs. Cassocks, that's what they were. He hurried to keep up with the priest.

Father Joseph stopped and opened a door, which he held open for Lawrence. "Come on in, young man."

"Thank you." He removed his hat, which he realized he was still wearing.

Father Joseph moved to the other side of a piled-high desk and took a seat. He motioned to a chair and Lawrence sat. "Mr. Zumbrun, we're so excited about your program. I'd love to hear about your plans to include our orphans."

Given that he didn't have all the facts, Lawrence wasn't sure where to begin. There was something he did need to know, though. "Father Joseph, forgive me, but I had sent you an important letter asking about Miss Susan Johnson." He waved his hand behind him. "I believe I met her just now."

Heavy salt-and-pepper brows crowded together on the man's ruddy face. "Why were you asking about our Susan? What was it?"

He swallowed hard, so penetrating was the clergyman's intense, accusatory gaze.

Someone knocked at the door.

"Come in!" The priest fairly bellowed, and Lawrence flinched.

The clinking of metal against ceramic heralded a teacart as it was rolled into the office alongside of Lawrence, but he kept his gaze averted.

"I'll have my usual, Miss Fillman. And what would you like, Mr. Zumbrun?"

A teaspoon fell to the floor. As he reached for it the young golden-haired woman bent, too, and picked up the spoon. She locked violet-blue eyes on him, her cheeks reddening.

The maid cleared her throat. "Sorry, Father Joseph."

"Mr. Zumbrun, would you like tea or coffee?"

"Whatever you're having, sir."

"Fine. Miss Fillman, make that two of the same."

"Yes, Father Joseph."

"Now, Mr. Zumbrun, what were you asking about Miss Johnson?"

The maid brought a cup of coffee to the priest and set it on his desk. He smiled warmly at her, not looking at all like the curmudgeon he'd appeared to be moments before. "Thank you."

Lawrence exhaled a deep breath. "A family friend has been looking for a Miss Susan Marie Johnson whose parents died when she was young."

Hands trembling, Miss Fillman passed a cup of black coffee, resting on a saucer, to him. What had this girl so rattled?

"And this friend's name and her situation?"

Lawrence clutched his hat's rim tightly. "Mrs. Tara Mulcahey. She was one of the founders of a group called The Sugarplum Ladies which Mrs. Johnson, Susan's mother, had been manager of for some years."

Miss Fillman gasped. "Tara Mulcahey? Susan recently mentioned her. She knows her."

The priest cast her a glance that could have seared the tapestries hanging from the wall.

"Excuse me, Father, I spoke out of turn."

Eyes rolled slightly upward; the priest dipped his chin slowly.

Lawrence cleared his throat. "Tara is my mother's first cousin. So this has been a personal search within our family as well."

"Please go fetch Susan for us. Tell her that I'm meeting with Lawrence Zumbrun, who wishes to speak with her."

Instead of departing, the young woman sank onto a nearby wooden chair. "Lawrence Zumbrun?"

She was trembling.

The priest stood and rushed to her side. "Miss Fillman?"

The door opened and a nun wearing spectacles entered. "What's going on?" She went to the young woman and crouched beside her. "Valerie? Can you hear me?"

"Mr. Zumbrun, please leave us while we assist Miss Fillman." Clearly rattled, Father Joseph barked out his order. "Sister Mary Lou please show him how to get to Butterfly Cottage from here."

The nun nodded and then led Lawrence out of the room. When she closed the door, she leaned in. "Miss Fillman recently lost her parents."

This was not the time nor place to delve into all his questions. A sudden weariness descended upon him.

"Follow me and I'll show you a shortcut up the hill to the Wellings' cottage."

"Thank you."

As they headed out into the yard, they passed Miss Johnson. Prettier than her picture, her eyes held the light of someone with inner reserves that powered her life with joy and purpose. He fought the urge to go to her and tell her about Cousin Tara.

There would be time enough for that later.

What about Miss Fillman? Was there something about him that had triggered her strange response?

Or had it been her grief that had unnerved her?

Round Island

Crossing over the rocking waves, Susan wished she'd never agreed to Father Joseph's request. She'd never have made the journey to the lighthouse if not for Valerie's sake. Her stomach rebelled but she held it in check.

Finally, they reached the tiny rocky island on which the lighthouse sat.

Susan shivered as Father Joseph, Sister Mary Lou, and then she disembarked the boat with Billy Lloyd's assistance. The skiff on the beach indicated that Superintendent Dardanes already had arrived.

Billy scowled at the lighthouse. "I heard one of the new temporary lighthouse keepers goes back to his cabin on Bois Blanc Island, for fear of infection."

"Superintendent Dardanes assured us the entire place has been thoroughly disinfected and aired out." Father Joseph used his pulpit voice.

If the assistant didn't want to sleep there, were they in any danger at this point?

"Thank you for coming with us." Sister Mary Lou squeezed Susan's gloved hand.

As a breeze coursed through, they both clutched their wool capes closer around themselves.

"Brrr, let's get inside," Sister Mary Lou took quick small steps over the rocky soil, toward the lighthouse.

Superintendent Dardanes waved from the house's entry door.

Once they were all inside, Mr. Dardanes led them upstairs to the family's floor. He took their cloaks and hung them on pegs. The place was warm and the scent of wood emanated from a potbellied stove just inside. This had been the Fillman's parlor, *God rest their souls*.

Now to begin gathering whatever of their belongings that could be salvaged.

Was this what scavengers felt like? On the one hand, Susan wanted to find special objects that would bring Val comfort, but on the other hand, it felt wrong—to go through these belongings. Like being a thief.

Father Joseph clapped his big hands. "Well, this has to be done, to help dear Miss Fillman. So allow me to offer a brief prayer."

Dardanes cast the priest a skeptical glance before he bowed his head as did the others.

"Dear Father, guide us in our efforts, make our hands Your tools to find that which You have predetermined needs to be returned to Miss Fillman to bring her peace and comfort. Lord, we know You alone are in charge here, but make our eyes, our ears, our hands, instruments of Your efforts on this mission. In the name of the Father, and the Son, and the Holy Spirit, Amen."

"Amen."

"All right," Dardanes pulled an index card from his suit pocket. "I'm going to review the rules with you and assign you each a space. There are baskets here and wood boxes for the items." He pointed behind himself. "We'll need to catalogue what we are taking from here."

"Do you have the list of things the state owns, that remain here?" Father Joseph rocked back on his heels.

"We've tagged them all. My assistant and I were very thorough, so you should have no worries that an untagged item isn't property of the Fillman's."

"You didn't tag the lighthouse's beam, though, did you?" Sister Mary Lou laughed at her own joke, and Susan grinned.

Dardanes's dark brows knit together. "If you'd like to walk up all those steps to ensure my helper tagged the Fresnel light, feel free." He gestured toward the entrance to the lighthouse stairs.

When he named the number of steps, Sister Mary Lou pushed her glasses higher on her pert nose. "I believe we should trust him on that, Superintendent."

"All right then. Let's get started."

Soon they were each sent to different rooms. Susan hesitated as she entered the Fillmans' bedroom. This felt like such an invasion of privacy, even though the couple had already been buried on the mainland. From the looks of things, Dardanes had spoken the truth. The stripped bed had been tagged as had the chest of drawers, bedside tables, and lamps, and the walnut desk that sat by the window. The empty armoire was also tagged.

Dardanes stuck his head in the room. "Remember, although the furniture may all be tagged, any contents remaining within them will be the Fillmans'."

"Thank you." Susan moved toward the armoire. No clothes, as all soft goods had been burned. She pulled the drawers open. Only an old cigar box full of letters. She opened it. Letters to Dorcas lay on top. That would go back to the orphanage. She set it on the bed and then headed toward the desk to check the drawers.

As she crossed the floor, a floorboard near the desk creaked loudly. She pushed the narrow desk aside and bent to examine the board. It flexed. She bent and jiggled it but the plank wouldn't come loose. Then she stood and stepped down hard on one end and it lifted. Beneath, in the floor cavity, sat a metal candy box, the kind used for special occasion candies. From the bits of rust on its ornamented top, painted with doves, hearts, and swirls, it had to have been at least a few decades old. Her mother had possessed a very similar one that she'd kept old photographs in. Whatever had happened to that memento box? Mother said that Susan's grandmother had presented her with special chocolates for her twenty-first birthday.

She removed the tin from its hiding spot and set it on the desk. Then she pried off the top. A pair of fine leather, young child's shoes lay atop. Maybe this wasn't the Fillmans' box. She removed the expensive shoes. Beneath nestled an envelope that held long curls of silky blond hair reminiscent of Valerie's hair, only lighter. She set the envelope aside and gasped as sunlight caused the gems in a tiny golden bracelet to sparkle.

Were those diamonds? She lifted the jewelry, her breath catching in her chest. Then she spied the photographs beneath. The bracelet slipped from her fingers.

Her mother and father looked back at her in the picture. Hands trembling, she lifted the photo to view the next ones. Her and father in the fields. Mother and little Susie holding a basket of apples from the Wenhams. The next image was of Paul and her at the Scholtus's farm. And then pictures of Mother when she'd been a Sugarplum Lady all those years earlier.

"What's this doing here?" she mumbled aloud.

A memory of the strange woman and her little girl who'd brought them their last basket of apples skittered through Susan's mind. The nervous woman, who'd reminded her of a scarecrow, had arrived when Mother was "being sentimental" as she called it. She'd been seated at the kitchen table with her photo box when the two had arrived. They'd been staying at the Wenhams' farm. The little girl's hair was so short that at first, Susan had mistaken her for a boy.

"What's that, dear Susan?" Sister Mary Lou stood in the doorway.

Susan pressed a hand to her temple, suddenly lightheaded. "This candy tin—I believe it was my mother's. Some of our family photographs are inside, along with some odd items." She pointed to the bracelet and shoes. "When I asked about my mother's treasures, from her chocolate box, the social service workers had insisted that they'd not found it. And I'd thought they'd simply chucked it out with so many of my parents' other belongings."

How had it gotten here?

Chapter Ten

*V*alerie hummed as she attacked the windows with a solution of vinegar water aided by newspaper sheets. With Susan and Sister Mary Lou gone all morning, the place remained quiet except when the children went to lunch and onto the playground.

Earlier, Lawrence Zumbrun had walked by when she was outside, but he didn't stop to speak with her. Perhaps he feared she'd have another fit. Her face heated at the thought. As she wiped the acrid solution from the mullioned windows, she spied a stranger walking toward the building. Attired in work clothes, the ginger-haired man sported a neatly trimmed beard. He tilted his head back to look up, presumably at the upper stories of the imposing structure. The mid-day sun illuminated his handsome features.

Valerie sucked in a breath and pulled back lest he see her staring at him.

One of the newspaper sheets fell to the floor, and she bent to retrieve it. The social section featured a picture of a salt-and-pepper-haired woman in fine attire and an equally well-dressed man. "Mr. and Mrs. Booth-Moore Sponsor Fall Gala" read the headline.

Val squinted at the images. That sense of familiarity overwhelmed her—again. She had to stop believing that strangers had connections to her.

Sister Mary Lou entered the building, the scent of fresh air surrounding her.

"When did you get back?"

"We just arrived, but I'm afraid you'll have to be patient with us. We'd like to look through what all we found there before we have you take them. There's something odd we'll have to ferret out, first."

"Oh?" She placed a hand on her collar, the lace edging tickling her fingers.

"For one thing, poor Susan got a bit of a shock when she discovered her *own* mother's candy tin beneath the floorboards."

"What?" Valerie stiffened.

"Evelyn Johnson's box, with pictures and such." The nun shook her head. "Susan is a bit. . . overtaxed by the trip. I've sent her up to her room to rest."

"I'll be sure to not interrupt her then." But oh, how she wanted to speak with her friend.

"I'd appreciate that." Sister Mary Lou glanced at the newspaper page, a smile tugging at her lips. "The Booth-Moores are lovely people and great benefactors."

Should Val mention that the two seemed familiar? *No.* She'd already spouted far too many strange comments to the dear nun. But she couldn't hold back. "Sister Mary Lou, I have a recurring dream about a woman who looks like this Mrs. Booth-Moore."

"And?" Sister Mary Lou's brow furrowed more than Valerie had ever seen.

Her face flushed. "Mrs. Booth-Moore looks like an older version of the woman in my dream who gifts me with. . ." she'd told Susan, why not tell Sister Mary Lou? "She always gives me the same thing— a sparkling bracelet that causes light to reflect on the ceiling of a fancy room full of children having a party."

The color drained from the nun's face. "A diamond bracelet?"

"I don't know."

Father Joseph's voice echoed from the hallway, followed by another man's response. Perhaps the handsome stranger she'd seen entering the building.

Sister Mary Lou gestured for Valerie to sit on the rose velvet settee and then took a seat beside her. "Please allow us some time to go through your mother's things—as well as that of Susan's mother."

"Yes, I will. I understand."

"And we have returned the Lighthouse Association's library books to Mr. Dardanes."

Those had been her treasures. Her escape from the multiple isolated lighthouses she and her family had inhabited. But all had been on loan. Their only "owned" book was Pa's family Bible. And Mum had only pulled that out to read when she was in one of her frenzies. Then she'd hold the Bible between herself and Valerie and blame her for the fit she was having. Everything had always been Val's fault. But not the terrible swift illness that had taken them. Tears slipped down Valerie's cheeks. Her brother and sister, both afflicted with infirmities, were now receiving appropriate care on the mainland, and reported to be making good recoveries, thank God.

"We need to speak of your next steps, especially if your siblings are placed in your care later." Sister Mary Lou pushed her glasses onto the bridge of her nose. "Mr. Dardanes advised us that he's selected a new lighthouse keeper from the candidates."

The interim no doubt needed to move on.

"The government will do the final hiring." The nun adjusted her habit. "And of course, the gentleman would have to accept the position."

"Of course." Val shivered. That poor man would have to go where her parents had died. "I wish there were more jobs available here on the island for me so that I didn't have to rely upon the orphanage's charity, Sister Mary Lou."

"Valerie, we want you to stay. Both Father and I."

Val dipped her chin, tears threatening. "I'm very grateful."

"We'll ask the entire parish for help in placing you in a position, but positions are few in the off-season."

Val held up a hand. "I understand. Even Susan's friends, the Christys, can't give me a job right now."

"And the medical bills for your brother and sister are exceeding the sums provided by the lighthouse benevolence fund."

"By how much?"

"We have to find you a paying job."

"There are none to be had."

"Services will end soon if you can't continue on your own to pay those bills."

"But I thought Mabel and Timothy were improving." What would happen if their treatments stopped?

"They are." The nun pressed a hand to the back of her neck. "Father said to tell you that the new lighthouse keeper prospect requires care for his daughter."

No, she couldn't mean that she expects me to help. Not there.

"I haven't told Susan yet, but the applicant is her childhood friend—Mr. Scholtus."

Gaping, Valerie repeated dumbly, "Paul Scholtus?"

The office door swung inward. Father Joseph entered, followed by the stranger. This close, the man was even more handsome than he'd appeared through the window. Taller than the priest by half a head, the man's red-gold hair curled around his high collar. He clutched a smoky-colored bowler hat in his broad hands, his work-roughened knuckles suggesting he was a laborer. Hadn't Susan said he was a farmer? Sadness was etched across his high cheekbones and around his light green eyes that spoke of tragedy.

Father Joseph rocked back and forth on his heels, a nervous habit of his. His black cassock swayed as did the tassels of his cincture. "This is Mr. Paul Scholtus, a candidate for the Round Island Lighthouse position."

Valerie tried to keep from gaping. Here was the very person Susan had spoken of so frequently—whom she'd begun corresponding with by mail. Whose family sounded so wonderful that Valerie had daydreamed that she lived in such a household.

Mr. Scholtus nodded curtly.

"Mr. Scholtus, this is Sister Mary Lou, who is in charge of the orphanage."

When a broad smile grew on his face, he became even more handsome—if that was possible. "Sister Mary Lou Kwiatkowski? My mother is a friend of yours."

Sister Mary Lou smiled warmly, her cheeks reddening. "I'm so glad our Jack shared the island newspaper with you."

Father Joseph's brows drew together. "What's all this?"

"Remember the picture of Susan with me in the paper?"

"Yes. Nice article, too."

"It was." Sister Mary Lou beamed. "And it helped reconnect me with my dear friend Mary, who is Mr. Scholtus's mother."

"I see," said the priest, looking a little bewildered. "We can talk more about that later, but let's finish introductions."

Paul dipped his chin.

Father Joseph gestured toward Valerie. "This is Miss Fillman, who has been with us a short while. The young lady I was speaking of."

To suggest her for possible childcare for his daughter?

The handsome stranger's lips parted, and his eyes widened. "Miss Fillman?" He clamped his lips together and frowned. "The former lighthouse keeper's daughter?" He cast a quick look of confusion at the priest.

"Yes, she also served as an assistant to her father."

"I did." And more. *Much more.*

"Mr. Scholtus needs someone to help him at the lighthouse."

As Sister Mary Lou had mentioned—but surely that would be Susan. There was no way on earth Val would be going out to the lighthouse again. She shrugged. "He'll have relief workers."

"That's not exactly what I need." He pressed his lips together. "I have a child."

"He's unmarried." Father Joseph announced this fact as though the potential lighthouse keeper was helpless. Or was he implying something?

A strange sensation of both dread and fascination shot through Val. Was Father Joseph suggesting Val should help at the one place she wished to never return? It would be completely inappropriate for a young woman to be at the lighthouse without another woman there. Or was he hinting at something else entirely?

"I am a widower." His mouth drew into a thin line beneath his neat mustache. "I am *not* an unmarried man."

Mr. Scholtus sounded like he was claiming he was still married. It was like when a few children had asked Valerie if she was an orphan and she'd told them she wasn't. But she was.

The lighthouse keeper applicant stepped forward, light suddenly piercing through the clouds outside and filtering through the windows.

"Miss Fillman, I have a very young daughter and she's the reason I'm here at the orphanage looking for help."

Had he sensed her misgivings? Could he have any notion of the thoughts running through her mind? Heat seared her cheeks.

Sister Mary Lou patted Val's hand and leaned in. "Could you imagine being out at the lighthouse again?" she whispered.

No wonder Susan and Father Joseph had both asked her the same question the previous day. Valerie had thought they'd wanted her to go with them to the lighthouse—to take another look around the place. Susan had suggested that being there might help her remember something more in the quest to learn of her true past.

Father Joseph clasped his hands at his waist. "Let's leave the two to discuss Mr. Scholtus's situation, shall we, while we get ourselves settled after that trip?"

'No!' Valerie wanted to scream. Susan was the one who should be here, not her.

But Susan was needed at the orphanage, wasn't she?

"Is there some reason Susan isn't being considered?" She was playing the devil's advocate, but wouldn't it be the devil's plan for Valerie to be sent back to that hellish home?

Father Joseph cast a hard look her way. "Yes. But I don't need to explain those reasons."

Valerie's cheeks heated at the rebuke.

"Mrs. O'Brien will be here shortly." Father Joseph didn't explain why about that, either.

Was the cook being considered for the position, too? Relief edged through her.

Sister Mary Lou pointed to the door. "We'll be outside in the hallway if either of you should need anything."

"Thank you," Paul said.

But Valerie simply watched as they left, leaving the door open behind them.

This beautiful young woman was not the matronly type he'd had in mind for his daughter's care. Sweat broke out on Paul's brow, and he wiped it with his handkerchief before sitting down across from her.

"Do you like to fish, Mr. Scholtus?" Miss Fillman clasped her hands so tightly together that her knuckles grew white.

Was he so frightening? Paul swallowed. He would never want Hetty to be in the situation this woman now faced. "I do. But, being a farmer, I haven't gotten to as much as I'd like."

This elicited a curt laugh. "You'll have plenty of opportunity if you're a lighthouse keeper at Round Island."

"I hope to teach my daughter to fish, too."

Miss Fillman glanced toward the window. "A fun pastime for both boys and girls. My brother and sister love it."

No one with the commission had mentioned her siblings. "Are they here with you?"

Her blond eyebrows rose high. "No."

"Where are they?" He shouldn't have asked. What if they were deceased, like the lighthouse keeper and his wife?

"They're both on the mainland, where they can receive medical care for some. . . problems they have."

"I understand St. Ignace is a thriving port. That's good to know if Hetty ever needs special care or if we need to purchase something special."

"That's correct. But you'll find many things that you need right here on the island. You can send for them or you can come in on your free day."

A knock sounded on the door as Mrs. O'Brien entered. "Father Joseph said come here, so here I am."

"Welcome." Paul took command of the situation.

"Where would ye like me to settle myself?"

Valerie patted the seat beside her. "I was just telling Mr. Scholtus about the lighthouse. I'm sure he'll have questions for you about the position he has available."

Mrs. O'Brien's lips twitched downward as she joined Valerie on the settee.

"Mr. Scholtus has a little girl who will need care, but no doubt he'll need some help with housekeeping as well."

So much for taking control. Miss Fillman had grabbed it and run. "Mrs. O'Brien is an excellent cook, Mr. Scholtus."

The woman pulled at her cap. "I could say the same of ye, especially yer bakin'. Yer biscuits could near about float right off the plate."

"Thank you. I learned in a logging camp from the ladies in the cook shack." She turned her pretty violet eyes back on Paul. "I was explaining about the lighthouse. Was there anything more you wish to know before I leave you to interview Mrs. O'Brien?" There was an edge in her soft voice.

"Interview me?" Mrs. O'Brien pressed a hand to her chest. "Has he already finished with you?"

Paul needed to redirect this conversation.

Father Joseph had said that Valerie was in need of a position. That she had ongoing bills to pay. But he'd also said there were two candidates for the position. Somehow, he'd assumed Susan would be one of the women and the other would be a widowed matron who needed the work.

"I need Miss Fillman to stay. I have more questions." He shifted in his chair. "And Mrs. O'Brien, what is your situation?"

"I've a full-time position here, Mr. Scholtus." The Irishwoman's accent was heavy but she was easy to understand. That would be important for little Hetty.

Mrs. O'Brien rubbed her fingers together, in her lap. "Och, I enjoy me work. Mostly."

Miss Fillman touched the other woman's arm lightly. "You'd have a chance to cook, though, if you went out to the lighthouse."

"But we were goin' to be doin' tha' this summer—at the program," the cook argued.

Clearly, neither woman wanted to come out to the lighthouse. "What is this program?"

Miss Fillman locked gazes with him. "A training program coming to Mackinac which will provide all kinds of opportunities."

He raised his hands. "I am in great need of care for my Hetty. She's lost her mother. We'll be leaving the only home she has known. I need someone to care for a wonderful three-year-old girl who will be far from those she loves. But we need this new start. I need this. For us."

The look on Miss Fillman's face transformed from fixed determination to refuse, to that of concern and regret.

"I. . . I know that would be very hard for her." The young woman sat straighter. "She needs someone who understands."

Could this be the one who could help Hetty cope?

Miss Fillman gazed directly at him. "Could you give me until the hour before the last ferry leaves?"

Paul exhaled in relief. She was willing to discuss the position, and to consider it. "That's more than fair. Especially considering…" Considering that she'd lost her entire family on Round Island. But he certainly didn't need to point out what she was certainly already struggling with herself. She'd have to be an exceptionally brave young woman to go back and face her losses. And here he was running from his. What an unlikely pair they'd make if she agreed to take the position. He cleared his throat. "Considering what you've gone through, Miss Fillman. And please accept my sincere condolences."

Her lips were compressed so tightly they paled, but she dipped her chin in acknowledgment.

God, you know what I need, and what this young woman needs, but this wasn't what I was asking for. The matron beside her—isn't that the one for us?

Chapter Eleven

*L*awrence surveyed the massive room that would become his gymnasium—not *his*, but the Social Affirmation Society's gym.

"Whatcha doin'?" Jack called out as he jogged over to join Lawrence.

He shook his head slowly. "Looking this place over. It's amazing."

"Yup." Jack swiped his arm, covered by a striped athletic shirt, across his nose. "And we'll be usin' it before long, eh?"

"Sure looks like it." He patted the boy's shoulder and felt muscle. The kid was growing up.

"I gotta get in that mileage you asked me for." Jack waved and ran off.

A foghorn blasted and Lawrence flinched. He turned, imagining the construction site as it would be when fully finished.

Heavy boots thumped in the anteroom. A man in work clothes stomped through the door, glaring. He jerked a thumb away from the building, the gesture unmistakable. *Get out.*

Raising his hands, Lawrence departed.

When he stepped out of the construction zone and crossed the street, he decided to head for the water. How nice to be nearer the Great Lakes than in Lansing. To be surrounded by water. He'd always enjoyed his family's visits up north in the summer. Wintertime could be interesting, but no doubt beautiful as well. He heard stories of the blue ice that built up in mid-winter, that was supposed to almost glow ethereally.

He walked across the meadow, now fallow, and toward the benches that crouched along the shoreline. One bench was already occupied, the other vacant.

As he neared an empty bench, the woman on the other looked deep in thought, as she petted a calico cat that lay in a thick scarf on her lap. She startled as he sat, and looked in his direction. "Miss Johnson?"

"Yes."

Lawrence wanted to know more about her. He rose. "Would you mind if I joined you?"

She scooted further down the bench, making room.

He joined her, pushing his coattails aside as he sat. "You looked deep in thought."

She took a deep breath and then exhaled it sharply. "I had a bit of a surprise this morning."

"Oh?"

Miss Johnson swiveled slightly to face him. "If you knew someone very well, and while looking through their papers you found some disturbing things, what would you do?"

He straightened in his seat. "First, I wouldn't assume he had acted upon those things. Second, I'd inquire if they really were his. Had they gotten placed there by someone else? And the nature of the information would be important."

She nodded. "What if you found newspaper articles on making poisons and on. . . other very distasteful things, wouldn't you wonder how well you knew that person?"

"Again, I'd not assume they were his things." He shrugged. "My father is an attorney, and he collects all manner of terrible clippings. Helps with his work. Were these things pertinent to your friend's occupation?"

"No. And there were two people's belongings mixed in this one box."

"Ah! There you go then." He grinned. "But did you know them both well?"

"No. That's the thing. It's very strange." She blushed. "I confess that I cannot believe I'm telling you all this. I don't even know you."

He hung his head. "If we shall begin confessions, I have a big one for you." He turned toward her.

Miss Johnson cocked her head at him. "What could that possibly be?"

"I believe you're the Susan Marie Johnson that my mother's cousin, Tara Mulcahey, has been searching for—"

"You're related to Tara?"

"Yes."

"This day is getting stranger by the moment." She pressed her fingers to her temples. "Are you some kind of detective or something?"

He laughed. "No. I'm here for the Social Affirmation Society's new program."

"Tara was my mother's dearest friend."

"She will be so delighted when she gets to see you this summer."

"How will she do that?"

"She's one of the Sugarplum Ladies that Mrs. Welling invited to come teach cooking and catering skills to participants."

"The Sugarplum Ladies are coming?" Her brown eyes grew round.

92   *Mackinac Island Beacon*

"Yes. I understand your mother was their manager."

"She was."

"Like mother like daughter then." He grinned.

She frowned at him. "How do you mean?"

He blinked. "Father Joseph agreed that you would oversee and manage some of the programs."

From her silence, she obviously didn't know. She stared out at Lake Huron.

He leaned closer. "Father Joseph didn't have clippings on poisons and nefarious things, did he? Hate to think we're about to be. . ." he made a slashing motion at his throat, "done away with before we've even gotten started."

A chuckle began low in her throat. "No. Not him."

Lawrence elbowed her arm gently. "I'm handling the athletic and health endeavors."

"You're Jack Welling's coach, aren't you?"

"Yes. And until recently, I directed a young men's athletic center in Lansing."

"I can't believe no one has mentioned this change to me." She frowned. "I have been working with the orphanage for several years."

"I don't know why. But given that you shared some concerns with me just now—do you think you and I could be good partners in crime? I mean in managing all those young people desperately seeking skills this summer?"

She laughed. "Dear sir, I was one of those not-so-young people looking to advance my cooking skills this summer."

"Oh." He clamped his lips shut. How ridiculous to be teasing this young woman whom he'd only recently met. "But you look young to me. I'm nearing thirty myself."

She scowled. "No, you are not." Her voice sounded just like his sister's did when she was about to scold him.

"Twenty-seven." Still unmarried. *Jilted by my college sweetheart.* She'd been an obstetrician, the first female medical doctor in her class. She went on to marry a surgeon—and she'd broken Lawrence's heart.

"That's not thirty." She shifted her cat and stroked its fur. "About Tara—did she come to your father for help? Does he have an investigator who works for him?"

"He did a long time ago when she first started looking for you."

"I've always wondered if anyone had."

"She did. But every jurisdiction where you lived claimed that Cousin Tara had no legal standing to pursue custody of you."

"No legal standing."

"Because she was not related to you."

A wan smile blossomed. "It's refreshing to hear she did look and try. But how awful that some bureaucrats refused our reunion over lack of blood relation."

He shrugged. "That's the conundrum."

She draped the cat over her shoulder. "I'd better get back. I've got some things to take care of and I'm going to work on a letter for Tara, if you'll be so kind as to give me her address."

He rose and offered his hand as she stood. Her small hand was warm in his. It felt right, somehow. *Enough silly thoughts.* "Happy to offer her address in return for something."

The cat swiveled its head and looked at Lawrence as if it was considering hissing at him. Instead, it raised one paw and licked it.

She arched one dark brow. "What is it?"

"Do not let the proverbial cat out of the bag," he motioned toward her pet. "Don't tell Father Joseph what I said."

She sniffed. "I won't say anything about this summer's work."

He wasn't going to lie, but neither was he going to inform her that she'd begin working with him on the program much sooner than summer. "Will drop Tara and Bertie's address off later."

"Thank you."

Tentatively, he reached to pet the cat, who began purring.

"I think Lizzie likes you."

"Don't tell my dog."

A sly grin crept over her face. "I only promised to keep one secret."

What had been the point of Paul familiarizing himself with the shops on Mackinac Boulevard when he might not be able to accept the position, if confirmed? He'd asked at every open shop if they knew of a steady islander girl who might be available.

None.

A thin stream of sunlight broke through the clouds as he returned to the orphanage.

What did he really know about the former lighthouse keeper's daughter? She'd reportedly had a limited education but seemed well-spoken. She had cared for her two younger siblings, both of whom suffered infirmities. And she knew the ways of a lighthouse. But from her negative reaction to the notion—would she be willing to return to the site of the tragic demise of her family?

No. He couldn't see it. He'd need to speak with Mrs. O'Brien privately. But she, too, seemed to have no desire to help him. If only Susan had been available.

He continued past the pharmacy and Doud's grocery store, which he'd stopped at earlier. In another quarter of a mile, he reached the church. He strode up the steps and entered the foyer. A young woman knelt near the alter. *Miss Fillman.* He drew in a deep breath as he moved forward to the last pew.

Lord, I have to give this to You. You have it anyway. That whole thing about not my will but Thine, I guess that's it, God. Amen.

If Annabelle had heard Paul's prayer, she'd have laughed. His prayers had sounded nothing like that when she'd been so ill. He'd railed at the Lord. Yelled. Demanded. Begged.

He closed his eyes.

A short request to the Creator was all that was needed. Or was it needed? Didn't the Holy Spirit intervene? Or was that for when you no longer had the words? Poor Anabelle. Poor Hetty. *God help me.*

The creak of the wood floor alerted him to Miss Fillman's steps.

He looked up.

Wide-eyed, she looked around the narthex. "Mr. Scholtus?"

"One and the same." He had to be bold. "The new lighthouse keeper—if you'll help Hetty and me."

She straightened and pushed her slight shoulders back. "Possibly. Perhaps for a season."

"A season?"

"This fall." Her lips twitched. "When I have my brother and sister with me in the spring, then we'll need another place."

He was slow to understand sometimes, but not now. "You wouldn't want them out there."

"Correct." She ran her tongue over her upper lip. "So if I helped you now, you'd need another worker once the lighthouse re-opens after winter.

Relief coursed through him that she was seriously considering the position. His cold hands, still locked in prayer, began to warm. "I am very grateful that you may take the spot."

She looked around once more then sat in the pew ahead of him and angled her body toward him. "Obviously, you are a praying man. That's good."

"Is there anything else we should discuss that may convince you to accept the position. . . for this autumn?"

"Do you raise your hand to your daughter?" Her accusatory tone made him cringe.

"Never. And neither shall you." He rubbed his forehead. "If you take the job."

"Do you yell and curse?"

His cheeks heated. He was seated in a church after all. "I've been known to curse in frustration—the same with yelling—but I've tried hard not to do that in front of others."

She tipped her head a bit. "Are you successful at that?"

He chuckled. "I live on the family farm. My ma makes sure we all behave—even my brothers who are well into their thirties." He grinned.

"How does she do that?" Genuine interest tinged her tone.

"We don't want to disappoint Ma. We all love her. Can't stand to see disappointment on her face."

She blinked those lashes that were surprisingly dark, given her blond eyebrows. This young woman was far too pretty to be unmarried for long. But if she'd stay for the rest of the fall, maybe he'd find someone new.

"Do you have any questions of me, Mr. Scholtus, before you leave Mackinac?"

"Did you enjoy helping with your younger sister and brother?"

"Yes. I love children. Not as much as Susan loves them, but. . ." She shrugged.

"She was an only child and always loved being around my big family." Susan used to pretend that one day they'd marry and have a huge family. If he was honest with himself, Paul preferred the notion of a smaller family. But never had he thought he'd be a widower with only one child to raise by himself.

"She said that."

"She did?"

"Susan loved being around your family on the farm." She cocked her head. "But have you ever worked at a lighthouse?"

"I was an assistant lighthouse keeper downstate—on Lake Michigan."

"Good. What was your favorite thing about it?"

"Got to fish in my free time. Always had trouble with my nets, though." Darned things tore frequently.

Miss Fillman leaned in. "I enjoy repairing nets, Mr. Scholtus, so don't fear."

He laughed. "My great-grandfather sailed on the Great Lakes. He taught me to make nets which I don't mind—it's the repairs that bother me."

"Not as satisfying as creating that new thing."

"Exactly."

"And the lighthouse work?"

"Enjoyed all the mechanics working with the lighthouse—even the repairs." Almost as comforting as tilling the earth and inhaling its loamy scent. This would be the first year in his life that he'd not be there for the planting and the harvest. *Might never be again.* He drew in a deep breath. Was he making a mistake?

No. He had to recover. Had to make a new start. "Are there any suggestions you have for me for my daughter coming here?"

She offered him a tremulous smile. "You might ask the island library to stock a few more picture books."

"The lighthouse board assured me they'd send us young children's books." Paul brushed hair away from his eyes. "And some sporting books for me."

"Good. I could ask the library for more, though."

With her golden hair and good looks, Valerie appeared nothing like the older woman he'd imagined would care for his child. How was this going to work out? He needed help, Hetty needed someone to watch her, and that was that. He'd best keep any feelings of attraction under strict control. "Miss Fillman, I'll also request some women's literature that a wife would enjoy. I mean, that *you* might like." He couldn't help staring at her. What had he just said?

The young woman's cheeks turned pink. Did she expect more than a position providing childcare? He had no plans to remarry. But Hetty could benefit from a mother. Why was he even thinking these things? Why had he said such a thing?

"Yes, I'd like some lady's books and magazines. Mum rarely asked for those, but they are available." She touched the scarf wrapped loosely around her slender neck. "If I take the position, will I be able to go from Round Island to Mackinac Island on my own?"

"Of course. The days my substitute mans the light, you'll be free to come and go from Round Island to Mackinac Island."

"Good." She exhaled in obvious relief.

"But for safety, I'd prefer that we travel together, Miss Fillman. If you take the position, that is."

She flushed and averted her gaze. "Of course."

Good heavens, she'd not even started the position and already she was thinking about getting away from him? Still, she was his only candidate. "There are two boats—a canoe and a rowboat—and we'll have access to a small sailboat during full season. But I expect you already know that, don't you?"

She nodded but said nothing.

He needed an answer today. *Now.*

Sunlight pierced the stained-glass windows on his right revealing tiny dust motes in the air and the shadow of something, or someone, beneath one of the pews. Concerned, he rose.

"What is it?

Paul took two quick steps into the aisle. "I see you," he called to the small figure on the floor.

As he moved closer, the girl shoved something into her mouth. She began to cough.

Miss Fillman rushed forward. "Francesca?"

"It looked like she shoved an entire biscuit into her mouth."

Miss Fillman pushed past him. She went over, pulled a handkerchief from her pocket, and shoved it at the dark-haired girl. "Spit."

The child didn't react.

"*Sputalo Fuori, Francesca.*"

Part of the item came out, but she began to choke.

"Let me help." Paul touched Miss Fillman's back.

She bent and pulled the child to her feet. "I think she'll cough it out."

More bits and pieces of biscuit continued to fly onto the hymnals.

"She needs water." Paul ran to search for a canteen. It had been nearly empty. He'd not yet refilled it. He hurried to the pew where he'd left his daypack, pulled out his canteen, and shook it. "Not much in here, but some."

Hands pressed to her throat, Francesca was deadly silent.

Paul removed the top and handed the canteen to Miss Fillman.

"Francesca, drink," she urged.

"It could help the bread get unstuck. It could soften and wash it down." Paul moved to the pew behind the child. If he had to, he'd turn her upside down, like he'd once done with Hetty to get some stuck sourdough bread out.

Miss Fillman held the container to the girl's lips. She swallowed. Dark eyes grew panicked.

"Give her another," Paul commanded. He readied himself to lift the girl.

Another drink as tears poured down pale cheeks onto a frayed collar.

Silence.

Paul reached to lift the girl when she grabbed the canteen and drank more. Then Francesca gasped and coughed.

What a beautiful noise! The child sank onto the cushioned seat.

Paul bent and patted the child's shoulder. "Take some slow breaths."

The child turned toward Miss Fillman and wrapped her arms around her. "*Va tutto bene,*" she whispered into the child's hair.

"Francesca!" Another woman's voice called out behind them.

The little girl broke free and ran toward the dark-haired woman who stood at the entrance and threw herself into the attractive lady's arms.

"That's your Susan." Miss Fillman inclined her head toward the stranger.

He stood to his full height. "Susan Marie Johnson?" *After all these years.*

Miss Fillman hurried toward Susan.

Paul tentatively followed, suddenly tongue-tied.

An image of Annabelle's face, twisting so quickly into anger that he'd almost missed it, when Susan had joined them in play at his parents' farm. The fleeting smug expression on Annabelle's childish face when she'd heard the social workers had taken his friend away after her parents' death. Behaviors that had caused him alarm. Still, he'd overlooked them. It wasn't until after they'd married that he'd realized how manipulative and cold she could be.

He drew in a steadying breath. The photograph in the paper couldn't begin to do Susan's fine features justice. She had grown into the brown-eyed beauty he'd thought she would become. And clearly, she loved children, as her friend had affirmed.

Miss Fillman spoke with Susan, but he couldn't hear her soft words.

Susan locked gazes with him. "Paul? Is it really you?"

"In the flesh."

She glanced between him and Miss Fillman. "And did she say, yes?"

For a split second, Val thought Susan was asking if he'd proposed. What a ridiculous thought. From Mr. Scholtus's blush, had he inferred the same? "Yes. I did agree to go out to the lighthouse." She'd assist this kind man who showed by his actions that the fine boy Susan had remembered from childhood had become a remarkable man. "He just saved Francesca's life."

"I saw that." Susan pressed her hand to her chest. "Thank God you were both here."

Francesca ran back and kissed Paul's cheek. The expression of paternal joy on his face pierced her heart.

"You, too, *bella*." The girl brushed her lips against Valerie's cheek, too. Soft as butterflies' wings.

Francesca ran back to Susan. The way she stood by her suggested proprietary ownership. Francesca considered Susan *hers*. Her person.

"I guess we ought to shake on our agreement, Miss Fillman." He extended his hand to her, and she took it.

The warmth of his firm touch traveled through her, connecting her to something. What would it be like to be *his* person? "Our agreement?" She couldn't seem to release his hand and he held hers longer.

Amusement shone in his eyes as lines crinkled at their corners. "For you to come out to the lighthouse and watch Hetty for me."

"Yes, I agree."

When he released her hand, she resisted the urge to rub the missing warmth back into her fingers and palm.

"I'll see you when I return then."

Chapter Twelve

Mackinac Island

*H*ad Valerie really told Paul Scholtus yesterday that she'd go work at Round Island when he returned in a week with his daughter?

She shook her head as she began dusting Father Joseph's cavernous office.

Even with all the tumultuous changes in her life, she possessed a modicum of peace, as she awaited her meeting with Father Joseph and Sister Mary Lou. Val stood in the center of the room and pressed one hand to Mabel and Timmy's letters nestled in her apron pocket. Her new job could pay for their treatments. Both reported being happy and healthy and determined to do their best to make progress.

She turned in a slow semi-circle. This place evoked hominess. Leather-bound books filled the walnut-stained bookcases that covered the three walls without windows. She'd been allowed to read as many of them as she wished in the short time since she'd arrived—and she had. The priest even made sure that she went to the island's library, too, to select more books. A world had truly opened up to her between all those pages of religious doctrine and history. God was a loving god not one intent on inflicting maximum punishment, as Mum had insisted.

Father Joseph's desk supported stacks of official church and orphanage papers. Sister Mary Lou had taken the papers from the lighthouse, though, to the meeting room to examine them. Strewn atop his desk were also hand-scrawled notes from former orphans, now adopted, and an array of trinkets he'd collected on his many travels.

"It's a mess," she murmured. As much as she fussed about those mementoes as she dusted them, Valerie smiled when she feathered off the motes from the tiny statuette of a boy and girl, hands outstretched. Crafted in bronze, the artwork occupied a place of prominence in the center of his collection. He'd said that they represented the children who came to the orphanage looking for help.

Someone rapped on the oak door frame, startling her. The door opened and Mr. Hammond, the janitor, a slim man, peered inside. What was he doing there?

"Ha' penny fer yer thoughts, Miss Val?" The janitor's British accent reminded her of her father's, making her uneasy.

"Just waiting on Father Joseph." Not that it was any of Hammond's concern. Since she'd arrived, he had the habit of showing up unannounced. She was being silly. It was probably his accent, so much like her parents', that was what bothered her about him.

His moustache twisted above his narrow lips as his sandy eyebrows drew together. "He should be right along, miss."

Mr. Hammond dipped his pointy chin. "I'm right sorry, I am, about yer folks."

He seemed sincere. She regretted her negative thoughts about him. "Thank you."

He disappeared almost as quickly as he'd arrived.

Father Joseph, clutching his Bible, strode into the room. The chandelier overhead, a gift from a patron, illuminated his thick, wavy, silver hair.

Val dipped a curtsy. "Good morning, Father Joseph."

"Good morning, child."

Valerie resisted the urge to laugh. No one had ever treated her like a child at home much less referred to her as one. Father Joseph and Sister Mary Lou treated her more like family than her own parents had.

The dear priest waved her toward the settee, an uncharacteristic frown puckering his forehead. He sat down behind his desk as she adjusted her skirts to sit.

"First off, we're grateful for your work at the orphanage." He raised his hand, the gems in his gold ring catching the light. "Second, it was a noble sacrifice for you to accept the position watching the new lighthouse keeper's child."

"Thank you."

He shook his head. "We thank you."

Val had been the one to teach her brother and sister to say, "Thank you," to the few other people they saw. *But who taught me?* The thought skidded through her mind but unlike other memories, she grasped this one. Examined it.

A dark-haired lady, finely dressed, had instructed Val to say the words, while a servant—a cook—nodded approval. And somewhere, nearby, stood Mum, in the shadows. Dorcas—not Mother.

Pain seared her scalp as a headache threatened.

"Miss Fillman?" Father Joseph sat behind his desk.

"Yes. Sorry."

"As I was saying, we're glad you're able to accept the position, but we're a little concerned."

As am I.

Soft rapping on the door announced Sister Mary Lou, who shut the office door behind her. "Sorry I'm running a little late. We had one child who couldn't find a pair of shoes. But all's well now." She offered Val a tight smile before sitting beside her.

Father Joseph's eyebrows arched high. "We're concerned about your recurring nightmares."

Heat singed Val's cheeks.

"We're sorry about those terrors about your family." Sister Mary Lou patted her hand.

Val chewed her lower lip. The dreams weren't about her family. They were about strangers and places she didn't remember when she awoke. "Susan thinks all the changes in my life have stirred them up. I've not had them so regularly in years."

"So you've said. But Sister Mary Lou has asked Dr. Duvall to meet with you if you're willing."

The psychiatrist. She'd heard his name before. Mum had said psychiatrists did the devil's work. But she was gone.

"Might be good to speak with him before you start at Round Island, my dear." The sweet nun had just as dulcet a voice.

"Let me consider it."

"Good." He clapped his hands. "Now, how about you get me some tea and those little cakes you've been baking with Cook?"

"I'll bring the tray right back."

"And Valerie, we'll speak with you about what we know so far, about those papers, when you return."

"Susan told me a little bit about the box—about her mother's things."

Sister Mary Lou nodded. "Yes, it's very strange. We've yet to discern how that happened."

A tentative rap sounded on the doorway, accompanied by, "*Il carrello del tè, signore e signori!*"

"*Si accomodi*, Francesca!" The priest called out. He smiled at Valerie. "She's bringing in the tea cart, so please stay."

The girl pushed the cart toward them.

"Francesca, I believe Miss Susan asked you to speak in English." Sister Mary Lou sighed.

Valerie hated to hear the girl be admonished, but Susan had been adamant that Francesca would never fit in if she didn't try harder. And all of them were concerned about the possible adoption of a child who didn't have mastery of English.

"Madame Mirandette teach the catechism in French. How this is different?" Francesca's defiant words were accompanied by a look of penitence. She'd make a great little actress, because Valerie discerned that she felt no remorse.

Father Joseph didn't correct the girl. "Latin is very close to Italian. If my staff can't generally understand you, then how are they understanding my homilies? *Capire l'omelia di Padre Giuseppe poi capire* Francesca."

Francesca pushed a strand of long dark hair over her slim shoulder. "Si, Padre Giuseppe."

"Don't worry, child." Father Joseph shook his head and waved the child away. "*Non preoccuparti.*"

Valerie stood and poured the tea, inhaling the familiar scent of orange pekoe. She carefully plated the petits fours onto the floral embossed plates and then distributed them.

Father Joseph took a sip of his tea. "We have concerns about your parents."

The priest and nun exchanged a long look. "Father and I suspected, when your father took his post, that something was very wrong with your mother."

"Very secretive." The priest shook his head.

"And very odd with you and your brother and sister." The nun rubbed the knuckles of her left hand. "We grew concerned about her outbursts, too, when she came to the island."

Her mouth dry, Val sat back on the settee and drank some of her tea. She knew all about her mother's nature.

"You know a great deal of their belongings had to be burned." Children's hoots of laughter outside didn't distract Father Joseph but made Valerie's teacup wobble in her hand.

Val's gut clenched. "Of course." All of the cloth items. She'd had to replace her clothing with items from the mission bin. Her brother and sister had required clothing, too.

"But we now have that box Susan found and a few other things." Concern flickered over the priest's face.

Sister Mary Lou gazed past Val, toward the window, through which the children's voices continued to carry. "Father and I sorted the papers but haven't had time to go through them individually yet."

Father Joseph rubbed his brow. "We found some we deemed very important."

"While there were birth certificates for your brother and sister..." Sister Mary Lou and Father Joseph exchanged a glance.

"There was no record for you." Father Joseph ran his thumb over the teacup rim. "Also, Dorcas Fillman would have been perhaps only fourteen or fifteen when you were born."

So young.

"We found an old letter to her younger sister, Lettice Woods— there was a London address and a card from her in the box." Sister Mary Lou clasped her hands in her lap. "Apparently, Woods was Dorcas's maiden name. Did she ever mention her other family?"

"No. Nor did she receive letters from family members. But she and Pa were from England."

"We have sent a letter to her and are hopeful she's at that same address."

Father Joseph shrugged. "But if she's married and moved on, who knows?"

"What did my aunt say? She could be our only living relative, though honestly Mum never mentioned her."

Father Joseph pulled open his desk drawer.

A shriek of childish joy pealed from outside, startling Val. She set her teacup back in its saucer.

He handed her the envelope, which had been sent from Lettice Woods in East London. She opened the letter, written in almost childish script, so much like Mum's.

Dear Sister, Johnny says ye've got his child so he has to go over there. His folks are in a right fury. Why do ye claim to have a daughter when ye've never told him afore?

"Claimed?" Val raised her head, which began to pound.

Tis over two years ye've been gone. What are ye up to? Yer friends have left ye there alone. Why did you wait so long to tell Johnny? He was going to marry me. I'll hate you till the day I die.

Valerie raised her eyebrows. "Sounds like her sister and she had a lot in common." She exhaled sharply.

Father Joseph sighed. "Found nothing from Lettice after that."

Val sat up straight. "My mother never spoke of having any kin."

"We can send inquiries about Dorcas's family to London." The priest tugged at his collar.

"I see."

"Seems odd Dorcas hadn't told them she'd had a child." Sister Mary Lou patted her hand.

"Obviously, her disclosure had the intended result, because Pa came to New York."

"Leaving the other Miss Woods behind." The priest's lips pulled in.

"Perhaps I was adopted? Could that be why she'd not mentioned me?"

Father Joseph shook his head. "Not by a single girl in her late teen years."

"And there were no adoption papers. We'll go through and log every item and every date."

"Maybe some other young girl gave birth to me, and then my mother took me in and raised me?" She'd read of such things.

Sister Mary Lou set her teacup down. "Valerie, the year of their marriage was 1882. And you're how old?"

"I'm…" Truth be told, she wasn't quite sure. "I was told I will be nineteen in February." But she'd always been certain she was older. Perhaps twenty in February.

Father Joseph's jaw dropped open. "You don't know?"

She shook her head, tears spilling down her cheeks. Everything she thought she knew could be wrong. A life based on lies. "Mum always said I was smarter than my years and taller than other children my age."

Sunlight shone through the window and Val stood and turned. The children played happily outside. Susan chasing them through the yard. Here were orphans seemingly happier than she'd been in her entire life.

Sister Mary Lou came alongside her. "Those nightmares about being a young child may hold some clues, and we'd like you to start writing them down for us."

Father Joseph sounded like he was rummaging through his desk.

"And the Stevens asked for you to come back to their cottage." Sister Mary Lou sounded the most excited that she had since Valerie had arrived. "They told Susan to send you this afternoon. Colonel Stevens has some questions for you."

"Susan said the place was triggering memories for you." Father Joseph joined her at the window and handed her a leather-bound journal. "Write anything down that you recall when you visit the veterans' home."

Valerie chewed her lower lip. "They mentioned having us help with an event at Apple Blossom Cottage." But then they sent word that they wouldn't need them because they'd canceled due to the September winds being too rough on the water that weekend.

"Do you mean Tumbleston Refuge?" Sister Mary Lou frowned.

"The name given by the original owners was Apple Blossom Cottage." Father Joseph came to the window. "Mr. Mott died near on thirty years ago. Rarely saw his daughter and her family when they came for summers on West Bluff—and they stopped coming long ago."

"Valerie, I can't send Susan with you today." Sister Mary Lou offered her a wobbly smile. "Could you walk up? It's a good half hour or more."

Her shoe leather was nearly worn through and there had been nothing her size in the donation barrels. "Do you know what the colonel wants?"

"Susan said that you'd pointed out some things you believed might be on the property. He didn't say, but she wondered if he had the veterans trim back those bushes by that spot you asked about."

Her cheeks heated. How embarrassed she'd be if there was nothing there. "Should I set out now?"

Sister Mary Lou checked her watch that hung from a chain on her bodice. "Yes."

"One last thing." Father Joseph tapped his finger on his blotter. "We have an item that we are investigating. But we'd like you to give us some time before we discuss its possible significance. Superintendent Dardanes gave us permission to investigate the provenance of a piece of jewelry in that box that contains items belonging to both you and Susan."

"Jewelry? Mum had her wedding ring, that's all."

"It's children's jewelry, and we're going to research it."

"Grab your coat and hat because that wind is determined to blow today." The nun pointed outside. Autumn leaves of yellow and orange fell outside the window as the children's voices again lifted in glee.

Lawrence hadn't expected so much excitement over a new kickball. The orphans had squealed with delight. A red-haired older boy grabbed it and ran off.

Lawrence patted his pocket housing the illegible letter from Colonel Benjamin Stevens, crumpled by the mail carrier. Today, the Wellings had offered him the use of their carriage for a trip up to the West Bluff to visit at what had been Apple Blossom Cottage, the Gladstone's summer home when they'd lived in the States.

"Hey, she ain't out there, Larry!" Jack called from the carriage. "She just went in."

He knew exactly who the boy meant—Susan Marie Johnson. He ignored Jack, hoping she'd come back out.

One of the nuns emerged from the building, waving her hands as her black habit flapped around her like wings.

"Aw," the boys chorused.

They brought the kickball to Lawrence, but he raised his hands. "No. It's a gift."

The nun must have heard him because she nodded her approval and smiled.

The children formed a line.

A little dark-haired girl, her back to the group, didn't follow the others, so Lawrence approached her. "The children are going in now."

Her tiny features pulled in. "*Mi scusi?*"

His Italian was a little rusty, but having had Latin drilled into him, it had been his foreign language of choice in high school. "*Gli altri bambini. . ,*"

"*Parlo solo loco.*" He explained his limitations, bent, and smiled at her. "*Devi andare, piccola signorina.*"

She ran off toward the line. Then she turned. "You speak good Italian. *Grazie.*"

He searched for the words to explain that the children were going inside. "*Stanno entrando adesso.*"

Happiness flicked over her face. "*Tu parli italiano*?" She rattled off something in Italian so quickly that he missed all the words except for 'happy.'

The line moved forward. The brief happiness had fled. Loneliness emanated from the child in her entire demeanor with her head bent, shoulders slumped, and the shuffling motions as she moved forward. This was the child who'd never be chosen. Not for the games, not for confidences, not for adoption.

And I didn't even notice her while we were playing. That would change. One day he'd have a houseful of children, Lord willing, and he'd take in kids like this girl—ones who didn't have a proper home.

The wind blew and tousled Jack Welling's hair. "Come on, Larry."

"In a minute. Where'd you find that get up you're wearing?" And why did he wear a topcoat, dress pants, and spats?

Satisfaction painted the younger man's features. "Found it in the old carriage house up at Butterfly Cottage. Must be at least fifty years old." He turned his head toward his shoulder and sniffed. "Smells like it, too."

Lawrence shook his head, but he couldn't help laughing. "Glad I'm not sitting next to you." Jack was driving the carriage today.

"Oh no, you'll be in the back, my dear man." Jack used a strong fake British accent.

"Don't take up acting as a career."

"I'll have you know, sirrah, that I've been in many a fine play."

Lawrence pushed open the gate. "Elementary school productions no doubt."

Jack crinkled his nose. That kid—his nose was going to get stuck wrinkled like that one day.

As Lawrence stepped onto the walkway, Valerie, the young woman he'd seen in Father Joseph's office, emerged from the front entrance to the orphanage. Sun rays danced on the golden hair that peeked from beneath her bonnet and framed her face. Not whom he'd hoped for, though.

Jack waved. "Looking for a ride, milady?"

Eyes widening, Valerie glanced between Jack and him. "Did the colonel send you?"

The colonel? Did she know the Stevens?

"No, milady. You see this carriage was a pumpkin, and I'm here for Cinder Ella—but there's no prince—just him." He waved toward Lawrence.

He huffed a sigh. "Please ignore Jack. He's dramatic."

She took a few more steps. "I see. This is your carriage ride then." Disappointment tugged at her even features.

"We're going up to the colonel's, milady." Jack scowled at him. "And we have room aplenty in our pumpkin turned carriage."

She glanced between him and Jack, wariness warring with hope as she turned toward the conveyance.

He'd not address her by her Christian name. "Absolutely, Miss. . ."

She clutched her reticule tightly to her waist. "Miss Fillman."

He moved closer, to assist her into their ride. "I'm Lawrence Zumbrun."

Miss Fillman stiffened. Was he that frightening?

Wide violet eyes, a shade he'd never seen in anyone else's eyes except his friend's little sister's, locked on his—except he'd never seen hers looking terrified. *Valentine. . . Valerie. . . could it be? No.*

"We are going up to Tumbleston Refuge, to see Colonel Benjamin Stevens. You're most welcome to join us." He pointed to Jack. "This is Jack Welling, a phenomenal athlete and one of the foremost runners in America. You have no need to fear him despite his odd behavior."

A stifled laugh slipped past her lips. "I'll accept the offer."

Susan had spoken in such an animated fashion about Lawrence Zumbrun the previous night, that Valerie had almost expected the man to wear knight's shining armor and not be attired in a tan plaid wool jacket and brown pants.

"My reputation precedes me." Jack smirked at her.

"I've heard you're a fast runner, yes."

Lawrence assisted her into the carriage. His hand was warm, and firm, but it didn't feel like Mr. Scholtus's had when he'd shaken her hand goodbye. The widowed father's grip conveyed something she'd never felt before. Something Valerie couldn't quite fathom.

"Larry is my coach. He used to be almost as fast as me." Jack flexed his shoulders. "But not quite."

She caught Lawrence rolling his eyes heavenward.

"And how have you heard my name mentioned?" The gentleman asked. He must be in his mid-twenties or so from the look of him, though his manner seemed like someone older. The same could also be said of her friend, Susan. The world and life did funny things to people.

"Susan mentioned your name last night." She bit her lip. She'd not tell him how Susan had found him handsome, witty, kind, and charming. "She said you'll be running the summer program that we're anticipating."

Disappointment flickered across his strong features as he settled across from her. "That's all she said?"

"A lady does not reveal confidences." She quirked her eyebrows upward.

A smile tugged at his lips.

"Ready milord and milady?" Jack looked over his shoulder at them.

Seagulls squawked and soared overhead.

"Yes." She was ready to explore the cottage further.

But was she prepared for what she might yet find?

Chapter Thirteen

*P*erhaps Cinder Ella's mice had shown up and magically transformed into yard workers instead of horses. Valerie pressed her hands to her mouth. "Those veterans have transformed the place."

The place looked immaculate, with neatly trimmed bushes and the autumn lawn raked clean. "Colonel Stevens must have worked them hard—or perhaps it was his wife's doing."

"You said you've only met them once?" Lawrence swept his gaze from one side of the massive yard to the other.

"Yes, over a week ago and the yard looked nothing like this."

Jack parked the carriage and then Lawrence assisted her out. "Thank you."

"You're welcome."

"I'm goin' over to the Canary to see my little cousin, Aunt Sadie, and Uncle Robert." Jack had indicated the yellow cottage when they'd driven by just now. It was several homes back.

Lawrence checked his watch. "I'll come get you afterward."

"Thought you were walkin' back."

Valerie's face flushed. "I can do that."

"Just kiddin', eh?"

Beside her, his coach huffed a sigh.

With all the hedges trimmed in front, what had they done to the back? She had to see if the birdbath was still there, hidden beneath that tangle of overgrown bushes. But had they removed them as she'd suggested? "I'm going to walk around for a bit if you don't mind."

He shrugged.

"I'll let you and the colonel have a little time alone together."

"Fine. But be on guard. I don't know how well these veterans behave if alone with a young woman."

Instead of responding, she hurried off around the right side of the cottage, past the wide porch, and up the driveway that led to the carriage house, now in disuse and overgrown. She raised her skirts and hurried up the drive. Would it be there?

She held her breath as she rounded the back corner. Every bush had been cut low.

She expelled a short breath and then forced herself to breathe normally as she all but ran toward the marble birdbath surrounded now by low-cut azalea bushes. Now visible was the circled path around the birdbath, rimmed with remnants of what had once been beautiful roses.

She could almost feel her finger being pricked by one of the many thorns. Her sister had grabbed her hand as blood oozed out, and she'd begun to wail. *This was real.* It had to be a real memory of her hand being pressed to a white handkerchief to stop the bleeding. She pulled her journal from her cloth bag. She looked for the benches that should be there.

Valerie moved away from the birdbath, which someone had thoroughly cleaned and filled with water, and searched out the benches.

"Lookin' for somethin', miss?" One of the veterans, whom she'd seen on their last visit looked up from clearing debris by the walkway.

Then she saw it. *The black hitching post with the lion's head.* Just like she'd told Colonel Stevens. But it had been nowhere in sight then.

She needed to sit down before she fainted. "Is there a bench?"

"Sure, miss." He gestured a few yards past him. "A few concrete benches by those old apple trees."

"Thank you." She walked to the hitching post and ran her hand over the polished lion's head.

It's good luck, Val! Go ahead and rub his mane and you'll have a great day. The boy had said that. Her older brother it seemed.

She walked to the benches and sat. The scraggly apple trees had been long neglected. What a shame, for they could have produced fruit for the men. She remembered beautiful pink blossoms and her dark-haired sister running underneath, hands uplifted.

Valerie pulled her pencil out and began to write.

"I got your letter, Colonel Stevens, but it was completely illegible." Lawrence held the mangled envelope aloft.

"Darned mail service. Can't trust them to do their jobs."

Lawrence held back a response. "But I'm here now—"

"You made a trip all the way up to speak with me?" The colonel's eyebrows rose.

"No, sir, I'm beginning a new job on the island with the Social Affirmation Society."

He rocked back on his heels. "Are they already here then?"

"I'm the first program director, and the Wellings are here, too."

"Didn't know Peter was involved with this."

"He and Mrs. Welling are both helping."

"Ah, yes, Ada Fox, the one who worked up at the Grand."

"I don't know about that. I've only met them when I began coaching their son."

"Her stepson."

"Yes." But the Wellings didn't make that distinction.

"Jack is back then? Quite a good fellow. Always running."

"He drove us here."

"My wife saw some character in an old-fashioned frock coat pull up. Thought it was some kind of a prank."

"No. That was Jack being, well, Jack."

"Come in and we'll have a smoke."

Lawrence raised his fingers. "No thanks for the smoke, but yes, I'd welcome a chat."

"Through here."

He followed the man to a dark-paneled office heavy with the scent of pipe smoke and cigars. Burgundy leather chairs looked well-worn but sturdy while the upholstered divan could use replacement. He sat in the first chair and the colonel sat across from him on the divan and lit a cigar. "I wrote you about a young woman, the former lighthouse keeper's daughter. Paid us a recent visit."

"Miss Fillman?"

"You know of her?"

"Yes. She came up with us."

"Good. I wanted to show her the backyard."

"She said it's been rehabilitated."

He laughed. "You could say that. We had to do it for the soiree that got canceled. But while the crew was in there, we did find a few things that she'd mentioned should be there."

Dizziness threatened—whether from the smoke or the conversation he wasn't sure. "And what did your letter to me say?"

Stevens inhaled and then blew cigar smoke out slowly as he fixed his gaze on Lawrence. "Let you know we had another possible claimant. A potential Gladstone connection."

Lawrence looked down at his shoes. "I thought we'd put this to rest."

Stevens scooched up on the edge of the settee. "This is why I wrote. I didn't want to go to your father until I got your thoughts. You see Miss Fillman claimed she remembered this cottage. Pointed out a few things only someone quite familiar with the building should have known. Told us of items we should find beneath that overgrown mess in the backyard."

"Are they there?" He swallowed hard.

"Yes." Stevens scooted back in his seat.

Valerie. Violet eyes. Knows hidden items in the yard. Can it be?

Lawrence tapped his fingers on his knees. "I'll contact my father, who is a dear friend of Lord Gladstone's, and we'll see what he says."

"But if it were up to you?"

He flexed his shoulders and shook his head. "I would not want to upset that family unless I had more proof."

"Good man. I'll leave this to you, then. That she knows the yard's features gives a connection of some kind." Stevens tapped ash into a nearby tray. "But what if she'd simply visited this place?"

"True."

"The Gladstones are coming here this summer, you know." A muscle in the colonel's jaw jumped.

Lawrence's mouth dropped open. "No. Why?"

"Something to do with that program of yours."

He frowned. Susan had mentioned the cooking program being led by. . . "Lady Gladstone was the founder of those Sugarplum Ladies, my father said."

"Yes. The letter said Lady Gladstone would be reuniting with her old friends."

"If there were substantial indications her daughter is alive and here on the island—if I were her, I'd come sooner."

"That's impossible. The Straits will be frozen over within the next few months."

"That's a few months away."

"After all these years do you really think you'd have solid proof?"

"I don't know."

"Let's go seek her out, and you can observe her."

The two of them left the house and found Valerie. But in the following fifteen minutes or so, she'd been silent as the grave.

"What do you think, Miss Fillman?" Colonel Stevens gestured toward the hitching post, then a ring of rosebushes now dead. "Are they as you remember?"

Lawrence stepped closer, then paused. "I remember being here once with my family, long ago." Lawrence blurted out the words before he could stop himself.

Two sets of eyes locked on him. He marched toward the hitching post. "This is the lucky lion. I gave it that name. Nathan Gladstone, my friend, said he'd keep the tradition going."

"He did," Valerie said softly.

The colonel's face softened. "You told me that when you were here."

"And about the birdbath." She pointed to the center of the roses.

Lawrence focused on the poor old bushes. "Those roses were—"

"Red!" She crossed her arms over her chest as if daring to correct him.

"Yes. They were red."

"Colonel Stevens, if you wish to ask me your questions, please proceed." Her body trembled as if she was cold or in distress.

"Already answered them." His lower lip tugged over his upper. "Wanted to show you this backyard and see if it's as you recalled."

"There were buds on the apple trees and roses in bloom in the memory that I have." As a gust of wind blew, she pressed her hand to her hat. "But with these improvements it is very similar."

Colonel Stevens ran a hand along his chin. "And you don't remember your parents—the Fillmans—being with you?"

She shook her head slowly, then moved toward Lawrence's side. "I'd like to leave now, please."

He extended his arm to her. "Certainly."

"Good of you two to come by." Colonel Stevens' face flushed. "When Lord and Lady Gladstone come to the island, they may kick us out of our housing. I expect that we'll begin looking for another spot soon."

Lawrence had no idea what to say to the former military man, so he simply dipped his chin and led Miss Fillman away up the drive toward the street.

Was this young woman beside him his friend's sister? The missing child? Attired in ill-fitting well-worn clothing? Could it be? He wanted her memories to be true.

When they reached the walkway, Jack ran toward them. "My nephew is takin' a nap so I left."

"What about your sister and brother-in-law?"

"Aw, he's out hunting down some story about some social do-gooder who speaks against the evils of alcohol and also against some of the crazy stuff they do to the inmates in the mental asylums."

"What does that have to do with the island?" Jack's brother-in-law, Ben Steffans, was a journalist as well as a talented pianist.

Jack scratched his chin. "Can't remember the reformer's name but she's gonna come speak at that program my mom set up. I mean that the Social Affirmation Society has started."

How much influence did Ada Fox Welling have then? "Could be good to include with the health sciences program."

"Looks like you two are ready, so let's go" Jack ran to the carriage.

Lawrence assisted Miss Fillman into the carriage and soon they were on their way.

She pulled a notebook from her bag and a pencil and began to write something.

"What's that for?"

"I'm keeping track of things that I remember. Like just now when I left the cottage and recalled that there is a hidden side entrance to the left of the building."

"I see." He didn't remember it from his visit all those years ago.

She finished writing and closed the book.

If she was really Valentine. . . Should he? "May I have permission to draw something for you?"

"Draw?"

"Yes. I'm not an artist but I do enjoy sketching." And he'd often given little Valentine sketches.

"Alright." She handed him the notebook and pencil. "But I don't see how you'll draw while we're in the carriage and Jack is apparently racing with himself. I had a hard time writing my few notes."

"Hey Jack! Slow down a bit."

"Spoilsport!" But the youth brought the horses to an easier pace.

Lawrence quickly sketched the outline of a sparrow—like the one he'd drawn for the card he'd given Valentine. Then he began to shade it and fill in with lines to bring the bird to life.

"What are you drawing?"

"One of my favorites of God's creatures."

"A dog?"

He laughed. "No, but that's a good guess. I have a—"

"Hound."

He looked up. "How did you know?" The Zumbruns had always kept hounds.

"I don't know. Maybe Susan said. Do you?"

"Yes. My father will be bringing him up next week."

"That's lovely. I enjoy Susan's cat. It's good to have a mouser around."

After Jack rounded the corner, Lawrence resumed sketching. Soon his sparrow, perched upon a branch, began to take form.

"May I look?"

He shook his head. "Not until I'm done."

They rode on past the brilliant azure waters of the Straits, topped by rippling white waves today. At least with the sunshine and Indian summer day temperature, he was reasonably comfortable.

"The lighthouse looks close from here." She placed a hand above her eyes to shade them. "Yet when I was on Round Island, this bluff looked impossibly far away."

"Funny how perceptions change depending upon where you are situated."

"Or your life situation."

He glanced at her and caught her pensive expression. With the right clothing, she'd be a beauty. *No more so than Susan, though.* He raised his eyebrows at his own thought. Susan Johnson kept popping up in his mind. And his dreams last night—one in which she greeted him at the door of a cozy house, with children's voices calling from inside. Heat seared his face, and he focused on finishing the image.

For twenty years he'd wished he'd never written *Good-bye* on that stupid card he'd given little Valentine Gladstone. When he'd become an adult, and sent out inquiries about her for his father, he'd remembered that avian figure on the card. For His eye is on the sparrow—and I know He watches you, little Valentine. Sometimes he'd sing the Bible verses aloud from that passage. *Someone really should compose music to go with those inspiring words.*

Another carriage rolled past in the other direction. Lawrence kept his head down.

Jack skillfully drove them down a back street past some charming shops, many of which were closed. They also passed by many state park buildings, also closed for the season.

"Aren't you done yet?" She leaned forward but he pressed back into his seat.

"I have the eyes to work on." This was cruel to do if this young woman truly was Valentine Gladstone. If she recognized the bird from the card and remembered him giving it to her, and yet she was separated from her entire actual family—wasn't he causing more harm than good? He ceased drawing and held onto the notepad as Jack turned down a side street. In a few moments, he directed the horses back onto the main road.

No steamers at the docks. Some fishing vessels moored. Workmen repairing the dock buildings, their hammers loud on this quiet day.

As Jack pulled up by the orphanage, Lawrence hesitated, but then passed the notebook to its owner.

Eyes widening, she stared at the sparrow and then at him, then back at the drawing. "I have a drawing just like this."

"A drawing?" he repeated dumbly.

"It's a card I kept from when I was a child."

Was it possible? Before he could ask her more, she rushed from the now-stopped carriage and headed into the building, calling, "Wait for me!"

He got out and stretched his arms heavenward. *Have I just opened a can of worms? Or have I lit a fuse for dynamite?* He'd write or telegraph his father immediately. He'd suggest that Father contact the Gladstones if he believed what Lawrence now suspected—that this young woman could be the missing child. But if they came to the States and this wasn't Valentine—Lady Gladstone would be devastated. That would be cruel.

Ada Welling pushed a pram toward him. "Hello, Lawrence. I'm so glad we've run into you. I wanted to tell you about a special guest I've invited to visit us. She may speak at our summer program."

Little Sally waved her stuffed rabbit at Lawrence, and he bent to take it.

"Tell me more. I wonder if this is the social crusader Jack mentioned to me."

"Georgina Gladstone is a—"

"Georgie Gladstone?" He gaped at the woman. He'd not even sent up a prayer, but God had answered.

"Bun-bun!" Sally reached for her toy, and he returned it to her.

"Do you know her? She's an outspoken critic of some of the travesties taking place in our sanitariums."

He briefly glanced down at his shoes. "Not in that capacity."

Valerie came running back out of the building, holding a card in her hand.

He knew even before she reached him that it would be the one that he'd given her. He ran both of his hands alongside his neck, where perspiration formed despite the air's chill.

Mrs. Welling raised her eyebrows. "Are you alright, Lawrence?"

He opened his mouth, but his lips wouldn't move.

"Look!" The young woman held his childish card up for him to see the sparrow, which matched the one he'd just drawn. "It matches almost perfectly." She pulled her notebook out to show Ada Welling.

"That's remarkable." Her mouth formed an "O".

"You have no idea, Mrs. Welling." *No idea whatsoever.*

Emotion gripped him. Had he finally found Verity "Valentine" Gladstone? Surely he had. But his mind warred with his spirit, which urged him to not get disappointed again. But where could she have gotten this old drawing of his? It was her. It had to be. He forced himself to breathe normally.

"Mama go!" In the stroller, Sally kicked and flailed her arms.

Mrs. Welling turned and patted the girl's cheek. "We're on our way now, darling."

A young man passed by on his bicycle, trailed by two younger boys. How Lawrence and his brothers enjoyed cycling together. He missed them.

Lawrence bent and took Sally's chubby hand. "Want to bike ride later? Bike bike?" Being around Sally more, he was getting used to speaking in baby talk.

The toddler clapped her hands.

He turned to Mrs. Welling. "That enclosed wagon, attached to the back of the bike, works great. Jack is a genius with anything mechanical."

"Early dinner, so you may take her afterward. But for now, we're going to the apothecary to pick up some salts for Mr. Welling's dyspepsia."

Lawrence could use something himself because his gut was beginning to churn.

"Have you tried baking soda in warm water?" Valerie clutched the drawings to her chest.

"Yes, but it's time for magnesium salts for my poor husband. Enjoy the rest of your afternoon, you two."

As they left, the little girl strained out the side of the pram to look back at them. Lawrence and Valerie waved at her, and she waved her bunny back, then settled into her seat.

"She's full of energy like her brother." Lawrence shook his head.

"If that was Mrs. Welling, then is Jack her brother?"

"Yes."

She held the pictures out. "Mrs. Welling agreed then that this is the same hand that produced both works."

"Yes." The faded paper still clearly showed his original artwork. He'd set that interest aside, rarely sketching, after Valentine had gone missing. And here she was standing in front of him.

"So you knew me when I was a small child then?" She compressed her lips.

Conviction smacked him on the head. "Yes."

"And you were acquainted with my parents?"

This was her. He'd found the missing child. "Your father was my father's dearest friend."

"How did he know my father?"

Father would finally be free from chasing down a child who couldn't be found. "My father was an attorney in Detroit, and I believe that's how they met."

"Was mine in some difficulty?"

"No."

She cocked her head. "Did your father do my adoption?"

"Adoption? No, you weren't even born yet." He shook his head.

She straightened. "But my father lived in England."

His breath became shallow, harder to draw in. "He had, but he made his home in Canada, in Windsor."

"Was da' a lumberjack then? This is very confusing." She tipped her head back.

"A lumberjack?" She was speaking of Fillman. How did he tell her? "No. Your father was a barrister. Your mother was the daughter of a wealthy Detroiter and was a social crusader when they met and for some years afterward." He had to say their names.

"You aren't talking about the Fillmans then."

He took her elbow and led her over to a nearby bench. "Sit down."

"Tell me from the start how you made this drawing and gave it to me. It was one of the few things from my early childhood that my mother let me keep when we left to come to Michigan. I had it in my little bag, which is long since gone, with a few other things."

"The little girl I gave this to. . ." He touched the card. "She was the daughter of my father's friends. Percy and Eugenie Gladstone."

"Then why was I raised by my parents?"

"Those people weren't your parents. Verity is your true name, and Valentine is a nickname because of your birthday. You went missing in New York City as the family was departing for England."

Red maple leaves drifted down toward them.

"It was in the fall. Like now." Her eyes looked like she was viewing something far away.

"Yes."

"You had been three, almost four, and a high-energy little girl. That was one of the things your brother and I liked about you. You were always up for a game."

She slid the card into her notebook. "I always thought I had another family. But this is. . . too much."

"I plan to send word to my father to contact your parents—"

"No." She raised her hand. "You speak of this brother, who must be an adult. But I have both a brother and sister—children."

"The Fillmans' children."

"My brother and sister nonetheless, and if I lost them. . ." Tears glistened in her eyes.

She would have no legal claim to them. "I can ask my father what your rights would be in this situation."

"A couple in St. Ignace with no children have already asked if they might seek adoption even though they are older." She shook her head. "I want them with me. They're my real brother and sister even if we don't share blood."

He nodded. "I know they are dear to you but imagine how your true parents feel. They need to know."

Tears trickled down her face and her hands shook. "Maybe I have that card because someone gave it to me. Maybe it's not mine at all. Maybe you didn't sketch it for me as this Gladstone child."

"You just said you remembered me drawing it for you."

She shook her head.

She was distraught. Violet eyes, similar blond hair as the child's had been though darker, facial features that even with his basic artist's eyes were the adult version of the girl's. Possessing memories of being at the Gladstone's cottage. This was Valentine. And her parents needed to finally see her again.

"Promise me that you won't send anything to the Gladstones until Timmy and Mabel's situations are settled, and I am not cut off from them any more than I already am."

How could he promise that? When was her older sister, Georgina, coming to the island? Could he persuade Ada to invite her to come sooner?

Valerie squeezed his hand. "Promise me."

He exhaled hard. "I will seek my father's legal advice for your siblings only. For now."

"Thank you." She swiped the tears from her eyes. "I'm to begin work at the lighthouse soon."

Lord and Lady Gladstone's daughter working at the lighthouse. Why had the priest even put her name forward? "Won't that be difficult for you?"

She blinked rapidly. "I think now, after discovering what may be, I could put some demons to rest."

"Has Mr. Scholtus considered how this may not work out?" Lawrence had mulled over the possibility that Susan might be forced to take her friend's place, putting her farther away from him.

Why did everything keep coming back to Susan? He'd have to figure that out, especially if he was going to work with her.

"I don't know. But I must raise the funds to cover my brother's and sister's expenses. Tomorrow, I'll have a better idea what that will mean for me."

Her biological parents could pay those bills. Perhaps even Father would help until Valentine consented to the disclosure. Or until poor, dear Georgina spilled the beans.

But with Georgie's emotional struggles, would she even acknowledge Valerie as Valentine Gladstone?

"I'd best go in and finish my packing for Round Island." She stood. "Thank you for the picture."

"You're welcome."

Her eyebrows drew together as she held up the notebook and the card. "Thank you for both pictures."

This was Verity. This was truth—like her name meant. *Veritas.* But he'd promised he'd not tell the people who most needed to know.

Why did I do that?

Chapter Fourteen

*R*eplacing her with a petite French-Canadian great-grandmother wasn't exactly what Susan had expected Father Joseph to do. She exited his office steaming mad. The poor lady already worked herself to the bone. She volunteered to teach the French-speaking children catechism, participated in baking for the Sunday coffee hour, and opened rooms in her home to guests.

Spying Sister Mary Lou, she strode toward her. "Really, Sister Mary Lou? A new job for me while poor overburdened Madame Mirandette takes my place?"

"Now, now, it will be all right. You'll see."

"I don't see how." Susan loved these children and didn't want to leave them.

"All things work together for those who love the Lord." Sister Mary Lou's sing-song voice had the desired effect—it made a smile tug at Susan's lips.

"But I'm not ready to leave so soon."

"Pish posh, as Valerie, would say."

"She does have some funny expressions, doesn't she?"

"And her odd accent. A mix of Midwestern and aristocratic English."

"Her parents being British probably explains it."

Sister Mary Lou cocked her head. "Did you talk with her brother and sister?"

"I did, the few times I saw them at church. And they conversed with the other orphans a bit."

"Didn't they sound"—the nun raised her shoulders—"like their parents? Like English people from a more. . ."

Susan cast her a quick glance. "From a lower class?"

"Yes."

"The children did sound a little like that."

"Yet Valerie does not."

"No."

"But both parents did, as well."

"Right." Susan rubbed her neck. "Very strange. But why is Valerie different?"

"The good Lord only knows, but we're going to get to the bottom of this."

"Yes, and find out what all her mother did. Those writings of hers concern me."

"I agree. Between her rambling journal and the poison clippings, which we're now quite sure are hers, I have to wonder what kinds of things she may have done."

Valerie rounded the corner, Lizzie in her arms. "Oh, Susan, can you take her? She was up a tree and Francesca scampered after her and got your kitty down."

Father Joseph ducked his head out in the hallway. "Valerie and Sister Mary Lou, please join me."

"Has he always been so bossy, and I've never noticed it?" Susan asked in a hushed voice.

The nun rolled her eyes heavenward.

Susan accepted Lizzie from her friend and whispered, "They've let me go. I'm to work full-time with the Social Affirmation Society."

"What?" Valerie gaped at her.

"You better go. Father Joseph is in a foul mood today." Susan huffed a breath. "And now so am I."

Lizzie chose that moment to dig her claws through Susan's sweater and blouse. "Ow!" She pulled up her sleeve, revealing five tiny marks. If she didn't live here, would her landlady allow her to keep her cat?

As Susan headed up the hallway, Madame Mirandette emerged from one of the classrooms. She smiled benevolently at Susan and then pointed to Lizzie. "May I pet her?"

"Yes, but be careful. She just scratched me, and that's not at all like her."

Dark brown eyes locked on hers. "She must sense you are upset. Do you want to come talk about it?"

The tiny lady mustn't realize that Susan was being displaced.

"Before you leave for the lighthouse, we'd like to ask about a particular item found." Father Joseph gestured for Valerie to sit.

Sister Mary Lou also joined her on the settee.

"We think this may have been yours." Father Joseph held a small wooden box aloft. "Susan found it under a floorboard at the lighthouse."

He came around his desk and handed it to Val.

Behind her spectacles, Sister Mary Lou's pale eyes lit with a question. "Do you recognize this, Valerie?"

"No."

"Open it." Father Joseph sat down in the wing chair next to her.

Val lifted the top of the small rosewood box, the wood smooth and cool on her fingertips. Inside nestled a tiny glittering bracelet. Her heart pounded. The last time she'd seen it. . .

A pretty lady handed the gold-papered box to Val. Tied with silver ribbon, it fit perfectly in her small, outstretched hands. Red, white, and pink paper hearts were strewn on a table covered with treats. Three-tiered china plates with petits fours. Bowls of candy. A large white frosted cake at the center.

"Have her open it!" A dark-haired girl, a little older than herself, jumped up and down, as her creamy satin dress flounced around her. On her wrist dangled a sparkling bracelet.

The woman pointed to the bow. "Pull it!"

She'd pulled the bow and removed it. Then she lifted the top of the paper box. She stared at the wood box inside. How was she supposed to play with that? Maybe the toy was inside. She removed the box and pulled on the top.

"Oh, Carrie, it is lovely!" The lady said. She lifted a fancy bracelet out.

A young maid in a black-and-white uniform bent over and smiled at Val. She looked twitchy—like the dog did when it needed out of the house.

"Here, little Valentine." The lady's rose-scented perfume enveloped her in familiar warmth.

Disappointed that the shimmering jewelry wasn't a toy, tears began to well.

The maid knelt beside Val. "Mrs. Booth-Moore is a generous woman. You're a very lucky little girl." The thick East London accent belonging to the maid was that of Mum.

"Dorcas! You forget your place!" Carrie, the woman who'd invited them scowled at the maid. "Leave my goddaughter be! Our Little Valentine doesn't need you whispering to her."

The maid scurried out of sight—but not before she'd cast a look of pure venom at Val's beautiful dark-haired mother and her friend.

Val rubbed her head, where an ache had burst forth. "I don't know. It might be mine. . ." Her voice came out a whisper. For just a moment, she'd been in a beautiful room surrounded by laughing children and adults scented with perfume. The bracelet brought back a memory that some dark voice urged her to suppress.

A frown puckered Sister Mary Lou's forehead. "Unusual for a lighthouse keeper's daughter."

"I don't think I lived in a lighthouse then." Not when she'd received the bracelet.

Father Joseph leaned in. "How did you come by it?"

"I don't exactly know. It was a gift, though."

"What do you remember?" Sister Mary Lou patted her hand. "I'm pretty sure that's a diamond bracelet."

"Diamonds?" Val gasped and raised the tiny bracelet higher, causing sparks of light to dance around the room as a bright sunbeam pierced the windowpanes. "It's funny how the main thing I recall is disappointment that the bracelet wasn't a plaything."

"The box is from an elite jewelry store near Detroit, whom we've contacted. Vitellio's."

If she was not Mum's daughter, then what would happen to Tim and Mabel?

Marquessate of Kent, England

Eugenie stood in the center of her wardrobe room, the chandelier causing little glimmers to catch on the beadwork of her summer evening clothes, displayed on a portable rack to her right. On the left hung her daytime wear—tennis outfits, a multitude of tea gowns, walking suits, and more.

"We're going to air all these." The maid's sweet sing-song English countryside voice always made Eugenie smile. "We're workin' on getting the mothball scent out and we've gathered all the cedar balls we could find." The servant gestured to a small crate.

Eugenie felt like she, too, was being taken out of the mothballs If only being surrounded by cedars could have the same effect upon her spirit as it could upon these clothes.

But since Verity's disappearance, Eugenie could go for ages being all right, and then something would happen to trigger that reminder that her daughter had never been found. Her baby, her youngest child, had been a precious gift from God. A beautiful little blond girl with the biggest smile. *Dear Lord, if she's out there, somewhere, please reassure her that she's loved, she's missed, and if it is Your will, reunite us one day.*

"Lady Gladstone?"

"Yes?"

Maisy bent and pointed to the row of shoes. None had been polished. Eugenie frowned.

"Pardon me, madam," The girl blushed, "but many of these styles are no longer current footwear fashion."

Eugenie scanned the row of shoes, last worn when she'd been in the States all those years ago. "Heavens, I believe some of those shoes are almost as old as you are, Maisy."

"I didna want to say, milady. But I didna want you to be embarrassed."

"They'll have to be replaced. Ask the shoemaker to pay me a visit tomorrow afternoon."

The maid bobbed a curtsy. "Yes, milady."

"If anyone in the household wants any of them, they may have them. And then please donate the rest."

"Yes, milady." She pointed to the opened hatboxes, set in the bottom row on a triple-row shelf. "And would you like your summer hats updated a bit? The village milliner could add some feathers or bows."

"They're newer than those poor shoes, so yes. Thank you." She'd still attended church and they'd had services in their own little chapel over the years, so her headwear wasn't as pitiful as her summer footwear.

Next, Maisy pointed to gloves, lightweight scarves, summer handkerchiefs, and other accessories. "These all appear to be in excellent condition, Lady Gladstone."

"They should be fine for my trip. Go ahead and pack them."

What would Eugenie do if she spotted someone in America, who she was sure was her own little Valentine—but all grown up?

Nothing. She'd do nothing.

There'd been too many failures over the years—which was why they'd ceased their searching.

God would have to put her daughter right out in front of her with a sign on her neck, for Eugenie to believe it was her. Yes, there would have to be a placard sent by God upon which was engraved Verity Caroline "Valentine" Gladstone for Eugenie to accept that her precious child had been found.

❦

Mackinac Island

As Susan finished her coffee, in the cafeteria, the upcoming change in her status hit her full-on, churning her gut. Her hours would soon be split between the orphanage and her new job. Father Joseph had procured a position for Susan with the Social Affirmation Society— just as Lawrence had said.

She didn't have time to concern herself with something she had little to no control over. Susan prided herself on being a practical person. Today she needed to review all the information she'd found in the box from the lighthouse. *Mother's box—yet somehow Dorcas Fillman's.* But she'd also agreed to check on Valerie's siblings on the mainland and would need to catch the one ferry that left. She took the last sip of her coffee.

"Take your tray up, *signorina* Johnson?"

"Thank you, Francesca." She patted the girl's arm. "You're a dear girl."

Dark somber eyes pooled with tears. "You are dear lady."

Her own eyes grew wet. "Thank you."

The child scurried away.

Of all the children, this one would be hardest to leave when Susan was full-time with the society. She probably shouldn't have allowed it, but Francesca now sat with Susan's cat on her lap some nights, after dinner and before evening prayers. Sometimes when Lizzie caught a mouse, she'd bring it to Francesca. Most of the other children would have been horrified by a dead mouse, but the dark-eyed girl acted as though Lizzie had saved the world from destruction. The girl would heap Italian praise upon the cat for the "gift" Lizzie brought her.

Susan left the hall and headed toward the meeting room, where Sister Mary Lou was waiting.

"We sent the query about that diamond bracelet to Vitellio's, along with a photograph and description of it with measurements." Sister Mary Lou slipped her hands into her pockets. "I still can't believe Father Joseph scratched the window in his office just to prove those were diamonds."

"Me neither."

"We've got it locked up in his safety box."

"Good." *All diamonds.* What child wore something like that? Certainly not a lighthouse keeper's daughter. But had she?

The nun moved to the table where Susan's paper rested. They stood side-by-side.

"I see what you've done here." She pointed to the clippings about poisons. "You believe Mrs. Fillman cut those, correct?"

"Yes. So I put that index card with her initials on it to indicate I believe those were hers."

Light eyes slanted her way. "Makes you wonder, doesn't it?"

"Yes. Why did she want to know about those?"

"And the pictures are clearly of your family. I even saw one of my friend, Mary Pelletier Scholtus." She turned and smiled. "I'm hoping she'll come up to the Straits and see Paul and his daughter sometime next summer."

"But will you see her at Christmas?"

"If Father Joseph grants me leave, then yes, I'll make a trip to Shepherd this Christmas."

Lately, lots of things seemed up to Father Joseph. But he was the priest there, and he was in charge. Susan had been baptized in the Methodist church, where she attended the first part of her life. She chewed her lower lip. She'd attended every conceivable Protestant denomination over the years in foster care before ending up at the Catholic Church in St. Ignace, where she'd met Sister Mary Lou. Was Father Joseph having Susan leave because she'd never converted to Catholicism? Couldn't say she blamed him. He had warned her that her position was intended for a member of the parish. She drew in a deep breath and then exhaled. He'd kept her several years now without that change happening. It was time to move on. But the children. . . She loved them so much.

"Sister Mary Lou, Father Joseph told me that I'll go out to relieve Valerie on her free day."

"You'll get to spend time with Paul then. I enjoyed having him fill me in on his mother when we had a few minutes to chat."

She smiled. "I'm looking forward to catching up. We only got to chat for a little bit when I walked him to the ferry before he left." And he'd been quite distracted over his happiness at becoming the new lighthouse keeper. He'd told her about his brothers and their families and his little daughter. And he'd discussed several mutual friends and neighbors. But one thing they'd not discussed was Anabelle. That topic appeared off-limits.

With good reason.

Sister Mary Lou returned her attention to the oak table. "These clippings about the Sugarplum Ladies, which include some about Mrs. Tara Mulcahey, Carrie Booth-Moore, and of course the Founder, Lady Eugenie Mott Gladstone, I assume are ones your mother cut from the newspapers."

"I remember seeing those when I was young. She was very proud of having been a member." Tears pricked Susan's eyes for the second time that day and she swiped them away. "In fact, I'm sure this is Mother's box. She kept this in our dining room." She'd sometimes show the clippings to visitors—especially new ones, like the lady staying at the Wenhams' farm, who'd visited before they'd died. She frowned, concentrating on the woman's name, but it escaped her.

"What is it?"

"I was thinking about the last person I heard Mother tell about her time with the Sugarplum Ladies. The stranger was a twitchy kind of person, and I'd not stayed long because I had"—she shrugged—"an instant dislike of her."

"Twitchy like Mrs. Fillman?"

"Maybe. And I'd taken her little girl outside to play. She was quite a bit younger than me, or so it seemed at the time. We went to the barn." The child had said something strange then. It sounded like something from the Bible. Like verily, verily, I say unto you—but something else. Verity? It hadn't made sense.

"These other articles are about. . ." Sister Mary Lou pressed her hand to her chest. "Purging an unwanted child."

"Yes. It's horrible, what's in those."

The nun tapped the initials on the card above them. "You believe Mrs. Fillman kept those."

"The handwriting on some is not my mother's. And she and my father had wanted more children—they'd said so often." Susan pulled her mother's autograph book from her pocket. "Mother's handwriting doesn't match that."

"Have you checked to see if, by some strange chance, Mrs. Fillman signed this book? What's the connection? Why did she have your mother's things?"

Susan drew in a slow breath. "Let's sit down while I flip through the pages. I've read many of them, over the years." But it made her sad to think of all the people who'd known and loved her mother but had abandoned Susan, so she'd not read them all.

"What about this article about Lord Percy Gladstone arriving to search for his daughter? That looks like it's well after your parents died. Because look— right next to it there's a small column about President Chester Arthur dedicating the Washington Monument. That was in 1885 I believe."

It felt like a chunk of that monument had fallen into her gut. "That had to be kept by Valerie's mother."

Sister Mary Lou quirked an eyebrow. "Or someone else—her father, maybe?"

"Perhaps. But why?"

"Oh my, and this ambrotype of the infant. That's. . ."

"I wondered if that was a picture of Valerie when she was a baby."

The nun's cheeks quivered. "Oh, no my dear. I'm afraid this child was not among the living when this image was made." She made the sign of the cross.

"What?" Susan leaned closer.

"See how the eyes are closed and the limbs are so. . . floppy?"

"I thought that was a sleeping child. I knew it wasn't me because on the back it is embossed with New York."

The nun shook her head slowly and removed her glasses. She rubbed the bridge of her nose. "The last time I saw a picture like this, the mother had asked a photo vendor to make the image before bringing the infant to be prepared for burial."

"Poor baby." Dark hair, similar to Susan's, protruded from beneath a lacy cap. A simple gown covered her thin frame.

Sister Mary Lou flipped the frame over. "I see something etched into there—like someone used a pin to scrape a date, but I can't quite make it out."

"Knock, knock!" Lawrence Zumbrun stood in the doorway, his tawny hair waving around his handsome face perfectly. Attired in a charcoal single-breasted daytime jacket and matching trousers, his checked black-and-white waistcoat sported large natty buttons.

"Oh, you're here." She sounded like a schoolgirl. *Of course he's here.*

He dipped his chin. "Good morning, ladies, I'm here to whisk Miss Johnson to the mainland on an errand for Val. . . Miss Valerie Fillman."

"You'll bring us back a report on the children, then, Mr. Zumbrun?" Sister Mary Lou gave him a benevolent smile.

Wasn't Susan's word enough? *Pah—I'm being sensitive.*

"Father Joseph says the Jeffries have been getting medical care for both and placed them in public school."

"I believe they are both educators?" The nun pushed her chair slightly back and Susan followed suit.

"Only Mr. Jeffries is. He recently became principal at the elementary school." Susan had never met the man. "Do you remember Mrs. Jeffries' bakery in St. Ignace?"

"Ah, yes. She's our own Mrs. Christy's sister-in-law, and I'm not sure I could pick whose baked goods are better."

Susan would opt for Rebecca Christy's tea as best and Jo Jeffries' pastries as a smidge better, although she'd never say. She made a motion as if buttoning her lips.

"I wonder how Mrs. Jeffries runs her bakery while caring for her young child and both of Miss Fillman's siblings." Sister Mary Lou pulled at her habit's long sleeves.

Lawrence smiled in that charming way of his. "We'll have to look into that."

"Her sister-in-law manages our island bakery and a houseful of children." Susan stood.

"I'd love a home filled with children." Lawrence flipped both palms. "And if the Lord guides my future wife to constructive work for His benefit, then who would I be to stop her?"

Both Susan and Sister Mary Lou gaped at the young man. *What a refreshing, yet unusual sentiment. Times were changing. But not for most men.*

When neither woman responded, his cheeks reddened.

Susan lifted the autograph book and slid it into her pocket. "Please pray that we have smooth weather both coming and going."

"We already have," Sister Mary Lou said. "We need you back here tonight for Harvest Festival planning!"

Susan would miss seeing the kind nun every day once she moved to her new position and new residence come springtime.

Round Island, Michigan

Val perched on her narrow bed beneath the window in her lighthouse room, darning a hole in her stockings. She hummed *What a Friend We Have in Jesus* but switched to softly singing some of the lyrics out loud. Thousands and thousands of times she'd sung this song over the years, to remind herself that at least she had that one friend—Jesus. Now, not only did she have Jesus as friend, but a real, genuine pal in Susan. But her chum was on the mainland, and Val was at the lighthouse.

Still, since her arrival that morning to the freshly scrubbed and painted family quarters, her dread about being here had fled. With little Hetty now tucked into bed and Paul manning the light, she had finished her evening ablutions and was taking care of personal chores. Satisfied that the sock was repaired properly, she set it in the drawer with its match.

She pulled her notebook from the drawer and a pencil. Lifting her head, she caught her reflection in the pretty wood-framed mirror that Paul had placed there for her convenience when brushing her hair. The oil light behind her made her golden hair glow in the reflected image. Before she'd left for the lighthouse, she'd searched the donation barrel to see what she could take with her. She pressed her hand against her pin-tucked bodice embellished with embroidered roses and the right size for her. She'd never worn anything so fine. She frowned. At least not that she remembered.

Paul had brought all manner of clothing for Hetty. The child had an entire chest full of things from pastel-colored sleeping gowns to hand-knit sweaters with lacy edging to coats for all types of weather.

Were Timothy and Mabel properly clothed? Had the Jeffries family taken care of those needs? Did she need to repay them?

Valerie extinguished the oil lamp, slipped into bed, and began to talk to her Friend. He always listened and was always there.

God was there when all her clothes had been burnt. Jesus was there if she had none. He always made a way. He would now.

He had to—because Valerie could only do so much. Her dearest Friend had to help her now.

Paul stood in awe of his view of the Straits of Mackinac from the lighthouse. The colors were beautiful, ranging from tan, to aqua, to deepest sapphire blue and topped with frothy white waves. From this aspect, he could see nearby Mackinac Island and across to Mackinaw City. Were his fellow lighthouse watchers preparing all up and down Lake Huron and Lake Michigan for the dark to descend? Soon the Fresnel light would glow in its glory, guiding ships through the dark waters. Would this thrill of helping those mariners be something that would continue as the days and months passed by? And why did that zing in his spirit immediately connect with Valerie Fillman?

Something inside him had melted when he'd heard her reading stories to Hetty that afternoon. Even after Valerie had spent much of the day unpacking their belongings, she'd made sure his daughter got to hear her beloved stories. The woman had a pure beautiful voice, despite all the sorrow she'd known. To have lost her parents and yet come back to this place—what a tough spirit she must have. And what kindness to help him.

He exhaled sharply.

He had to help her, too. The only thing she'd asked of him was to give her freedom when they went ashore on their days off. He'd make sure she had that.

And he could be a friend. If anyone needed more friends, it was this young woman.

He'd freely give her his friendship—no holds barred.

Chapter Fifteen

Straits of Mackinac

*L*awrence may soon spit blood onto the ferry's floor if he had to keep biting his tongue about Valerie being Verity Gladstone. But he'd promised Val. Georgina couldn't get there fast enough for his liking. But Ada had said over breakfast that Georgie's arrival wasn't for another week yet.

He and Susan clutched the seatback in front of them as the boat took another slow swell. Still, the ferry was as comfortable as could be expected on waters full of low whitecaps.

"I don't understand why Dorcas would have anything of my mother's. It's baffling."

He extended his hand. "May I have it?"

Susan released the seatback and lifted the book from her lap. "There's one in here from Carrie Booth-Moore that makes my mother sound similar to myself."

> *Fudges and cookies*
> *Perhaps you've not mastered*
> *But now organize us all*
> *With your management skills!*

Susan chuckled. "But I need to look through the rest of these names and see if Mrs. Fillman ever signed her autograph."

He took the book and flipped it over. "You looked past the middle, right?"

"Yes. I've read to the last third."

Lawrence flipped to the back of the autograph book. "My mother had one of these."

"We had so few visitors that I don't remember Mother having people sign—except Mrs. Scholtus, because we made a big fuss."

"We?"

"Me and my best friend, Paul Scholtus, her son."

"Ah." He compressed his lips. The new lighthouse keeper, a widower, would no doubt rekindle his relationship with this beautiful woman and give his daughter a new mother. *Lucky man if he does so.*

He pointed to the last entry. "There! Mrs. John Fillman—isn't that her?"

Susan leaned closer—her shoulder warm against his. "Yes! The other ladies signed their Christian names and most added their married names second."

"It's dated."

She frowned. "That's a week before my parents died. It's when the Wenhams' guest came to visit."

"So this guest may have been Dorcas Fillman?" Verity's abductor?

"I. . . I think possibly."

"That sentiment reads more like a threat than delight at meeting someone new."

> *We never know*
> *Who we'll meet*
> *Sometimes life*
> *Is all too fleet*
> *Mrs. John Fillman*

"Oh my. I am a pragmatic woman, but yes, I can see that. It's a strange message."

"I agree."

"Mrs. Fillman had cut articles about poisons and. . ." She couldn't bring herself to say what the others were about. Her mind was whirling.

"Your parents died within a short time after Mrs. Fillman, a newcomer, visited. Possibly not a coincidence. With how disturbed Dorcas Fillman appeared, would it be too far a stretch to wonder if she poisoned her entire family?"

Susan's features scrunched together. "From all accounts, Valerie's parents succumbed to an illness that has been rampant in our area."

"All right." He scratched his cheek. "And Dorcas would have ended up killing herself in the process."

"Their symptoms were similar to what others in the area had from this bad flux." Susan's lower lip curved downward. "Maybe Dorcas cut those articles out to protect her family from poisoning?"

"But Susan, what about your parents?"

She locked her pretty brown eyes on him. "What about them?"

"How exactly did your parents die? And why weren't you affected by whatever killed them?"

"Food poisoning, is what I was told." She flexed her fingers. "Someone had sent a meat pie—my father loved them—and they'd eaten it for supper the previous day."

"But not you?"

"I hated those things. And it upset my parents' stomachs because they were ill much of the night."

"Was it tested for poison?" It should have been from the sounds of things.

"I don't think so. Why would they?"

"Why not?"

"Small community. Besides, I believe one of their friends sent it over, as they'd done regularly. They were devastated."

"Did they, did you, eat anything else that night?"

"I mainly had bread, butter, and some apples that. . ." She pressed her hand to her mouth.

"What?"

The ferry ploughed into a large wave, lifting the vessel, and then setting it down hard. Lawrence grabbed Susan's hand as they almost lifted from their seats.

She huffed out a breath. "Oh my."

"A little tricky crossing the Straits in the autumn sometimes." They'd been warned.

"Yes, indeed." Susan looked a little green around the gills.

"You were speaking of your last meal with your parents."

"Those apples were what Mrs. Fillman brought that first time she came. We'd eaten them all. And the ones at dinner were new."

"So she brought more?"

"If so, I didn't see her."

"Perhaps the proverbial poisoned apples like in that children's story?"

Susan shook her head, her brown curls bobbing around her pretty face. "I would have died, too."

"Hmm." He pressed back in his seat, but released her hand, as the ferry steadied. "Arsenic poisoning looks a lot like food poisoning. And it's used on orchards."

They sat there silently for a moment.

"Sister Mary Lou has sent a message to Mrs. Wenham, the farmer's wife who hosted the lady and her daughter who visited our farm."

"Who we now understand to be Dorcas Fillman."

"And that had to be Valerie who came to play with me."

They both sat quietly, again. He couldn't let this synthesis of what they understood end just yet. "A message was sent to whom?"

"Mrs. Thomas Wenham. I wasn't sure of her name until I saw it in my mother's autograph book."

Lawrence tapped his toes. "Perhaps she'll have some answers, then."

"Yes." Susan leaned away from him.

Dorcas Fillman, Verity's kidnapper, had passed herself off as her mother. But he couldn't tell Susan his suspicions because he'd promised Valentine. "Suppose Mrs. Wenham confirms that Dorcas Fillman, her husband, and their daughter did indeed stay with them during that time."

"Yes? And?"

"And what if they also confirm that the Fillmans left the area immediately after your parents' deaths?"

"Could be coincidence if so." She shrugged.

"What if these Wenhams have knowledge of that deceased child pictured in the ambrotype? Who would have been the same age as Val—"

"Sugarplum!" Susan burst out.

"What?"

"What if Mother told Dorcas about being a Sugarplum Lady and what if that child was Eugenie Mott Gladstone's kidnapped daughter? What if Dorcas believed Mother was a threat because she'd been one of Lady Gladstone's Sugarplum Ladies?" Susan frowned. "Mother may have received pictures of the child."

"And at that point, pictures of her were in the news. More so in New York, but possibly in Michigan papers as well."

"What did she look like then?"

"Long blond hair, almost to her little waist."

"Dorcas must have cut it short. That's why we found those long golden locks of hair in the box."

"But Dorcas could have panicked that your mother might figure out who she was."

"Or that Valerie would say something to me. She didn't allow us to play for very long." Susan scrunched up her face. "She did say something odd to me that I never understood."

"What was it?"

"I thought she said a Bible verse, like verily, verily, I say unto you, but I think she said verity, verity."

"Oh." Lawrence closed his eyes and tipped his head back. It felt as though a box of bricks from the new site had dropped atop his chest.

"What is it?"

"We called her Valentine, because of her birthday. But her given name was Verity. None of the kids called her that, though."

"Verity. She was trying to say Verity was her name." When Susan had just stared at the little girl, and then laughed, the child had run off.

"Did Dorcas hear her?"

"I can't remember exactly where she was. But it's possible she was outside the barn door."

"And then Dorcas plotted how to. . ." He didn't want to say the words.

Susan leaned forward and placed her head in her hands.

Lawrence patted her back. "We could have this all wrong." He was pretty sure, though, that they'd just hit on the truth.

He could feel the impact in his spirit.

Susan tried to focus on what Mrs. Jeffries was telling her about the Fillman children, who were seated before her. How was she supposed to listen when all she could think about was that her new friend had been abducted and that the woman who'd passed as her mother may have killed Susan's parents. These children, in this room, were born from that evil woman.

Josephine Jeffries smoothed out her deep blue skirt. "Timmy has a wonderful mastery of math, and he's fascinated by engineering principles."

The boy blushed. "Mr. Jeffries has been making sure that I have access to all the books and materials that I need now that we're on the mainland."

Tom Jeffries handed the boy a notepad. "Show them your work."

Timothy Fillman raised the notebook, and Lawrence scooted to the end of his chair. "I see you've made the association between avian flight and uplift factors."

"Yes, it keeps me up at night." Timothy grinned at the two men, while the females in the group sipped their tea.

"The young man I coach—"

"Jack Welling—everyone knows about him!" Timothy interrupted. "Best runner in America. You must be a great coach."

"Yes, he is, but I can't take credit." Lawrence gave a self-deprecatory smile. "Anyway, Jack has a training location in Ohio— near some young fellows who're interested in flight, too."

Mrs. Jeffries raised her hand. "Next you'll be telling us they plan to fly a crate to the moon."

"Now, Josephine." Mr. Jeffries cast a stern glance in his wife's direction, but his lips twitched as though he was resisting a smile.

"Ladies, let's go to my bakery and grab a table in the corner where we can discuss things other than math, science, and engineering principles." Josephine rose and gestured for them to follow.

Mabel, who'd not been talkative when Susan had met her at church, chatted nonstop with her foster mother as soon as they exited the house. She mentioned the girls at school, the new dress she saw at a shop, the boy who'd given her a dried apricot at lunch, how her stockings were getting too small, and how she very much wished to go to the library after dinner. She barely took a breath between comments. The only sign of her hearing loss was when she turned her head slightly to the side when being spoken to.

Once inside the bakery, yeasty scents mingled with that of cinnamon, maple, and cloves. Mabel hurried to the largest table and pulled out the chairs that ringed it. "There! Now you'll all be comfortable. And I shall take your orders if you wish."

What had happened to the terrified little mouse whom Susan had previously met?

Jo gave the girl a motherly pat on her shoulder. "Ask Katina to do a mixed assortment of pastries for us."

"Oh, good—then we can choose. I shall wait till last, of course— like you have taught me."

Jo smiled and waved Mabel toward the glass-cased counter. "You'd think she'd lived with us all her life. She's fit in so well with our family." Her bright smile quickly faded though. "Of course, we understand that her sister wishes to reunite the family."

"Yes, very much so." With the Jeffries' child home taking a nap, and Mabel at the counter, this was the opportune time to ask what Susan thought the truth may be. "Do you believe the children might be better off with you? Here on the mainland?"

The young mother tugged on her embroidered collar. "From what those two kids have said, it's a wonder they made it out alive from that crazy household."

Susan stiffened. "Tell me more. I mean I've heard from Valerie, but what have they said?"

At the counter, Mabel was laughing with the girl who was fixing their tray.

Josephine huffed a sigh. "Honestly, both children have shared that they wished they could find what they hoped were their real parents—they've always wished they had another family who would take them away."

"Val said something similar."

"Also, and I hate to say this, but because their sister often tried to get in between their mother and them when she was having a spell, both Timothy and Mabel associate Valerie with their mother. It's affected their relationship. As much as they love her, they also somewhat fear her, even though both report that she never harmed them—only tried to protect them from their mother's mental illness."

"I'd say Dorcas was beyond mental illness and a criminal." Had she been criminal enough to kill Susan's parents?

"Yes. I hesitate to share some of the even more unseemly things Mabel and Timothy have shared."

Later, they said their goodbyes to the Jeffries and Tim and Mabel. Lawrence and Susan walked out to the front yard, where trimmed-back rosebushes clustered behind a white picket fence.

He tugged at his coat collar. "We've got to get to the ferry."

"What a nice tidy home." She gazed wistfully at the home.

"I like them. Good people." And this was a wonderful man standing beside her.

"I pray Francesca finds a home like this one."

"I could picture that." Lawrence angled his body closer to hers. "But with a beautiful brunette adoptive mother."

He was outright flirting with her. Susan could not be imaging what he was suggesting. "And I suppose she'd have a handsome adoptive father with sandy blond hair?" And golden amber eyes like the rich caramel sauce in Jo's Bakery.

"Could be." His husky voice sent a shiver through her.

Lawrence was the first man who seemed to appreciate her as a woman. Did he reciprocate her growing feelings?

She was a spinster.

No. What had Jack said the other day?

She was a bachelorette. The youth claimed this was the new word for unmarried women.

Bachelorette. And Lawrence was a bachelor.

Perhaps there was hope for them both to change their marital statuses.

Chapter Sixteen

Round Island Lighthouse

Why, oh why did I agree to come out here again? Valerie stopped dusting Hetty's room and patted her pocket. The letters from Tim and Mabel practically burned through her apron. Hopefully, Susan and Lawrence would have good news about them when they returned from their trip to St. Ignace. But Valerie would have to wait another five days to hear what they'd found—unless someone came out and brought her news. Billy Lloyd could be counted on if they sent a message.

"You done? I want stories." Hetty jumped up on her bed.

It was almost time for the girl to try to take a nap, but Valerie hadn't had any luck with that the previous afternoon. Instead, they'd snuggled, and she'd read several books to the child.

"Come sit." The imp patted the pretty pink quilt that covered her bed. Paul's mother had made it for Hetty.

Valerie set her dusting cloth aside and sat down on the bed, careful to not sit atop the appliqued woman in a fancy bonnet and hoop skirt that centered the quilt. The previous day, Hetty insisted if Valerie sat on the lady's image that it must hurt the Southern belle. Hetty had an imagination, that was for sure.

Valerie kicked off her shoes and laid back on the end of the bed, her legs overhanging.

"Do you want the one about the boy and his hound?" She suffered from dreams about Lawrence Zumbrun, as a young boy, chasing a dog while another boy, possibly her older brother hooted and hollered.

Hetty crossed her arms across her chest. "No. I want a new one."

"Hmm, let me see." Valerie startled as a warm arm flung across her abdomen. She angled toward the child. "Aren't you worried about the pretty lady on your quilt?"

"No. She's asleep. Won't notice."

"Ah. Okay." Valerie shifted as Hetty snuggled her soft curls against her shoulder.

Outside, seagulls squawked and the wind pushed hard at the window.

"Once there was a lady who lived on the lake."

Hetty lifted her head. "On top the lake?"

"Sort of." She patted her arm. "Where do you think she could live?"

"A big lily pad. Like frogs."

"The lady of the lake lived on a lily pad and was lonely. And one night when she'd cried new tears to fill the lake—"

Hetty angled her head back. "Tears make lakes?"

"Just in the story. Not for real. But you have to pretend."

"She cried a lot then."

"Yes. A very lot." This was not a good story for a child. Valerie would change it up. "But that next day, a man with. . . ginger hair—"

"Like daddy's?"

"Yes. Like his."

"Okay."

"The Ginger Man—that will be his name—floated out to the lily pad on a raft."

"A raft?" She popped fully up in the bed.

This wasn't turning into a good naptime story. On the other hand, Hetty was learning some new things. She'd explain rafts later. "I was wrong. He floated out to the lily pad on a huge maple leaf that had fallen into the water. It was so big. . ." she opened her arms wide, "that it held him and a wee little babe."

"Was she this big?" Hetty held her hands a few inches apart.

"Yes, she was so tiny, and he'd heard. . ." she searched for something to add, "Ginger Man heard that the Lady of the Lake could make his tiny child grow bigger—for she'd been that size for many years."

"Oh no." Hetty shook her head. "She stay like a baby."

"Right."

"Babies sleep lot don't they?" Hetty yawned and stretched.

"They do. They have to sleep so they grow. So that's the first thing the Lady of the Lake told Ginger Man when he arrived."

"That his baby take nap?"

"Right."

Hetty laid her head back down on Valerie's shoulder. "I not a baby."

"Nope. Me neither—but sometimes I take a nap."

"We close eyes, Val."

After spending that day and the previous one putting away all of hers and Hetty's clothing and setting up the household, Valerie was sorely tempted. "All right. And I'll tell you a little more story."

"Good." The girl sighed and snuggled closer.

Valerie reached to the foot of the bed and pulled a crocheted afghan up and then covered the child with it. "Your auntie made a beautiful covering, didn't she?"

"Uncle Ron can't make them."

"My brother, Tim, doesn't crochet either."

"Boys don't." The child pulled the afghan under her little chin.

"Let's close our eyes, just like Ginger Man's daughter's. And the Lady of the Lakes pulled that maple leaf boat right up next to hers, and she moored them together. Then she dipped her finger into the water and dropped one little bit onto the girl's eyes. And the next thing Ginger Man knew, his daughter had grown a full inch."

The soft whiffling sound of Hetty's breath was all she heard. Then soft footsteps carried into the room. She opened her eyes.

As Paul stood in the doorway, Valerie raised her fingers to her lips.

When she looked at his celadon green eyes, the deep love she saw there pierced her heart. His pure unadulterated love for his daughter was something she'd never experienced from John Fillman.

But in her heart, she knew that she had seen that same fatherly love on another man's handsome face. Different eyes. Unusual ones with more than one color.

As Paul turned and left the room, tears coursed down her cheeks. She could fill the Great Lakes with them—just like the Lady of the Lakes.

This isn't what I wanted, but this is what I have—I'm here at the lighthouse but without Annabelle. Yet somehow, Paul sensed that he and Hetty would be all right. God would provide. He already had, providing childcare for his daughter.

With reverent care, Paul unpacked his silver-framed wedding photo and propped it on his bedside table. He ran his thumb over the image of Annabelle's beautiful face. The dull ache in his chest that had thrummed all these years had begun to quiet. Outside his window, seagulls squawked and swooped and dove into the sapphire-blue water. A gentle breeze rustled the Swiss Dot curtains that his mother had sent with him—a reminder of home but which would soon lack the warmth needed for October weather. Still, he'd leave them there for now.

If he'd come here to forget, then why had he brought the picture and the curtains? He huffed a sigh and sat down on the bed.

"Daddy?" Hetty stood in his doorway, index finger in her mouth. "Aren't you taking a nap?"

Hushed steps he'd quickly begun to recognize as Miss Fillman's, hurried toward his room. "I'm sorry, Mr. Scholtus. I thought Hetty had settled." Her stricken face seemed out of place for the severity of her perceived crime.

He opened his arms to his daughter, and she ran to him. He scooped her up. "Don't worry, I know this little rascal's tricks."

Hetty leaned away from him and then poked his cheeks. "Made you smile."

"Yes, my little love." Indeed, his daughter was one of the few people who had been able to get a grin out of him in the past few years.

"I'll put her back down." Miss Fillman's tone was dubious, though. She'd mentioned the previous evening that her younger sister never napped after age three.

"How about we all go down and work on the nets?"

Miss Fillman smiled gently in apparent approval.

Paul set Hetty down.

"Go wading?" she pleaded.

"It's very cold water." Miss Fillman feigned shivering. But excitement seemed to bubble up in her, and he was once again shocked at how well she could adjust to being here where her parents had perished.

Hetty crossed her little arms. "Grandmom says I got warm blood." Which was why she'd sometimes strip off her day clothes and into her thin sleeping gown even for naps.

"My child has been known to run outside in a snowstorm attired just as she is now." Paul touched Hetty's cotton sleep dress.

"No!" His daughter lifted her foot and wiggled her toes. "Wif boots."

Paul raised his hands in surrender. "True. In winter you have the sense to put your boots on."

She ducked her chin.

"It's settled then." Miss Fillman took his daughter's hand and led her from the room.

"I'll be down in a moment." Paul returned his focus to the picture of him and his wife. What kinds of things would they have done together with Hetty, had Annabelle survived? His chest tightened, recalling the haunting poem by Edgar Allan Poe, *Annabel Lee*.

> *It was many and many a year ago,*
> *In a kingdom by the sea,*
> *That a maiden there lived whom you may know*
> *By the name of Annabel Lee;*
> *And this maiden she lived with no other thought*
> *Than to love and be loved by me.*
>
> *I was a child and she was a child,*
> *In this kingdom by the sea,*
> *But we loved with a love that was more than love—*
> *I and my Annabel Lee—*

> With a love that the wingèd seraphs of Heaven
> Coveted her and me.

He and his Annabelle had been childhood sweethearts. They'd been so young. And now she was gone. She forever young, while he continued on—some early stray gray hairs gathering at his temples. What would Annabelle say if she were here? She'd tease him, no doubt.

There had been another childhood friend, Susie. And she was here—on Mackinac Island. Regret stung him. When Annabelle had come along, he'd let his and Susie's friendship dwindle. They were kids, though. Why had Annabelle wanted to exclude her from their playtimes? And why had he, when he'd seen how hurt Susan looked, not pushed harder for her to stay and visit with him and Annabelle?

He'd become fixated on Annabelle from the moment he'd met her until she died. And like Poe, her loss devastated him. But was that kind of love the right sort?

Hetty's squeals of delight carried up through the window. Fatherly love was all he needed to have right now.

Or perhaps ever again.

Val laughed so hard at Hetty's antics in the water that she feared she'd tear a seam in her too-tight gray plaid work dress. She pressed a hand over her mouth as the child jumped over chilly waves, twirled like a ballerina, and then imitated a seagull. The child was so free. *Free.* That was something Valerie had not been in years.

The door behind them closed, and Hetty's father joined them. Strange how in only two days the new lightkeeper had established his presence there. He seemed naturally inclined toward the position and had spoken about his previous placement at another lighthouse in Lower Michigan.

When Hetty once again attempted a pirouette in the chilly water, her father moved forward, lifted her up, and held her high overhead as she laughed in delight.

The streaming sun from behind them darkened their image, and for a moment Val could feel the arms of a very tall man holding her. The scent of cigar smoke, strong tea, and something spicy clung to him. She frowned as the memory surged over her. Suddenly dizzy, she leaned back on the rocky beach. But John Fillman was average height, didn't smoke, drank only strong black coffee, and smelled mainly of strong soap. And the only time she remembered him carrying her was when her mother had chased after her, intending to. . .

"Valerie? Miss Fillman?" Mr. Scholtus set his daughter down and they came up on the beach.

144

Was that memory of her real father, Percy Gladstone? She'd tried so hard, the previous night, to imagine him at Apple Blossom Cottage—to no avail.

"Yes?" She sat up again and pressed a hand to her brow. "I was dizzy. But I'm all right."

The handsome lighthouse keeper cocked his head, frowning. "You look like you've seen a ghost."

"No ghosts, I assure you." But she shivered. Her parents had died here. "I don't believe in such nonsense."

"Good." He patted his flat stomach. "I've worked up an appetite for tea and cookies."

"Cookies!" Hetty clapped her wet hands, sending droplets flying. "Grandmom's, please."

Val sighed. "I'll have to learn to bake Hetty's favorites."

"No need. Mrs. Christy and I have an arrangement." Mr. Scholtus winked at her.

"Oh?"

"The teashop will provide us baked goods each week if we bring them whitefish, bass, and so on. Her husband is too busy with his off-season crafting work at the Grand Hotel to fish."

"You've only just arrived." She smiled. "You work quickly, don't you?"

"It was the first place I stopped when we arrived. The dock workers told me about them."

Valerie laughed. "I think everyone must know about their cookies."

"They are the best."

"'Cept for Grandmom's." Hetty's lips pulled into an adorable pout.

Valerie tweaked Hetty's nose, like she had to Mabel and Tim when they were younger. "If only life could be so easy. If only a cookie solved our problems."

Hetty ran back toward the lighthouse, and they followed her. Mr. Scholtus stopped just outside the entrance. "Miss Fillman, may I please call you by your Christian name? I'm a farmer. Was a farmer anyway." He ran a hand through his thick hair. "And I'm used to keeping things simple. Please call me Paul."

A niggling of unease was accompanied by a chill breeze from Lake Huron. "Very well, Paul. You may call me Valerie—but only when we are here alone. People might misconstrue our arrangement."

When she looked into his green eyes something warm chased away her chill. He squeezed her hand. "I have only respect for you, Miss Fillman. . .Valerie."

He released her hand. Why did his words leave her wanting more than respect? They were becoming friends after only a couple of days at the lighthouse. She crossed her arms. She had friends on the island. That had to be enough for her in her station in life. But was that really her situation—or was she the daughter of an aristocrat in England?

She couldn't picture Mabel and Tim separated from her forever, if the Gladstones claimed her as their missing child.

"Don't forget to make a list for when our relief worker comes in." Paul gestured to the bigger of the two boats. "We'll take that one over. I'm hoping Hetty won't be too scared. She got a little upset on her trip here."

"I'll hold her tight and tell her stories while we cross."

"Thank you." Paul ran a hand over his neat beard. "I don't know what I'd do without you."

With Mr. Welling's enthusiasm, it was hard for Susan to not get swept up in his vision for the program. She followed him as he led her through the classrooms and offices that circled the gymnasium. They were almost finished.

He cast a glance at Lawrence and Jack who were heading out the door for a run. "Your office is adjacent to Lawrence's, but you could pick any one of these." He cast her a knowing look. "But perhaps you'd prefer to have him nearby?"

She bit her tongue. It wouldn't do well to let her growing feelings for Lawrence have her lose her new position.

Sister Mary Lou strode determinedly through the doorway. Spotting them, she continued on. "I have a letter from Mrs. Thomas Wenham."

Mr. Welling's lips tugged. "From Shepherd?"

"Yes." Susan angled her head toward him. "Do you know her?"

He expelled a sharp breath. "They are neighboring farmers."

"The letter is for Susan." Sister Mary Lou reached them and passed her the missive. "But you know the family?"

"Of course. I grew up there and live there again. Obviously not now since we're on the island."

Susan opened the letter. "Oh, my, this is a long letter. Should I read it out loud?"

"Would you, dear?" Sister Mary Lou pointed to the benches and chairs that encircled the walls, ready for positioning in the new classrooms and offices. "Let's sit, though."

"Near that window." Mr. Welling strode toward a large window on the wall without classrooms. He pulled several chairs closer together.

"Thank you." She sat and began to read the letter.

Dear Susan Marie,

First off, I am delighted that you are doing well on Mackinac Island. I'm glad you wrote to me. Your questions confirmed suspicions I held about my old friend Dorcas Woods, who married John Fillman. A young child was brought to our farm with them not long after John arrived in America. But she did not appear to be the same child Dorcas had with her in New York.

My husband and I arrived in New York with Dorcas. She and John hadn't yet married. Dorcas was brought up in the Catholic faith, but John being Protestant, her parents refused the marriage. We were emigrating and had plans to eventually try for a land grant farm, which, praise God, we finally did. Dorcas lived with us in our New York tenement until we departed. She'd gotten a maid's job quickly after arrival. When she realized she was pregnant, the other maids told her to hide her condition, which she did. A baby girl was born with a large distinctive dark birthmark on her back. Dorcas, a superstitious girl, took this as an omen. She didn't tell John about the baby and when he still hadn't come to America after a year, she began to grow worried he'd not ever come. I watched the baby while Dorcas worked for the Booth-Moores, and my husband also watched her when he wasn't at the docks, employed as a laborer.

When we learned of our opportunity for a land grant farm in Michigan, we begged Dorcas to come with us. She refused, claiming John would come soon, and he'd not want to travel so far. Since the baby, she'd lost a great deal of weight, having once been a plump girl. She began claiming that the baby was possessed by a demon. My husband and I grew more concerned. I regret that we didn't make Dorcas come with us. She remained in New York for another year while we settled on our farm. I received regular letters in which Dorcas mentioned Valerie's new skills. But in one, she said the couple who were watching Valerie had taken the baby to a physician, and she had bad croup. In subsequent letters, she stopped talking about her daughter. I wondered if possibly the couple had adopted the child or if the child had died."

Sister Mary Lou gasped. "Oh my. Do you think that's the child in the picture?"

"Possibly." She angled toward Mr. Welling. "We found an image of a toddler, who appeared to be. . . ."

"Oh." He gaped. "I've seen some of those morbid pictures—more than I cared to see. But please resume reading."

Susan found her place again.

>*"John confided in a letter to my husband that he'd changed his mind about following Dorcas. It was only after she'd sent a long rambling letter talking about their child that he'd finally booked passage. So he arrived almost three years after we'd left. Dorcas insisted they follow us to Michigan immediately after he'd gotten to the country. Since we had work for him, and he knew us, he brought her and Valerie by train to Michigan.*
>
>*The beautiful little girl they brought here had unusual eyes, almost violet, but Valerie's had been a regular shade of blue when we'd departed. I grew very concerned when, during a bath, I saw this child had no birthmark on her back. Dorcas claimed it had gone away—that God had removed it and the stamp of her sin. But I knew. God forgive me for not doing something more, although I don't know what that could have been—but in my heart I knew this wasn't her child. Within days of me confronting her about these changes in the child, Dorcas and her family left."*

Susan stopped reading.

"So everything is adding up that Valerie was taken by Dorcas." Sister Mary Lou clutched her hands in her lap.

"Yes, but she writes more."

>*"Your parents, dear Susan, died during that time. There were a few other people who'd passed away from illnesses that when Dorcas and her family left, we were glad to have them go."*

Susan chewed her lower lip. "I wonder if she was concerned about Dorcas having been at our home near the time my parents died. But since it's believed they had food poisoning then why?"

"I remember hearing about the Johnsons' passing after I'd returned to Mackinac Island." Peter Welling's face grew thoughtful. "I had been visiting my parents in Shepherd and had taken a walk around the fields. Just looking around, I guess. And I saw a woman carrying a covered basket toward the Johnson's farmhouse."

"Mrs. Nelson? The lady who made the meat pie?" Poor thing had died not long afterward.

"Oh no. Mrs. Nelson was very elderly. This woman was young. A stranger to me."

Susan closed her eyes. What had Dorcas worn to their house? "Wearing a dark cloak with a hood."

He pointed toward her. "Exactly."

"So you were there?"

"As I said. I was married and living on the island with my wife and daughter, Maude, but I'd come home to see my folks."

"Lawrence and I talked about my recollection of that time." Susan pressed her hands to her mouth. "We thought Dorcas may have done something. Now I think I know."

Sister Mary Lou touched Mr. Welling's arm. "We found many articles on poisons in Dorcas Fillman's box."

"My *mother's* box—which Dorcas had stolen. She took Valerie from her family, and she put poison in that meat pie my parents ate. I'm sure of it." Susan's hands trembled. "Mr. Welling, you've just given me that final piece of the puzzle."

"It all makes sense—but in such an evil way." Sister Mary Lou shook her head.

"So it wasn't the apples. But I still wonder about arsenic."

"Arsenic can't be detected after a decade, though." Peter blushed. "Read that in one of my crime novels."

A headache pounded at her temples. "I think I need to lie down."

"Go ahead, dearie." Sister Mary Lou stood.

Susan rose, a bit unsteadily, and Mr. Welling took her elbow.

Jack surged through the door, panting. "It's gonna rain so I ran back." He looked at them. "What's wrong?"

"Nothing that concerns you, son." Mr. Welling led Susan forward. "But let's get Miss Johnson to the orphanage."

"She don't look too good." Jack frowned. "Better not let those kids see you lookin' like that."

Susan was about to give a retort when Lawrence came through the door. "What's going on? How can I help?" He jogged across the gymnasium toward her.

When he reached her, pent-up tears escaped. Mr. Welling released her elbow and Lawrence grasped her arms. "What's happened."

"We have news about Val." She trembled. "But, Lawrence, Mr. Welling saw Dorcas headed toward our farmhouse before my parents died."

Lawrence stared at Mr. Welling. "You were there? You saw her?"

Mr. Welling shrugged, his cheeks red. "I saw a strange woman, dressed in a dark cloak with a hood carrying a basket toward the Johnson's home. She was coming from the direction of the Wenhams. Didn't know them then—they'd only immigrated from England a few years earlier, and I'd already left home."

"I'm very sorry to hear this, Susan, but it fits with what you conjectured had happened. But what about Val?"

Susan handed him the letter. "The Fillmans were at their home. The Wenhams had last seen Dorcas's child about a year earlier. This was not the same girl."

"A tortured mind can cause many a person to go astray." Sister Mary Lou pushed her glasses back.

"Why did she have to take so many people with her?" Susan hurried from the room, as Lawrence called after her.

Only when she'd reached her garret room, did she allow herself to let all the anger and tears run freely. She threw herself onto her bed and sobbed into the pillow, pounding her hands against it.

Lizzie pounced onto the bed and settled beside her waist.

"Signorina?" The soft voice carried from the chair turned toward the wall and covered with an afghan.

"Francesca?" She lifted her head and sniffed. "What are you doing up here?"

"Il gatto era triste. Avevo bisogno di stare con lei."

"Francesca. Say in English. Please." Susan sat up, spying Lawrence standing in her doorway.

"She said that your cat is sad, and she came to comfort her." Lawrence shrugged. "That's why I'm here, too."

"We hug Lizzie, yes?" Francesca lifted the cat from the bed as Susan stood beside her.

Lawrence joined them and wrapped an arm around Francesca and Susan.

Was this what a circle of love felt like? If it was, then Susan wanted to stay there forever.

Lizzie meowed and then jumped from Francesca's arms.

The girl cocked her head. "If Father Joseph see you, *serai nei guai.*"

Lawrence put a finger to his lips and motioned for Francesca to follow him out.

She didn't need to understand Italian to know the child was warning him he'd get in trouble.

At the doorway, he swiveled back. "Dinner tonight? Astor's? Five o'clock?"

"I don't know if I'm up to it."

He gave her a look of disbelief. "We're going to talk about all of this over dinner—if you want. I'm hoping it will help you feel better. Share the load."

Some of the angst seemed to fly out of the room as she answered, "Then yes."

Chapter Seventeen

Round Island

Sunlight illuminated the supply boat's full white sails as it skimmed along the water toward Round Island, and Val's heart skipped a beat. A giddiness she'd always felt at the boat's arrival welled up. The suppliers brought news and books, which made her feel more connected to the outside world. But the intense, almost desperate, elation was different now. *A little softer.* All because Paul had made her world safer. Had made the lighthouse a place of comfort and. . . home. Like a real home could be.

Paul followed Val outside the lighthouse. He held Hetty's hand as she waved to the crew of two. "The mail has come." Val knew he'd waited on word from his parents and other family members. Would she have letters, too?

She turned and bent down to Hetty. "That means our books have arrived, too!"

Paul released his daughter's hand. Valerie scooped her up and twirled her around.

When the child's squeal began to sound like distress, Val set her down and patted her shoulders. "I didn't mean to scare you."

"Dizzy." Hetty patted her strawberry-blond curls. Val had wrapped the child's hair in rag rollers the night before and pinned them until they dried. Perfect ringlets framed her gamine face.

Val tweaked her nose. "You're a pretty little girl even if you are dizzy."

Hetty made a face and then plunked onto the ground.

"I'll get our deliveries." Paul headed toward the short pier.

Knowing Mr. Haapala never stayed for tea, Val didn't offer to make any for him. But she kept a watchful eye in case, for once, the older man had changed his mind. She suspected he didn't stay because of his heavy Finnish accent, which made conversation with him difficult. One of these days, she'd simply bring him out a basket of cookies and a mug of tea. The thought made her smile. Next delivery by Mr. Haapala, she would do it.

Hetty picked up her stick and began practicing drawing a straight line, as Val had been encouraging her to do. Those lines would eventually turn into the number one and also start the letter *H*. This practice was just like she'd helped her brother and sister with their numbers and letters.

She frowned in concentration as a dim recollection overcame her. A pretty auburn-haired girl in a pink muslin and lace dress had stood Val beside a small blackboard. "Write a *V*, Verity! That's the first letter of your name!" She shivered, as the girl's gentle laugh echoed in her ears. Her older sister. That memory, that girl, was her older sister. There were two older sisters, one with dark hair and one with auburn. Tears pricked her eyes.

She blinked and Hetty stared up at her, head cocked. "Sad?"

Val wiped her eyes. "I'm ok. I was thinking of someone."

Hetty dropped her stick, and took Val's hand. "Mommy?"

Not Mum. She'd not yet had a clear memory of another mother. Maybe she'd blocked those. "My sister." *One of them.*

"Come on inside," Paul called over his shoulder as he carried the large crate into the lighthouse living quarters. "Both you and I have bundles of letters."

"Lovely."

"And many books." Paul set the crate down in the center of the braided rug in the parlor and then headed toward the kitchen, an oilcloth pouch beneath his arm.

Hetty dropped to the rug and patted the box. "Open!"

"In a moment."

"Patience, my little love." Paul rejoined them and produced a knife.

Valerie needed patience, too, to learn what letters had arrived for her. But she didn't have time to read them now.

He cut the twine and then carefully sliced open the heavy oil paper covering the wood crate. "Nailed shut. Let me get my pry bar."

Both Val and Hetty leaned much closer, peering through the slats. Val pointed to the top book. "I see Thumbelina."

"Fairy wings." Hetty pointed to a cover embossed with tiny fairies.

"Oh my, that's very pretty, isn't it?"

"Yes! Want it."

"All right, just a moment." Val sighed when she spotted Emily Dickens's name. "I see a poetry book."

Hetty clapped her hands. "Book with a doggy!"

"But I asked for a cookbook for girls who love pancakes." Val cocked her head at the child. "It has only recipes for panny cakes in there. Can you believe it?"

Her tiny eyebrows drew together. "You're fibbing."

Val laughed. Hetty would eat pancakes morning, noon, and night if her father allowed.

"You're right. But there is a cookbook in there. I can read the title. Oh, and a letter book for you."

"I learn letters soon."

Val sat down beside the little girl. "Yes. Let's sing our ABCs until your father gets back."

Although a little off-key, they commenced singing and had gotten through their ditty twice when Paul finally returned.

Soon they'd "oohed" and "ahhed" over each book until the lighthouse keeper picked up the last one—a large tome covered in grass-green cloth.

"Never ordered this." A pucker formed between his tawny eyebrows as his lips parted. *Farming in Small Spaces.* Paul opened the book and a slip of paper fell out. Mr. Dardanes's even script was easily identified.

"What does it say?" Val encouraged.

"Tell us, Daddy."

Paul drew in a deep breath, the furrow between his brows relaxing at last. "The inspector suggests I learn how to prepare a garden next spring on what little land we have here. They'll bring in soil amendments in the spring since we're basically living atop rock."

"Does he not recall that you were a farmer?"

"I *am* a farmer." The way he said it, so emphatically, reminded Valerie of when he'd said he was a married man.

Was he having second thoughts about returning to lighthouse work? Or was working the soil so much a part of his constitution that he'd always consider himself a farmer?

Paul set the book back in the box.

She found the cookbook and raised it. "Here's my all-pancake cookery book, Paul. Isn't that what the cover says?"

He made a comical face as he scanned the front. "Recipes to make with children."

Hetty wrapped her arm around Valerie's shoulder. "Can I help?"

"Of course, you'll help, you little cookie!"

"Not a cookie. I'm a girl."

Val pressed her nose into the child's curls. "You smell sweet as a cookie."

Hetty stood and raised her arms to her father. "Tell her, Daddy."

Laughing, Paul pulled his daughter up and he, too, inhaled the sweet scent of his daughter. "You do smell like a sugar cookie."

"It's vanilla," Val confessed. "She asked for perfume, so I put a dot of vanilla essence in her hair."

"Not perfume?" Hetty leaned back and looked at her father, her lips in a pout.

"That's little girl perfume, sweetie." Paul leaned his head toward his daughter. "Didn't you know?"

"Oh." Placated, she grinned and wiggled to get down. Her father lowered her.

"Paul, what mail did I receive?"

He laughed. "A lot. A lot of mail from a lot of people. There's one big envelope from Susan that may have several inside it."

"Oh." How thrilling. But what might it all reveal? "If you'll set it on my bed, I'll read it after Miss Hetty is tucked in tonight."

"I'll do that." Paul grinned. "I think everyone in my entire family sent me a note."

"Get up." Hetty suddenly pointed at Val.

No one had to tell her twice. Val sprang to her feet, feeling the color drain from her face. Only *once* had she not immediately obeyed this directive to stand. She could still recall the sting of Mum's switch on her bare legs. She flinched. But this command was from a child. A girl who simply wanted Val up off the floor.

"Are you all right?" Paul touched her arm briefly, sending reassuring warmth through her.

Pa had simply ignored Mum. Looked the other way the majority of the time—especially where Valerie was concerned.

"Maybe get up a little slower next time, Valerie. We don't want you getting dizzy and falling." His kind voice was low and sincere.

She gazed up at him. Such a pleasant and considerate man, a wonderful, loving father. What a lucky woman his wife had been. What kind of woman had she been?

Val swallowed hard, averting her gaze from that of the handsome lighthouse keeper.

She was only here for a season.

The sun streamed through Paul's window in his room overlooking the Straits of Mackinac. Sitting in his desk chair, he tucked his parents' letter into his Bible. What strange questions they'd asked. Had he found a new wife? Would she be a good mother for Hetty? What was Valerie like? Just because many widowers with children quickly remarried, why did they believe he'd now suddenly go wife hunting? Still, their prodding made him consider when he might be ready again.

Annabelle had loved being the center of attention, had a quick wit, and would have made a wonderful actress. Because she'd grown up having been doted upon, she hadn't learned skills that a farmer's wife needed. Ma had warned him that the adjustment would be hard. During her difficult pregnancy, she'd spent most of her time on the settee in their parlor. He frowned as he recollected that her happiest times were when her mother and father came calling. She'd always perked up then.

He broke into a sweat as he recalled a memory he'd squelched—that of his wife asking her mother if she could return home with her. If her father hadn't put his foot down, would Annabelle have left him? Or had she simply been having a difficult day in her pregnancy, as her mother had insisted?

He rubbed the dampness from his forehead.

While Annabelle had been self-absorbed, Valerie appeared almost too empathetic with others. Although with Annabelle, he'd not let himself see her flaws, with Valerie he had to admit that something was not right. When she laughed, it was like something bursting forth, and almost childlike. Suppressed joy that had been restrained. He saw that joy bursting out when she engaged with Hetty in play and didn't realize he was observing. There was a childlike innocence and wonder that emerged during those times. And although Valerie accepted affection easily from Hetty, when she was with her friends in town, and they reached to hug her, she would go almost limp. As though someone had hurt her. What had happened in her life with the former lighthouse keeper and his wife?

Paul's thoughts returned to the time when he'd worked at the sanitarium. He'd met so many tortured souls there. But one stood out. Georgina, whose beautiful face resembled Valerie's.

He thumbed open his Bible, which had gotten more use in the past month than it had since before he'd become a father. He'd been deep in his grief and had less time to spend in the Word with taking care of his daughter as her only parent. Ma and everyone helped, of course, but he hadn't liked to impose.

Had he imposed by reading the senders on Valerie's mail? The letter from Lawrence Zumbrun, on top of the stack, had him wondering. Wasn't he what most young women were looking for in a husband? Educated and polished and an athlete as well and from a very good family. And they apparently had some kind of connection with one another. Why did that bother him so much? He definitely wouldn't let anyone take advantage of this young woman who'd suffered through so much. He'd keep an eye on that fellow and his intentions.

He finished reading his chapter in Luke, and then Paul knelt on the rag rug alongside his brass bed and prayed. *Lord, help me assist this young woman. I don't know what to do, Lord, but You do. Guide me. Be with us now, Lord. In Jesus' precious name, Amen.*

Hetty had, for once, settled into her nap quickly. Val slipped into her room and closed the door behind her. The letters on her bed beckoned to her, and she skimmed through the names on the envelopes. Lawrence, Mrs. Tom Jeffries—that had to be Tim and Mabel's letters, the thick letter from Sister Mary Lou which likely held something from Susan, too.

She opened the letter from her siblings' caretaker. She'd sent it with Susan and Lawrence and had been delighted to meet them. Timothy and Mabel were doing wonderfully well in school. The teachers couldn't believe they'd never attended any public school. Tim's letter outlined all of his thrilling new activities and friends. The same with Mabel.

She dropped the letters into her lap. They were making a life without her. Then it hit her. They were where she'd always tried to get them—away from their parents. Away to another life. *Thank You, Lord.* Not that she'd wished her parents dead. But as Father Joseph had said during the eulogies, God's will—not our own.

She opened the envelope from Sister Mary Lou. The nun said that Valerie would be surprised to learn that Mr. Welling helped confirm something Susan and Lawrence had worked out about Dorcas. And she had a letter from Mrs. Wenham, in Shepherd, that they'd share with Valerie once she returned to the island in a few days. Francesca drew a heart and what looked like a cat on the bottom of the letter. Susan said she missed her and looked forward to seeing her and they had a lot to discuss. And that she'd gone to dinner with Lawrence. Valerie re-read that line. Was Lawrence courting Susan? Happiness for her friend made her face warm. Lawrence's letter was brief. He said Georgina could not be reached. Also, his father sent word that only blood relations had precedence over vetted foster families as far as the state was concerned. Just as Lawrence had said they'd learned when they'd tried to intervene on Susan's behalf.

Maybe it was for the best that Georgina wasn't found. Valerie could save all her income and when winter arrived, she'd. . .

She'd what? She'd take Timothy and Mabel away from a place where they were happy?

If that was true, then she'd not uproot them. But for now, she felt too far away, even though only a few miles of water separated them. She'd have to make plans to go see them for herself.

Chapter Eighteen

Mackinac Island

*T*he first freeze had nipped in, so Susan donned her heavy hooded cloak over her best wool winter dress. She didn't want her trip with Lawrence to be cut short because she grew cold. As she stepped outside the orphanage, sunlight pierced the gray clouds.

Jack waved from the carriage, and she smiled.

He sported a top hat and the old-fashioned coat, pants, and spats he'd worn the previous time. Beside him, on the driver's seat, rested several pumpkins in various sizes.

Lawrence sprinted toward her; hands upturned. "He's practicing for the Harvest Festival."

Gaping, Susan stood stock still. "He can't be giving the children rides in the carriage." She'd heard from Val about his difficulties.

"He can and will." Lawrence raised his eyebrows. "But he needs more practice and he'll be limited to only one block rides with the Pumpkin King."

"Who pray tell, is this Pumpkin King?"

Lawrence took her arm. "You're taking a drive with him right now to look at housing options."

"Oh heavens. Should I simply refer to you as PK now?"

"Better not." He raised his index finger to his lips. "It's supposed to be a secret."

"Ah."

"But there's another reason Jack is with us."

"Which is?" Her back hurt just thinking about what the youth might put them through on the drive.

"He knows most people on the island and who has boarders."

That would help things.

Soon they were off in the carriage. Lake Huron, with its uneven waves on varied colored water, appeared agitated today.

Jack pointed to the right. "That's Pine Cottage on the left up there."

The three-story structure stood proudly on the steep hillside on Bogan Lane.

"It reminds me of that beautiful home we saw in St. Ignace." Susan took in the large yard that fronted the home. *Lots of space for children to play and plenty of rooms to house them.*

"Great space for children to play at that one near Mrs. Jeffries' bakery. Plenty of rooms to keep them in, too."

Susan's eyes widened as he put her thoughts into words. "Yes, but it looked rather forlorn now."

"It's empty. But some blessed couple will fill that place up, again." He gazed into her eyes intently.

She couldn't look away. Surely, he wasn't implying that the two of them could be that couple. She'd never been courted by a man. Was Lawrence merely making conversation? Of course he was. She averted her gaze, her heart hammering out a rapid unsteady beat like the Chippewas did on their drums to entertain tourists.

"Astor House has plenty of rooms. But I bet you'd like to have heat in your room."

"So it's only a summer place?"

Jack directed the horses to turn at the corner after the pharmacy, and they drove up the short street.

The Astor House, which dominated the left corner, had been filled with happy guests over the summer. Now, it stood empty, piles of orange and red leaves clustered in the yard that surrounded it.

As they drove onto Market Street, Jack pointed to a small house. "That lady's a witch. You don't wanta stay there."

"Prone to exaggeration," Lawrence muttered.

"But he's driving much better today."

"Under threat by his father."

"Hey! I heard that." Jack flicked the reins and the horses picked up speed.

"Did you want your running coach to resign from training you?" Lawrence called out.

The carriage immediately slowed, and he threw his arm across Susan's waist to keep her from lurching forward.

"That's more like it." Lawrence removed his arm. "Are you all right?"

With him there beside her, she was more than all right. "Yes." She sounded breathless. Which she was.

He took her gloved hand in his. "May I? In case he speeds up again?"

Susan nodded her assent. Even wearing gloves, she could feel the warmth of his hand over hers. It felt right. Lovely. Reassuring. She wanted to enjoy the sensation for as long as she could. Whatever Jack and Lawrence were saying about the other homes, she vaguely heard.

The next thing she knew, they were almost back to the orphanage.

Lawrence's shoulder pressed into hers. "I could tell you weren't interested in the others. I'm guessing Pine Cottage, near the children."

"Or Madame Mirandette's, closer still."

One day, would they have a place of their own?

When he released her hand, she realized Jack had driven beautifully the rest of the drive. Lawrence hadn't needed to hold her in place. When he assisted her out of the carriage, his expression wasn't that of a helpful co-worker or a new friend. It was more. Much more.

Her world was changing—fast.

Gratitude and love swelled her heart.

"Paul will be back from the island tomorrow. Will you be spending time with your old friend?"

Was that jealousy she heard in Lawrence's voice? But was he trying to tell her something? Doubts swooped in. Perhaps he was simply clarifying.

"I imagine so. And you'll be seeing Valerie?"

"Definitely."

He didn't sound uncertain at all about that. Jealousy was definitely nipping at her heart. Susan turned to Jack. "Thank you for taking me around to look."

Jack removed his top hat. "The Pumpkin Carriage Master is happy to serve you."

Was the Pumpkin King happy to help?

Mackinac Island

The freedom that Valerie had once expected to enjoy, upon arrival at the Mackinac Island wharf, evaporated as Paul and Hetty waved goodbye and headed toward the ice cream shop. She'd asked him for this, but the pain of their separation stabbed at her as she walked toward St. Anne's.

A dray loaded with crates rolled by. Soon Valerie arrived at the orphanage where she discovered Sister Mary Lou seated on a bench.

The nun waved a missive high. "We received word from Vitellio's."

This wasn't quite the welcome Val had expected. She swallowed hard. "Good to see you, Sister Mary Lou."

"Yes, dearie, you, too." The nun laughed. "You look well."

"I am." Better than she'd been in ages.

The October breeze swirled leaves around their skirts as Valerie sat beside Sister Mary Lou. Thankfully, the sun shone down this chilly morning, but Valerie clutched her threadbare cape closely around her.

"What does the message say, Sister Mary Lou?"

"Mr. Vitellio had only seven custom orders for this bracelet." Sister Mary Lou's voice was full of excitement.

"Seven?"

"Yes," her eyes grew wide, "but only one person commissioned them."

"Who?"

"Mrs. Carrie Booth-Moore."

Carrie is the name of the lady in my memory.

"She was a Sugarplum Ladies founder and a friend of Susan's mother as well as what Susan would call a 'bosom friend' of Eugenie Mott Gladstone."

Shivers coursed down Val's arms. "Will you send Mrs. Booth-Moore a letter? To ask about the bracelets?"

"Father Joseph is putting ink to paper as we speak. He may even wire her."

Val inhaled slowly. "Thank you for helping."

"Don't worry, we'll get to the bottom of this. Trust God to help us."

Had she trusted God to help her? *Sometimes.* Valerie sniffed.

"How are things at the lighthouse?" Sister Mary Lou touched Valerie's hand. "What do you think of Mr. Scholtus?"

"He seems very kind." *Thoughtful, protective, intelligent, and a wonderful father.*

"And handsome, too?" Sister Mary Lou quirked her eyebrows.

She cast the nun a questioning look. "Yes, he is handsome, especially with that auburn hair."

"My favorite color, I'll admit."

"I was expecting you to ask if he was devout. Which he is, but not a fanatic." Not someone who twisted God's words, like Mum had.

The nun nodded solemnly. "I may have to pray my rosary extra times for asking you about Mr. Scholtus's good looks. I'll see what Father Joseph tells me to do during confession."

"Hopefully, he'll be lenient." Valerie suppressed a grin, imagining the serious priest responding to that confession.

"Oh, I think he'll be in a snit."

Hooves sounded in the nearby roadway as a carriage driver rode past, an older distinguished-looking lady inside.

"Why is he grumpy?"

"Our Susan attempted to help with baking duties and was shooed from the kitchen when her shortcakes burned. Father Joseph had her return to cleaning up the classrooms."

"Then she can't come walking with me? I was hoping to hear news about Tim and Mabel while we went up to the Veterans' Home."

"Ladies?" Lawrence Zumbrun jogged up to them, attired in a ridiculous-looking striped shirt and loose pants cuffed at the bottom.

Val couldn't help gawking at him, he looked so strange. Jack, in similar attire, ran up to join him and whacked his coach hard on the back.

Lawrence swiveled and threw an arm toward the boy, who threw his hands high as he jumped backward and laughed.

"Mr. Zumbrun, thank you for joining us since Miss Johnson is. . . preoccupied."

"In trouble, ya mean, dontcha?" The boy snickered. "Good thing she ain't got a husband. Can't cook for nothin'."

"Jack." Sister Mary Lou drew out his name in warning.

"Miss Johnson possesses attributes far superior to mere cooking skills." Lawrence sounded completely smitten.

Jack's chin drew in. "Sounds like the Pumpkin King found his queen."

"Not a bad idea." Sister Mary Lou grinned. "Dear Susan could keep Lawrence company, and she'd look splendid in an orange cape."

"She would," Lawrence agreed.

"Pumpkin King?" Valerie cocked her head.

"Larry's role in our Harvest Festival."

Valerie didn't believe Jack meant Susan to play some role as queen.

"Dunno if those two could be trusted alone in the pumpkin carriage." Jack crinkled his nose. "Larry was holding her hand the other day in public."

Lawrence's high cheekbones turned pink.

What had happened in the week since she'd been at the lighthouse? How could she judge her friend, though, when Valerie's admiration for Paul had blossomed so quickly?

"Lawrence is Susan's co-worker. Perhaps you'd nudged your horses a little faster when those two were in your carriage?" Valerie arched her eyebrows at him. "And that's why he kept hold of her hand?"

Jack's face fell. "I mighta done that."

Lawrence needed to get Jack away from the orphanage before his runner said anything more about him and Susan. They were keeping their courtship quiet until he'd had a chance to speak about it with the Wellings.

"My brother and sister—how are they?" Valerie looked pensive.

"Very fine indeed." He pressed his hand against his sweaty running shirt. "I've got to go clean up while Jack does another run around the island."

"Through the island." Jack winked. "I've got a great trail run through Harrisonville."

"Harrisonville?" Valerie stood.

"Where a lot of workers on the island live. It's in the center." Jack ran off without a by-your-leave.

The three adults shook their heads.

Lawrence was just relieved that Jack was gone. Loose lips sink ships and all that.

The nun pointed toward Jack as he swept out of sight. "If they could harness that energy and use it on the mainland, then they might not need that new hydropower plant on the St. Mary's River in the Soo."

"Maybe you should write the engineers a letter and suggest that." Lawrence gave her what he hoped was a charming smile.

The nun smiled as she slipped past them and back toward the building.

"Lawrence, before you make your ablutions," she gestured toward his messy condition, "is there anything you can tell me about your impression of my siblings?"

He shrugged. "They are perfectly happy and well taken care of. The Jeffries are delightful. One would think they'd always been a family." He frowned, recalling the jealous pang he'd had as he'd left their cozy home.

"I see." Her lips rolled inward. "But they have a family. Me."

He couldn't make himself reply to that.

She had another family.

The Gladstones.

"I can't believe I fell asleep on Father Joseph's couch." Valerie rubbed her eyes as Lawrence roused her from her unintended nap.

"I ran into your employer, Paul Scholtus, downstairs with Susan." Irritation flitted over Lawrence's features. "He said you've been working hard. No wonder you're asleep."

"No more effort than when I lived there with my parents—in fact, less." But the reminders of them were everywhere, along with the absence of Mabel and Tim. "But a three-year-old does require constant supervision, especially one who is determined to give up her naps."

"One day I hope I'll know those pleasures."

She stood and stretched, her body achy from her ride over and sleeping scrunched on the settee. "You wish to have children?"

"I'd like a very large family. Perhaps foster or adopt children, too, especially now since I've seen the Jeffries with your sister and brother."

That stung. It sounded as if they'd already taken them away from her.

"I'm disappointed I've not gotten to speak with Susan yet." *But Paul had.*

"Too bad she's spending her few free moments with your employer."

"They are old friends." She chewed her lower lip.

"Scholtus wants to come to Apple Blossom Cottage." He shrugged. "I'm not inclined to bring him, but if you insist—"

"I prefer he comes with me. But I don't think Hetty would do well there. It's full of too many nooks and crannies and places to hide."

With a rush, her memory flooded back of hiding beneath the stairs, clutching her rabbit. Lawrence told her to be quiet or Georgina would hear them. Then they would be "it," but she didn't really know what it was. He explained they'd be put out of the game they were playing, and she must be quiet.

She flinched when he touched her arm.

"Are you all right? Dizzy?"

"I'm fine."

"Sister Mary Lou said Hetty can stay with Madame Mirandette's class. They are mostly French-speaking children, but speak some English, too."

"That's the older woman who is taking over Susan's responsibilities?"

"Yes."

"Poor Susan. I wonder if she feels like she's being flung off."

"Have no worries, we're going to pull her into the Social Affirmation Society with welcoming arms."

Given what Jack had implied, Lawrence may well be opening his arms wide for Susan. "Where will she live?"

"She's here for now but we've got staff quarters being built."

"Will they be appropriate for the off-season?"

He straightened. "We're still looking, but she may accept Mrs. Mirandette's offer to stay. She has a house right behind St. Anne's."

"The big white wood-sided house?"

"Yes. Then she can be near the children."

If Lawrence had his say, by next off-season, with the program up and running for future summers, Miss Susan Johnson would become Mrs. Lawrence Zumbrun. Of course, there'd need to be a fair amount of courtship between now and then. They'd live wherever Jack was training in the off-season. The society also planned to purchase staff quarters in the Lansing area for the core workers. And if he could adopt Francesca with Susan. . . "Don't fret about Susan. All will be well."

"I certainly hope so." Valerie turned and headed out the office door, Lawrence following.

As they headed down the hallway, Paul stood at a doorway, hat in hand. Madame Mirandette, a petite older woman with wispy white hair pulled up in a bun, took Hetty's hand. Hetty waved goodbye as she entered a room filled with children's happy voices.

The door shut and the new lighthouse keeper still stood there, clutching his bowler hat.

"Keep squeezing that hat and you'll crush it." Valerie marched up to her employer and snatched the hat.

"Thank you. I think." Scholtus's face showed a mixture of amusement and surprise.

"Are you coming with us, then?" Valerie's tone with him sounded less like a servant and more like. . . A bossy sister? A wife?

"*Oui, mademoiselle.*" Paul bowed. "That's all the French I know. A good thing Madame Mirandette didn't speak in her native language."

Susan emerged from a nearby classroom. She smiled at Lawrence with warmth, and his face flushed. He recalled feeling her hand held in his. They'd been spending a lot of time together but even when she wasn't with him, he was thinking about her.

Susan hurried to Valerie and hugged her. "I've missed having you here. And Lizzie has been meowing for you every night."

Valerie inclined her head toward her employer. "Paul promised to get Hetty a cat."

The lighthouse keeper placed his hand over his heart. "If I don't find a kitty by the time we return tonight, I may be in very deep trouble."

Lawrence laughed. "Susan and I have been feeding an abandoned kitten at the docks. I'm sure she'll be happy to go home with you."

Susan's cat strolled down the hall, waving her tail majestically.

"She's the sweetest thing ever—except for Lizzie." Susan smiled, the warmth in her brown eyes making his breath catch. "Hetty will love her."

Valerie bent and picked up Lizzie. "Have you named the kitten?"

"We call her Little Bit for now." Susan cast him a conspiratorial look. "But Hetty will want to give her a special name, don't you think?"

"Of course." When the cat meowed and stretched, Valerie set her down.

"We'd best be going." Lawrence strode to the end of the hallway and looked out the mullioned windows. "Jack's still watching the carriage for us. Don't want to keep him waiting."

Nor Georgina, who was at her parents' cottage.

If Georgina kept her word and stayed in the background while Valerie and Lawrence visited, then he could get her opinion as to whether she believed as he did—that this definitely *was* her younger sister.

Paul locked eyes with Susan. "I'd love to see you again tonight, Susan."

Lawrence pushed back his scowl as he took Valerie's arm and left the building. Paul may love seeing his old friend, but Lawrence wasn't too keen on the notion. Memories of losing his fiancé, to a rival he didn't even know he had, resurfaced. But Lawrence had no right to these jealous feelings about Susan and no claim on her affections.

But could that change?

Chapter Nineteen

Zumbrun was lying about something—of that, Paul was certain.
What did Valerie need to see at that cottage? She'd already
visited the week before and had been upset afterward.

As they rode to the cottage, Zumbrun inclined his head toward a
dapper older gentleman who stood near Doud's Market with his
walking stick in hand. "There's Mr. Foley. Susan said he's taking
photographs of the orphans tomorrow."

Paul leaned forward and spied the sign for the photography
studio, situated on the second floor of the building. "I'd like to get one
done of Hetty and me sometime."

Valerie slanted a glance at him. She settled back into the carriage
seat as they continued on. Was she upset that he didn't offer to include
her in the picture? That wouldn't make sense.

"My parents never had a photograph made of our family," she
stated flatly.

"Frugal?" he asked, but from the things she'd said during her
week at the lighthouse, the caretaker and his wife sounded disturbed.

"My mother didn't want any images made of us. She had some
queer notions." She looked like she was chewing the inside of her lip.

As they rolled on, near the library, he called to Lawrence. "I
forgot to pick up some books for my daughter. Can we stop on the
way back?"

"Certainly."

They headed past the encampment of Chippewas, busy with
women weaving baskets as kettles heated over open fires, and then
made a turn up a steep hill.

"I bought a piece of beadwork in town, a beautiful deep blue
necklace for my mother. They said it was from. . ." he'd not use their
pejorative term, "ladies who lived in the camp."

"Mr. Welling said they'll return to the mainland soon." Zumbrun
sounded like such a know-it-all.

The other man, a few years older than Paul, seemed to have a
hold over Valerie that Paul didn't appreciate. He exchanged a quick
glance between the two.

Valerie appeared deep in thought, as she often was—unless she
and Hetty were together. Zumbrun's nose twitched ever so slightly—

as if he were a fox on the scent of something. And he kept shifting in his seat.

No, Paul certainly didn't have a good feeling about this trip.

Valerie, seated alongside him, pointed across the expanse of blue water toward the lighthouse. "West Bluff has one of the loveliest views on the island and what can you see?"

He shrugged. "The lighthouse?"

She laughed. That bubbling laughter, which had been absent at the beginning of the week, seemed to have grown more frequent with each day. But as they pulled near the veteran's cottage, her smile drooped, and her pink cheeks grew wan.

Zumbrun brought the carriage to a full stop in front of a huge mansion, which Lawrence and Valerie had referred to as a cottage.

A tall lanky man, dressed in gray work clothes, ran toward them, across the front lawn. "Can I help?"

Zumbrun and the man discussed the particulars as Paul assisted Valerie out of the carriage.

Lawrence joined them and extended his arm to Valerie.

Paul should be helping her right now—not this fellow. But this was Zumbrun's playing field, and Paul had invited himself to the game.

They walked toward the cottage that matched the opulence of the homes flanking it on the bluff. He trailed behind the two, irritation accompanying him.

When they reached the front door, a slender silver-haired man opened it. The servant's gaze remained steady upon Valerie as he welcomed them inside. Seemed strange to have a butler at a veterans' home.

Paul followed them inside and the servant took their coats and hats.

"Lawrence and Valerie, welcome." A handsome woman, dressed in purple and mustard greeted them.

"Lovely to see you again, Mrs. Stevens and Colonel Stevens." Valerie's stiff smile spoke volumes to him.

The colonel shook Zumbrun's hand vigorously before he turned his attention to Paul. "This the new lighthouse keeper then?"

Paul stepped forward and extended his hand. When the man's iron grip caused pain, he forced himself to not flinch. He stared into the army veteran's steely eyes until the colonel finally released his hand. Although he wanted to do so, Paul didn't flex his fingers, which were now red. Was this some kind of rite of passage? If this had been a ship captain, Paul would have been tempted to turn the Fresnel light dark for this fellow's vessel in the future.

"Tea?" Mrs. Stevens cast Paul a look of admiration. Did she know of her husband's peccadilloes when it came to meeting other men?

Valerie looked to Zumbrun, who nodded assent.

They ignored Paul.

"Come along, then." Mrs. Stevens gracefully pivoted and led them toward a parlor that had the air of decaying high luxury.

Even Paul, with his inexperienced eye, could see that the velvet had become shiny in spots and faded in others. The silk curtains bore evidence of repairs in spots, as if insects had gotten to what once had been stately window coverings.

They all took a seat in the large room, which featured a lit fireplace at one end.

Mrs. Stevens rang a bell. Someone entered from behind where Paul was seated on a divan.

"This place is an utter disgrace!" A high-pitched female voice, filled with contempt, was followed by a gasp as Valerie stood.

Gaping, Valerie pointed at the woman. "Mother!"

Zumbrun rose just as she fainted and caught her.

Paul came to Valerie's side and pushed the other man away. "Let me help her. Valerie, can you hear me?"

Reluctantly, Zumbrun released her, and then Paul lifted the beautiful young woman in his arms.

Paul swiveled to see Georgina—once one of the patients on his unit. He clamped his mouth shut. He wasn't going to violate confidentiality, even though it had been years since he'd left the institute.

"I didn't mean for this to happen. I'm sorry." Georgina gestured around the interior. "I just couldn't wait any longer and then I saw how decrepit our cottage has become."

What was she doing here?

And why had Valerie called her *Mother*?

Mum was dead—but this was another mother. Her real mother. Someone held her close, reassuring Valerie. When someone waved ammonia beneath her nose, Valerie pulled away, coughing, and opened her eyes.

She stared up at the dark-haired woman, attired in a day gown of fine emerald-green wool. Valerie pointed at her. "You. . . you can't be my mother—you're too young."

But the woman looked very much like her.

"Are you all right?" Paul still clasped her in his arms but set her on her feet. He had been the one whose comfort she needed.

"Yes, but—who are you?" She pointed at the well-dressed woman. "You can't be Georgina. Lawrence said he couldn't reach her. So who are you?"

"I am Georgina."

Woozy, Valerie closed her eyes. "Lawrence, you lied to me."

"I didn't lie. I told you Georgina Gladstone could not be reached."

The woman extended her left hand. Filtered sunlight through the windows and the overhead chandelier lit a large diamond and gold band. "I'm Georgina Hudgins now. My husband Lee and I—"

"You married Lee Hudgins?" Paul frowned. "The automobile designer?"

"Yes, I met him through Lawrence, in Detroit."

"He keeps a field near my family's farm and wreaks all kinds of havoc on the livestock with his racing. And now here you are, doing the same."

The room fell silent. Valerie stared at him, not believing Paul had said that.

He pointed at Lawrence. "You've got a lot of nerve bringing poor Valerie in here, who's just lost her parents—"

"They aren't her parents." Georgina stalked forward, her fancy shoes tapping ominously on the hardwood floor.

"Maybe they weren't, but they were pretty much all she's known." Paul's rigid posture was one Valerie had never seen before.

She raised her hands. "Stop! Both of you. I want to speak with Georgina alone."

Mrs. Stevens swiftly rose and gestured for Valerie and Georgina to follow her. As they departed the room, Lawrence grumbled something at Paul.

"That shows just what you know about Valerie. How long has it been since you've seen her?" Fear mingled with Paul's righteous anger.

Mrs. Stevens pointed down the hallway. "Let me take you to the lady's parlor."

Georgina swept past Mrs. Stevens. "This is my family's home. I believe I know where it is." Her imperious manner caused Valerie to pause in the hallway, Mrs. Stevens beside her—her cheeks red.

Georgina was at the end of the hall before she turned and looked back.

"You may be my sister by birth, but I will not tolerate you treating Mrs. Stevens with such disrespect." She locked eyes on the other woman, as her chin began to tremble.

Childhood memories, anger, fear, disappointment, outrage all welled up. She was three, almost four, and Dorcas had grabbed Valentine's hand and pulled her—taking her away from Georgie's side. Val hadn't wanted to go on the ship but neither did she want to go with the maid. Dorcas smiled at her. "I've got a kitty for you that Mrs. Booth-Moore wanted you to take on the trip. Your mother and father said you could. It's right over here. So let's grab her quickly." But the only thing grabbed had been Valentine as Dorcas continued to pull her through the crowd.

"You let go of me. You let the maid take me away." Valentine stood in the middle of the hallway, tears flowing down her face.

Her sister's face grew pale, her shoulders slumped, and she began to shake with sobs.

Valentine turned and ran to a place she knew would be safe.

Lawrence gritted his teeth as Georgina marched back into the parlor and jammed her index finger into his chest, her sharp nail making him flinch.

"Did you and this man put that girl up to this?" She stared with wild eyes toward Paul.

Lawrence shook his head. "What are you talking about? I asked you to stay back and just give me your opinion, not to come barging in here complaining because the place is run down." Even though Georgina had been very fragile for years, he wasn't going to let her get away with making false accusations.

She huffed a mangled sound. "This man told that girl what to say. Someone wants to put me back into treatment. But I'm not going. I tell you; it won't happen. Lee won't go along with this no matter what Mr. Scholtus tries to do."

She knew Paul's name. Had Lawrence mentioned it?

She whirled on Paul and pushed him, but he stood firm. "I can't believe you'd do this to me after all you saw me go through. How could you?"

Lawrence needed to calm her fast. "Georgie, how do you know Paul?" Had he looked vaguely familiar because Lawrence had seen him at the sanitarium?

"Did he tell you he'd never met me before? I'm sure he told that girl all about me. And what to say. How to get me to think she might be my missing sister. And you fell for it, Lawrence."

As disturbed as Georgina had been, she'd been stable for at least the last few years, which was why he'd introduced her to his friend, Lee. He turned toward Paul. "Is there any truth in what she's saying?"

Paul showed no remorse. No indication that he had anything to apologize for. "Mrs. Hudgins, if you wish to disclose our acquaintance, I grant permission. But I would never divulge any information I have."

"Not even to this young woman? This pretender? You want me to believe that all the things I shared with you were kept hidden in your heart?" She said this with mockery in her voice, her hands pressed against her bodice.

Mrs. Stevens came into the room and motioned to her husband, who'd been observing them in rapt attention. "Yes, my dear?"

"I can't find Valerie."

"What happened?" Paul demanded. The fellow acted as if he were a jealous husband and not her employer. Was it possible that Lawrence had misconstrued who Miss Fillman truly was? What was Scholtus's relationship with Georgie?

But no, Valerie had brought the drawing down to him.

"She got very upset and ran off, but she was inside the house. I heard no outside doors closing."

Lawrence had inspiration, from long ago. "I think I know where she might be."

"When we find her, I'm taking her back to the lighthouse." Paul followed Lawrence toward the closet beneath the stairs. "You're upsetting her."

Lawrence paused and made a motion with his fingers over his lips.

Gentle sobs came from within the hidden room under the stairs.

Lawrence pushed against the panel, which released the door.

Heels clicked on the floor behind him.

The door opened and Valerie, seated on the floor, held the bunny she'd left there long ago.

"You found it," he and Georgie said at the same time.

Tears streaming, Georgie got on her knees and reached toward Valentine. "You finally found your rabbit."

Valentine nodded and sniffed.

"And I've finally found you." She embraced her sister.

Valentine had mourned the loss of that stuffed toy from the time the family had departed the island that summer until the family had departed for New York and their ship to England to see her grandparents at their estate. And now she held the dusty old toy as though it held the answers to everything she'd wanted to ask.

"I think we should give these sisters time to themselves." Lawrence gestured for the others to move back.

Georgie scooted in beside Valentine and closed the tiny door behind them.

It was a hiding place once again.

He'd once fantasized that he'd come here and found Valentine hiding in that very spot with her bunny—that she'd been hiding there all these years. Of course, she hadn't been. A chill went through him. She was here now, and that was what mattered.

"Since Georgina brought up our acquaintance, I'll tell you." Paul rubbed his neck. He and Zumbrun sat on a bench in the hallway, waiting for the sisters. "I worked at the world-renowned sanitarium in Battle Creek. Georgina was one of the patients there."

"You were an orderly?"

"Basically. But she also confided in me." His face heated.

"She was devastated over Valerie's loss."

"Georgina blamed herself. She told me she was supposed to be watching her sister."

"Georgie never gave her name or specifics?"

Paul lifted his palm. "Not allowed. No last names. She did explain that her parents and brother and sisters were at the wharf with her."

"At the time I left the sanitarium, I wasn't convinced she was mentally stable."

Zumbrun harrumphed. "Muckraking journalists delighted in reporting on Georgie's mental instability, repeat stints in the asylum or health sanitariums, drug and alcohol use, and her tendency to go missing."

"So that continued on?" Paul pressed his back against the wall, surprised.

"Indeed."

"Our agricultural paper in Shepherd doesn't cover such things." Paul turned toward Zumbrun. "What about now?"

"Stable for about a year."

"She can't be all that mentally competent to have married Lee." Paul gave a short laugh.

"The man's a genius as is Grant Bentley, his business partner. Their automobiles are getting attention worldwide."

"Horseless carriages will never be found on farms."

"We'll have to agree to disagree on that."

He had to admit he missed the farm. The smell of the earth. The fellowship with his family. He was a lighthouse keeper now and far from the things that daily dredged up memories of his wife. But didn't he think of Annabelle every time he looked into Hetty's eyes?

Paul rose. "We need to get back to the orphanage."

Zumbrun stood and went toward the cupboard under the stairs when the tiny entry door opened.

Georgina clapped her hands, like a child. "We have a plan."

Val appeared dazed but happy. "I'd like to stay with my sister for a couple of days to get reacquainted."

"I have to return downstate soon, or Lee will come looking for me."

"Who will help Paul at the lighthouse?" Zumbrun said this, surprising Paul.

"I'll ask Susan," Val offered.

"And if she isn't able?" What would Paul do then?

Chapter Twenty

*A*da Welling, a wrapped crisscross wool hat covering her upswept hair, waved to Susan as she approached the worksite for the second of the new Social Affirmation Society buildings.

"Can you believe it?" Susan called out to the woman. "The housing dormitory building is nearly up, too."

"That's what happens when you pay top dollar."

Susan shook her head in marvel. "They said the roof is complete and they took a break to send for you, if you want to go inside."

Mrs. Welling laughed. "Which I do."

The two of them headed up the walkway to the building, the scent of fresh wood almost overpowering.

The older woman waved her hand over her face. "Wait until the paint fumes hit us next week."

"I don't think they'll let us in until it's all totally dry."

"But trust me, with that much surface to paint they'll need to air the place out well before the November gales start next month."

Susan patted her pocket. "Oh, I picked up the mail for the Society from the post office. There is something here from Mrs. Booth-Moore—"

"Carrie Booth-Moore?" Mrs. Welling stopped walking and extended her gloved hand.

Susan handed the missive to her.

A gust of wind swirled their skirts. "Let's go inside."

They entered the building, the large oak doors not yet painted nor stained. Inside, instead of the cavernous room she'd expected, the office spaces had already been framed out, walled, and had doors installed.

As Mrs. Welling surveyed the scene, a look of wonder washed over her face. "This never gets old," she whispered.

A strange thing to say. Susan bit her lip but wished for clarification of her new employer's enigmatic comment.

"Ah, they left us a few chairs. The desks and cabinets for the gymnasium and classroom building arrived and are at the wharf, ready for delivery."

"Already?"

"Mrs. Mirandotte's son regularly crosses the Straits. He advised us that we were safest to get the transport done early, since the weather has been reasonably cooperative this fall.

"Miss Johnson, why don't you look around while I read this letter?" It was a command—not a suggestion—and Susan took a promenade around the room, peeking in the indoor bathrooms as she went. This would be a luxury for many of the children.

When she returned, Mrs. Welling gestured to the seat beside her, a simple wood chair. "Mrs. Booth-Moore wants us to know that she's unsure what help she could be at our summer program, given her age and station in life."

Was that a glint of moisture in the older woman's eyes? "But will she still come? I was so hoping to see her."

"Do you know her?"

"Not exactly."

"She wishes to fund this entire gymnasium building in lieu of coming up to participate." From the sour expression now etched on Ada's face, she found this extremely distasteful.

"That would be so. . . extravagant and helpful."

"Not needed. We have the funds secured for years to come."

When Mrs. Welling lowered the letter, Susan glanced at it and frowned. She pointed to the signature. "That's not her handwriting."

"What do you mean?"

"That's not the handwriting in my mother's autograph book, where Carrie Booth-Moore signed."

"Autograph book?"

"Yes, my mother was one of the later Sugarplum Ladies—well, more of a manager of them than an actual baker or teacher, but—"

"Miss Evelyn?" The woman's face paled.

"Evelyn Singleterry—Evelyn Johnson after she married my father."

"You're her daughter?" Ada gaped at her.

Hadn't Susan just said that? She nodded. "I have the autograph book with me. I'll show you her signature." She pulled the book from her bag and handed it to the other woman, who stared at Susan's most precious treasure.

"I gave Miss Evelyn this." She drew in a deep breath.

"What?" Susan stiffened in shock.

Ada Welling ran her fingers over the decorated top of the leather-bound book. "So many years ago." Her eyes took on a faraway look.

"You're the Adelaide Fox who wrote in here?"

"Miss Evelyn believed in me and encouraged my math skills. She spent time with me when my mother was working. Taught me my earliest business management skills."

Susan leaned forward. "I am so glad. I wish I'd had more time with her."

"She's passed?"

"Yes, both she and my father died when I was only six years old."

"Oh no, I'm so sorry. I lost track of her after my mother died. I was in the Poor House in Shepherd—next door to Mr. Welling. That's our farm now."

"We lived in Shepherd, too."

"But Evelyn worked in the Detroit area when we had to depart. My mother was a very proud woman, and when she became ill and couldn't work at the Sugarplum functions, we ended up at the Poor House."

"I remember that place and wondered if I'd end up there when my parents died, but I entered into care." With many different families, basically as a servant.

"I'm guessing by your age that you were born not long after I left Shepherd, that was over twenty-six years ago." Mrs. Welling patted her hand. "We need to talk more about this over dinner, soon. Lawrence also knows Mrs. Booth-Moore."

Should she tell her that Father Joseph had just sent a telegram, about the diamond bracelet, to Mrs. Booth-Moore? It wasn't her place to disclose that information. "I'd like that very much. And I could make something in our kitchen to bring with me."

"I believe I'll decline." The woman's lips twitched. "Your baking skills are somewhat legendary on this island, already, Susan."

As she stared in disbelief, a low laugh bubbled up in the woman. "There's hope for you yet. Evelyn was forever bringing me burnt biscuits, inedible cookies that had to be soaked in coffee or tea to even bite into. She also baked loaves of bread that never rose and resembled flat drays rather than a fluffy Conestoga wagon-top effect."

"You must have been a child back then," Susan blurted out.

"I was in my early teens when I knew her. But show me her signature and let's compare."

Susan found the spot in the book and tapped it.

Mrs. Welling glanced down at the monogrammed letter. "This is her stationary. Ah, yes, she didn't actually sign it." She pointed. "Her secretary wrote this letter."

"Secretary? She has a personal secretary?"

"She does." Again Mrs. Welling laughed. "As do most very wealthy ladies of a certain set."

"I wonder what that would be like."

The woman looked deep in thought as she locked eyes on Susan. Then, suddenly, she turned and gestured around to the gymnasium.

"Some don't keep a personal secretary but put their extra funds into benevolence projects like this."

"Like Miss Mott did for the Sugarplum Ladies?"

"Exactly like Eugenie Mott, now Lady Gladstone, did."

Valerie's mother. "What an incredible woman she must have been—must be."

Mrs. Welling expelled a hard breath. "She was and made it possible for so many women, an entire generation of Civil War widows, and others, to make a living for themselves. It's just a shame that her daughter was never found."

"Perhaps soon." Susan bit her lip.

"At least, if all three of the founding Sugarplum Ladies did show up this summer, they could lend support to poor Miss Eugenie. That's something I pray will happen."

"And they'll be with another Sugarplum Lady—you." Susan gave her a pointed look.

"Yes. I guess I was, wasn't I?"

"Yes."

A smile washed over the woman's face, framed by her beautifully arranged hair. "But let me tell you about the autograph book."

"That was a sweet gift—especially since you were so young."

Ada waved her hand. "They were so popular back then, and Miss Evelyn was one of the youngest ladies—I thought she'd enjoy it. And I believe she did. She was so vivacious."

Unlike me. "She was very proud of it." To the point of showing it to Dorcas Fillman the day before her death. Had the woman killed Mother?

"She got an autograph from Alva Edison, the young telegram pioneer, and was excited to tell me about it. Such fond memories. I was so young then—barely past being a child."

"Those were exciting times for my mother. I'm so glad that I'm getting to know her better, as a young woman, through you, Mrs. Welling."

"You should call me Ada, please." Ada patted Susan's arm. "Wait until you see those three ladies together—they were magical. An inspiration to me. I wish I'd had such peers myself."

"But now they can be." Granted, Ada Welling was a matron with a young child, living on a small island and helping run a social organization. The other three must be in their fifties or sixties with grown children and likely grandchildren, too.

"I'll let you in on a little secret." Ada winked. "I'm the wealthiest woman in America."

That was amusing, but Susan resisted raising her eyebrows. Ada, although well-groomed, today sported a nice serviceable ensemble from the previous decade. Her sturdy shoes were well-worn but had been polished. "Oh?"

Ada laughed. "With my wonderful husband, Peter, my stepson Jack who I consider my own, and my little daughter, I'm blessed beyond measure."

"I hope to be just as rich one day." *There, that sounded good.*

"We'll see." Ada gestured around the building. "For now, though, let's get you up to speed on what we'll need you to do in your managerial role. We're going to make Miss Evelyn proud." She pointed upward. "Perhaps she'll get a glimpse from the heavenly realms."

Tears pricked Susan's eyes. What a shame she'd never gotten the chance to make her mother proud. Or was that why she'd always worked so hard—thinking that she had to keep performing to achieve love or recognition? Was that why Lawrence expressed interest in her? Regardless, she needed to take care of herself.

Quite possibly, no one else would.

"So Georgina and you will be spending a couple of days together on the island?" Susan repeated back to her friend what she'd just said. "And you're definitely Verity Gladstone?"

"Yes!" Val hugged her and then stepped back and grasped Susan's arms. "They called me Valentine because that's my birthday. And I'll be twenty on Valentine's Day."

"How wonderful. I am so excited for you. And now your nightmares will make sense I bet."

"I think so." Val's eyes shimmered. "But I need your help for a couple of days."

"Oh. Yes, Paul needs help at the lighthouse."

"Father Joseph said you may go."

"I'm sure Mrs. Welling will agree, also. It seems strange having to get permission from two people now."

"Until you go on full-time with this new position."

"Which won't be too long."

"Are you sure you'll be all right with Hetty?"

"You are jesting. I've helped with hundreds of children at the orphanage over the last several years."

Val's face flushed. "Of course."

"She's one little girl, and I'm sure she's just as adorable as you've told me she is."

"Yes, indeed."

Did it send a bad message to Hetty, though, that Val was so anxious to get away from the island already? "We'll tell Hetty that your sister came to see you, and you are having a visit."

Madame Mirandette stepped into the hallway, arms full of a squirming little girl. "Hetty says she is done. She heard you talking." The elderly lady set the child down, and Hetty ran straight to Val and raised her arms, but her friend shook her golden tresses.

Hetty smiled shyly at Susan—nothing like the coquettish smile Annabelle had possessed since childhood.

"You're Daddy's fren." She held up her arms—apparently trying for a lift when she'd failed with Val.

Laughing, Susan bent and picked Hetty up and kissed her soft cheek. "Yes, I'm your daddy's friend. And I was about your age when we started playing together on our families' farms."

Hetty's lip curled. "I miss my farm. And Granny. And Granpa. And Unkas."

"Those are all very good people to have in your life."

The child stuck her finger in her mouth.

Susan swayed side-to-side. "I knew all of those wonderful family members of yours—except your uncles' wives."

"I have aunties. There's dogs and kitties. An' chickens."

"I'm determined to bring a kitty out to you and your father. But we couldn't convince her to cooperate today."

"Why?"

Susan shrugged. "Shy."

"Give kitty one of Daddy's fishies."

"Great idea." She leaned in and rubbed her nose against the girl's tiny one and Hetty laughed.

"That tickles." She rubbed her nose.

Susan set her down. "How about I become an honorary auntie to you?"

"Ornery auntie?"

"Hmm, I hope you won't think I'm ornery, sweetie." Susan chuckled.

Val laughed. "Susan means like a pretend auntie. Someone who isn't auntie but who can be nice and love you like one."

Val hadn't thought much about all the relatives Hetty and Paul had been missing, although she should have. Having never been around a large extended family of aunts, uncles, and grandparents, and cousins, she'd not considered all Hetty had lost by this move. Yet, when Val was the same age, she had been separated from her family members.

Sweat broke out on her brow. She understood loss—but she was still so overwhelmed by her own situation, that she'd not been sensitive to Hetty's feelings. At least not like she ought to be.

Hetty stuck her tongue to the side of her opened mouth.

Susan hugged the little girl. "You'll see them again if your daddy takes you there for the winter pause."

Val gaped. She'd not thought of that. Paul didn't have to stay on Mackinac Island. He could go home once the light went untended during the winter.

The girl pulled her finger from her mouth. "Daddy says when ice comes, we go home."

"That's right," Susan kissed the top of the child's head. She was immediately more affectionate than Val was with her. "When the Straits ice over."

Paul and Hetty would be leaving her. And he'd never said a word to her about returning to Shepherd.

She'd be free to pursue custody of her brother and sister then, so why was her heart heavy instead of glad?

Chapter Twenty-One

*J*aw aching from clenching his teeth, Paul paced in front of the orphanage.

How had his well-laid plans crashed down in a single day? And by Zumbrun's interference. And Georgina—who could even trust that she was mentally stable? Her choice of husband certainly didn't bear evidence of clear thinking. Lee Hudgins was an annoyance at best and a pie-in-the-sky lunatic at worst with his crazy inventions.

God help me. Since Annabelle had died that had been his simple prayer so many times. Thousands of times.

He inhaled a sharp breath, entered the building, and then found his way to the younger children's playroom. But Hetty wasn't inside.

Little Francesca walked up the hallway, holding a wiggling cat. "*Buon pomeriggio, signor* Scholtus."

"Hello, Francesca. How have you been feeling."

"I feel good. *Grazie* for saving me when I choke."

He smiled. "Glad God put me there to help."

"Yes." She stroked the cat. "Lizzie is best kitty."

"There she is!" Zumbrun strode into the building as if he owned the place—just like he acted around Valerie.

Why was he intent upon finding the little girl?

When Zumbrun reached them, he lifted Francesca in the air and spun her around, the cat hissing.

"Let them down!" Poor girl was going to end up scratched.

Zumbrun glared at him while the cat mewled and Francesca tried to comfort Lizzie. The man suddenly beamed at someone behind Paul.

"Are you stirring up trouble, Lawrence?" Susan's clear voice carried as she came alongside him, Hetty in tow.

"Hold me, Daddy." Circles under his daughter's eyes told of her exciting day.

Susan bent beside Hetty. "Remember what I told you? I have to talk with your daddy alone."

Hetty nodded.

Susan huffed a breath. "Lawrence, could you keep an eye on the children while I speak with Paul?"

"Certainly. I'll take the girls outside." Zumbrun mussed Francesca's hair. "Unless you have somewhere you need to go."

The girl shook her dark head, and the trio turned and left.

Paul ran his hand along his jawline. Was Susan going to tell him Valerie wouldn't be coming back?

He needed Valerie there. Only she wasn't Valerie, the former lighthouse keeper's daughter—she was someone else entirely.

Wasn't she?

Or was something of their blossoming friendship real?

"Could you please bring a box to the wharf for me?" Susan tilted her head, just like she'd done as a child when requesting a favor.

This was her big concern? He pointed to his rucksack. "That's all I have to tote back with me. How big is this box?"

"I can carry my own bag, but I found a bunch of old books from our littlest orphans' room that I have permission to bring."

"I'll bring the books." It dawned on him that he'd been warned about Susan's cooking. "We have a children's cookbook that Val and Hetty have been using."

"Oh." She looked as guilty as she did when she'd snuck cookies from the cookie jar. "Does Hetty have any favorites in it?"

They could live on pancakes for two days.

Crisp late afternoon air, full of the musky scent of decaying leaves enveloped Valerie as she walked with Georgie along West Bluff toward Hubbard's Annex. Thankfully, the earlier gusty winds had settled to bare exhalations like that of an infant sleeping. "If you've only recently married, shouldn't you still be with your husband on your honeymoon?"

"How droll that you're more concerned about me than yourself." Georgie had changed into a fashionable tan tweed walking suit with low-heeled boots, while Valerie remained dressed as she'd arrived.

In truth, not only was she concerned about her shoes, whose leather soles couldn't take much more wear, but of more concern—had she made a terrible mistake? This woman, this stranger, talked so rapidly that Valerie had a hard time keeping up with her words, much less to consider them.

"As I was saying, Valentine, our parents spent a considerable fortune searching for you."

She flinched. The words felt accusatory. A little part of her burrowed deeper under her frayed cloak.

"To no avail. All those years we looked and looked." Georgie continued, but Valentine didn't pay attention.

To the left, the sometimes-wild waters of the Straits were calm today. She could remain placid herself. She only needed to go deeper yet inside, like she had all these years.

"And of course, our dear mother was broken—simply devastated by your disappearance." Georgie continued speaking about how everyone from their parents, to siblings, and friends had been crushed.

If I stay here, further in, if I tune her out like I did Mum—not my mum but Dorcas—I can get through these next two days.

She'd try something that helped when Mum, Dorcas, was on a rant. "Tell me about something happy. Tell me about Lee."

Georgie cast her a sideways look as they took the sharp curve toward the Annex. "Are you all right?"

"Yes. Perfectly fine." Val forced a smile, as she'd done thousands of times over the years. "Happy to find you. And I want to hear about your new husband."

Georgie sniffed as she focused her attention ahead on the dirt drive. "Beyond ecstatic to discover you, too!" Again, the accusatory tone.

Could Val last another day? No. She couldn't do this. An unexpected longing for the solitude of the lighthouse almost overcame her. "How much farther is the house?"

"You really don't remember, do you?"

"No."

"The Booth-Moores' house is that one." She pointed to a three-story white home with aqua-blue shutters. "Lee will love it up here. This home was always kept well-maintained."

Was her husband coming up? "Isn't he in Detroit?"

"He is, but I sent a few telegrams off."

Valerie stopped and stared hard at the woman beside her. Who had she told? "You said my disappearance was fodder for the yellow journalists for over a decade." Was the woman that dense? Even Valerie understood that if news of her reappearance got out then their parents, across the sea in England, would be devastated to read it in the news. She turned on her heel.

"Where are you going?"

"Back to town, even if I have to walk." Hopefully, she'd arrive before the sun began to set.

"Oh, please don't!" Georgie grabbed the back of Valerie's cape.

A rip sounded, as a breeze pierced her torn outer garment. Tears filled her eyes. "This is my only covering."

Georgie rushed in front of her and grasped her elbows. "Oh my! I'm the worst of sisters. I know it. I'm babbling on about me. I've not even noticed the condition you or your clothing are in. All I cared about is that you're here with me." She pulled Valerie into an embrace and began to sob.

Valerie sniffed as she patted her sister's back. "I've got to get word to our parents—that's why I must get to town. Don't fret."

"I've already sent word." Georgie pulled away. "And please don't do that—don't try to comfort me when you are hurting."

Her sister's face, just then, reminded Valerie of their mother's. She'd have that same wrinkled brow but with love etched on her features—unlike Dorcas's face when she was upset. Valerie dipped her chin as yet another gust made her shiver.

"Let's get you back to our cottage and into some suitable clothing." Georgie eyed her, head-to-toe. "I don't think my things will fit you. But we'll round up a dressmaker."

"It's off-season."

Blinking, Georgie stepped back, then swiveled to link arms with her. "We'll figure it out. There have to be people who can help us."

People who can help us. This was the first time, in years and years, that an abundance of helpers had finally appeared.

What had taken God so long to send them?

Off Bois Blanc Island

Pounding waves echoed Susan's heart, as she, Paul, and Hetty traversed the Straits of Mackinac. Billy Lloyd got them there in no time, despite the whitecaps threatening to form.

On the Round Island shoreline, three stacked piles of rocks of differing heights greeted them on the beach.

Hetty pointed. "Thems my rock peoples."

"Are they friendly?"

"They frensly."

Paul grinned at Susan as she began to rise.

"Sit tight, Miss Johnson, until we come ashore."

"Oh, yes! Sorry Billy!"

When they reached the shore, Paul held her hand as she got out of the boat, his grip warm and firm—that of a man and not the boy she'd once known so well. Did she really know him anymore? *I plan to catch up on all his news.*

"What do you think, Susie? Is it like you imagined it all those years ago?"

She blinked.

All those years ago, when she and Paulie sat in their sandpit out of sight of their mothers and filled it with water, then built a village with rocks.

Paulie piled a bunch of flatter stones on top of each other. "That's the lighthouse I'm going to be in charge of when we live by the water."

"And away from all this land." Susie, too, longed for a home by the Great Lakes, ever since their neighbor's son, Mr. Welling, had shown them a painting of his son's inn on Mackinac Island.

"But where are all the lighthouses at?"

"Oh, they're here and there. But I'm going to have a nice new one for my own."

"And I'll stay home and take care of our dogs and cats." She drew pictures in the dryer part of the dirt."

"What about children?"

"Two boys and two girls." She nodded emphatically. "And two dogs and two cats."

"All right then." Paulie tossed sand at her, and she hurled some back.

"You all right?" Paul asked, returning her from her memory.

"Yes." She pressed a hand to her chest. "I was just remembering that huge sandpit we had in your yard."

"A mud pit when it rained." A grin slid over his face.

"How our mothers fussed at us."

"Ha! Stripped us down and tossed our muddy clothes in to soak."

Her face heated, thinking of this as an adult. She hurriedly said, "We were the King and Queen of messes according to my mother." She straightened her skirt. "Speaking of which, I shall be Queen of the Pumpkins while Lawrence shall be the Pumpkin King for the Harvest Festival."

"Aha." A strange look crossed his face. "What does Val think about that?"

"I didn't tell her." Why should she?

Hetty, that sweet bundle of joy, raised her arms. "Carry me, Miss Susan! Pweez!"

Susan pressed her hands to her chest and feigned a sigh before she scooped the girl into her arms.

Billy Lloyd carried one last box up to the house. It appeared full of bakery goods from Rebecca Christy's shop. "Gotta shove off soon."

She nodded.

The boy's face was full of worry. "I hope you'll be all right out here, Miss Susan."

"Why wouldn't she be?" Paul gave the youth a penetrating stare.

"That Mr. Lawrence fella seemed mighty concerned about her."

Susan shook her head.

"Probably just jealous—with you two being old friends." Billy saluted, then pushed off.

Susan set Hetty down. "Go make another rock person, one for me." Then she turned to Paul. "I hope you don't think I said anything that would have made Lawrence jealous of you."

Val had told Paul that Susan had spoken very highly of him and his family. She'd said it had made her feel comfortable coming out to the lighthouse. Had Val said similar things to Lawrence?

186

The breeze from the Straits flapped Paul's jacket around him as the Lloyd boy maneuvered his boat toward Mackinac Island.

Hetty ran to him. "Daddy never asweep today!"

He'd pulled lighthouse duty the previous night and did need to sleep soon.

Susan lifted her skirts slightly as she stepped over the rocky soil toward them. "I'm so happy to be here."

"I'm sure you and Hetty will have great fun together."

"You, too, Daddy. We all have fun."

Susan laughed. "I think your father may be asleep most of the time I am here."

"Not the whole time." He must have blurted that out faster and louder than he intended because Susan's eyes widened. She'd become a beautiful woman. No wonder Zumbrun seemed so infatuated with her. "I'll be awake some, but I have to sleep before I man the light tomorrow night." Thank goodness for the relief worker and the assistant lighthouse keeper.

"Lovely. Let's play some games together and talk before you sleep." Susan leaned in closer. "And I bet I'll beat you lots!"

A chuckle began deep in his chest and grew. "That's what you always used to say to me."

"And I was right, wasn't I?"

He raised his eyebrows. "Often enough. Especially at marbles. I sure lost a lot to you."

Hetty slowly looked between him and Susan. "You good frens, Daddy. Not fambly though."

Susan scrunched her fine features. "No, not like your aunts and uncles and grandma and grandpa."

"Unka Ron make you laugh like her do, Daddy."

Susan grinned. "Oh my heavens, Ron was such a character. I bet he made you laugh, too, Hetty, you imp." She made an adorable face at Hetty and then touched her nose.

"I not imp! They bad."

"Not all imps are bad." Susan bent and cupped her hands around her mouth and whispered in his little girl's ear. "There used to be two very good imps on your grandparents' farm."

He grinned at her exaggerated whisper.

"Really?" Hetty's face reflected disbelief.

Susan straightened. "Yup."

"What their names?" Hetty took Paul's hand and squeezed.

Paul bent and kissed his daughter. "Paulie and Susie."

"And they had a lot of good fun together, those imps." Susan winked.

Good fun. That was just what they all needed to distract them. Because Val's absence had changed something for him on this tiny Round Island.

Would his Valerie return to them?

To him?

And why should he think of her as his when the poor young woman was only just discovering who she truly was?

"Come on, let's get you settled." He led Susan inside and showed her to her room.

"I think I'll grab my shawl."

"It's a little chilly in here today. We can add some wood to the stove."

"I'll be fine." She bent and pulled a pink, green, and light orangey shawl from her bag. "Do you remember this?"

She smiled, but inside, his heart fell. Annabelle and he had only been about thirteen when they'd gone to the fair with her parents. She'd worn the thick scarf and had complained about it. She wanted her father, a banker, to buy her a new one she'd seen in a vendor's stall there. "I remember."

As much as he wanted to enshrine his wife as a saint, her behavior that day became a consistent pattern over the years. She'd given Susan the pretty shawl out of a desire for something more—which her father later supplied when she explained how she'd gifted her own to "that poor Johnson girl whose parents died." When her mother praised Annabelle for her act of charity and kindness, Paul had forced himself to bite his tongue—a habit that he endured for years to come.

"I thought it was very kind of her." Susan wrapped the now well-worn wrap around her shoulders.

Kindness was what Valerie Fillman displayed every day—always thinking of others. He rubbed the back of his head. Annabelle would have been an excellent actress. "I'm glad you think so." He clapped his hands. "Now, let's see who'll win our first game of dominoes."

"I gonna win. I gonna knock 'em all over."

Paul needed to take his wife off her pedestal and knock that over to make room for a future for his daughter and himself. Having Susan there may help with that process.

🍁

Lawrence surveyed the domestic scene before him. Ada on the settee with her daughter on her lap, reading a picture book to her, Peter in his upholstered chair, and Jack on the red wool rug.

"Are you certain your family is fine with my father bringing my dog here?" Lawrence re-read the telegram from his father.

Peter looked up from reading the Detroit Free Press. "Poor thing is probably out of condition." He pointed to Jack who was doing the push-ups Lawrence had requested. "Unlike my son, who has run and biked and performed calisthenics every day."

Lawrence closed one eye in consideration. "Darby can't do calisthenics nor bike, but he does need to run with Jack and me. My father's idea of a brisk walk is once around the block, stopping to speak with each of his neighbors as he goes."

Peter nodded. "Sounds like most pet owners—not fanatics like you."

"Now, Peter." Ada cast him a quelling glance. "But we do have to think about future housing for Susan and Lawrence with his dog and her cat."

"We'll get to that when we have to," he harrumphed.

"Your favorite saying." His wife sighed.

Lawrence couldn't stay with the Wellings indefinitely. But the employee housing wouldn't be built until the spring. Perhaps Susan could continue living with Madame Mirandette. Or maybe. . . Pine Cottage would be the perfect size for a young couple to fill up with pets and. . . more. He could picture children in that large yard.

Ada turned the book's page. "I'm grateful Robert and Sadie are bringing our materials for the Harvest Festival with them. They found some fun things in Detroit for us."

Jack collapsed onto the rug, feigning exhaustion. "I think you're trying to kill me."

"You saw how things were last spring at the American Marathon in Boston, son."

Jack sat up. "Their first one was amazing. But what about the one at the Olympics?" His eyes lit up.

Lawrence had been shocked when he'd learned the Wellings had traveled to Greece for the Olympics in 1896. He began working with the youngster shortly after they returned.

"Thank goodness for your sponsors, Jack." Mr. Welling turned his attention back to his newspaper.

"Oh, yeah, I'm grateful." Jack's lips scrunched up like they did when he was contrite. "But hey, Larry, how's Susan gonna know her pal Tara is arriving here tomorrow?"

Lawrence expelled a slow breath. "Billy Lloyd said Susan and Hetty will come to town tomorrow while Paul is sleeping. Then Billy will take Val and Hetty back later to the lighthouse."

Peter lowered his paper. "Billy will make two trips tomorrow, so we can't ask him for more. Susan will hear the news when Billy picks her up tomorrow."

Jack nimbly rose from the floor. "Mr. Hop can tell her about the telegram."

"Mr. Hop?" Lawrence hadn't heard the name before.

Mr. Welling waved toward the door. "If you can catch him."

Jack was out of the house like a shot.

"Darling, you know Mr. Haapala's English is limited. How would she understand him with that Finnish accent?"

"Doesn't matter." Peter chuckled.

"Why?" Lawrence rose from his seat at the desk and stretched.

"Haapala leaves like clockwork with supplies—has to be gone by now."

"Then why did you send him?"

"You were going to have him run extra today anyway, so why not now?" Peter went back to reading his newspaper.

Lawrence grabbed his jacket. "I'm going to Mrs. Martin's to check on rooms for Cousin Tara, her husband, Bertie, and my father." And while he was there, he'd ask the lady what she knew about the big house across the street—Pine Cottage—and its availability in the spring.

Chicago

"Another telegram, Mrs. Booth-Moore." From the high color on Lucy's cheeks, this message was important—either that or the young woman had a fever. Her assistant quickly padded over the Aubusson rug to Carrie's desk.

"I only just dashed down my thoughts on the previous one." Her chest squeezed, and she resisted the urge to grab another of her heart pills. Valentine Gladstone's petite, diamond, Vitellio bracelet had emerged after all these years. Her hands trembled as she accepted the new telegram. "Did you read it?"

"Yes, ma'am." She curtseyed. "As instructed."

Carrie rotated her hand in the air, irritated. "So tell me." Still, she reached for her reading glasses.

Miss Gladstone has been found.

Hands spasming, the telegram dropped to the desktop. The telegram, from Georgina Gladstone, stated 'Valentine here on Mackinac Island' in the first line.

Dear merciful God, thank You. But was it true? Georgie, for all her foibles, had seemed perfectly fine at her wedding this past weekend. And her husband, Lee, although high-strung, was a rock for the young woman.

"Lady Georgina asks if she may open Wedding Cottage for her sister, since Apple Blossom cottage is occupied by all those—"

"Veterans?" Carrie sucked in a breath. "Yes, of course." She scanned the rest of the message. *Nothing.* Was the moment really here?

"Mrs. Booth-Moore?"

"Yes?"

"You can count on me to keep this quiet, of course, but. . ."

As the realization hit her, Carrie opened her top drawer, removed her tin of pills, and swallowed two. "Come take a response. And we have several other telegrams to send, too." Before any journalists got wind of this. *Oh Georgie, why couldn't you have used the code we'd created for just such an event?* Was it those years of dissipation? Had they affected her mental faculties? Or was it the joy of finding her beloved long-lost sister?

Lucy strode to her ow

n nearby desk, sat, and then retrieved her writing pad and fountain pen.

"Before we start, I have to do something." Carrie rang the summons bell. There was so much to be done.

Where to start?

Telegrams.

Chapter Twenty-Two

Straits of Mackinac

*T*ara Mulcahey practically buzzed with electricity—like all those wires going up around the country were conducting. She'd never been on a Great Lakes ship before, but that wasn't the cause of her giddiness. *I can hardly wait to see Susan Marie, after all these years.*

Captain Robert Swaine, who wasn't steering the ship that day, led Tara and Bertie, her husband, followed by Christian Zumbrun and a hound dog, to the side windows. Swaine pointed out over the turquoise waves of Lake Huron to Mackinac Island, which was finally within view. "We're almost there."

Her husband quirked an eyebrow at her. After so many years of marriage, she knew exactly what he was thinking. *Who're all these people in this motley crew and are we really considering staying here?*

Mrs. Swaine, a pretty young blond woman and trained nurse, remained seated at their table where they'd played cards. The Swaines' son, Robbie, peeked out from beneath the linen tablecloth. "Go home?" he asked.

The captain retrieved his boy and hoisted him aloft. "Almost there."

Robbie patted his father's bearded cheeks.

"He wants you to shave off that infernal beard." Sadie Swaine's voice held what Tara recognized as an unspoken wifely threat. She resisted the urge to chuckle.

Christian Zumbrun turned from the window. "Makes him look like a genuine captain."

"Makes him look old," Sadie mumbled.

"Mature." Bertie wrapped an arm around her.

"Please do not be referring to me as mature-looking," Tara warned him. She whispered, "Mature is a euphemism for old."

"Never old nor mature-looking, lovie." He kissed her forehead.

The steamship's horn blared, the hound barked, and then howled. Sadie covered her ears. Tara did the same as the men simply cringed.

Christopher sat on a bench by the window and pulled the dog, which had to be a good forty pounds, onto the lap of his green plaid business suit. His waistcoat buttons strained—possibly more from the luscious meal they'd been served aboard ship than from any extra bulk he carried. "Lawrence loves this dog like a child. I'll be darned glad—"

Sadie cleared her throat. "Ladies aboard."

"Yes, sorry. Jenny and I will be awfully happy when our boy takes a wife and gets the dozen or more children he's always wanted."

"A dozen kiddies?" Bertie's Cockney accent thickened whenever he spoke of children. "Why I'd 'ave been 'appy wi' even one." When everyone looked at him, his face flushed, and he shrugged.

Christian continued patting Lawrence's dog, which he was returning to him. "Full house and all that—like we had at home. Not that we made it to a dozen, though."

"Lots more little cousins for me, thank you!" Tara had loved visiting her cousin and her children, and they'd regularly received holiday invitations.

"And lots more hounds amongst all yer kiddies." Bertie gestured toward Christian. "Ye started Lawrence on the hounds all those years ago."

Christian scratched behind the hound's ear. "Darby is happy now that he's getting petted."

Captain Swaine grinned. "I'm happy, too. I won a round of pinochle, two rounds of Aces, as well as a checker game on the trip up." Swaine gave a short laugh. "And my poor wife didn't have to entertain Robbie on her own."

"We were happy to play with your sweetie." Tara had read the boy several books, sang with him, and watched him during his nap so that the captain and his wife could walk the ship alone for a bit. Bertie had stacked blocks with Robbie after his nap and had worked puzzles and then carried him around as though the boy was a ship plowing through the water. Frankly, though, she was a bit worn out, even with the rest during the card games. She wasn't a spring chicken anymore.

"You two need some grandchildren to spoil. . ." Christian cut himself short. Was he thinking about the fact that they'd asked about adult adoption? About their intent to make Susan their heir of whatever earthly goods they had when they were both gone? Or was he hopeful, as they were, that perhaps Susan and Lawrence might one day secure a future together and produce said grandchildren?

What if Susan didn't want anything to do with Tara once she got there? Her letters had been very encouraging, though. And Lawrence wrote that he'd explained to her about how she and Bertie had tried to seek custody, but to no avail.

Swaine and his wife, who weren't privy to the discussions, exchanged a strange look. Robert set his son down, and the boy toddled under the table again. "My parents are gone, God rest their souls, as is my mother-in-law, and my father-in law is—"

"Somewhat of an invalid," his wife finished for him. "But we have many islander friends who've made up for the grandparenting Robbie has missed out on."

Tara knew Christian, her cousin's husband, felt terrible about the advice he'd given as a young attorney, to Jacqueline Cadotte Swaine, the captain's mother. Christian hadn't specified what Mrs. Swaine had done, only that she'd sought to provide for her children and grandchildren when she was gone. Christian had met with Captain Swaine, who'd kindly offered to transport not only Christian but Tara and Bertie up to Mackinac Island on his ship. What a kind gesture, especially since Christian said he wasn't sure what more he could do for the captain and the other family members.

The door to the wood-paneled room opened and the steward stepped in. "Ship's ready to dock, Captain, if ya care to join the crew."

"No, thanks, Lasley. I'll stay right here."

The fellow saluted Swaine. "Suit yerself, sir." He spun on his heel and departed.

"Better sit, folks, while we get docked." Captain Swaine motioned those standing to sit.

Tara and Bertie stepped to the table and took their seats. She followed Sadie's example and began gathering the cards and placing them back in their containers.

How would the rest of their cards play out today?

A sudden wind whipped around Susan and Lawrence as they stepped out of the orphanage, where she'd left Hetty in the young children's room. The little girl seemed happy to have playmates.

Lawrence pulled his shoulders higher. "Glad it was calm when Billy brought you back."

"And when the ship came in." Susan shook her head in disbelief that Tara was really there. "Can't believe we're heading down to the docks to greet Tara."

They crossed the street since the approaching dray was far enough off to safely do so. Then they hurried toward the docks, gusts of intense wind puffed and then disappeared. *Not many people out.*

A horn blasted, but Lawrence didn't react.

She turned to him. "I'm proud of you."

"Oh?"

"You didn't jump."

He grinned. "I guess I'm becoming a Mackinac Islander."

"I guess you are!" She wanted to hug him and kiss his cheek.

"Tara and Bertie will be here soon. Are you excited?"

She rubbed her arms. "Yes." How would things go?

As they approached the wharf, workers rolled carts toward the end of the dock. A wildly waving flag fell flat as the wind settled.

"Sister Mary Lou is expecting some items for the Harvest Festival." Lawrence took her arm.

Her breath caught in her throat. He felt so right—being there beside her. She looked up into his amber eyes. She could lose herself in those golden depths.

He quirked his eyebrows. "Captain Swaine promised to have a few things picked up in Detroit."

"Anything unusual?"

"Not really. Just a lion, a monkey, and a tiger."

She turned toward him. "What?"

"The look on your face is priceless." Lawrence laughed.

"Let me guess." She pressed her index finger into her cheek. "Are those costumes?"

"They are." Lawrence inclined his head closer to hers. "Jack said he is dressing up for the bit with circus animals devouring all the pumpkins, corn, and other vegetables that have been harvested. But they won't touch the green stuff—no spinach or broccoli for them."

"Jack is a delight."

"My father says he's glad none of us were like Jack, though—he wouldn't have known what to do with him."

"Mr. Welling and his wife seem to know what to do. And to hear Jack tell it, you're like a second father to him."

"I'm his coach, not a second father. Good gracious, I'm not old enough to be his father."

"It sounds like you possess the same fatherly instincts that Mr. Welling has."

"I hope so." He looked down at her with those warm assessing eyes.

What did he see? A spinster hanging on his every word? A woman with no prospects? A fellow employee and co-worker? Those eyes seemed to say more—much more. Would he ask her to dinner tonight, or would he be with his father while he was here? Susan would be with Mr. and Mrs. Mulcahey, so she'd be busy, too.

The ship, now moored alongside the wharf, let down its ramp. A large man in a navy coat and tan work pants rolled three huge, stacked boxes forward. He tipped them back on the dolly, and carefully brought them down to the dock.

Captain Swaine, a handsome man with prematurely graying hair, and his wife descended the ramp. Behind them, an older gentleman carried their son, while a matron, attired in a wool day suit moved alongside the two.

Susan pressed her hands to her mouth. "Auntie Tara."

Tears pricked her eyes. It'd been twenty years since she'd seen her mother's dear friend. Her hair had grayed, but as Susan rushed toward her, that spark in Tara's light eyes shone as she opened her arms to Susan.

"Susan, it's so good to see you again after all this time."

Susan held Tara close, her face soaked with happy tears, and she inhaled the woman's peachy rose scent—the same as she used to wear.

A dog barked.

Susan stepped back to spy a distinguished-looking man struggling with a hound.

Then the pup broke loose and ran.

The carriage Georgina had procured dropped Val at the docks. She stepped out and hurried to the wharf's edge. By the ship, Lawrence shook hands with Captain and Mrs. Swaine, while Susan embraced an older woman as a man holding a toddler watched.

A hound dog bayed and pulled free from the suited gentleman holding him. It charged toward Lawrence and jumped into his arms.

Val stopped where she was as her head began to ache.

"This is our family dog, Valentine. She's a hound. She has lots of babies. Puppies that is." Young Lawrence scratched his nose. "One day I'm gonna have one of her grandpuppies for my own."

"Now, son, don't count your chickens before they're hatched."

"Don't you mean eggs, Dad?"

"That's not the expression."

"Besides, dogs don't have eggs, and they don't give you chickens. You get puppies." Lawrence grinned at this bit of wisdom, which made sense to Valentine, so she nodded.

"Never mind." Mr. Zumbrun patted the dog. "She's a good girl, aren't you?"

"She's the best. But I want my own one day."

"I'm gonna have ten or twenty on my grandfather's estate one day." Her brother asserted.

"Nuh uh." Georgie crinkled her nose. "Father won't inherit so you won't live in nasty old England where it's cold all the time."

"Isn't that why we're going over there? I thought our granddad was givin' us the place." Her brother scowled.

"I don't think your father would like to hear you bragging about your grandfather, the Marquess." Mr. Zumbrun shook his finger at them. "He'd tell you that's not good form."

That imitation did sound just like Father, with his funny accent.

"Here, Valentine, you hold her." Lawrence shoved the pup at her.

The dark-eyed dog licked Valentine's face and she laughed.

At the end of the wharf, Lawrence pushed the dog down and bent to pet it. The man with him said something. That had to be his father. He looked between Lawrence and Val and even from this distance, she could see that he'd paled. He removed his handkerchief from his coat pocket and pressed it against his brow.

Mrs. Swaine turned toward them and then she shouted as Lawrence's father sank onto a large wooden bench. The lawyer clutched at his chest as his white handkerchief fluttered to the wharf's walkway.

Val hurried toward them. Captain Swaine and Lawrence each took Mr. Zumbrun by a shoulder and laid him down on the wide bench.

"Bring my medical bag!" Nurse Swaine called to a porter.

What had happened?

Why had he told his father about Valentine right here? Lawrence mentally kicked himself. As soon as Lawrence had explained to him about confirming her identity, Father had broken into a sweat, his ruddy complexion paled.

"Do you have heart problems, Mr. Zumbrun?" Sadie leaned close over Father and took his pulse.

Father stared up wide-eyed but didn't respond.

"He doesn't as far as I know." Lawrence fisted, then opened, his hands.

Sadie fixed hard blue eyes on him. "Did you just subject him to a shock?"

"Yes. I told him news that upset him."

"Greatly disturbed him, quite obviously." She frowned.

If something happened to Father. If he died of a heart attack because of shock over Valentine Gladstone, then what would he do? For one thing, he'd be done with that family once and for all. She was moving toward them now. He had a good mind to tell her—

"Lawrence, does your father have any significant ailments?" Sadie directed her question toward him as she took her kit from the porter. She pulled out a stethoscope.

"He smokes a pipe. Mother hates that—wants him to quit."

"I mean does he see a physician for anything?"

Lawrence had left home and gone to school farther away from the family than had his siblings. He'd grown weary of the recurring, and upsetting, conversations about Father's friend, Lord Gladstone, and his missing daughter. Yet it had been Lawrence who'd resumed the search, albeit tentatively, after his father and brothers had given up their efforts.

Lawrence leaned in. Father was breathing but his face contorted in pain. His fingers had that odd appearance they got in winter if he'd not donned gloves—like now.

Sadie opened Father's waistcoat and listened to his heart. All fell silent. Only the squawk of a seagull and someone coughing nearby competed with the sounds of the waves lapping against the wharf.

"Normal," she announced.

"My chest hurts." Father took a shuddering breath.

"His fingertips are turning blue." Mrs. Mulcahey pressed her hand to her mouth.

Susan's dark eyes widened in horror.

Sadie lifted his left hand. "Yes, and they're cold."

From the panicked expression on Father's face, did he believe he was dying? Lawrence moved forward and took his father's free hand.

"Tell Jenny. . . tell your mother that I've always loved her."

"She knows that." Lawrence assumed his best coach voice. "Nurse Sadie says your heart is beating just fine. Stay calm. Try to breathe normally."

Father gave an almost imperceptible nod. His lips began to open and close in a more rhythmic pattern.

"Good. Slowly breathe in and then out again."

Val had edged closer behind him. Lawrence wanted to yell at her to go away and leave them alone. Hadn't she done enough?

But what had she done except to survive? He was angrier at himself for not preparing his father better for this encounter.

Father locked eyes on Val's face and stared. "Those pretty violet eyes." He smiled. "So unusual."

"Thank you, sir." Val sank down beside him.

"But not so lovely a color on one's fingertips." Sadie pressed a hand against Father's forehead.

Valentine cocked her head. "I've seen this before—a long time ago."

"Where?" Lawrence blurted out. *Dear God, don't let her say that dying people manifested this change.*

Chapter Twenty-Three

*W*ith all eyes locked on her and poor Mr. Zumbrun lying there, Val struggled to find her voice. "A cook in one of our lumber camps had this discoloration happen when her hands got cold."

"Raynaud's?" Lawrence suddenly recalled Mother calling this oddity by that name.

"That's my thought as well," Sadie agreed.

Father lifted his hands. "Jenny called it Raynaud's Phenomenon."

Lawrence turned to face the nurse. "But what would that have to do with his chest pain?"

Sadie checked Mr. Zumbrun's heartbeat again. "Good, strong heartbeat but we'll get the doctor here and see what he thinks. My suspicion is that it's likely related to the Raynaud's. Or from this shock he's received." She narrowed her eyes at Lawrence, who blushed.

Val confessed her own ailment. "I get something like that, too. Here." She pressed the middle of her chest. "When I'm really upset. It's like a terrible squeezing, and I feel faint. But it goes away."

Sadie nodded. "That happens to some people when something upsets them terribly. But why is Mr. Zumbrun disturbed by seeing you?"

Color seeped back to the man's cheeks, and he struggled to get up onto his elbows, but Lawrence pressed him down. "Stay put."

Susan's friend, Mrs. Mulcahey, stepped toward Val. "Is it really you, Valentine? I see both Percy and Eugenie in you."

Nurse Sadie cocked her head. "Aren't you the lighthouse keeper's daughter?"

Mr. Zumbrun shoved Lawrence's hand away and sat up. "That's Lady Verity Gladstone, daughter of Lord and Lady Gladstone, who has been missing for more than fifteen years."

"Is that true?" Sadie Swaine gaped at her.

"I believe so."

Sadie huffed a sigh and put her stethoscope back in her medical bag. "I still think Mr. Zumbrun should see Dr. Cadotte."

"I'm fine. Just a shock, like you said." Mr. Zumbrun re-buttoned his waistcoat.

"Put some gloves on, Father. It's cool today." Lawrence removed his own and passed them to his father as the breeze lifted again, but calmer than before.

Val gestured to the ship. "Was it hot inside the cabin?"

The toddler began kicking in the stroller, and his father went to him.

Mrs. Mulcahey, who was still staring at Val, coughed. "It was a bit. . . I hate to say stifling in there, but yes, it was a bit warm. I was surprised."

Susan took the matron's arm. "But you're all right, aren't you?"

"The sun was streaming through the windows, that's all. So it was warm." Sadie turned her gaze on her son, who was stretching his arms toward his mother. "We should have opened the portholes."

Val moved closer to Mr. Zumbrun, whose fingertips still looked discolored. That nagging sense of guilt she always carried had intensified. "The camp cook had a few episodes like this—of chest pain—when she went from the hot cook house outside in the winter. The shift in temperature did something."

"Is that right? And she had this infernal Raynaud's thing?" Zumbrun pointed to his fingertips and then donned Lawrence's gloves.

"Yes. She couldn't afford to go back to the doctor. But the other cooks made her stay inside, and the camp boss put her and her husband in the shack closest to the cookhouse. That pretty much stopped her from having those chest pains."

"You should still see Dr. Cadotte," Sadie repeated, this time with a substantial bite in her tone.

"I'll get a taxi to take us to the clinic straightaway." Lawrence assisted his father to stand. "Are you okay to walk?"

His father stood. He smiled at Val. "I feel fine. Does Percy know?"

"My sister, Georgie, cabled him."

"Very good." He took two tentative steps forward. "I'm all right now. Just a shock. But a very good shock. I am delighted. So giddy—an unusual feeling. I confess I've not felt it since this one was born." He gestured to Lawrence.

"Well, you need to settle that giddiness down, Father, before you feel faint again."

"Yes." He stared at Valentine. "I cannot believe my eyes."

She angled her body away from the lifting breeze. "May I call on you before I leave for the lighthouse?"

"The lighthouse?" Mr. Zumbrun narrowed his eyes and looked between her, Lawrence, and Susan. "Lady Verity is living at a lighthouse?"

"She's staying at Apple Blossom Cottage right now, Father, but she'll be at the Round Island Lighthouse. And I'll explain it all later."

"Georgina and I discussed it, and Hetty and I could stay until tomorrow. We could return when Paul will be awake tomorrow afternoon instead of today. Give Billy a break."

Lawrence pointed toward the building whitecaps. "I'm not sure you'd have had a choice. It's getting rough out there."

"Before I forget," Val splayed her fingers, "Georgie asked Mrs. Booth-Moore if we could use the Wedding Cottage, if all of you would like to stay there."

"They have rooms at Mrs. Martin's, right across the way." Lawrence pointed toward Bogan Lane. "But thank you for asking."

Georgie hadn't heard back yet from Mrs. Booth-Moore, so perhaps this was for the best. But she'd told Val that she assumed Mrs. Booth-Moore would agree and Georgie knew how to gain entry to Wedding Cottage.

She went to Susan and gave her a quick hug. "Thank you for taking my place."

Susan grasped her elbows. "Will you really return to the lighthouse?"

"God willing." That was something her true mother used to say. And long ago, Val wondered if God had willed for her to be taken. Yes, there were forces that worked against the Lord, but His will was never for evil.

No matter what, she had to trust in the Lord, that was what Mother had said. And it was true. In her weakest moments, He was the thread she'd held onto—the presence she felt there and would never forget. As His Word said, God could return good for the evil done, and she was counting on that promise. He was already fulfilling it.

England

Eugenie set her needlework in her lap when someone knocked on Percy's office door.

"Enter," Percy called from his desk.

Her husband's manservant clutched something behind his back as he joined them. The normally placid servant had bright red splotches on his pale face. Something must be terribly wrong.

Percy pushed back from his desk. "What is it?"

"There are several telegrams for you, my lord."

"Urgent?"

The servants sometimes read their telegrams. The telegram operators weren't always the most discreet either. What was in there that alarmed the man so?

"Give them to me." Percy extended his hand. "I'm sure you've examined who the sender is, so don't try to pretend." His curt voice, so unlike his normal manner, made Eugenie flinch.

"One from Lady Georgina, one from Mrs. Booth-Moore, and another from—

"Georgie and Carrie both?" Eugenie set her work aside. "I hope all is well."

Irritation creased Percy's handsome face. "And the other?"

"Lord Gladstone, that one purports to be from Lady Valentine."

"What?" Eugenie and Percy blurted out the question at the same time.

If she hadn't been seated, she might have swooned.

But they'd been through so many imposters over the years. They'd both had enough of it. Percy scowled. "Hand them over!"

On unsteady legs, Eugenie went to her husband's side.

"Let's start with the one from Georgie." Hands shaking, he grasped the three telegrams and located their daughter's.

"Shall I await your responses, milord?"

"Not now." Percy barked.

The poor servant slipped from the room, closing the door as he went.

Eugenie peered over her husband's arm at Georgie's telegram.

Valentine confirmed by me and Lawrence present on Mackinac Island.

She re-read that line. "Does she mean Verity is there?"

"I believe so." Her husband pushed back his chair and rose to stand beside her.

Eugenie pressed a hand to her chest. She forced herself to breathe.

Percy pulled her into his arms, his heart beating a rapid tattoo against her ear. No tears came. She'd cried so many, an ocean of them. She had none left. "Our baby girl has been found."

He released her, his face ashen. "Let's read these all."

They moved to the divan and sat side by side. She clasped his forearm. "Did Georgie say anything else?"

"Yes."

Not a mistake. This is our Lady Valentine. Please advise if you will attempt trans-Atlantic crossing and when arrival may be. Send telegrams to Apple Blossom Cottage.

Eugenie eyed the next telegram, her mouth dry. "Let's look at Valentine's message."

"You take it." Percy, sweating profusely, passed the telegram with hands shaking so violently he almost dropped it.

Despite the strange, almost surreal, calm that enveloped her, tremors coursed through her fingers as well.

Please sit down as you read.

She eyed Percy. "Good thing we already did that."

I believe I have something you might wish to have.

"That's a strange thing to say." Percy took the telegram.

Bracelet from Vitellio's. Here on Mackinac Island. Rightful owner present and will gladly relinquish to you.

Tears threatened then. She did have some left after all.

Percy leaned forward. "The diamond bracelet Carrie gave her?"

She wiped her eyes. "Don't you see, she's trying to tell us she is there. Valentine. The rightful owner."

"Why the subterfuge?" Percy pointed to the next message, which was from Carrie Booth-Moore. "Carrie is the one who gifted her with those diamonds. Inappropriate gift for a little girl."

"Let's see what she says." Eugenie opened the last telegram.

En route to Wedding Cottage.

Eugenie pressed her fingertips to her lips. "Their cottage on Mackinac."

"Yes." Percy shook his head. "She demands we go at once before any YJ arrive."

She squeezed her husband's arm. "Yellow Journalists, it's our code."

P & E I will confirm my gift recipient's legitimacy myself but indicators positive per G. Will telegram again if disappointed. Send messages especially travel itinerary to Wedding Cottage. Please join me there.

Percy rubbed the bridge of his nose. "Always sounds so demanding, doesn't she?"

"Carrie is a high society matron used to getting her way—plus she's the mother to some very willful young women."

Percy took her hand. "Are you all right, sweetheart?"

"I feel a little heady."

"These messages are enough to do that. I find the tones all different."

"Just like the senders."

"Of them all, I believe the one supposedly from our Valentine seems the most thoughtful. I believe she considered our feelings."

"Yes, I'm glad we're seated. The three telegrams together deliver a powerful punch."

"Carrie sounds certain—enough to go directly up to the island. Yet she exerted some caution in how she conveyed her message."

"But Georgie, ever impulsive, got right to the message without considering who might read it."

Percy exhaled sharply. "Yes. We need to get ahead of the journalists who might have sniffed things out."

"Are you ready to do this?"

"My dear Eugenie, I've been ready for almost sixteen years."

"Me, too—together!"

Chapter Twenty-Four

*P*erhaps it's a good thing that Father Joseph has fired me." Susan inclined her head toward the three carriages, now parked by Wedding Cottage, that had been carrying them all around the island.

Lawrence tugged at his detachable collar. "I agree, or we would not have been able to tour with Mr. Danner and his crew today."

They'd parked the carriages at the bottom of the trail to beautiful Ferry Arch, and the entire group hiked up—even Lawrence's father, who'd declared himself perfectly fine and had refused to see the physician.

"I like the picnic best." Francesca, petted Darby. "By Arch Rock."

"Now there's a word that's the same in Italian—picnic." He grinned. "I'm glad Father Joseph allowed you to come with us."

"Si! But not Lizzie. No cats, he say."

"I heard that while Miss Johnson was at the lighthouse, Lizzie got spoiled by the younger girls and slept in your bed."

"Lizzie left *regalo* for Miss Susan by door. But Sister Mary Lou throw away *topo*."

Lawrence quirked his eyebrows. "No doubt the cat considered a mouse a worthy gift for her owner."

"I heard you kept good watch over Lizzie." Susan patted the girl's back. "Thank you."

Francesca grinned. Then she began chanting a children's song as she danced around in a circle, hands on her narrow hips.

Lawrence cast her a knowing look. "You missed her, didn't you?" He'd certainly missed Susan.

Darby barked three times in succession.

Susan chuckled. "I think your pet has weighed in, and it's a yes. But it was wonderful catching up on all the news of Paul's family. Hetty is a little doll."

How relieved he'd been to learn that Paul's and Susan's interest in one another was purely platonic—unlike Lawrence's feelings for the beautiful brunette.

He pointed toward Val and Hetty who were following Georgie toward the Booth-Moores' massive white cottage that featured stacked rounded turret rooms on each of its three levels. "It's quite beautiful.

Val said Hetty could barely sleep last night because she was so excited to sleep in what she called a castle."

"Can't say I blame her." Not that Susan had ever wished for a castle or a prince. She was too down-to-earth. If anything, she dreamed of farmhouses filled with children. But then again, she'd not pictured herself doing all the things required of a farmwife, other than managing the children.

Auntie Tara and Bertie gravitated toward the landscaping to the left of the house where boxwoods and other bushes made a curving pattern. Auntie Tara turned toward Susan. "Look at how this makes a serpentine pattern. It's remarkable."

Was she regretting that they'd stayed in town? Doubtful, since they were able to spend last evening in Mrs. Martin's parlor talking, laughing, and drinking far too many cups of their host's excellent tea.

"Ada and Peter said they've always wanted to see the back yard of this property." She pointed to the Wellings as they disappeared down the drive. "Can you believe Jack is watching his little sister today?"

"I can, because I hear no one spouting off nonsense."

Francesca stopped dancing. "You miss Jack's spouting? What is this spouting?"

Lawrence leaned in. "Little ears can still hear everything."

"I shouldn't have said that, Francesca. I'll explain it later."

Lawrence handed the girl Darby's leash. "Here. Take him down to the corner and back."

"Come on, puppy." She darted off.

"Her English is improving." Every day that Francesca spent more time with her and Lawrence, the child's language was clearer, her accent a little softer.

"My father plans to frequent every open establishment in town tonight." Lawrence raised his eyebrows.

"I still can't believe he refused to see Dr. Cadotte."

"I can. He's hard-headed." Lawrence stepped closer. "Or maybe he just knows what he wants—like I do."

His amber eyes smoldered—and she was pretty sure she knew what he meant.

✤

Thank God, Father is back to his normal jocular self. He'd confided this morning that he approved of Susan. Not that Lawrence had asked him, nor had he spoken of his affection for her. Still, it was good to know he liked the woman Lawrence was falling in love with.

Unfortunately, Lawrence and Susan were co-workers. Once their relationship changed—if it did—then what would that mean for Susan and her position? She needed her job. So did he.

Lawrence pointed toward the massive front doors. "Did you want to go in and look around? I can stay out here with Darby, and you could take Francesca."

She gave her head a tight shake. "I don't think that's a good idea for Francesca."

But did she really mean for herself? He could never offer such a luxury—not in a main home much less in a rarely used "cottage." Did she wish to own a mansion like this, with a prominent view of the Straits of Mackinac? But he discerned no yearning on her face, other than when he'd leaned in and gotten a little too close to her a few minutes ago. When he'd locked gazes on her beautiful face, he'd almost kissed her. Luckily, he got himself in check.

"You go in. Talk with Val. She's going back to the lighthouse shortly."

They stood there for a moment, the chill late autumn air making Lawrence wish he'd grown a beard. Maybe he still would. But if they got moving, they'd warm up. Laughter carried from the backyard.

Susan tapped his elbow. "What do I do about Auntie Tara wanting to ride bikes later? I doubt she and Bertie have been on one in ages."

"He said the last time he'd been on one was a quadricyle for two, which was over a decade ago."

"Oh my."

"Let's promise them we'll get them accustomed to the modern bicycles when they're here for the summer program."

"I guess they didn't tell you. . ."

"What? Did we lose yet another Sugarplum Lady? Ada told me about the owner of this home not coming to help." Mrs. Booth-Moore did have some health issues.

"The Mulcaheys would like to stay."

He blinked. "Through the winter? What about their home?"

"She said your mother would close it up for them."

"I imagine she would do that for Cousin Tara. But she's never experienced a winter like they have here."

"Neither have you."

"True." And Susan had been almost glowing, more enthusiastic than he'd ever seen her, since Cousin Tara and she had been reunited. "Did you know she's my godmother as well as yours?"

"She told me she could now be cousin, auntie, and godmother all in one place." Susan beamed.

"But where would she stay?"

"Mrs. Welling told her Pine Cottage was at her disposal if they chose to stay."

He lowered his head. Mrs. Martin had told him the place had been sold, but she hadn't said to whom.

"You don't want them to stay?" Susan took a step away from him.

"It's not that." He swiveled toward her. "I was hoping to rent the place for myself." And one day have Susan there with him.

"I don't see why you couldn't move there with Darby. It belongs to the society now."

Why hadn't Ada and Peter mentioned anything? He exhaled the breath he'd been holding. "That's a good idea. Give the Wellings their home back."

"It would be lovely for the four of us—and Darby—to be able to visit there together. I peeked through the windows one time and saw that huge front parlor on the one side and the dining room on the other."

"Susan Johnson, did you really peek through someone's windows?"

She shrugged. "I knew no one was living there."

He, too, could imagine them there together. "We'll need to get their wood hauled in for the winter."

"Bertie says Ada already arranged it."

"Jack and I can help stack it."

"If Bertie lets you. He's in his fifties—not nineties."

"What about his job?"

"Ada is bringing him on staff for maintenance."

That woman was like everyone's fairy godmother sometimes. "This could be an interesting winter. And with Tara here, we'll be able to get the cooking program fully planned before spring even arrives."

Valentine and Georgie emerged from the house with Hetty. They each carried luggage.

"Let me go help." Lawrence jogged up to them. "I'll carry these down for you."

"I imagine Lee will be fretting if I don't arrive on that boat in Mackinaw City." Up close, Georgina looked years younger—almost restored, now that her younger sister had finally been found. "I still can't believe he brought his automobile up to test on the roads over there."

"I can believe it," Lawrence muttered. "Nothing says honeymoon like dust flying in your face on a back road."

Georgie tried to swat him with her free hand, but he backed away.

Val looked heavenward. "Paul would agree that Lee isn't exactly a commonsense type of man."

Her sister sniffed. "Neither am I—so we're a perfect match."

Hetty leaned her head against Valentine. "I want Daddy."

Georgie handed Lawrence a new-looking valise as did Valentine.

He inclined his head toward Georgie. "Could you walk Hetty down to the carriage?"

"Certainly. She is, after all, the first child to ever make me wish I had children." She took the child's tiny hand in hers, but then Hetty raised her arms.

Georgie carried the three-year-old down the walkway.

Pride swelled his chest. To see his old friend finally free from her many demons, married, reunited with her sister, and now to glimpse a vision of her possible future. . .

Lawrence took Valentine's hand. He had to treat her as if she were his own sister. "You sure this is what you wish to do? Go back to the lighthouse?"

"Yes. I'll be fine." She raised her chin and gave a small nod. "I always meet my obligations."

Did Paul realize he was simply an obligation to her?

Chapter Twenty-Five

Round Island

Val let the warm suds squish through her rag and over the dishes, lost in thoughts of her pretend parents. Paul played his accordion for them while Hetty made "rock people" at the table from the stones they'd collected on the beach. What a far different scene this was from when she'd lived here before.

It was easier, now, to think of the Fillmans by their given names and not as Mum and Pa. Doing so dampened the negative emotions she had toward them. When she'd lived with them, Dorcas often would lie abed while she, her brother, and sister took down clothes from the outdoor line. After Val made dinner, Timothy and Mabel would fold and put away clothes while Valerie cleaned up. John would leave to tend the light.

It was Valerie's job to make sure that neither Mabel nor Timothy went up to the Fresnel lens. Children's, or anyone's, greasy fingerprints could wreak all manner of havoc if they got on the precious light that guided ships through the precarious straits of Mackinac.

Poor Tim and Mabel—they'd not had much happiness in their lives. At least they'd had their books, and she'd read to them every night—until they'd become independent readers. She'd had to read slowly and clearly to Mabel. Her faux sister had lost hearing in one ear when Dorcas viciously boxed it for a minor infraction.

Val had comforted them. She'd sung for them. Taught them during the times they'd been kept out of school and lived in remote locations. Both had become voracious readers and had blossomed in their knowledge of their specific interests. Yet Susan and Lawrence had hinted that Timothy and Mabel seemed to resent her. She'd see them herself in a few days and make her own decision about that.

Val hadn't been able to attend but a few years of school herself. She'd been a precocious reader though. Georgie said their mother had read to them every night. She's said Val had an excellent vocabulary for a small child, and she'd been able to memorize and sing songs that only much older children did. Maybe that was why she'd continued to have the nightmares. Her mind wanted her to remember her past that Dorcas had tried to steal from her.

Val had cherished the quiet times when Dorcas had been kind and rational. And even though she didn't direct her affection toward Val, she'd been grateful for the kindness Dorcas had lavished on the other two during those brief and intermittent times. What had tortured the woman? Was it guilt over what she had done? *She stole me. And she likely murdered Susan's parents.* How did she explain to Tim and Mabel about that? Should she?

Paul, who also seemed lost in his thoughts, stopped midway in his polka refrain and looked at her. "What's wrong?"

She stopped washing the blue-speckled enamel pot. "Let's go outside after I'm done. It's not too cool, with the sun shining right now."

"All right." Paul set his accordion back in its case. "I have something I've wanted to ask you."

Her chest tightened. Would he once again convey his concern that she must discover who she truly was? Must go with her parents once they arrived—for they surely would. She felt pressured, as though he wished for her to leave.

When she'd finished the dishes, the three of them, dressed in warm coats, went outside to stroll on the Round Island beach. They circled the lighthouse twice and then Hetty settled on the sand. She gathered rocks to make designs—one of her favorite activities.

Paul stepped closer. "I can tell this whole situation is bothering you—especially not knowing when your folks will arrive."

"Yes, but I feel. . ." She shook her head. She would not say that she felt safe and secure with him and his daughter. The poor man must feel more windblown than a stormy afternoon at the Straits, with his daughter's care on the most tenuous of terms. "I don't know who I am anymore. But when I'm with you and Hetty, things seem like I always imagined a normal family would be." She fisted her hands, then forced them open.

He gave her a long look, filled with compassion—and something else. "My mother would laugh if she heard you. Always thought I was too much of a dreamer—that I should act more like the other men with families."

Hetty stood and wiped the sand from her skirt. "Is Auntie Georgie fambly?"

"Miss Georgina, I mean *Lady* Georgina, is Miss Val's sister, she's not in our family."

Hetty and Paul were a family. Paul and his wife and Hetty had been. And Paul would take Hetty back to the Scholtus farm at the end of the season—to his extended family. "I think I'll head inside. I'll give you some family time with Hetty."

She entered the lighthouse building and closed the door behind her. He'd follow her in soon. And later, after books and stories, she'd put Hetty to bed. As the caretaker. Not the child's mother. Not Paul's wife. Not the Fillmans' daughter. Nobody.

Not the Gladstone's daughter for years and years. Not part of their family. Not the sister that Georgie remembered, the sister whose disappearance had almost destroyed their world. Maybe better to be nobody, belonging to no one.

Mine. You are mine. Always mine, and I am here, too.

Val shivered and hugged herself. She didn't need to escape God. She needed to let Him embrace her and bring healing.

Mackinac Island Orphanage

Susan, Lawrence, Sister Mary Lou, and Jack sat around the large oak table in an empty classroom, assembling paper flowers for the Harvest Fair.

"Was it nice spending time with your old friend Paul?" Sister Mary Lou's pink cheeks suggested to Susan that the nun was reading more into their relationship than was true.

"Yes, and his daughter is a delight." Susan smiled, but when she looked at Lawrence, his brows were drawn together. "As Lawrence also got to see today."

"Scholtus was a farmer wasn't he?" Lawrence wrapped a wire around a paper carnation. "What made him fit to be a lighthouse keeper?"

She stiffened at his accusatory tone. "He'd been an assistant keeper." *Not an especially nice place by his description.* Which begged the question as to why he'd wanted this position.

"And so now once the season ends, he'll be in town. Is that correct?" Lawrence sounded like his attorney father might if he was in court.

"I believe he and Hetty will move into a snug cottage in town."

Paul had confided that he already had doubts about his lighthouse keeper position. And his mother was pressuring him to return home. He already planned to take his daughter for a quick trip to see his family before he returned to the island. But would he actually come back?

Sister Mary Lou gave them an assessing look. "But if Miss Fillman—Lady Valentine, leaves then won't you go out and help him, Susan? That could be for at least two months still, I would think."

Lawrence cleared his throat. "Susan has responsibilities here. I believe Mr. Scholtus can find someone else to watch his child. Or he can leave."

All eyes locked on Lawrence.

Jack began to laugh. "Green don't suit you, Larry."

"Green?" Lawrence looked down at his navy coat and matching waistcoat.

Susan's cheeks heated, as she understood the boy's inference. "Jack," she hissed in warning.

Sister Mary Lou set her work aside. "Now why would Mr. Zumbrun be jealous of Mr. Scholtus?"

Jack crinkled his nose. "My dad says if Larry doesn't ask Miss Johnson to marry him soon then that lighthouse keeper will sure as shootin' do the trick."

"That truly is beyond the pale if you're gossiping." Susan gaped at Jack. She looked to Lawrence, hoping he'd correct his protégé.

"Jack, don't be making up stories," Sister Mary Lou chided.

He raised his hands. "I ain't. You can ask my mother. She'll tell ya. She and Miss Tara are even planning their wedding already. They say Miss Johnson needs a full true sew, though what that is, I don't know. I mean is there a false sew kind of thing as compared to a true one?"

"Trousseau." Susan got the word out of her suddenly dry mouth.

"That's what I said." Jack slapped the table.

The nun pushed up her glasses. "A trousseau is things ladies have put together for when they get married."

Lawrence narrowed his eyes at the youth. "It's clothing and other things, special items, for a wedding and honeymoon."

"A honeymoon? Larry, you can't do that! We've got training to do for when I'm in the Olympics."

"That's enough, Jack!" Lawrence's deep voice brooked no argument. "Now I'm sorry you lost your mother, but you've a fine new stepmother who is taking excellent care of you. You've been extended a wide berth which is now going to be narrowed."

When Jack opened his mouth, Lawrence raised his hand. "And by berth I mean as in a ship's berth, which I know you understand so do not make a joke of it. Furthermore, I extended you the courtesy of using my Christian name, which I now rescind since you've continued to mock me with a nickname I despise."

"What's wrong with Larry?" Apparently Jack couldn't help himself.

Lawrence raised his eyebrows. "Do you mean if I called you Jackal, which is a funny nickname, you'd not mind that?"

"Jackal?" Jack scratched his chin. "That's kinda different."

"You wouldn't want to be called Jackal then?" Susan couldn't help herself as a chuckle welled up.

"Of course not," the boy mumbled.

Lawrence reached across to Jack. "I promise you, Jack not Jackal, if this wonderful woman ever agrees to become my wife, then I will not take her on a honeymoon while you have a race or are in the middle of intense training. Otherwise, all bets are off."

Jack crossed his arms and leaned back in his chair. "Well, then, you have my permission."

Susan shook her head. Clearly, it was going to take some doing to bring Jack into line. But she'd miss all the information they gleaned from him once that happened.

🍁

Did Lawrence understand what he'd just heard? Ada Welling was not only agreeable to his and Susan's blossoming relationship, but she already had them married off? Wasn't he doing the same thing, by imagining himself with her at Pine Cottage? Adopting Francesca and raising a family there? Taking in the Clancy boys Susan loved to complain about? And sweet Mandy?

While Susan coiled another paper rose, Jack jerked a thumb toward Lawrence. "Did old Larry, er, I mean Mr. Lawrence Zumbrun, tell you he wants a dozen kids?"

Susan smirked. "Goodness, we'd have his father working on the adoption of ten of those children before we ever reach the altar."

"That's right." Lawrence rubbed his eye. "Father will do it pro bono."

"For bones? Thought only Darby worked for bones."

"It means for free." Sister Mary Lou snipped a piece of wire to wrap around her crepe paper carnation.

Jack shrugged. "You'd still have to feed and clothe 'em all even if the adoption is free."

"There's plenty of fish out there in the lake." Susan fluffed out her paper rose. "I'm sure Billy will take them out in his boat to catch our dinner every day."

"Or they can cast a line down by the docks." Lawrence needed to get Susan to come fishing with him soon.

"You gotta be kidding. That ain't enough." Jack twisted wire around the one lone flower he'd managed to make.

"I'll learn to bake and cook in our summer program, and I'll prepare seven-course meals nightly."

Jack tipped his head back and hooted. "Now I know for sure, yer pullin' my leg. Everyone knows about your cooking. Inedible is what Sister Mary Lou said."

The nun's cheeks turned pink. "Jack, you know I'm going to have to speak with your parents about this, don't you?"

Jack's expression transfigured into one of extreme penitence. Might be hope for him yet.

"I'm a good cook." Lawrence took in their astonished looks and grinned.

214　　　*Mackinac Island Beacon*

Susan beamed at him in what looked like relief. "On a different topic, other than our impending marriage, the adoption of ten children, and my failures in the kitchen—what has anyone heard from Mrs. Booth-Moore?"

"Nothing." Lawrence hadn't nor anyone he'd talked to about it.

"Lady Georgie told my folks she ain't got word back. Neither have they." Jack scowled at them. "That ain't gossip—that's factual."

"Perhaps she's not able to make it." Sister Mary Lou started on another flower, rolling the paper tightly together.

"She has a genuine heart condition, unlike my father's situation."

"That was scary." Susan locked gazes with him. "If Carrie Booth-Moore has that going on, wouldn't she at least send a message?"

"Maybe she couldn't." Georgie would be upset, and possibly Valentine, too. "But we've had no word from Val's parents, either."

"It's all in God's hands. They'll get here when they get here." Sister Mary Lou's confidence encouraged him.

"That's certainly true."

Lake Michigan and Lake Huron juncture

If nothing else, this terrifically awful trip had convinced Carrie that her decision to remain home in Chicago that coming summer was for the best. The return of the Sugarplum Ladies? Who had come up with that cockamamy idea? They were all matrons with adult children and grandchildren now, except poor Tara who'd not been blessed with children. Still—Tara had now been reunited with Evelyn's daughter. Tara might yet enjoy those tender moments. But to think that the three of them, along with Ada Welling would now help run catering instruction—the entire thing was ludicrous. Her pounding head testified to the truth of that fact.

Male voices rose outside her door aboard the Great Lakes ship.

"Step aside, man, I intend to speak with Mrs. Booth-Moore." The captain's commanding voice must have swayed them because a heavy rap sounded on Carrie's chamber door.

She winced and tried to raise her head from her pillow. "Enter." She laid her head back down and closed her eyes. Her headache threatened to explode.

Several heavy steps approached, then stopped. "Oh. Begging your pardon, Mrs. Booth-Moore."

She opened one eye to look in the direction of the baritone voice. The captain held his hat in his hands. "What is it?"

"Madam, I apologize, it's just that the crew. . ."

What about them? She couldn't force out the question. She'd been ill with stomach distress and headaches since the trip began.

"Well, given that our ship is the namesake for Lady Valentine's family. . ."

Carrie tried to focus her thoughts. This was her husband's ship—one of many.

"This being the *Gladstone*, ma'am, we thought. . ."

The *Gladstone*? Had she realized that at the beginning? *No.* One of several that Percy had invested in with her husband decades earlier. "You thought?" she managed to ask, as pounding increased at her temples.

"We figured Mr. Booth-Moore picked this ship in particular to send you up to reunite with her. The whole crew got wind of it."

How? She wanted to ask, but couldn't.

"We're entering the Straits and as we pass the lighthouse they want—they demand—to sound a proper salute."

"Demand?" If her husband heard that they'd demanded anything, he'd likely sack the whole crew.

"I told them you're ill, but they want to acknowledge her."

Opening her eyes she stared at the man. Did he mean what she thought he meant?

"Might we blast the horns to give her a proper welcome back, Mrs. Booth-Moore?"

"Indeed!"

A lone ship made its way toward the channel, but as strange noises carried toward the lighthouse beach Val became alarmed. "What's wrong out there, Paul?

"I'm going to get my binoculars!" Paul ran back inside.

Hetty pointed from where she sat on a blanket. "Why they waving?"

Val shielded her eyes from the sun. An almost solid dark line ran along the top deck, but like Hetty said, something was waving. Men's arms? What was wrong?

Paul rejoined them and looked through the lenses.

Val squinted and read the name of the ship, painted on its side. "*Gladstone*?" She'd never seen it at the Straits. "I didn't know there was a ship by that name."

What sounded like cheers echoed over the water as the ship slowly drew closer.

Paul sucked in his breath. "Those men were waving at us, but now they are covering their ears."

"Cover your ears, Hetty!" The first honk was so loud and long that it made Val jump.

A series of long, short, low, and then higher sounds blasted from the ship's horns. At the end, a continuous burst of hooting and hollering commenced. Then all became silent, except for the chug of the engines and squawking of seagulls as they dove for fish.

"Look! They do this." Hetty put her hand over her heart. "Like for flag."

They meant that for me. Tears welled in Val's eyes as she realized that every man, including a gentleman in a fancy suit with a hat, who must have been the captain, stood with their hands over their hearts. The crew of the *Gladstone.*

"They know." Paul's whisper was laden with meaning.

If that ship full of men knew, then who else now knew where Val was? And what would that mean for them?

Val waved, then laced her hands together over her heart and pressed them to her chest.

Another cheer went up.

Then a song carried across the water. "Rock of Ages, cleft for thee, let me hide myself in Thee." This was one of her favorite hymns and had gotten Val through many a difficult night.

I crept into a crack in the rocks that protected my heart, and I've hidden there.

Was it time to come out? To be free?

To be healed?

Something blossomed inside of her, and out of the darkness of her past shined a light of hope.

It was time to start anew.

"What do you think they meant with the salute?" Who was on board? Paul had never experienced anything like it. "That ship doesn't travel this way, and they look to be heading to the Haldimand Bay harbor."

Valerie's lower lip curled in. "I think it's for me."

"I agree." Who was aboard, though? Would they swoop her away? "Let me check the ship's logs for ownership."

"Mr. Booth-Moore I bet. Georgie told me he owned ships. It has to be his. Which means. . . Carrie Booth-Moore may be on board."

"Georgie telegrammed her?"

"Yes. And my parents, too, as did I. But no word yet."

What was he thinking—that she'd stay with him and Hetty? He raked his fingers through his hair. "We've got to get you back to Mackinac Island."

She blinked at him. Then her face lit up. "I'll take Hetty back with me again. Mr. Haapala arrives within the hour."

"Are you sure?"

"Positive."

"If it doesn't work out, could you see if Susan can come out?"

"We won't stay too long. I just want to find out what's going on."

She would return? "So a day or two?"

"You'll be coming on your break day then anyway. So we can come back together in two days."

But would she? Would whoever was on that ship keep her ashore? Regardless, Paul wanted only the best for Val.

🍁

Susan stood awkwardly by the door, awaiting Jack's return to Butterfly Cottage.

Auntie Tara, Miss Ada, and Mrs. Booth-Moore were clustered near the fireplace, heads together over tea and saucers—laughing and talking far more than drinking their tea.

Lawrence came alongside her and leaned close, his breath warm on her cheek. "Dare I interrupt them?"

She shrugged. "For what reason?"

"To tell them the roof is finished on the third building."

"No. They need to catch up."

"True."

Jack came through the door. "Mr. Hop said he'd bring Val and Hetty back with him. At least that's what I think he said." Jack scrunched his face, looking very much like the older Finnish man. "I bring dee lady und ked wi' me,' is what it sounded like."

Lawrence gave Jack a thumbs-up.

The youth grabbed a plateful of cookies from the table and returned. "Want some?"

Neither accepted them.

"Suit yourselves. Wasn't that ship's salute something special?"

"It was unbelievable." And somewhat disturbing. The *Gladstone* crew knew where Val was.

"Maybe not," Lawrence said. "Not only is Mrs. Booth-Moore here but the first few newspaper articles appeared today.

"My brother-in-law wants first crack at interviewin' Valerie." Jack passed the cookie plate to Lawrence then made a rolling motion with his hand as he bowed. "Or shall I call her Lady Valentine?"

"That title would only be used if we were in England," Susan explained.

Lawrence took a cookie. "Or Canada."

"Oh." Jack grabbed the plate back. "The way them ladies are chatterin' and chucklin' over there, I bet they'll all end up helping." Jack shoved three cookies in his mouth.

"With the summer program?" Susan dropped her voice. "Didn't you hear Mrs. Booth-Moore say her heart problem won't allow her to participate?

"But she said she'll come to help." Lawrence placed his arm around her shoulder, and she looked up at him.

"Help with what then?" Susan was becoming frustrated.

Jack swallowed his cookies. "Help Mom with the catering stuff for the wedding."

She flipped her palms over. "What wedding?"

"The one they're planning for August." Lawrence kissed her cheek. Right there in the Wellings' home. Her face heated. "Ours."

"Ours?"

"But I'd prefer it be in June before our program kicks off."

"Good thinkin', Larry!" Jack jogged over to the women.

As Susan gaped, the youth jerked a thumb their way. "Hey, they wanta get hitched in June, not August."

Chapter Twenty-Six

*W*ind from Lake Huron rose and then fell as Mr. Haapala expertly guided his craft over the water to Haldimand Bay. Valerie clutched her hat for a moment, gazing out at the sapphire-blue water. For the longest time, water had been her enemy—keeping her isolated. But it hadn't truly been the Great Lakes—it had been her mother's iron will that ruled them all. Except for the days when Mum had medicated herself into a stupor. Those had been the blissfully quiet days. A lone tear trailed down her cheek.

"Sad?" Hetty wiped the moisture away.

"Yes. But happy, too." Because Carrie Booth-Moore may be on the island. She pulled the girl closer.

She glanced down at her threadbare skirt. She should have made herself a new dress, like the pretty ensemble she liked in *The Delineator*. Now she'd have to wait to get something ready-made in town or in St. Ignace. She'd order the pattern for the dress she liked and one for a new church dress for Hetty.

What was she thinking? Hadn't Georgie told her to get what she needed? Order what she wanted? But it hadn't felt right. Now, with this possible meeting, she suddenly felt ashamed of her appearance. And she wanted Hetty to wear pretty garments. Georgie had reminded her of the beautiful ensembles she'd had as a young child.

Mr. Haapala smiled at them. He and she had laughed together when they'd both asked, at the same time, about him taking her to Mackinac Island. He was a kind man. One day soon she'd make that tea for him. Finnish tea that Mrs. Christy could special order.

Would she have many special orders now?

What would that feel like?

She patted Hetty's head. *How could I spoil this precious little girl? And her father?*

For now though, she needed to get to the Wellings' home, as Mr. Haapala had tried to explain in his broken English—to see 'Meez Carrie'.

Carrie gasped when Valentine entered the room, a wide-eyed girl in tow. She clasped her hands to her chest, where her heart beat frantically in recognition. "Oh, I see the resemblance." She opened her arms to the young woman, who stood staring at her.

"Father said the same thing." Lawrence gestured from Valentine to Carrie. "This is Mrs. Booth-Moore, whose ship gave you that salute."

"Which was much appreciated." Val moved forward. "And I remember you."

Carrie embraced the young woman for whom she'd prayed all these years. Her dearest friend's youngest child. "I was much younger then."

"And I was a child." Val stepped away and gestured for the child to come forward. "This is Hetty Scholtus."

"Lighthouse keeper's daughter," Lawrence supplied.

"Hello, Hetty." Carrie bent and extended her hand, but to her surprise, the little girl wrapped her arms around her legs.

"You look like Granma." She raised her arms.

Carrie laughed as she lifted the girl. "I am a grandma." She was blessed to be one.

Valentine patted the girl's head. "Hetty's grandma lives not far from the Wellings' farm."

Carrie swiveled to face Adelaide. "Do you know the Scholtus family?"

"We haven't met yet, or rather I haven't met them due to all our excitement." She pointed to where Satilde lay sleeping on the divan. "But Peter knows them."

How wonderful for Adelaide to have been blessed with a child this late in life. It seemed like only yesterday she was near Jack's age and now Little Adelaide was in her forties.

"Let's get your coats off." Lawrence reached for Valentine's cloak.

Carrie set Hetty down and helped her remove her jacket. "You have the prettiest strawberry-blond hair."

The girl nodded, as if in agreement. Joy swelled Carrie's heart. *Children are our future.*

Adelaide went to Jack and whispered something to him. The youth ran over to them. "Hetty, you want to do blocks with me?"

The child stuck her finger in her little rosebud mouth.

"Nah? How about puzzles?" Jack swooped her up, and she giggled. "I'm gonna take you out and put you on the swings. You'll go way up in the sky."

"Yes!" Hetty pointed to her jacket. "Gimme coat back."

Soon Jack and Hetty went out into the yard, and Valentine went to the window to watch them. Carrie could see how much she cared about the little girl. Possibly for her father. Was God bringing something good out of what had happened?

Carrie moved closer and touched Valerie's arm. "Your mother and father should arrive in New York within a week."

Alarm skittered over her pretty features.

"I didn't mean to upset you." She'd thought Valentine would be glad. But what all had the young woman been through in all these years?

"Since your parents left for England, I'm the only one of our set to see them regularly. My husband and I travel there yearly."

Valentine said nothing.

Carrie gestured to the two nearby chairs. "Why don't you ask me anything you'd like to know. Then when you see them, perhaps it won't be as difficult to catch up."

Tears filled her violet eyes. "Thank you."

Compassion swelled and Carrie took her hand and led her to the chairs. "Anything for my goddaughter." Anything except another diamond bracelet. But from what she'd heard from Lawrence and Susan, Dorcas Fillman had been insane and had never sold the jewelry. Carrie could at last release that guilt. What a relief.

As a squeal of laughter carried from outside, Carrie smiled. Another diamond bracelet may be forthcoming.

Val held Hetty's hand as she, Ada and Sally, Carrie, and Tara followed Bertie and Peter to the big field where the Harvest Festival would take place the following day.

"Where Jack?" Hetty's curls bounced beneath her cap as they walked.

"Over there." Val pointed to where Jack, attired in his absurd outfit, was brushing off his very tall and crooked top hat.

As they arrived, Sister Mary Lou pointed to the hay bales that marked off the "theater" area for the Harvest Festival. "All of you performers, come forward for rehearsal!"

Susan, dressed in a black and red checkered medieval style dress, with a crown sporting a gauzy fabric tail, rose from the front hay bale. Lawrence, similarly attired, but with no embellishment on his crown, followed and then Jack.

All of Val's group took seats on the hay bales that faced the makeshift stage.

Val couldn't help thinking about her parents. Her father was a marquess now. They were aristocrats. What did they have in common with her anymore? Her brother was a barrister living in Ontario. Leonora, her other sister, married a duke. Even Georgie, with her issues, had been raised in affluence and privilege. The crazy thought that she should slip away, like she'd slipped away into her head growing up, made her wonder if that might be for the best for all of them.

But was it?

Or was that thought born of fear? Fear of change—even change she'd spent years longing for.

Jack blew a horn and bowed. "Ladies and gentlemen, I present the King and Queen of Pumpkin Land."

Lawrence led Susan onto the raised wooden structure. She made a commendable curtsey. Would Val be expected to curtsey to all manner of people? Would she need to learn all the rules of British society?

Hetty crawled onto her lap. "I want ice cream cone."

The child couldn't have picked a more perfect time. Val leaned toward Carrie. "I'm taking her for a walk. She's restless." As was Val.

She and Hetty headed toward town.

Even last night, at Wedding Cottage, Val couldn't tamp out the sensation of being out of place. It was different than when Georgie was with her. Carrie had brought temporary staff with her on the ship. They'd opened more rooms for Mother and Father—it seemed strange thinking of them as such. And the workers made sure the accommodations were up to Mrs. Booth-Moore's standards.

What if her real parents found her not up to their standards? Would they consider the man she'd come to care for as beneath them? His precious little girl, too?

Hetty pulled free and, quick as a wink, ran down the wood walkway that edged the buildings. Val lifted her skirts and ran. "Hetty! Stop!"

She'd come within a block of catching her when Hetty's cap fell off, but the little girl kept going. Val bent and grabbed the red wool hat. But when she looked up, Hetty was nowhere in sight.

Panic hit her like a strong gust off Lake Huron. Where was her girl? Not her girl—Paul's, and she was responsible for her. Her heart hammered. She couldn't have gone far. But the wharf wasn't far away, and she'd wanted to stop there on the way down in the taxi. Carrie had told her she'd have to wait until they returned to the cottage. Val looked across the street. Other than adult male workers, there was no one.

Had her mother panicked like this? Had she searched frantically for Val at the wharf in New York? Tears of commiseration filled her eyes. Shame flooded her that she'd contemplated running away from those parents who'd searched all these years.

"Boo!"

Val spun around.

Hetty peeked from the recessed entryway to a store closed for the season. "I scare you?"

Val hurried to her and crushed the little darling to her chest as tears rolled down her cheeks. How terrified Mother and Father had to have been. She released the child and clasped her shoulders.

"Promise me you'll never run away again."

And neither would she.

Paul should arrive any time and here they still were at the Booth-Moore cottage, getting ready for the Harvest Festival. Sprawled on her tummy on the satin brocade coverlet for the large bed, Hetty raised her head and pointed to the mirror. "You look pretty."

Ceasing her efforts to pin her hair into what Val hoped was an elegant coiffure, she examined her reflection. Her new pin-tucked Batiste shirtwaist fit beautifully, as did her cadet-blue linen skirt. She fingered the cameo at her neck, a gift from Mrs. Booth-Moore. With the shawl knit by Sister Mary Lou and the glittering hairpin from Susan, she looked. . .

Movement behind her distracted her and Paul's image filled the mirror, his face reflecting a longing that pierced her soul. His eyes said that he loved her—or at least he admired how she looked. Something inside her broke. Tears pricked her eyes, and she turned from the looking glass.

"You're beautiful."

Hetty scampered off the bed and ran to her father. "You're peeping!"

"Peeking," Valerie gently corrected. She blinked back the moisture in her eyes.

Paul lifted Hetty overhead until she could touch the ceiling. "What fine-looking females I get to accompany." The child giggled until her father lowered her to the rag-rug-covered floor.

"Mrs. Booth-Moore says you are both served notice of departure." Paul adjusted Hetty's hair bow and kissed her forehead.

"Coming."

Soon, they'd all gotten into the carriage and headed for the festival.

Val cast a glance at Paul, his handsome profile making her smile and sending a different kind of warmth through her.

Paul clapped as the Harvest Festival theatrical production ended. Their entire group had participated in a pumpkin judging contest, eaten pumpkin pastries, played ring toss, and more—yet his daughter didn't look tired as the event wrapped up.

Hetty poked his arm "You promise libry."

Val's eyebrows shot upward. "You still want more, even after all that?"

"Like my girls." Mrs. Booth-Moore lifted her chin.

"You promise." From the wobbly chin, tears would soon follow.

"To the library we shall go."

"Do you want the carriage?" Mrs. Booth-Moore offered.

"We'll walk."

"I'm coming with you." Val had told him what happened the previous day. She took Hetty's other hand. "I need to talk to Mr. Steffan before we leave."

He still couldn't believe Valerie intended to return to the lighthouse with them.

"His inn is near the library."

They walked through town, occasionally swinging Hetty between them.

When they reached the Winds of Mackinac Inn, Val said her goodbyes and kissed Hetty's cheek. She gave him the longest look, as if. . .

He drew in a deep breath and crossed the street to the library. Inside, a silver-haired woman welcomed them, her blue-gray eyes gentle. She was a handsome woman of about sixty. "May I show you our children's section?"

"Yes, please."

The librarian came from around the desk, the scent of lemon verbena soap wafting from her. "How old are you?"

Hetty's eyebrows pulled into a slim auburn line. "I'm three." She held up three fingers.

"I'm Paul Scholtus, the new lighthouse keeper." He pointed toward Round Island, where the lighthouse was now being supplied by his relief man. "And this is my daughter, Hetty."

"What kind of books does Hetty like?"

"Val read me Thumblina."

The librarian offered her hand to Hetty. "Thumbelina is one of my favorites."

His baby girl eagerly clutched the stranger's hand and walked ahead of him. She was growing up a little more each day.

The librarian reminded him of his mother-in-law. Sweat broke out on his brow. Painful memories of his in-laws' hurtful behavior surfaced. They'd not once come to see Hetty. Strange how people could be so self-absorbed in their own pain that they couldn't see the needs of others.

Val clearly had her own demons with which to wrestle. How could he have been so selfish to have brought her back to the very place where her family had perished? Desperation, pure and simple had motivated him. Desperation to have his way and to escape his own pain. But there was no escaping it, there was only moving through it. But as his Bible showed, if God could restore Job, then He could help anyone.

Val's muffled cries in her sleep had drawn him to her door repeatedly. But her repetition of "Don't take me! Stop!" and other protestations left him perplexed. When he'd gone into her room to look in on her, lamp aloft, she was always asleep.

She'd said her parents would be arriving possibly within the week. How could he dare keep her from them? She needed to be with them to have time to repair their relationship. He'd either have to find someone else to help him or he'd have to quit this job.

But hadn't he accomplished what he'd really come there for?

I have.

Chapter Twenty-Seven

Round Island Lighthouse

*H*etty is—I am not making this up—taking a nap." Val went to the parlor table and began picking up the pieces of a simple wooden puzzle depicting farm life.

"She loved that puzzle, didn't she?"

"I think she's missing your farm."

"It's the family she misses." He patted his chest. "Me, too."

"I'm sure they are looking forward to seeing you soon." She set the puzzle in its small wooden box.

As Paul sipped his coffee she cupped her hand around her ear. No horns sounding, no seagulls' squawks carrying from the outside—just the crackle of the wood-burning stove. No little girl laughter or chatter or tiny feet running around. "I guess Hetty has a few naps left in her after all."

Paul laughed. "Told ya so."

Val pulled another puzzle from the drawer. "Want to try this one?"

"That's a doozy." He drank deeply from his coffee mug.

The puzzle showed a scene of lumberjacks taking down woods on the left and then transitioning to a new small town on the right. "Reminds me of my early life."

"On the run?"

"Kind of—but I didn't know it then. I sensed it. And I'm remembering why I felt so frightened for years."

"I imagine at first you expected your folks to show up."

"Right. And when they didn't. . ."

"You got upset." Paul set his coffee mug down.

Paul patted the sofa, beside him—where Hetty had sat. Val poured the pieces of the puzzle onto the tabletop and then settled next to her favorite man in the world. He draped an arm around her.

The sound of giggling carried down the hall from Hetty's room.

Val playfully touched Paul's hand, on her shoulder. "Careful now, Daddy, little eyes might be here soon."

"All right." He removed his arm and leaned toward the table. Quickly, he began assembling the frame.

She found the pieces to make a massive white pine that the lumberjack was going to fell. "I used to look at those beautiful trees. I. . ." She swiped at her eyes. "Sometimes I felt like I was that proud tall tree, and I was being chopped down."

Paul pulled her close and kissed the top of her head. "It kind of was like that. Dorcas pulled your world away."

"Yes." She sniffed and leaned into his warmth, the sound of the crackling wood reminding her of one place of solace at the camps. "But the ladies at the cook shacks were always nice to me. Said I had the best manners of all the children in the camps."

"You held onto those manners that your parents had instilled into you before Dorcas grabbed you."

"I never really thought of it, but yes." She pulled away and looked into his eyes. "The other kids used to mock me for being polite—even the ones whose parents tried to teach them the same things."

"A little part of you wouldn't give that up. You were hanging onto who you really were."

"Which was hard." She straightened and reached for the pieces for the lumberjack. "Some of those places were rough."

"And rough men?"

"Yes." She pieced the man's red Frenchman's cap together. "But that was an advantage of having John and Dorcas being so secretive. They kept us secluded from everyone as much as they could. I only got to help in the cook shack because it meant Da', that is John, got extra rations."

"A saving grace, I guess."

She gave a curt laugh as she assembled the man's muscular arms and hands holding an axe. "I felt so lost."

"You're found now."

"Yes. Yes, I am." She swiped at her tears.

He gave her a warm hug and she inhaled his piney scent. She could stay in his embrace forever, but Hetty would be up soon, and she needed to feed this man dinner before he went up into the tower. She began to pull away, but he held her tight.

"You're thinking about all you have to do, aren't you?" He kissed her forehead. "But why don't we sit like this for a moment more?"

"You know what I feel like?"

"Like you are loved and appreciated?"

"That wasn't it, but thank you, I feel the same way."

"Good." He tugged her a little closer.

"I was going to say, that my old life was like this puzzle. And my life with my parents is another. And yet more is to come. And all the pieces of my life's puzzles are broken apart."

"And it's like someone has thrown them in the air?"

She pulled away and locked gazes on him. "Yes. How did you know?"

"It was like that after my wife died. I hate to bring her up, but it's the truth."

She nodded. "Can you imagine God creating an amazing puzzle with everything thrown up into the air and reassembled just right?"

"I believe He could perfectly straighten it all out."

"And make something beautiful of our lives."

Paul lowered his hand and patted his pocket, where a letter from his mother seemingly burned a hole. He'd gotten his yearning for experience at a lighthouse out of his system, and now it was time to make decisions. What if he couldn't find someone to watch Hetty?

Val emerged from the kitchen, two coffee mugs in her hands. Hetty carried a plate of Mrs. Christy's cinnamon rolls aloft, as though she carried a plate of gold.

Golden goodness, for sure and for certain.

"Breakfast is served!" Val announced.

Hetty's lips formed an adorable pout. "Storytime today, Daddy."

"She says it's your turn."

"Today?" Paul accepted a steaming mug of black coffee, the brief touch of Val's fingertips warming him more than the cup had.

Valerie smiled up at him, a blush tingeing her cheeks. Had she felt the effects of that contact as he did? When he looked into her eyes, he knew she did, and he couldn't help grinning.

"Today, Daddy!" Hetty set the plate of rolls on the table. "I tell 'bout the Ginger Man."

"Ginger man?" Paul laughed as Val used a spatula to transfer a roll onto his plate. "I believe you mean the Gingerbread Man."

"No." Valerie's cheeks looked even more rosy than usual. She looked pointedly at Hetty as she raised a finger to her lips.

"The Ginger Man." Hetty cocked her head at him. "He has ginger hair. Green eyes. Saves the Lake Lady."

"Sh!" Valerie bent and whispered something in his daughter's ear.

"It's secret." Hetty sat in her spot. She bit into her cinnamon roll, frosting smearing white on her pug nose.

"A secret?" He sipped his coffee. "Is the Ginger Man handsome?"

"Of course," Valerie answered, too quickly.

"Daddy." Hetty rolled her eyes. "Of course. He look like you."

Was this his daughter's idea, or Val's? From Val's guilty expression and knowing that she'd helped his daughter with the story, he drew his own conclusions—and grinned even bigger.

His feelings were likely reciprocated. And this Ginger Man may need to find a ring to put on the Lady of the Lake's finger one day.

The six days at the lighthouse passed so quickly, that Val couldn't believe they had already returned to Mackinac Island's wharf.

The time had been filled with laughter, games, hugs with Hetty, lots of books, and many conversations with Paul about faith and about his life in Shepherd. She'd shared more, much more, about her difficult times growing up. He'd listened, becoming upset when he'd heard about Dorcas's cruelty and what he called John Fillman's neglect. He was an even better listener than Susan, which she'd not thought possible.

"Miss Fillman?" One of the port message boys, whose blond hair stuck out like straw around his large ears, ran toward her from dockside. "Sorry, I mean Lady Gladstone? I read that article Ben Steffans wrote. That was some pumpkins what he wrote!"

Hetty made a quizzical face.

Paul leaned toward his daughter. "That's a silly expression that means something amazing or unusual."

"Sister Mary Lou wants to see you." The youth handed Val a note and extended his palm.

As she scanned the missive, Paul gave the boy a tip, and he ran off.

"I need to head there now, Paul."

"Should we go with you?"

"No. I'll be fine." Her parents were there. Paul didn't need to witness this.

Hetty tugged at her father's hand. "Come on, Dad!"'

To Val's surprise, Paul pressed a quick kiss to her cheek, right there in front of God and everyone as their witness. Her breath caught in her throat. She was in love with him. Oh, how she wanted to shout it. But that simply wouldn't do.

"We'll come to the orphanage after our errands."

"See you then." Father and daughter strode off to the left and away from the wharf as Valerie headed toward the orphanage.

As she neared the church, apprehension filled her, and she slowed her pace.

Outside the building, a tall gentleman with dark hair generously streaked with gray, paced. His attire bespoke wealth. Was this her father?

He looked in Valerie's direction. His jaw slackened, and his mouth dropped open. "Verity? Valentine? Is it you?"

She took several tentative steps forward.

"I'm Percy Gladstone." His gray-green eyes, rimmed with deep blue, were the same that had stared at her with adoration as he'd sung lullabies to her.

Tears pricked her eyes.

Sister Mary Lou emerged from the building. "Come in out of the cold. We're ready for you."

Lord Percival Gladstone extended his arm to her, and she accepted it. He looked as nervous as she felt. They followed the nun to Sister Mary Lou's office, which smelled of cloves, oranges, and tea. "Come in, dearie."

Val's breath seemed stuck in her throat.

Inside sat a beautiful matron with dark silver-streaked tresses upswept beneath a broad-brimmed hat. An older version of Georgina, with dark eyes, so unlike Val's, and ivory skin. Lady Eugenie Gladstone, her mother, was the picture of elegance in her burgundy velvet brocade ensemble. She rose effortlessly, one hand clutching leather children's shoes and an envelope bulging with long silky blond curls. She looked as anxious as her husband had.

Sister Mary Lou slipped from the room and closed the door behind her.

"Verity," Mother whispered the name. "It's really you, our Valentine."

She really was Verity "Valentine" Gladstone—possessed of a past that hadn't included only misery.

"We looked for you for years."

"Detectives, Pinkerton agents." Lord Gladstone, standing by the wingchair, looked as lost as Val felt.

"Then one day, I realized that if I didn't accept God's will, His help, I'd lose my mind." This woman, her mother, had suffered, but in a different way than Val had. She held up the shoes and envelope. "I tied these very shoes on your little feet the day we were to depart from New York."

"And that's the very color of your hair—our only child possessed of spun gold curls." Percival placed a hand over his heart.

"She cut my hair." Val swallowed hard, recollecting the tears as her long tendrils had been chopped off, the terrible scents of stale liver and onions making her stomach queasy in that tenement building.

"To change your appearance."

"I looked like a boy." She'd been put in trousers, a shirt, and a cap until the train had reached Michigan. Then she'd been dressed in girl's clothing.

"Your face is too pretty for that." Lady Gladstone shook her head slowly. "You look much like Georgina."

"Georgina was especially affected by your disappearance."

Val's spine stiffened. "I know. She's told me all about it." And she didn't wish to hear of Georgina's suffering again.

"Your absence, your kidnapping, changed all of our lives." Percy Gladstone tugged at his ascot tie.

"Would you sit beside me?" Her mother pulled her toward the settee. "I have so many questions."

"As do I" Val's pent-up questions burst forth. "Where did I live those first few years of my life?"

"My family home, the Motts, in Detroit, is one where we spent some limited time. Your older brother Nathan and his family split time between there and their home in Ontario, now."

"I barely remember him."

Her father sat in the chair across from them.

Her mother patted her hand. "You were so young."

"My Ontario home in Windsor was where we primarily stayed." Her father's voice held a mix of British and Canadian accents. There was so much she wanted to know about him.

"Your older sister, Leonora, and her husband live in England not far from our estate." Her mother squeezed her hand. "We were on our way together to see your grandfather at the estate. We were in New York, when we lost you."

Val shook her head. "I was stolen. You didn't lose me."

Her parents exchanged a look of intense grief.

"What happened the day Dorcas Fillman took me?"

"We were staying in New York. We'd been visiting with my friend, Carrie Booth-Moore, and her family. Business had brought her husband there for an extended time."

Her father leaned forward. "We stayed and visited with the Booth-Moores before we were to depart for England."

"We were taking you there for the first time." Mother fingered the strand of pearls at her neckline.

"To see your grandparents and the rest of my family."

"We didn't go then, after all, because you went missing."

"Georgina was watching over you. Something happened that she lost track of you."

Both parents bowed their heads briefly.

"I remember looking up at all these people around me, like a sea of tall people in jackets. Then Dorcas took me and led me away." Val unfisted her hands, which had been balled tight. "Life was never easy after that." To say the least.

Her mother embraced her. "You can tell us all in due course."

No need to probe that wound anymore today. Val sat back, as did her mother.

"We'd like to do whatever is needed to help you." Her father pulled at his waistcoat. "We'd love to bring you back into the family. Everyone wants to see you. But you are, first and foremost, our priority."

"Do you have any ideas, Valentine?"

Paul was returning to his family's home with Hetty at season's end. If she could stay with him until the lighthouse closed, perhaps they had a chance. . .

"I made a promise I intend to keep, to watch a precious little girl named Hetty until the lighthouse closes for the season. She has no mother and is the same age I was when I was taken."

"You wish to remain there?" Mother squeezed her hand.

"Yes. And I have a brother and sister raised with me. I intend to spend time with them before I come visit with you and the others."

"Percy, couldn't we stay here and take care of the business with our cottage? Then we could see Valentine on her free days. Maybe we could even help with little Hetty."

"The Stevens have found a new place for the veterans in town—a long rambling home with most of the bed chambers on the first floor. We could help them with the transition and assess what needs to happen to Apple Blossom Cottage. But regardless—I'd have slept in Skull Cave if that meant we could see you, Valentine." His upper lip quivered.

"That would be wonderful." She turned toward her mother and then her father. "I can't believe you're here. My prayers have finally been answered."

"And ours."

Paul carried Hetty back the last half mile, his little angel asleep from the excitement of the day. And it wasn't over yet.

Jack ran toward them. "You meet Lord and Lady Gladstone yet?"

"What?" He stumbled then caught himself and clutched Hetty close in his arms.

"They're touring the new Social Affirmation property. My mom actually knew them a long time ago. Pretty interesting to hear about when she was my age."

Would Valerie stay? Would she leave with them? She should go and reacquaint herself. He'd stop by Father Joseph's office to see if he'd found anyone willing to come out to the lighthouse until it closed for the season.

"Mind if I walk with you?"

"No."

Jack jerked his thumb to the left. "I'll take those stairs up the bluff, behind the orphanage, to my house and get changed for dinner."

What kind of dinners did Lord and Lady Gladstone have? Nothing like he and Val and Hetty had at the lighthouse, he was sure. Paul's steps slowed as he continued toward the orphanage. Val had insisted, all week, that she intended to keep her commitment to stay for the duration, which was only another month or two. But once she saw her parents, surely she'd relent and go with them.

"Hey! I think we may have a ride." Jack waved.

A closed carriage pulled to a stop alongside them. Mrs. Booth-Moore waved from inside. "Get in, it's chilly out there!"

Paul passed Hetty to her and the woman placed her on her lap. "She's tuckered out, isn't she?"

"No more so than her daddy."

She laughed. "I can see that. But are you ready for a night at the Wedding Cottage?"

He frowned. "I thought we'd return tonight."

"Oh no, dear young man, your evening has been all marked out by the Gladstones."

Was Val's future all worked out by them, too?

"We'll pick them up with Val and head to the house. Then we'll have a scrumptious dinner while I catch up with them and you and Val and Hetty can utilize the playroom that has long gone unused."

"I have to get back over by tomorrow night to tend the light." He arched his neck back. "Oh no, I need to stop and see Father Joseph to secure help for when Val leaves with her folks."

"Unnecessary. She's going back to the lighthouse with you."

"What?"

"But first she's gonna see her brother and sis. My mom says Hetty could stay with us. Make some messes with Sally." Jack scratched his neck. "Val can bring Hetty back out with Mr. Hop in a coupla days."

He could trust his little girl with the Wellings, but. . . "Who's accompanying Val to the mainland?"

"Mr. Christy." Jack sniffed. "His sis is the lady who took in the Fillman kids. He takes a lot of people over."

Garrett Christy, by all accounts, was a God-fearing man but Paul had never met him. "Is he someone who could handle any persons who might bother Val? Like journalists?"

Jack chuckled, deep in his chest. "His nickname is Ox. You coulda used one of him instead of two of your brothers to work your fields. His arms are—"

Paul cut him off as the youth flexed his arms in a muscle man stance. "I get the idea."

But he didn't have to like the notion that he wouldn't be with Val when she went.

Paul couldn't always be there. But God would be. And the Lord provided. No matter what happened between Val and himself, God would still be there for both of them. That he could count on.

St. Ignace, Michigan

Val's brother and sister looked just as nervous as her parents had the previous day. She sat across from the two in the Jeffries' parlor, who were dressed in nice new clothing. "I am so happy to see you."

They nodded mechanically—like those little figures at the curiosity shop—but said nothing.

"I enjoyed your letters." She raised her eyebrows, hoping for a response.

Timothy grinned. "I liked the one about the X-ray machine."

"Tim might get an X-ray one day." Mabel adjusted her dainty silver necklace. *Another new thing.*

"But the doctors say they aren't safe right now."

"He does exercises that help his leg, though."

The two were clearly still as attached to one another as they'd been growing up. But did they have room for, or want, Val in their life? "My friends said you like it here in St. Ignace."

Timothy raised his arms and made circles. "They even have electric lights on the street here."

They exchanged a quick look.

"Tim and I can walk around after dark and go to the library."

"I've got an engineer from the electric plant who's interested in motors, too. He goes to our church."

"I like our new church. I've got two girlfriends I've made in Sunday School class." Mabel almost looked like an entirely different person.

Her sister had never had any friends, nor had Tim. They weren't allowed. "How about you, Tim, have you met some guys your age?"

"We have a Math Club that Principal Jeffries leads." He tapped his chest. "I'm the new president of it. And all of us fellows are buddies."

Val couldn't help gawking. Tears pricked her eyes. Her brother was doing amazing things now that he was out from under their parents' rule.

"We get to do all kinds of things we couldn't do before. We read newspapers and magazines every day now." Mabel ran her hand over her dark gray dress. She was dressed in mourning, yet her very being had transformed into happiness. Was she thinking of that?

"We're glad for your letters." Tim patted his black trousers. "Sounds so different out at the lighthouse now."

"Games, music, and fun trips to Mackinac Island—we didn't have that, did we, Valerie?"

Guilt poured over her. "I tried my best."

Tim leaned forward. "We know you did. It's just that. . ." He turned his hands over, palms up. Those hands were getting larger. He was becoming a young man. He needed the opportunities now being presented to him.

"I'm glad you're getting to do so many things here." She clutched her trembling hands in her lap. She'd explain everything to them before she left later. "How about school classes?"

"I love going every day." Mabel crossed her hands over her chest.

"It's so good here. Everything." The look in Tim's eyes dared her to take him away.

"Mrs. Jeffries already told me that you'd like to stay."

Both nodded, their lips pulling tight.

"It may be that we'll have no other option." She drew in a deep breath. "There's a reason your parents didn't allow us to read much outside news. Or engage in all these activities."

"Don't you mean our parents?" Timothy frowned.

Apparently, news hadn't quite reached St. Ignace yet about Verity "Valentine" Gladstone being found. Either that or Mr. and Mrs. Jeffries had kept those papers from the two. "You'll likely see it in the papers soon. You see, you and I are not actually related." She gestured between herself and the two youngsters that she considered her brother and sister no matter what the law said. "So I will have no legal ability to obtain custody of you. But I do intend to help support both of you."

"How?" Tim frowned.

"Are you marrying the new lighthouse keeper?"

"No." She couldn't rule that out—one day. "My real parents have a trust fund settled on me."

Mabel rose and sat beside her on the divan. "Your real parents?"

"We always wondered." Tim gaped at her.

"It's a long story but let me tell you what I know."

Hours later, Val settled beside Garrett Christy on the ferry. The man might not have been as muscular as he'd been as a young lumberjack, but he still had a commanding presence. After the emotional long day, she felt entirely spent. She was like Mabel's old rag doll when the cotton fabric had ripped, and all the sawdust fell out.

"How did it go?"

"They're staying." She'd explained on the way over who she was and how she had no legal standing with her brother and sister.

"As you reckoned."

"It's for the best. Your sister and brother-in-law are amazing people." If only Tim and Mabel had been born to them instead of Dorcas and John.

"They're good folks. My pa is only two throws yonder from their bakery. That big ol' hotel on the main street. Tom's ma owns it."

"I didn't realize that."

"Like gettin' two for one, ain't it? A grandpap and grandma to boot. Plus a ma and pa."

"That's a double win." She grinned.

He tapped his small black Bible. "The good book says God gives us double for our trouble sometimes."

"It's like that for me and my friend Susan. We both had nothing. Then Paul, from her childhood, and Lawrence, from mine came, to Mackinac. And it's like we're doubly blessed."

"Rebecca's already hopin' to bake the wedding cakes when you all get hitched."

It felt a little like she was becoming part of the Christy and Jeffries family with Tim and Mabel now in their care. "You're part of a big loving family. Will they accept Tim and Mabel?"

He turned and gave her a long look. "You ever see the old folks who live with us?"

"Aren't they your grandparents?"

"No." He laughed. "Frenchy and Pearl are grandpap and grandma to our older kids."

"So Rebecca's parents?"

"Nope. Met 'em both in the lumber camps. Those children were at the orphanage. But they were Pearl's grandchildren. She didn't know where they were." He rubbed his beard. "Point is—you don't have to be blood kin to make a family."

"You just need love."

"And plenty of it." He tapped the Bible. "And God's blessing to cover you all."

Chapter Twenty-Eight

Mackinac Island, Michigan

*W*hen Val exited her and Hetty's guestroom at Wedding Cottage, where the little girl slept, Paul awaited her in the hallway.

Warmth flowed through her. "I'm so glad Superintendent Dardanes got a relief worker for you."

"Me, too. I couldn't leave and not hear what happened with your brother and sister. Awfully glad Tim enjoyed that article on Roentgen's discovery of X-rays."

"He's excited to think that one day a doctor will be able to see what's wrong with his legbones."

"And maybe fix them?"

"That would be something."

Val pointed toward the closed door. "Hetty enjoyed her bath, and she's asleep with the kitten that Lawrence and Susan found for her."

"I couldn't believe Mrs. Booth-Moore agreed to that."

She shrugged. "I think she saw how excited Hetty was when they gave him to her."

He stepped closer, and she drew in Paul's piney scent. "We can't let her name him Larry, though, like Jack suggested."

"Little Bit isn't a good name, either." She pressed a hand to his warm chest, covered in a dress shirt this evening. He placed his broad hand over hers.

She drew in a breath. "Paul, I know you and Hetty are returning to your parents' home after the lighthouse closes."

"But—"

"Let me continue, or I won't say it. I'll go with my parents to Detroit and Windsor to meet, or rather see, my brother Nathan. We'll spend some time together."

"I understand."

"My parents, like they said earlier over dinner, intend to remain on Mackinac and we'll all get to visit weekly. That is—if you'd like that."

"I'd love that." He looked into her eyes with such affection that she closed her eyes, anticipating her first kiss.

Paul drew her into his embrace. Warm, sheltering, reassuring arms surrounded her and pulled her close against his chest. Then his lips covered hers. Moved over hers. Promised more. So much more.

She could trust this man with her heart. She knew it with all her being.

As Carrie headed toward her friends in the dining room, she spied Jack through the open office entryway door. He read a mechanical engineering book, which he held in one hand as he rocked his sister in a wooden cradle with the other. One day, he could make a good father full of verve. She continued past the parlor where Lawrence and Susan inclined their heads over a game of chess. Those two were becoming best friends and that was a great start to a future together.

She strode through to the dining room. Her servants brought the coffee service in on a silver tray and poured for her friends.

The scent of the Arabica coffee tempted Carrie, but she stood firm. "No coffee for me." She patted her chest. "My heart doesn't need any extra stimulation." Especially after almost interrupting Valentine, who was kissing Paul as Carrie had returned from upstairs with her shawl. She took her seat.

Using the silver tongs, Eugenie dropped sugar cubes into her coffee. "This is just like old times."

Tara pressed her hands together. "I still can't believe after all these years that little Adelaide brought us all together."

Adelaide patted her hair. "When I reunited with my father a couple of years ago, it got me thinking about all the people who had touched my life in special ways. And of course, I married the most special person."

"Peter is a darling." Carrie found his humor droll, much like her own husband's. She missed him.

"Yes, but I'm still glad the men retreated to the billiard room." Adelaide smiled. "And we get to chat."

Carrie fingered the tablecloth. "I'm thrilled to have you all here."

"It's like a dream come true—what with us Sugarplum Ladies here and our long-lost girls finally found." Tara's hands trembled on her coffee cup.

Carrie focused her attention on Adelaide, the one who'd set the die in motion. "Did you ever think that your efforts would bring Tara and Eugenie to the place where they would finally find Valentine and Susan?"

"Never." She shook her head. "I only thought of myself if I'm honest. I wanted to see you all so badly. You were like older sisters or mother figures to me. Having Satilde made me long for that connection."

Tara, who sat beside Adelaide, patted her shoulder. "I understand that's perfectly natural for new mothers."

"It is a perfectly natural inclination." Eugenie set her gilded cup in its saucer. "And now that you've found Susan, I expect you'll feel like a new mother yourself."

"She needs you, Tara." Carrie patted the linen tablecloth.

Eugenie raised her hands and turned her palms over. "We all need each other."

"Yes," Carrie, Adelaide, and Tara chorused.

Those connections, that love, those friendships—they all intertwined and were part of God's plan for each and every one of them.

Adelaide beamed at her. "And now that our officially named Mackinac Island Beacon program is launched, I pray that you'll return each summer!"

Love's light, which emanated from all her friends, would surely draw them all back.

Round Island Lighthouse

This season wasn't ending as Val had imagined. *Not whatsoever.* But God wasn't limited by her imagination. Instead of moving to Mackinac Island, she'd stay first in the Mott home in Detroit and then in Canada, getting to know Nathan and meeting his family.

But oh, how she'd miss Paul and Hetty.

Val packed Hetty's tiny clothes as Paul surveyed the room, looking for their cat. She picked up a sweater that Mrs. Scholtus had knit and folded it. "Can you believe those Sugarplum Ladies insisted they each take turns staying out here?" Carrie had returned to Chicago at her husband's insistence—he'd even sent another ship to fetch her, but Mother, Tara, and Ada had taken turns coming out.

Paul snorted. "Mrs. Booth-Moore was right. They're trying to protect your reputation."

Her cheeks heated. "We're alone now."

"Lady Gladstone is with Hetty in the parlor right now."

"Shhh!"

"I'm simply speaking the truth."

"No, shhh! Hear it?"

They were silent. A mewing sound came from the blankets.

Val pulled the quilt back and then the wool blanket. The tiny calico stared up with frightened eyes. Beside the kitten lay Hetty's rag doll. "I still can't believe she named you Dilly."

"Maybe that's why she's hiding."

"She said she's a dilly of a cat, so it kind of makes sense."

"Speaking of what makes sense—do we have a plan for this winter? For us?" Paul took the kitten from her. "You'll be in Detroit and Windsor."

She resumed folding Hetty's clothes. "Where you are welcome to visit."

"I appreciate your parents' invitation."

"And you'll be at your family's farm."

"Yes. No doubt Hetty will tell them she wants you for her new momma."

"What have you said to them?"

"Not much."

"My sister Georgie and her husband Lee had dinner with your parents last week." She'd been saving this little tidbit to drop like a hot potato.

"They did?"

"Yes." She moistened her lips. "You know Lee Hudgins owns that farm down the road from them."

"Don't I ever." He laughed. "But I'd not thought about his new wife being there, too."

"I'll stay with my sister and her husband when I come to Shepherd."

"Oh. Might I hope that could be often?"

"Possibly," she drew the word out. "You know how she likes to talk."

"Yes."

She folded the last undershirt and turned to face him. "And I write to Georgie regularly as does my mother."

"Aha. So you can get word from Georgie about me, and you can come visit us and spend time with my big family."

"That's about right."

Paul wrapped his free arm around Val. "It'll be hard being away from you."

It was so nice being close to him. "Yes." *Kind. A good father. A thinker. Conscientious. Makes lovely music. Makes me laugh. Loves God.*

"I love you, Val."

My handsome Ginger Man loves me. "I love you, too."

He kissed her gently, his mouth warm and right against hers. He pulled away and leaned his forehead against hers. "I've wanted to do that again for so long."

"Maybe it's good the ladies came out." She leaned in and kissed him.

He returned the kiss with more fervor, then stepped away. "Yes, that was a good idea."

Her heart hammering, she couldn't help but grin.

Footsteps sounded in the hallway. Mother came in, followed by Hetty, who rushed to grab her kitty.

"Dilly!" She kissed the cat all over its tiny face, until it meowed loudly.

"Hiding under the covers," her dad told her. "Like you do sometimes." He pressed his index finger playfully on her little nose.

Hetty skipped off down the hall, clutching Dilly.

"Looks pretty well packed." Mother gestured around the room. "So much easier than it was for the Stevens to get all the veterans packed and moved. But they love it in town."

"Has to be easier to have them on one floor," Val said.

"And what about you and Mr., um, Lord Gladstone. Have you lined up a winter work crew?"

"We hired all available workers who're not on the Social Affirmation Society worksite. So by the time next summer comes, Apple Blossom Cottage can hold any and all of our family members and our friends."

The way Mother's lips twitched she must be leaving something left unsaid.

"Anything left besides this quilt my Ma made?" Paul went to the bed and folded the beautiful pink and white quilt.

"I think that's it in here," said Val.

"Then we're almost done with life at the lighthouse." Paul looked wistful. He'd not decided yet if he'd return the following year.

"One benefit of being at the lighthouse. . ." Mother's face grew serious, "is that you've not been bothered by gawkers and journalists."

"True."

"And she's had me and Hetty with her, Lady Gladstone." Paul winked.

"Hmm, I'm wondering if you two heard about the Sugarplum Ladies' first contract for the Social Affirmation summer program?"

"No. What's it for?" Her mother's eyes sparkled as she added, "Who?"

"Lawrence and Susan's wedding."

"That's so exciting." Val raised her steepled hands to her mouth.

"Not only that, but they plan to take in that little Italian girl."

"Francesca?"

"Yes. And those big red-headed boys."

"The Clancy brothers? All three?"

"That's what Adelaide told me. They'd have taken Amanda, too, but she's just been adopted."

"Praise God for all that, but where will they live?" Lawrence and his dog had moved into the cottage with the Mulcaheys.

"Pine Cottage, after the honeymoon. The Mulcaheys will help them get the place ready this winter, and then they'll move to the employees' housing building. They've refused both Carrie's and my offers to stay in our cottages." She shrugged.

"They remind me of my folks. Probably don't want to impose." Paul leaned against the doorframe.

"Speaking of parents, Susan had no father to obtain permission from when they began courting in earnest." Mother inclined her head toward her. "But Valentine does."

Paul straightened. "I, um, yes ma'am, Lady Gladstone."

"And you'll do well to ask Lord Gladstone for permission later, again, if things. . . progress."

That distinctly sounded like they already had approval.

Val wrapped her arms around her mother, grateful that her friend's push for a Sugarplum Ladies reunion and that Lawrence and Georgie's autumn arrivals had brought her parents there before the Straits froze over.

God had worked things out for their good.

Chapter Twenty-Nine

Mackinac Island
June, 1898

*C*ould it be a more perfect day?" Susan, attired in her wedding finery, peered out her third-floor window at Wedding Cottage.

"No, dearie, it couldn't." Wistfulness tinged Sister Mary Lou's words.

"And there couldn't be a prettier bride." Auntie Tara sniffed and pulled a handkerchief from her long sleeve.

Someone rapped on the door. "It's time."

As they left the room, Bertie met Susan in the hallway. "I believe I'm blessed with this honor." He extended his arm, and then they went to the stairs.

Once they'd descended to the foyer, harp music carried through the open front doors.

Here I am—the spinster once living in a garret, now attired in a gorgeous Worth wedding gown given by Mrs. Booth-Moore. Susan was about to join in marriage with her wonderful co-worker at the society and the man of her dreams. Could her heart be any fuller?

Her bridesmaid and best friend, Val, emerged from the parlor holding two bouquets, the larger one full of white roses for Susan. Francesca held a white wicker basket of flower petals.

For weeks now, the Sugarplum Ladies had practiced the recipes they planned to teach the program participants. They'd had to pull Rebecca Christy in to help with the catered wedding, though. Her friend had been delighted to be part of the celebration.

The scent of lilacs carried in on the breeze and mingled with that of the roses in the bouquet that Val handed to her.

With her free hand, Val adjusted Susan's veil. Susan's hands were trembling so hard she feared she might drop her flowers.

Auntie Tara moved closer. "Remember this—at the end of the day, you and Lawrence will be man and wife no matter what else happens."

Val pulled a stray hair from Susan's dress. "So if the Sugarplum Ladies' tarts are sour and Rebecca Christy's wedding cake topples over and if seagulls dive into the crowd seated out there—you're still going to be Mrs. Lawrence Zumbrun after you both say, 'I do.'"

Susan's knees wobbled harder. "Now you've only made it worse. What if that all happens?"

Jack strolled by the open double doors. Then he paced back again.

"What's he doin'?" Bertie grouched.

Jack ran up the steps and fell on his knees on the carpet, in front of Susan. "Oh Pumpkin Queen, pray thee, do not wed Master Lawrence Zumbrun! Instead, make me your Pumpkin King, or I shall forevermore be aggrieved!"

She stared at the goofy boy and was tempted to do something very unladylike. She crinkled up her nose like Jack often did and expelled a hard breath.

Val put an arm around her. "At least he's not wearing that crazy outfit he had on for the Harvest Festival."

I know how to get rid of this pest. She handed her roses to Val, lifted her trailing skirt, and headed toward the door. With enthusiasm, she called out, "Where's your carriage, Jack? Let's run off together!"

"Huh?" His face fell. Then the youth dashed off—presumably toward the outdoor seating area and not for his carriage.

Susan swiped her hands together as she turned and accepted her bouquet again.

Her anxiety fled and determination swept in. This was her day, surrounded by a multitude of friends, making new family, and entering into a union blessed by God.

And she'd enjoy every moment.

Val sat beside Paul at the table of honor, for the bridal attendants, contemplating all that had happened in the past five months. Servants carried plated food to each table, beginning with the radiant bride and groom.

"Maybe for our reception, we could catch our own fish and fry them up and serve them on our blue ware plates instead of sending for those fancy prawns?" Paul pointed to the crystal cocktail goblets laden with prawns and spicy tomato sauce.

"I'd probably catch more whitefish than you."

"Nope. But you could fry them up better." He quirked his auburn eyebrows.

"Definitely." She adjusted her linen napkin on her lap.

"We sure have had a busy few months, haven't we?"

"Yes. The trickiest part was working out with the Jeffries and Timothy and Mabel how we could be a team. Lawrence's ideas really helped with that." She leaned over to smile at Lawrence and Susan, who were gazing into each other's eyes, and were completely oblivious to her.

"Hetty loves seeing them more, now that they're enrolled in the summer program here on the island."

She elbowed him. "What's your favorite part about our crazy courtship so far?"

"When we went to your parents' estate in England with my mom and dad."

No one in his family had ever traveled abroad, but she knew what he most valued. "Your father gave mine some excellent advice about the problems he'd been having with the crops."

"And he got that no-account manager fired who should have known what to do." Paul grinned. "I was glad we saved your folks and the villagers from what could have been a heavy loss this coming harvest."

"Yes, but that's not a very romantic memory."

"Neither was the unforgettable time when we were at Georgie and Lee's and almost got blown up by one of his new engines."

"Absolutely terrifying and not romantic."

He ran his hand over his handsome face. "Okay, what about when we went to your brother's home in Canada and he and his wife watched Hetty while we walked through the snowy lanes by moonlight?"

"It was so gorgeous beneath the full moon." She feigned a shiver. "But it was freezing out."

He leaned closer. "I don't remember being cold at all. I'm pretty sure I warmed you up."

Her face heated. She trusted this man with all her heart, soul, and mind. "I can't wait to be your wife."

"Even if that means you end up being a farmer's wife? In a small town?"

"You're my beacon, whether you're at a lighthouse or standing in a field full of potatoes."

He touched her nose. "Not a romantic picture with those spuds."

"If my Ginger Man is in it then yes, it is."

"And I'll go wherever my Lady of the Lake wants to take me—back to England, to lower Michigan, or here at the Straits of Mackinac."

Susan touched Val's hand, the sunlight catching on the new Mrs. Lawrence Zumbrun's gold wedding band. "The Mackinac Island Beacon program accomplished more than its planner had ever intended. Don't you think?"

"I do."

Lawrence leaned over and gestured between himself and his new wife. "That's what we both just said. I do."

"That's what we'll soon be saying, too." Paul placed his arm around her shoulders.

246

God was blessing them all. As He'd intended.
He was their beacon all along.

The End

Author's Notes

The original novella, which gave this novel its seminal start, was published as "Love's Beacon" in Barbour Publishing's Great Lakes Lighthouse Brides Collection. My rights reverted back to me two years ago and I let the story sit as the fictional character, Susan Marie Johnson, nudged me to write her story, too. This book quadrupled in size, with much of the original story changed or deleted altogether. "The Sugarplum Ladies" originally published in *The Victorian Christmas Brides Collection* (September, 2018) from Barbour, and now re-published as its own novella (2021) includes important characters in this novel. Those who have read "Dime Novel Suitor" in the *Seven Brides for Seven Mail-Order Husbands* romance collection may remember Deanna Tumbleston now married to Colonel Stevens in this book. That novella will be available under separate imprint soon.

The Valerie/Valentine/Verity character had been through so much turmoil that as a former psychologist I wasn't happy with the previous version of her recovery from everything that had happened to her. She needed more page time, too.

I was a psychologist for twenty-seven years and I also was a corrections officer (briefly) for the state of Michigan. Unfortunately there are a number of disturbed people, like Dorcas, who have suffered a traumatic loss and also have mental health issues. In her case, there is also a spiritual issue. Dorcas's behavior is truly evil. And her husband is neglectful with his failure to help his children in any kind of meaningful way. And yet there are people, like the characters Susan and Lawrence, who love children and want to take in as many as they can and help guide them.

The real-life mother of the actual namesake Valerie Fillman is a lovely Christian woman completely unlike Dorcas the fictional "mom" who kidnapped fictional Valentine. Real life Valerie Fillman is an amazing cosmetologist with her own salon in Newberry, Michigan, and she's just as sweet as Val in this story! I borrowed so many names, with permission, from many friends. Paul Scholtus was my next-door neighbor and my best friend in early childhood. He's a talented carpenter and a spirit-filled Christian man like fictional Paul. Sister Mary Lou

Kwiatkowski is my actual friend who is a nun in Pennsylvania. She's a dear sweet person like her fictional counterpart. Susan Marie Johnson is my long-time Facebook friend, Pagels' Pals member, and has been a stalwart Beta reader for my books. She shared the names of her family members and even her cats, Lizzie and Dilly. Sadly, her mother Evelyn Marie Singleterry, whose name was used for a character, passed away recently before this book was published. Christian Zumbrun, the father of Lawrence, in real life is C. J. Zumbrun, my friend Christy's son, who serves our country in the United States Navy.

My hero, Paul, in this novel, had an almost obsessive love for his deceased wife. That's why I chose Edgar Allan Poe's Anabel Lee for the inspiration for their relationship. My own grandfather, Lloyd Earl Fancett, Sr., grew up on a farm in lower Michigan, like Paul in the story. He was the inspiration for Paul and his first wife. My grandfather married his childhood sweetheart. I was told they loved each other greatly. She died young leaving him a widower in his early twenties, and he went out West to be a cowboy for a while—not to a lighthouse! If that hadn't happened to my grandfather, though, I wouldn't be here—and you wouldn't have read this book.

There are two lighthouses in the Straits of Mackinac nowadays. At the time of my story, only Round Island Lighthouse (brand new at the time, built in 1895), existed. The Round Island Passage Lighthouse was built later. Visitors to Mackinac Island recognize the iconic "schoolhouse" design of the Round Island Lighthouse. It is one of the most photographed of all the Great Lakes lighthouses.

When I worked on Mackinac Island as a teenager in 1975, a fundraiser to save and restore Round Island Lighthouse was launched. I believe I paid a one-dollar donation for my button to wear, showing I proudly supported this effort. Who'd have thought that one day I'd be writing a story set at this very lighthouse?

Clarke Historical Library at Central Michigan University has a wonderful "Life in a Lighthouse" article available online at their website. The Round Island Lighthouse Preservation Society also has a very helpful website, including a virtual tour inside, history, and a brochure. Since the Round Island Lighthouse isn't normally accessible to the public, I found the information at the Old Mackinac Point Lighthouse, open for tours through the Mackinac State Historic Parks, to be very helpful.

His Eye is On the Sparrow was not written until 1905, after the time of this story. It's one of my favorite hymns.

A whistling tea kettle was not invented until after the time of this story, but I think Bertie and Tara Mulcahey would have enjoyed having that feature!

Bye, Baby, Bye: A Lullaby sung to Jack's sister was an American popular song issued in 1890, lyrics by Eudora S. Bumstead and composer Fred C. Hahr. *Sweet Rosie O'Grady* by Maude Nugent was an actual song popular in the 1890s.

Believe it or not the hydropower plant in the Soo (Sault Ste. Marie, Michigan), built beginning in 1898, still operates today and powers the electricity to the EUP where I grew up.

There really was a famous Mackinac Island resident, Madgelaine Laframboise whose former residence is now a hotel on the island.

Aaron Thompson, a Facebook friend and resident of Mackinaw City who is the administrator of several Mackinac area Facebook groups allowed me to use his great-great-grandmother's name in this story and he sent me some clips about this remarkable woman. "Dame" Madame Marguerite Mirandette (1823-1910) lived in a home that still stands behind St. Anne's church. She was reported to be one of the first white women to live on Mackinac Island, having come there from Quebec. I can only imagine all the stories she could have told! She did teach CCD classes at St. Annes Catholic Church.

Thomas "Alva" Edison spent part of his childhood in Michigan, and his father continued to live there. His father had been a lighthouse keeper, too! We know that near the time of our original Sugarplum Ladies start-up, after the Civil War, Edison worked on the railroads with the telegraphs and was moving on to research. I don't think it is too much of a stretch to imagine him bumping into our fictional ladies in Detroit!

ACKNOWLEDGEMENTS

I thank God that He has allowed me to write this story despite my infirmities. Much appreciation to my family, who support me and my writing—especially my husband, Jeffrey. Thank you to all my friends who've allowed me to use their names in this story, in a fictional manner, especially Susan Marie Johnson, Sister Mary Lou Kwiatkowski, Valerie Fillman and Paul Scholtus. My best friend, Tara Mulcahey, has shown up in other books, too. Carrie Booth-Moore's name is a conglomerate of the amazing book media specialist Carrie Booth Schmidt's and reader Carrie Moore's names.

Thank you to Pegg Thomas, my amazing editor for her hard work. Thank you to my critique partner, Debbie Lynn Costello, for taking many calls from me.

What would I do without my Beta Readers? Gail Mundy, a newer Beta reader rocks! Andrea Selaty, a brand-new Beta reader and aspiring editor did a great job. I'm truly humbled! Tina St. Clair Rice may have Beta-read so many of my books that she qualifies as a Superstar Beta! My newer Beta reader, Melissa Main, is an author and an editor. Melissa Henderson, a fellow author, also stepped up to the plate—much appreciated.

Thank you to new reader, and already an Advance Reader, Robin Auten! Thanks, Beverly Duell-Moore, Linda Matson Thomas, Betti Mace, and Rory Lemond for being Advance Readers! Thank you to Sherry Moe, my Yooper friend, and fellow Mackinac Island addict who is always there for me. Thank you to my dear friend, Joy O'Steen Ellis, for advance reading, also. God knew I needed you here in Hampton Roads when He blessed me with your friendship! Much appreciation, to the real Susan Marie Johnson, who was an Advance Reader despite the recent loss of her mother. Susan's fictional namesake hijacked my plot on this book in such a good way!

Thank you to my Early Readers: Rebecca Tellez, Brenda Murphree, Paula Shreckhise and Sonja Nishimoto. And I'm grateful to my Pagels Pals group who support my writing ministry.

Thank you to Aaron and Bianca Thompson for advance reading and for feedback. Their ancestors' histories are richly woven into the fabric of Mackinac Island and the Straits area. Appreciation also to the Addicted to Mackinac Island Facebook group and the administrators who share their love of all things Mackinac, including books set there.

With much appreciation to Mary Jane Barnwell, the owner of The Island Bookstore, and manager Tamera Tomac, for their support of books set on Mackinac Island and to their amazing team. They are ever-gracious hosts when I am at the store for book signings.

I'm so grateful for Dr. Renata Kowal, for her wonderful chiropractic care and her staff, Kaitlynn Whitehead and Faith Miyamura. When I first went to Atlas Specific Chiropractic months after my previous chiropractor unexpectedly retired, I was so stiff from my arthritis that I was barely functional. I don't know how I'd have completed this novel much less gotten the first draft of my next novel, a contemporary Women's Fiction novel due out in 2025, without Dr. Kowal's intervention. And much appreciation to Dr. Ugur Yilmaz Anatolian, my new neurologist, who battled the insurance company to get my migraine medication returned to me. I had recurring almost daily migraines while completing the last section of this novel and during my self-edits before my editor received the manuscript. With Dr. Anatolian's help, I was able to get my medication resumed and was feeling better when my edits were returned to me.

Thank you, too, for being a Christian fiction reader! Where would we authors be without our readers supporting our writing ministry? Many blessings to you!

Other Books in the Mackinac Island Romances Series

Associated Novella for Mackinac Island Beacon

Mackinac Island Romances Books 1 & 2

Associated Novel for the series

Book One
My Heart Belongs on Mackinac Island
Maggie Award winner and a *Romantic Times* Top Pick.
Journey now to Mackinac Island where...
A Tangled Gilded Age Love Story Unfolds.

Book Two
Anchored at Mackinac
Gilded Age Romance on Mackinac Island
As 1895 comes to a close, will hearts be broken when choices are made—or will all hoped-for wishes be fulfilled?

Associated books:
Behind Love's Wall (Barbour Publishing)

The Sugarplum Ladies – A novella

The Substitute Bride – A novella

Bio

CARRIE FANCETT PAGELS, Ph.D., is the multi-award-winning author of over twenty-five Christian fiction books, including ECPA and Amazon bestsellers. She loves a good cup of tea and keeps her teacart well stocked! The family dog, an Aussie Kelpie, walks her almost daily! Twenty-seven years as a psychologist didn't "cure" her overactive imagination! Carrie grew up in Michigan's beautiful Eastern Upper Peninsula. Although she now resides with her family in Virginia, she vacations most summers at the Straits of Mackinac—where many of her stories are set.

You can connect with Carrie through her website www.carriefancettpagels.com.

If you enjoyed this novel, a review is always very much appreciated!!!

Made in the USA
Middletown, DE
16 May 2024

54430389R00146